FUEGO

By

J.E. McBee

Pat,

Thanks for all your help!

Gunther

For Christopher and Sarah

"I've never been the man I used to be."

- Jim Harrison

ACKNOWLEDGMENTS

I would like to thank an extremely talented group of friends and colleagues who have provided significant contributions to this work of fiction – without their insight, knowledge and assistance, this story would never have reached the printed page.

Many thanks to Pete Malamas, who once again created an evocative and singular cover design. The cover photo of the harbor in Key North was provided by Tim Weintraub.

Thanks also to Linda Chamberlain, Pat Maher and Thomas Sharp for their early review and astute critiques of this work in progress.

Also of immeasurable help were Kevin O'Shea, Eddie Padron, Pete Jarvis, Wayne Hammond, Kevin Baxter of the Florida Wildlife Commission, John Richard Rodgers, U.S. Air Force (Ret.), Margo Sullivan and Dallas Diamondz, all of whom provided invaluable information in their particular areas of expertise.

1

He was jolted awake by a garish image, a familiar feeling of dread engulfing him as he shifted slightly in his bed in the dark to read the glowing red numbers on the clock radio resting on his bedside table: 3:57. He groaned to himself. He'd been unable to sleep through the night for two weeks, since the morning he'd discovered a dead body on Anclote Key.

A day before that macabre encounter, he'd discovered something else on the narrow uninhabited sandspit that formed the southern tip of Anclote Key: a battered wooden boat half-buried in the sand along the western shore a few feet from the tide line, likely deposited there by the storm surge generated from Hurricane Irma in September. Nearby lay an outboard motor that had been separated from the boat's stern, almost completely buried, its protective cowling missing, the vital interior components of the engine choked with sand. Had there been an occupant?

He'd returned to the key just after dawn on the morning after he'd found the boat with his camera to take some pictures of the derelict vessel before the tide or a salvage crew could dislodge it from its resting place. He'd secured his skiff on the eastern shore of the key where it was shielded from the Gulf currents and was striding across the sandy tip when he saw the body, which hadn't been there the day before.

Zachary Rheinhart's first thought was that the man – he could see it was a man as he approached – was an early sun worshipper, out to catch a few rays before the heat of midday set in. He waved to the man, who was seated in one of those lowrider beach chairs, legs on the sand extended in front of him, head tilted forward. No response. Maybe he hasn't seen me, thought Rheinhart. He took several more steps and was about to speak when he noticed a small rectangular white object protruding from the man's right hand that stopped him in his tracks. Something wasn't right.

"Hello? Are you alright?" Rheinhart asked tentatively as he approached. Still no response. He took another step, close enough now to see that the item gripped in the man's hand appeared to be a business card. As Rheinhart reached to remove the card from the unresponsive man's hand, his wrist brushed against the man's arm.

He recoiled in horror, somehow managing to maintain his grip on the card. The man's flesh was cold, rigid. No wonder he hadn't responded to Rheinhart's greeting. He wasn't unconscious. He was dead.

Rheinhart stepped back, breathing rapidly, shaken. After a few moments he stepped forward again and placed his hand gingerly beneath the man's chin, trying to raise his head so he could get a good look at his face. Rigor mortis had set in, however, and Rheinhart couldn't move the man's head from its slumped position without applying considerable force.

He took several steps back, heart pounding now, and fished his cell out of his cargo shorts, trying to figure out who to call. The Coast Guard? No; the corpse was on land. He Googled the number for the Pinellas County Sheriff's Office and punched in the numbers. In a few moments a tired voice answered. "Pinellas County Sheriff's Office. How may I help you?"

Rheinhart cleared his throat. "I'd like to report a dead body."

He had the deputy's attention now. "Male or female?"

"Male."

"Are you sure he's dead?"

"He's not breathing and his skin is cold to the touch. I'm pretty sure he's dead."

Exasperation crept into the deputy's voice. "You touched the body?"

Rheinhart nodded reflexively. "It was an accident. I thought he might be sleeping and I was trying to wake him up when my wrist brushed against his arm. He felt like he'd been in a refrigerator all night."

"Where are you?"

"In the Gulf, on Anclote Key," Rheinhart answered. "The southern tip."

"Have you disturbed the scene in any other way?"

Rheinhart looked at the business card he held in his other hand and made a snap decision. "No."

"Good," the deputy responded. "What's your name?"

"Zachary Rheinhart."

"Could you spell that, please?"

"R-H-E-I-N-H-A-R-T."

"Okay, Mr. Rheinhart. Is there anyone else on the key with you?"

"No. I'm by myself."

"Here's what I want you to do, Mr. Rheinhart. I'm sending a marine unit out immediately. Please step back from the body and try not to disturb the scene anymore than you already have. Is that clear?"

"Yes, sir."

"Good," the deputy said. "The unit should be there in thirty minutes. One of our sheriffs will want to take a full statement from you, so don't go anywhere. And if you see anyone else on the key before our boat arrives, keep them away from the body."

"Will do."

"Thanks, Mr. Rheinhart. You did the right thing."

He looked at the business card in his hand and thought: I hope you're right.

*****

Rheinhart noted the time on his watch, then got to work. He wouldn't have much time before the sheriff's boat arrived. He took several pictures of the business card with his Nikon digital camera before bending down to replace it in the man's hand. He knew his prints would be on the card, but he'd already come up with an answer if the sheriff pressed him on it – he thought the man had been asleep in the sun, not dead, when he spotted him. The card had slipped from his grip when he'd nudged the man's arm in an attempt to wake him before his skin began to burn.

As he bent down to return the card to its original position, he noticed that the man's mouth was open. He dropped to his knees on the sand to get a closer look and made another gruesome discovery: the man's tongue was missing. Lying on the sand, he took several shots of the man's face from below before rising to his feet and looking up and down the length of the key. There was no boat other than his own skiff anywhere in sight; how had the victim arrived?

He stood up and took several pictures of the corpse in the chair, then walked swiftly back to his skiff, where he stowed his camera in one of the live wells, beneath several chamois cloths he used to clean the boat. He'd watched enough cop shows on television to know that the cops would confiscate his camera as

16

evidence if they knew he'd snapped pictures of the body, and that it would be a long time, if ever, before it would be returned.

Rheinhart walked back to the lifeless man in the chair and scanned the area for any signs of activity. Other than Rheinhart's own footprints and the marks on the sand where he'd lain down to photograph the victim, there was nothing around the body to indicate how it had been deposited there. In a boat, under cover of darkness – it was the only thing that made any sense, since he hadn't been there the day before.

He looked more closely at the man. He had dark hair, cut short, pale skin and was wearing a white polo shirt over khaki shorts, barefoot. Rheinhart guessed he was in his late 30s or early 40s. He looked like any other tourist seen on any other Florida beach, except for the rigor mortis and lack of breathing. And the missing tongue.

What kind of transgression resulted in having your tongue removed? Rheinhart's mind drifted to *The Godfather*, wondering if this was mob related, retribution for singing to the feds. He shuddered as he considered the prospect of having his tongue cut out. He hoped the man was already dead when it happened.

He shielded his eyes against the morning sun and scanned St. Joseph Sound past Fred Howard Park for the sheriffs' vessel. As he looked for the patrol boat he reviewed the story he would tell the cops: he'd seen the wooden boat and outboard washed ashore on Anclote yesterday, but his phone had run out of juice on the key and he'd been unable to get any pictures. He'd returned first thing this morning with a fully charged phone and was walking across the sand toward the boat and motor when he'd discovered the body. The man failed to respond to his greeting as he approached; he thought the man had fallen asleep. He'd reached out to jostle the man's arm gently, to nudge him awake, causing the card to fall to the sand. That's when he felt the dank flesh and knew the man was dead.

There'd be no mention of the digital camera, no mention of missing body parts. The smart play would be to act as ignorant as possible without raising suspicion and then move on. Leave it for the cops to figure out.

2

Thirty minutes later, two marine units from the Pinellas County Sheriff's Department slowed as they approached Anclote from the south before anchoring side by side just offshore, near Rheinhart's skiff. He watched with interest as the passengers disembarked. Two officers, a man and a woman, walked directly toward Rheinhart. The woman spoke. "Mr. Rheinhart?"

He nodded as she removed a notebook and pen from a back pocket and motioned him away from the body, off to the side. "Let's give our forensic team some room to work," she said as the group from the other boat, laden with equipment, trudged across the white sand toward the victim. "I'm Detective Kullmann and this is Detective Profeta." Profeta nodded silently; Rheinhart nodded back.

Kullmann glanced at her notebook, then looked up. "You discovered the body, correct?"

"Yes."

"What time was that?"

"A couple of minutes after I landed on the key. I left the marina just after dawn, around 6:30. It takes fifteen minutes to get here, so I guess it was a little before seven."

"Which marina?"

"The Crooked Snook, in Ozona."

Profeta finally spoke. "Why so early?"

Stick to the script, he reminded himself. "I wanted to take some photos of a wooden boat and outboard motor I'd seen on the key yesterday. They looked like they'd been washed ashore after Irma. I wanted to shoot in the morning light for the best effect, so I left at sunrise."

Kullmann glanced up from her notebook. "Why didn't you take any photos yesterday?"

He tried for a sheepish grin. "My phone ran out of juice, so I came back this morning. I beached my skiff and was walking across the sand when I noticed a man sitting in a beach chair. I waved but he didn't respond. His head was bent forward. I thought he might be sleeping and I didn't want him to get a sunburn, so I walked over and gave him a nudge, trying to wake him up. That's when I felt how cold he was. The only reason for him to be that cold under this sun was that he was dead, so I dialed 9-1-1."

Kullmann jotted a note. "What part of the body did you touch?"

"His right arm. There was a business card in his right hand. I accidentally knocked it out of his hand and it fell to the sand when I tried to wake him up. I picked the card up and slid it back between his fingers."

Profeta's dark eyes bore into Rheinhart's. "Did you read the card?"

"Yes."

"What did it say?"

"Chad Middleton, Junonia Realty, Captiva, Florida."

Kullmann spoke without looking up from her notebook. "Does that name mean anything to you, Mr. Rheinhart?"

He shook his head. "No. Never heard of him."

Profeta watched Rheinhart's eyes intently as he responded to Kullmann's question, looking for that downward glance that denoted duplicity. He didn't see it.

Kullmann continued. "Did you touch any other part of the body?"

Rheinhart shook his head vigorously. "No. I called 9-1-1 immediately and they told me to stay clear."

Profeta scanned the shoreline on both sides of the narrow key. "Did you see any other boats?"

"No. I wondered how he got here, so I checked along the shoreline after I called the sheriff's office. I couldn't see any boats or any sign that one had been here."

Kullmann looked at him and spoke calmly. "Any idea on how he might've arrived here?"

The first trap had been set. He knew that cops always suspected anyone who discovered a body. He was on tricky ground here. He returned Kullmann's querulous gaze with what he hoped was a neutral expression and shrugged his shoulders. Just keep it simple. "Beats me."

"Do you have any identification, Mr. Rheinhart?" Profeta asked amiably.

He reached into the pocket of his cargo shorts and retrieved his wallet. He extricated his driver's license and tried to hand it to Profeta, who directed him to give it to Kullmann. Shielding her eyes from the morning sun, she jotted down his essential information and handed the card back to Rheinhart. "Do you mind if I ask what you do for a living, Mr. Rheinhart?"

"I'm retired."

Kullmann checked her notes, then looked at Rheinhart with renewed interest. "According to your license, you're fifty-five

21

years old." She looked at Profeta, who like Kullmann was in his forties, then back at Rheinhart, smiling. "Must be nice to be retired so young."

There was a moment of silence before Rheinhart responded. "Not exactly."

"What do you mean?' she asked, looking at him expectantly, pen poised over her pad.

Idiot! He raged at himself for his careless response before composing himself once again. Both detectives were looking at him with interest – surely they'd seen his lack of emotional control when posed a seemingly innocent question. Too late now; he had to tell them. "Uh, it wasn't a voluntary retirement."

"Really," Kullmann said, trying to keep her interest under wraps. "What did you do for a living?"

"I was a designer."

It was Profeta's turn to look puzzled. "Designer? What does that mean?"

"I'm an architect." Rheinhart said. "I design buildings."

"Who did you work for?" Kullmann asked.

Rheinhart looked at her, trying to keep exasperation from his voice. "Is that information necessary to your investigation?"

Kullmann saw that she'd struck a nerve and pressed forward. "Just a routine question. What we're doing here is trying to eliminate you as a suspect. Following up with your employer—"

"Ex employer," Rheinhart growled. His eyes widened as her words took hold. "What do you mean, suspect?"

Profeta swept his arm across the horizon. "According to you, no one else has been here this morning. Like it or not, until we clear you, you'll remain a person of interest."

"You mean witness, don't you?"

"For now. Until you're cleared."

Kullmann interjected. "Let's not get sidetracked. It's a simple question: who was your employer?"

"Gunn Design, in Jacksonville."

She looked at Rheinhart with interest after she'd jotted down the name. "What happened?"

After a moment Rheinhart replied. "How much time do you have?"

"As much as it takes."

He told her the whole story, how he'd been a hotshot designer with a promising future in Gunn Design's headquarters in Grand Island, New York, north of Buffalo, when the firm had landed a plum government contract: the design of the new Duval County Courthouse in Jacksonville. Historically, the firm had made its name in the healthcare field, designing hospitals, and this courthouse contract was their first big break in the lucrative government contracting and design field.

The owner of the firm, Skip Gunn, had selected him personally to manage the design and construction of the new courthouse. It was the type of opportunity no ambitious design professional could pass up, so he sold his house in New York and moved into a condo along the St. Johns River in Jacksonville. He and his hand-picked team came up with a design that was approved by the mayor of Jacksonville, who according to Florida state law was the managing entity for the project, and work began.

Finalizing the design took two and a half years. During that time there were significant change orders that sent the project's cost skyrocketing in excess of $230 million, a figure which outraged both government officials and taxpayers. The escalation in cost of the courthouse was the prime factor in the incumbent mayor being defeated in the next municipal election, and his replacement wasted no time assigning his new legal staff to find a way out of the contract, which they succeeded in doing in three months.

Someone in Gunn Design had to take the fall for such a disastrous outcome. The obvious choice was the project designer and manager – Rheinhart. He was forced to "retire" from the firm as part of a plea deal to avoid a lawsuit being brought against the firm by the city of Jacksonville. He negotiated the best severance package from Gunn he could under the circumstances, packed his belongings and moved across the state to the Gulf coast to lick his wounds. Finding a similar job was out of the question, at least for now – his name and reputation had been effectively destroyed in the architectural design field once he was convinced to take the fall for the firm.

Kullmann was scribbling furiously, getting as much of Rheinhart's story down as she could. When she was caught up she looked at Rheinhart. "How did your family take the news?"

Rheinhart looked down at the sand. "No wife, no kids, no family. It's just me."

"Sorry to hear that," a grinning Profeta said in a tone that indicated he wasn't sorry at all.

Kullmann shot her partner a withering look before returning her gaze to Rheinhart. "We're just about done here. All I need is your telephone number, in case we have any follow-up questions. And someone from our forensic team will want to take your fingerprints so we can match them against any prints we might find on the business card, and footprint impressions to compare to the footprints surrounding the body." She stuck out her hand, along with one of her business cards. Rheinhart took it. She had a strong grip, stronger than her slight frame indicated. "Thanks for your help, Mr. Rheinhart. We'll be in touch."

3

When Rheinhart's boat was on its way back to the marina in Ozona, Betty Kullmann turned to her partner and asked, "What do you think?"

"About Rheinhart?" Ted Profeta responded as he reached for a cigarette. "Not much."

"You made that clear earlier. I mean, do you think he has any connection to this?"

He lit his cigarette and shook his head. "Nah. I think he's just some schmuck who ended up in the wrong place at the wrong time. He seems pretty full of himself, but initial impression? I don't think he has the *cojones* to cut out a man's tongue – that's got pro written all over it."

They were seated in one of the marine units under the craft's bimini, shielded from the sun, waiting for the forensic unit to finish up before heading back to the mainland. Kullmann dabbed at a bead of perspiration on her forehead and reached for a bottle of water from the cooler near their feet. "I think you're right," she said. "We'll follow up on his Jacksonville story. Once we confirm that, my gut tells me he'll be out of the picture."

"Speaking of your gut—"

Kullmann, who'd put on a few pounds in the last year and was hyper sensitive concerning any mention of her weight, broke in quickly. "Don't go there!" she warned in a menacing tone.

Profeta took a drag on his cigarette and smiled. "Bit touchy, aren't we? I was just going to ask how you think the body got out here in the first place. No signs of a boat, no prints around the body other than Rheinhart's, no blood at the scene. Looks like he was killed someplace else and dumped here. Rheinhart said the body wasn't here yesterday, and no one else reported seeing it. It must've been dumped sometime during the night, which means it's someone who knows their way around the local waters, how shallow it is out here."

"Which is anyone who owns a boat. Probably about half the state. Ace detective work, Poirot."

Resentment boiled in Profeta at her teasing tone, and he struggled not to respond. Kullmann had a history of self-conscious and defensive behavior concerning male subordinates – in fact, that's why he was paired with her now. There'd been an incident between Kullmann and her last male partner seven months earlier which was still the subject of lingering gossip around the house. He knew better than to push that button. "What about a chopper?" he asked tentatively.

She thought about it for a moment. "Could've been, I suppose," she conceded. "Harder to avoid detection in the air, but possible. We'll check with DHS to see if they picked up anything unusual last night."

Profeta leaned over and doused his cigarette in the water before wrapping it in a napkin and carefully placing it in his pocket. Since they'd become partners, he'd been lectured several times by Kullmann, one of those ex-smokers now fanatical about their smoke-free status, for leaving butts at crime scenes. "I know someone at the Coast Guard. I'll give them a call later."

"Okay." Kullmann was thinking ahead, laying it out in her mind. This wasn't going to be easy. It was early in the game, but what she'd seen so far told her that clues pertaining to this case would be hard to find. She sighed. Nothing like a professional hit to usher in the holiday season.

*****

Rheinhart knew it was futile to try to get back to sleep, so he switched on the light on his bedside table and rose to go to the bathroom. He'd slept with the bedroom window open last night and noted the house was still warm, so he slipped on a pair of shorts when he was finished peeing and headed for the kitchen.

He'd purchased the small bungalow nestled beneath the cypress and sea grapes on Bay Street in Ozona with proceeds from the sale of his condo in Jacksonville. Despite that condo's seemingly desirable location overlooking the Intracoastal Waterway, he soon discovered that he disliked urban living and wanted to return to a home where he felt more comfortable, away from nightmare traffic, off the beaten path.

Ozona, a sleepy community at the western terminus of Tampa Road, fit the bill perfectly. He'd originally been interested in Tarpon Springs and had scouted several prospects online, but when a real estate agent he'd been dealing with heard about a small one-story home in Ozona that had just gone on the market, he wasted no time scheduling a viewing.

It was love at first sight. He embraced the laidback vibe of the tiny community, where most local traffic consisted of golf carts and bicycles. He also loved the fact that he could be in downtown Tampa or St. Petersburg in less than an hour if he wanted a cultural change of pace. He'd made an offer that day, the owner had countered and Rheinhart accepted the counter offer. As soon as the house was inspected, he arranged to have what furniture he hadn't sold with the condo moved to his new home.

He brewed a pot of tea and turned on the small flat screen perched on the counter beneath the microwave in the compact kitchen to check the day's weather and tide charts, but his mind kept slipping back to the dead body. He'd expected a call from one of the detectives to follow up, but that call had never come. And

28

there was this: he'd scoured the *Tampa Bay Times* and other local media outlets, looking for news about the case since that first day, but had found nothing. How in the world does the discovery of a dead body on a deserted island under highly suspicious circumstances manage to go unreported in this age of 24/7 news coverage?

After ten days of media silence his curiosity drove him to call Detective Kullmann. He'd left several messages on her voicemail before he finally connected with her three days ago. She was on her lunch break in Dunedin, munching on a fish taco when she answered. "Detective Kullmann."

"Detective Kullmann, this is Zachary Rheinhart." He paused. When she didn't respond after a few moments he continued. "The guy who found the body on Anclote Key a month ago. I was wondering how things were going on the case."

"It's good to hear from you, Mr. Rheinhart. But I'm afraid I can't answer your question. I'm no longer assigned to that case."

He hadn't expected that. "Who is?" His voice was laced with bewilderment.

"I don't know that either."

"What happened?"

She finished chewing her taco before answering. "I'm afraid I can't tell you that, Mr. Rheinhart. Have a nice day."

He stared at his phone, stunned, as the line went dead.

*****

Profeta, who was sitting across from his partner and had heard her end of the conversation, wiped his mouth with a napkin. "Rheinhart?"

Kullmann nodded. "Wanted to know about the investigation."

Profeta's features clouded over as he arched his balled-up taco wrappers like a three-pointer into a nearby trash can and stood up, brushing some tortilla chip crumbs from the sleeve of his shirt. "Join the club."

4

Rheinhart spent the rest of the morning as he had most mornings during the last two weeks, scouring the Internet, looking for any mention of the murder of Chad Middleton, finding nothing. By 11:00, his search once again proving fruitless, he'd finished the tea in the pot and jumped in the shower. He'd wasted enough of another glorious sunny morning chasing this mystery.

It was Wednesday, the day of his weekly luncheon with Steve Morrison at Kitty Galore's Raw Bar. As he stood under the refreshing spray, he wondered once again if he'd lapsed into obsession when it came to the dead body he'd discovered, but just as quickly found himself pushing back against his own characterization as he sometimes did: who *wouldn't* think that something very unusual was going on here?

When his hair was dry he threw on a Toronto Blue Jays T-shirt and a pair of khaki shorts and sandals and headed out the door on foot. The late morning sun was warming on his neck as he strolled up Bay Street. He smiled. Just another day in paradise.

If there was any place that qualified as the hub of life in Ozona, Kitty Galore's Raw Bar was it. Located on Orange Street, a two-minute walk from Rheinhart's small bungalow, the two-story white clapboard building had originally been built during the early 20th century by one of the Tampa Bay area's most notorious rum smugglers as his private home. It had changed hands several times before Florence Leaf bought the building in 1985 and converted it into a restaurant which opened the following year. At the suggestion of his realtor, Rheinhart stopped in for lunch on the first day he viewed the bungalow he would eventually buy and instantly felt at home. The grouper sandwich recommended by the bartender was delicious, and the lunchtime crowd was an eclectic mix of all ages, most of them, the bartender replied when asked, locals. The bar buzzed with conversation and laughter as the blond female bartender hustled to keep ahead of her thirsty clientele, and waitresses wearing Kitty Galore tank tops and black shorts shuffled back and forth to the kitchen carrying trays loaded with mostly fresh seafood offerings from the nearby Gulf of Mexico.

From his first visit, Rheinhart felt a visceral attraction to the place, instantly comfortable among the collection of kitsch that adorned both the bar and dining areas, at ease with the variety of characters perched on barstools and the stuffed game – moose, deer, a wild hog and a variety of tropical game fish – mounted on the walls. It reminded him of a cracker version of that television bar, *Cheers*, and he wondered idly how long it would be until everyone here knew his name.

Steve Morrison was seated in his usual position at the end of the bar, nursing a Yuengling draft, when Rheinhart walked through the door. Gracie Fenton, the daytime bartender who missed very little, spied him first. "Hey, Sherlock," she called out, an impish smile on her face. "Morrison is already working on his second beer."

Morrison looked up from his beer and smiled, indicating with a nod an open seat to his left. Rheinhart took it as Gracie, without need of a prompt, filled a glass with his favorite local craft beer, a Big Storm Wavemaker, and dropped it on a coaster in front of him. "Any new clues?"

Rheinhart grimaced. From the moment he'd mentioned finding the body on Anclote Key, he'd been mercilessly teased by Gracie, who began referring to him as Sherlock, a moniker he openly disliked, which only made her use it more frequently. "No news," he said, reddening slightly. "You'll be the first to know if I hear anything."

Gracie smiled. "I hope so," she said. "We're all waiting for some evidence to back up your claim." Her blond hair was cut short, parted in the middle, just covering her ears. She had mesmerizing blue eyes, a quick wit and an encyclopedic memory of personal drink preferences that amazed both customers and friends. From owner Florence Leaf's perspective, she was Kitty Galore's most valuable asset.

Rheinhart shook his head. "I never should've said anything about that day, especially here."

Morrison winked at Gracie, getting in on the fun. "Don't worry about it, Zach. We're glad you did. Where else could you get this kind of support?"

Rheinhart took a healthy swig of his ale before replying. "Support? You call this support? You must be high."

Gracie bent over the bar, making a show of looking into Morrison's eyes. "Pupils seem fine. I see no evidence of your claim." Before Rheinhart could respond, she smiled, straightened up and headed toward a waitress at the other end of the bar, who was waiting impatiently at the service bar to place an order.

"Gracie says the oysters are especially good today, a fresh batch trucked in this morning from the panhandle. You game?" Morrison said after she departed.

"Absolutely."

"Good, because I ordered us a dozen. Should be out any minute."

At the other end of the bar Gracie was engaged in spirited conversation with Marcia Alvarez, another lunchtime regular who lived in a condo on the causeway leading to Honeymoon Island in

Dunedin with her elderly father, Clement. Alvarez was venting – Morrison and Rheinhart could see her gesticulations but couldn't make out what she was saying - while Gracie appeared to be attempting to restore calm to her animated customer.

Like Rheinhart, Steve Morrison was a transplant in Florida. He'd moved to Ozona from Los Angeles two years earlier after being named sole beneficiary in the will of his uncle, Merle Benson. Benson, the younger brother of Morrison's mother Betty, was a retired flight engineer for NASA, never married, childless, who was enjoying his retirement in a three-bedroom ranch on North Street in Ozona when he died of a massive coronary, despite having previously exhibited no evidence of heart disease.

The inheritance came as a complete surprise to Morrison, who'd had little contact with his uncle since he'd moved to California from western New York at eighteen to pursue a passion for surfing. Morrison had been a straight A student and member of the National Honor Society at Riverton High School, but had rejected his family's pleas to attend college. Instead, three days after his high school graduation he packed a military-issue duffel bag he'd purchased at the Army/Navy surplus store in Buffalo and set out on a road trip with two high school friends that eventually landed him in a small community of hippies and surfers in the Ocean Beach section of San Diego. His parents had been furious, certain he was throwing away a life filled with unlimited potential for that of a beach bum, and had cut off all contact, including financial support, with their only son.

Morrison and Rheinhart were kindred spirits, refugees from lives that had soured elsewhere, and had bonded quickly since meeting at Kitty's shortly after Rheinhart's move across the state from Jacksonville. Morrison was ten years older than Rheinhart, but held similar political outlooks and shared a passion for the water which provided much common ground between the two.

Their friendship evolved quickly after they'd been introduced to one another by Gracie at the bar.

Their oysters arrived. They lived up to Gracie's billing, fresh and cold, and were consumed with vigor. "So," Morrison said after he finished the last of his allotment and wiped some stray cocktail sauce from his lip with a napkin. "Have you tried to contact those detectives again?"

"Kullmann and Profeta? Nah, they stopped returning my calls after the first week. Claimed they weren't assigned to the case any more." Rheinhart was grateful in Morrison's interest, which for the most part was sincere and supportive. Unlike Gracie's constant ribbing, which often was delivered in a taunting tone that frustrated Rheinhart.

Morrison, who was the only person who had viewed Rheinhart's photos of the crime scene and the victim, photos that he'd concealed from the police, lowered his voice and leaned toward his friend. "Maybe you should show someone the photos. What about the media?"

Rheinhart looked at his friend. His voice was laced with alarm as he looked around to see if anyone had overheard. "Jesus, are you nuts? There has to be some reason that this murder hasn't been reported. Something really big." He took a sip of his beer, then continued with a rueful smile. "I'm pretty sure Chad Middleton was no normal real estate agent."

"Are you sure that was his business card?"

Rheinhart nodded. "I went on their website as soon as I got back from Anclote and checked. They have brief bios of all their agents, along with photos. Chad Middleton was the same guy I found. No doubt about it. But then something funny happened. I called the office the next day, asked to speak to Middleton. Told them I had been thinking about buying a place on Captiva and had

had a couple of conversations with Middleton. They told me he was out of the office and gave me his cell number, the same number that was on his card. I called; it went straight to voicemail. By then I knew something was wrong, so I didn't leave a message. But then something even weirder happened. I waited a few days, then went back to their website. Middleton was gone. His bio and picture were no longer there. I called the main number for the office and asked for him. The woman at the other end hesitated, then told me Chad Middleton no longer worked for Junonia Realty."

The image of Chad Middleton, tongue removed, rose in Morrison's brainpan. The words were out of his mouth without thought. "No shit, Sherlock."

Rheinhart looked at Morrison with a pained expression. "Not you, too?"

5

"He's drivin' me crazy. Absolutely fuckin' bonkers."

Gracie Fenton tried not to smile. It was a refrain she heard from Marcia Alvarez every time she came to Kitty Galore's for lunch. "What's he doing now?"

"The same old shit. 'Get me this, cook me that.' Like I'm his fuckin' maid." Marcia's voice was brimming with frustration.

Gracie thought: well, aren't you? "I thought the babysitters might help." She was referring to the two elderly women from the condo complex who took turns spending time with Clement Harkins while his daughter stole away for an hour of mostly liquid respite at Kitty Galore's each weekday.

"Them?" she snorted with derision. "I thought so, too. Figured they'd suck him in with kindness, being as they're both widows, each of 'em looking for a new meal ticket. But he's so goddamned ornery, I think they're both sorry they volunteered for this duty. Wouldn't surprise me none if they both up and quit." She reached into her purse and withdrew a pack of Marlboro Lights. "I need a smoke. Be right back."

Gracie watched as Marcia retreated to the outdoor smoking area and lit up, sucking smoke deeply into her lungs, as if nicotine would soothe her frustration. She shook her head. She was glad she wasn't in Marcia's position, having to care for a cantankerous elderly parent with multiple health issues whose mind was still agile, his tongue still a formidable weapon. Clement Harkins had fallen two years ago, breaking his hip, and now he was now shifting between a wheelchair and a walker, depending on his mood. He'd been a career Air Force guy, a paratrooper during the Korean War, and his lack of mobility had turned an already sour personality toxic. Even if he hadn't outlived his few friends, Marcia was sure they would've been long gone by now, driven away by the constant barrage of vitriol spewing from his lips.

Gracie appreciated the break from Marcia's rant and used it to check the bar. She saw Morrison waving his arm, trying to get her attention. She could see that both glasses were half full, so she grabbed a couple of menus and headed to the end of the bar, noting other drink levels on the way. Rheinhart and Morrison were as dependable as Japanese train schedules: beer, oysters, beer, lunch, beer, home. She was impressed by their discipline in limiting themselves to three drinks, since both lived close enough to walk home and obviously enjoyed the time they spent together at Kitty's. She knew both were somewhat damaged from hours of confessional banter across the bar, but still solid at their core, two of her most interesting regulars. She enjoyed the playful back-and-forth between the three of them. Plus, they were excellent tippers.

She held up the menus when she reached them. "Need these?"

Rheinhart looked at Morrison, who shook his head. He continued. "Nope. I'll have the grouper sandwich, blackened."

She looked at Morrison expectantly. "A bowl of gumbo."

Rheinhart turned to his friend, puzzled. "Dieting?"

"Trying to stay away from the fries," Morrison offered in explanation. He turned back to Gracie. "Have I told you this place has the best fries in the world?"

Gracie pretended to check a tally sheet on her watch, then looked up and smiled. "Every time you come in. Probably close to a hundred mentions by now."

Morrison smiled. "Glad you're paying attention."

"Just doing my job."

*****

The food was gone and they were nursing their third beers, delaying their exit, enjoying a rare lull in mid-afternoon activity, savoring the quiet. The crowd at the bar had thinned, a retired couple vacationing from Michigan the only other occupants. Gracie took advantage of the dearth of customers and stole away to the kitchen for a quick salad.

An overhead fan whirled slowly above Morrison and Rheinhart. They'd been talking about music, which J.J Cale album they preferred, inspired by "After Midnight" playing on the satellite channel in the background when, out of the blue, Morrison asked, "Did you ever call your insurance company?"

Rheinhart, whose house had miraculously suffered no damage from Irma despite being less than two blocks from the Gulf, shook his head. "No. I told you – there are enough people backed up out there with legitimate claims who're having trouble getting paid. Nothing happened to my house."

"They don't know that."

Rheinhart looked at his friend, dumbfounded. "Do you think they're just going to give me the money, take my word for it that I lost my roof or a tree fell on my car without sending an agent out to assess the damage? Are you serious?"

Morrison, who'd always been a renter before inheriting his uncle's house and was still largely clueless when it came to the nuances of home ownership, was unfazed. "I can get you damage photos to submit in an hour, no questions asked. Maybe less than an hour."

Rheinhart wondered: who has access to photographic evidence of customized storm damage on demand? "Thanks, but I'll pass."

Morrison shrugged. "Suit yourself. Personally, I think you're making a mistake."

"I'll take the chance. What about you? Did you file your claim yet?" Morrison's house, which was closer to the Gulf than Rheinhart's and not shielded from the brunt of the storm by cypress, banana palms, sea grapes and saw palmettos, was damaged when a sizable chunk of his neighbor's Australian pine sheared off and plunged through the roof above the guest bathroom. Rain pouring through the resultant breach had damaged the drywall in the bathroom; it was currently out of commission.

"Last week. The guy I talked to on the phone says they're backed up to their eyeballs, don't know when they'll be able to get a man out here."

"I told you not to wait," Rheinhart scolded.

Morrison waved his free hand dismissively as he raised his beer to his mouth with the other. "And how many times are you going to say 'I told you so'?"

"As many as it takes."

Gracie overheard their last exchange as she arrived with the check, chiding Rheinhart. "You sound like his wife." She held the check out expectantly. "Whose turn is it?"

Morrison nodded toward Rheinhart, his voice rising. "Give it to Sherlock. Ozona's own Righteous Brother."

"Opting not to commit insurance fraud makes me a Righteous Brother?" Rheinhart fired back indignantly.

Gracie struggled not to smile. She was on Morrison's side on this one. She thought the insurance business was one of the most venal for-profit American schemes spawned during the previous century, just behind the American healthcare system, holding both the tenets of the industry and its agents in contempt.

She dropped the check on the bar midway between the two. "You two can sort this out. I need to attend to some of my less volatile customers. See you boys next week." With a parting smile she turned and was gone, headed in the direction of an agitated Marcia Alvarez, impatiently waving an empty glass at the other end of the bar. "Ready for another, Marcia?" she asked, pausing at the beer taps, fresh glass in hand.

She glanced at her watch, calculating. "One more. Then I'm out of here."

Gracie laid down a fresh napkin beneath the perspiring glass. "Nothing to eat today?"

Marcia leaned back from bar and grabbed a handful of flesh from around her waist, crudely offering it to Gracie as evidence. "Been trying to cut back. Thanksgiving is in two weeks. We're headin' into the heavy calorie season." She took a gulp of beer. "Besides, I shoulda left an hour ago. Muriel's been texting me every five minutes, says Dad keeps asking where I am."

"His mind's still sharp, then?"

"Like a razor."

"What do you think he wants?"

"Dad? To make my life miserable. He's like that, pissed off that he can't walk no more, can't drive no more. If he's unhappy he wants everyone else to be unhappy. The fuckin' prick." She took another gulp. "I keep prayin' one of those bitches asks him to marry her. Take him off my hands."

Gracie saw Morrison and Rheinhart getting up to leave, a wad of cash left on the bar, and waved goodbye. She turned back to Marcia as they walked out the door. "Do you think there's a chance of that happening?"

"Naw," she said after a moment of internal debate. "They're crazy, but they ain't batshit crazy."

6

Morrison and Rheinhart walked home together in silence, each lost in thought, Rheinhart once again fixated on the mystery of Chad Middleton and the complete lack of reporting regarding his death, Morrison thinking ahead to the poker game he'd be attending that evening, wondering if he should stop by the bank on the way to withdraw some more cash.

When they reached Rheinhart's home, Morrison extended his hand. "Thanks for lunch. Next week it's on me."

Rheinhart shook his friend's hand. "My pleasure. Any plans for tonight?"

"I'm heading out to Land O' Lakes to meet some friends for a drink."

"Anyone I know?"

Morrison shook his head. "Someone I used to work with in California. How about you?"

"The Lightning are playing the Sabres. My two favorite teams – I can't lose."

Morrison, who was born in Niagara Falls, nodded in approval. "Buffalo started playing in the league the year I left for California. I still follow them a bit."

Rheinhart pretended to size up his friend. "Really? I never figured you for a masochist."

*****

Marcia finished her beer and withdrew her wallet from her purse. "What's the damage?"

Gracie handed her the check. Marcia gave it a quick once over and dropped a ten and a five on the bar. She looped her purse over her shoulder and pushed herself to her feet. "I guess I'll see you tomorrow."

"I'll be here," Gracie replied with a smile, sweeping up Marcia's empty glass and depositing it in the sink. She moved to the end of the bar and watched as Marcia got on her bike and pedaled south on Orange Street toward the Pinellas Trail bike path in the mid-afternoon heat. She glanced at the clock on the wall above the cash register. Three hours to go.

*****

When Marcia exited the elevator on the seventh floor of their building, she could hear her father threatening Muriel Drake, his lunchtime companion, in a bellicose tone as she approached their condo. "Quit, then. I don't give a fuck. You're nothing but a pain in my ass, anyway."

"Jesus, Dad. What's wrong with you?" Marcia exclaimed as she came through the door. Her father was leaning on his walker next to the dining room table, glaring malevolently at Muriel several feet away in the kitchen. Tears were streaming down the elderly woman's face as she cowered in a corner, collapsed in a chair, as if fearful of an impending attack. "I could hear you all the way down at the elevator."

"Ask her," he said, pointing defiantly at Muriel. "She's the one who started it."

Marcia turned toward the woman. "Muriel?"

The silver-haired widow dabbed at her nose with a monogrammed linen handkerchief. "Your father wanted tomato soup for lunch, but there wasn't any in the cupboard. I told him

44

you were out and he started screaming at me, telling me to go to Publix and get some. You told me never to leave him alone, which is what I told him. That made him even madder." Her voice caught. "Where were you?" Muriel asked Marcia imploringly. "You're over an hour late."

"I'm so sorry, Muriel. I lost track of time. It won't happen again – I promise you." Turning to her father, her voice frosty, she said, "Apologize, Dad. Right now."

"What for?" he said defiantly. "I didn't do nothin' wrong. All I wanted was my lunch. What good is she if she can't feed me my lunch?"

Marcia gestured toward the cupboard. "There's lots of food in there. You could've had something else."

"I didn't want something else. I wanted tomato soup," he replied with the petulance of a child.

"See?" Muriel sniffled. "That's what I mean." After a moment she continued, her voice wavering. "I don't know if I can do this any more. All he does is criticize me."

Marcia knew losing Muriel would be a disaster. She had to find a way to convince her not to quit. "This ain't your fault, Muriel. It's mine. I shouldn't of been so late. Please don't quit. I promise he'll behave."

Doubt flooded Muriel's face. "How are you going to do that?"

Marcia hadn't expected Muriel to call her bluff. In a moment she replied, "I'll take the TV out of his bedroom if he does anything like that again."

Clement Harkins howled in protest. "You can't do that! The TV's all I got."

"Then you better be nicer to Muriel. Edith, too. They don't deserve to be treated like something on the sidewalk you stepped in with your shoe."

Muriel wasn't convinced. "I don't know…"

"I'll call you tomorrow, when you're feeling better," Marcia said to Muriel as she helped her to her feet and edged her toward the door. "We'll figure this out."

Marcia guided the diminutive senior as she shuffled carefully out of the condo, toward her own place two doors down, repeating her earlier claim. "It won't happen again."

She watched until Muriel unlatched her door and was inside before turning back to her father, livid. "Are you trying to ruin what little freedom I have? I get out for an hour a day---"

"Two. Two hours today," he interjected.

"You're right, Dad," she said, exasperated. "I fucked up. You know why I fucked up? Because I was having a good time for a change, talking with my friend. My only friend. You'd know what that was like if you had any."

Her father, stunned, responded meekly. "I have friends."

Marcia stood facing her father defiantly, hands on hips. "Name one."

Harkins, whose memory had developed significant gaps during the last several years, struggled to come up with a name. After a long silence he tentatively offered, "Muriel."

Marcia laughed harshly. "Muriel? She's just a widow looking for a new husband. You can tell how desperate she is by the amount of horseshit she puts up with from you. What about those Army buddies you claim to have? Ain't never heard from a single one of 'em in all the years I've been living with you. Never visited, never even called."

"They're all dead," he said in a whisper.

Marcia was on a roll now, gaining momentum. "I believe that. But what about that FBI agent, the one whose name I can never remember? Ralph something. I think he was German. The one you sent that letter to."

Harkins eyes lit up excitedly. "Himmelsbach. Ralph Himmelsbach." He tried to form an image of the man in his mind, but failed. "He's my friend."

Marcia sighed. They'd had this conversation many times in the past, usually in the evening after Clement had consumed several bourbon and cokes. Her voice was gentler, sympathetic. "Dad, he didn't believe your story. He never answered your letter. How can you call him your friend?"

Harkins' voice was choked with emotion. "Because he didn't arrest me after I confessed. He wants to protect me – that's what friends do."

"He didn't arrest you because he didn't believe your story. Nobody does. If he believed you, you'd be in Leavenworth now." And out of my hair, she thought, with only a trace of guilt.

"You're wrong," he insisted, as he always did when the subject came up. "He *is* my friend. And you're wrong about the other thing, too. You'll find out, someday."

Although she already knew the answer, she asked the question anyway, attempting to keep her voice neutral, as if she was asking for the first time. "Find out what?"

"That I'm D. B. Cooper."

7

Morrison continued down Bay Street, following the bend where it reached the Gulf of Mexico, walking past the Crooked Snook Marina toward his house on North Street. On the far side of the navigation channel he could see a pair of kayakers nosing around one of the small mangrove islands, killing time in the waning late afternoon sunshine as clouds began to mass over the Gulf.

Morrison was worried about Rheinhart, specifically his obsession with the dead body and how it seemed to permeate every aspect of his life. Before that day on Anclote Key his friend spent most of his mornings in the Gulf on his boat, exploring the coast between Anna Maria Island and Cedar Key, becoming familiar with the fluctuations in depth, learning how to read the tides and decipher the clues to weather patterns that could change the nature of a pleasant day on the water to one of disastrous import in a manner of minutes. The only break in his routine occurred when the mandatory evacuation notice issued by Pinellas County officials ahead of Hurricane Irma's arrival forced him to secure his house as well as he could and head inland to higher ground, his boat trailered behind him.

Since that grisly discovery two weeks earlier, however, his boat hadn't budged from its position on the lift at the marina. Instead, he spent most of his time on his computer, trying to figure out how such a crime had thus far gone unreported. In the current climate of cable news, where the sensational was served on a platter on a daily basis, the absence of a single story about the dead realtor seemed unfathomable to Rheinhart, who had vented his frustration to Morrison numerous times when they'd been together.

"They cut out his tongue. *They cut out his fucking tongue!* Who does that? The Mafia?"

Morrison had no answer and was frankly tired of the question. He thought it was foolish to allow an issue that had no bearing on your life to disrupt your daily routine, so much so that it dominated your waking thoughts and interfered with your ability to sleep through the night. What Rheinhart needed was a clean slate, to move forward as if he'd never returned to Anclote Key to photograph that storm-ravaged skiff. Life was too short to waste time on anything beyond your control, no matter how ominous it may seem.

As he approached his house the blue tarp spread over the gash in his roof reminded him to call the roofers he'd lined up and see when they could fit him into their schedule. He knew all contractors were under extreme pressure in post-hurricane Florida, but it wouldn't hurt to keep planting a bug in their ear, to let them know he was still out there, in need of repairs. At least they were past the rainy season. He dialed the number and the call went directly to voicemail. He left his name and address and a request for a call back.

The house on North Street that Morrison had inherited from his uncle had come fully furnished and remained, for the most part, just as it had been when Merle Benson lived there. Morrison had few possessions to his name when he'd been contacted by Benson's attorney, telling Morrison he was the sole heir to his uncle's estate. His last few years in California had been difficult; the precipitous decline in his career coupled with the insane rise in monthly rental costs in the San Fernando Valley during the last eighteen months had forced Morrison to sell most of his possessions and join the increasing number of Californians who were living in their vehicles. Morrison might never have been informed of the unexpected inheritance he'd received if he hadn't fortuitously decided to fill out a change of address form and rent a post office box after he was forced to give up his tiny apartment in Reseda.

The single-story bungalow he'd inherited had the look and feel of a man cave from the previous century, the type of domain where women had rarely if ever entered. Merle had been a lifelong bachelor, and the cream-colored walls in the living room gave no indication of a female touch. They were covered with memorabilia from his time at NASA: pictures of him with his colleagues in one of the control rooms in Titusville, a shot of the Apollo 13 launch, and a picture of a smiling Merle shaking hands with President George H.W. Bush at the White House. It had the feel of a shrine to Morrison, featuring highlights from the impressive career of a family member he'd barely known.

It also infused him with a sense of guilt. Uncle Merle wasn't the only family member with whom he'd lost contact. When he'd ignored the pleas of his parents to attend college and instead had driven to San Diego at age eighteen with two of his friends to become a surf bum, his father had been so apoplectic he refused to speak to his only child and had kept that promise until his death. His mother never lost hope of reconnecting, sending him periodic postcards with images of Niagara Falls, his hometown, urging him to come home. But once he moved north to Los Angeles to pursue an acting career in a genre of film that could never be discussed at the Morrison dinner table during holiday meals, he felt the best path for all concerned was a complete break. At the urging of one of his new female colleagues he assumed the screen name Biff Bratwurst and began the second act of his adult life, severing all familial ties with the Morrisons and their extended clan. He knew that his decision to bypass college and hang out on the beach had proven to be a constant source of irritation to his parents, both of whom were college educated. There was no doubt in his mind they would have reacted much more poorly to the news that their son's new career involved him removing his clothes and inserting his penis into a variety of young women of diverse pedigrees. Steven Morrison vanished into the ether and Biff Bratwurst never looked back.

The story he'd given Rheinhart earlier that afternoon about meeting friends for a drink tonight wasn't the whole truth. There would be drinks available, but he was going to play a little Texas Hold 'Em with a group of people that included one of his former professional associates from California, Wai Tang, who'd moved to Florida five years earlier and had urged Morrison to follow him for several years before he'd received the letter from his uncle's attorney that had precipitated Morrison's cross-country move.

The game tonight was being held at Fuego, a sprawling 330-acre clothing-optional resort where Tang now lived on U.S. 41 in Land O' Lakes, a thirty-minute drive from Morrison's home. Tang had assured him there would be a bed available for him should the game run late, since it was the off season for the resort, which begins to kick into high gear at Christmas when wealthy European nudists arrive in droves to escape the harsh continental winter.

He was looking forward to this evening out, when he could let his guard down and be himself among friends. Tang had indicated that several other familiar faces would be at the table tonight, people he'd worked with previously or knew through mutual contacts in the industry. It would be the first time since Irma made landfall that Morrison engaged in any social activity other than his weekly lunch at Kitty Galore's with Rheinhart. He was overdue for a little fun.

He heated up a frozen dinner in the microwave and ate it while he watched the local news – still no mention of Middleton's body. When he was finished he rinsed his silverware and left them in the sink. As he was contemplating what to wear to the poker game, his cell phone rang. Caller ID indicated the incoming call was from a restricted number, so he let it go to voicemail. If it was anything important, they'd leave a message.

Tang had assured him that the game would be very casual, so he selected a navy-blue short sleeved shirt, tan shorts that were beginning to fray around the edges and sandals. Better to be underdressed when gambling – he wanted his opponents to underestimate him, to think he was an easy mark, some rube in over his head. "Besides," Tang had said when questioned by Morrison as to appropriate attire for the game, "we're playing at Fuego. Chances are 50-50 that Monique Monroe will show up naked. She thinks her boobs will distract the men at the table, give her a leg up." He chuckled. "She forgets most of us are used to seeing naked tits."

Morrison knew her from some work she'd done in LA several years ago. "She's playing?"

"It's her game – she runs it. She's been making noise about moving to Vegas to become a professional poker player as long as I've known her."

"She any good?"

"Not as good as she thinks she is."

8

The tale of how Steven Morrison first made it to California and then Florida has its origins in his upbringing. He was born during the final year of the Truman presidency in Niagara Falls, New York, the only child of William and Elizabeth Morrison, and was raised in Riverton, a small village along the Niagara River seven miles north of Niagara Falls, where he was a misfit from the beginning. Although both his parents were college educated, neither of them worked in professional jobs – his father was a foreman at the Bell Aerospace Laboratory in Niagara Falls and his mother was a stay-at-home mom.

During the post-World War II era, Niagara Falls was a vibrant place, filled with manufacturing facilities that had been essential cogs in the war effort and had continued to produce key components for the automotive, aviation, steel, paper and chemical industries for four more decades. Many of the top executives from these facilities lived in Riverton precisely because the picturesque village along the Canadian border was not Niagara Falls: a gritty cityscape where the land along the river above the majestic cataracts was dominated by belching smokestacks and clandestine waste sites instead of showcase homes with professionally landscaped lawns running to the river's edge.

Morrison attended the Riverton public school system along with the children of these executives, where his blue-collar existence placed him in stark contrast with classmates who were destined for Ivy League schools and trust fund lifestyles. There were few days during his adolescence where he didn't feel the economic and social chasm between him and some of his more privileged peers, didn't feel somewhat less in comparison with his friends, who ridiculed everything from his haircut to his wardrobe. By the time he was a teenager his thoughts were full of escape plans; he wanted nothing more than to get as far away from Riverton as he could.

Three incidents, all occurring when he was thirteen, provided powerful incentives for his thoughts concerning geographic relocation. The first and most important of these was his fascination with surfing, which began with his adoration of the music of the Beach Boys, Jan and Dean and Dick Dale and expanded from there to an obsession with the California surf culture. There was nothing in his limited world view that offered more of a contrast to his present travails than the lure of a life on the beach on the other side of the country. To stay as close to his dream as possible, he saved money from neighborhood landscaping jobs and pestered his mother to drive him to Mario's on Pine Avenue in Niagara Falls, the only store in the area that sold surfing magazines, which he devoured from cover to cover, savoring the revolutionary photography featuring the latest hot surf breaks and an abundance of barely clad bronzed surf bunnies.

The second incident involved that other bugaboo of adolescence, religion. Although neither of his parents were particularly religious, his mother attended the First Presbyterian Church in Riverton weekly, primarily so she could insist Steven attend Sunday School. When Steven turned thirteen, his mother enrolled him, despite his vociferous protests, in communicants' class, a series of educational sessions in which young boys were taught the basic canons of the Presbyterian faith. When completed successfully, these classes qualified all graduates to become members of the church.

These weekly classes were held after school across the street from the church in the apartment of Bradley Ervine, the 32-year-old assistant minister of the First Presbyterian Church. With his mesmerizing crystal blue eyes, wavy dark hair, dazzling smile and athletic physique, Ervine was the heartthrob of the congregation, the sort of man any mother would welcome as their son-in-law. As part of his apprenticeship, Ervine taught this class to a group of reluctant neophyte theologians, one of whom was Steven Morrison.

Morrison had protested long and hard to his mother about participating in the class, worried that he'd be called a religious wimp by the rich kids who already ridiculed him for his wardrobe, but his passionate pleas were in vain. Anyone who was anyone in Riverton who wasn't Catholic belonged to the First Presbyterian Church, his mother argued in response. Didn't he want to be included in such a group?

He didn't. But when his father stepped in and suggested it would be good for the condition of his backside to agree to his mother's request, he gave in and said he would attend. "But I won't like it."

It was after the third class when Reverend Ervine revealed his true character. Morrison and Hugh Truitt were about to leave when Ervine asked Morrison to remain behind for a moment. Truitt, relieved that he had avoided a similar summons, wasted no time gathering his school books and getting out the door.

When Truitt was gone, Ervine turned to Morrison with a smile and asked him to follow him into his bedroom to see his baseball card collection. Morrison followed innocently, unaware of what was about to happen.

Ervine stood next to his bed and motioned to Morrison to sit on the bed. Morrison complied. Then Ervine shifted his position until he was standing directly in front of Morrison and, still smiling, unzipped his pants and let them fall to the floor, an obvious erection straining his cotton briefs. Morrison sat frozen, stunned by the turn of events, as Reverend Ervine reached across the gap between them and wordlessly grabbed Morrison's wrist and placed his hand on his crotch, cooing, "It's not that bad, is it? Why don't you give it a squeeze?"

Confused and panicked, Morrison looked for a way to get by the minister, to get away from this nightmare. Ervine read Morrison's hesitation as acquiescence and relaxed, moving closer yet. Boxed in, unable to get away, the young boy slid his hand slightly down the shaft of the minister's erection and squeezed the man's balls as hard as he could.

Ervine moaned loudly and tried to pull away, but Morrison squeezed harder. Tears began to form in the corners of Ervine's eyes as Morrison finally released the man's testicles, gave him a shove and bolted out the door, grabbing his social studies book on the way, afraid to look back as he raced away from the church toward home, riddled with shame, his mind struggling to comprehend what had just happened, wondering: what had he done wrong to deserve this?

When he walked in the door of his home his mother was in the kitchen, frying bologna and onions for dinner. She glanced at the clock on the wall. "You're home early."

Morrison, his face flushed from his dash home, still out of breath, tried to be nonchalant. "Reverend Ervine let us out early because we did so good on the quiz on last week's assignment."

At school the next day, Truitt caught up with Morrison at his locker. "What did the rev want yesterday?"

Morrison thought: if you only knew. "He wanted to show me his baseball card collection," he replied, sticking to the ruse Ervine had used.

Truitt grinned. "Glad it was you and not me."

Morrison never mentioned the incident aloud, and when a sign went up on the church bulletin board the following Sunday, stating that communicants' classes were cancelled until further notice, Morrison was the only one of the class members or their parents who knew why. Reverend Ervine wasn't at services that Sunday, and after completing his sermon on the evils of temptation, the long-time minister of the First Presbyterian Church, Dr. Dennis Paulson, asked the congregation from the pulpit to pray for Ervine's recovery from a nasty virus that had laid him low.

The following Wednesday Ervine, who hadn't been ill at all but instead was terrified that Morrison would reveal what had happened in his apartment, fashioned a noose from one of his neckties, tied the free end to the doorknob and hanged himself in his bathroom. He left no note.

The third precipitating incident occurred that summer. The parents of one of his classmates, Scott Patrick, had gone to Toronto for the weekend to see a play at the Royal Alexandra Theatre. Morrison considered Scott one of the cool kids, above him in the social pecking order at Riverton Junior High, so he was shocked when he received an invitation to a party at Scott's house that Saturday night.

The party was held in the finished basement of the Patrick home, and soon the smoke was as thick as a cloud in the low-ceilinged space as several of the mostly eighth graders took advantage of the lack of parental presence and lit cigarettes they'd stolen from their own parents. Despite being invited, Morrison wasn't comfortable among this crowd and hung around the periphery, watching the action, declining several opportunities to drink from a bottle of vodka being passed around, listening to the music being played on the record player in the corner of the room.

When the family dog came down the stairs and made a beeline for Scott, rising up on his hind legs, cradling Scott's thigh with his front paws as he humped his master's leg, Morrison thought that would be the highlight of the party, the thing everyone would be talking about in school on Monday, replaying the hysterical laughter that spread through the room at the host's expense.

He was wrong. Three hours into the party, when couples had formed and began to disappear upstairs, Scott dropped the Beach Boys *Surfer Girl* album on the turntable. When the song "In My Room" came up, Morrison was approached by Andrea Herman, who asked him to dance. Of all the eighth-grade girls, Andrea had the most advanced physique, with softball-sized breasts that were the envy of her female classmates and twin objects of desire that generated countless crude and speculative comments from the boys. As the flabbergasted Morrison struggled to respond, Herman smiled, took his hand and led him to a corner of the dance floor, where she placed her hands on his shoulders and drew him tightly against her, her hips beginning to sway to the sultry rhythm.

He placed his hands tentatively on her back and his reaction was immediate. His penis leaped to attention as she ardently ground her pelvis against him, and he was flooded with shame and embarrassment at his lack of self control. He tried to pull away from her, to run and hide somewhere until his hard-on subsided, but Andrea would have none of it. She drew him in even closer, the hot points of her breasts mashed against his chest, one of her hands slipping down to cup his butt cheek through his jeans as she continued to massage his erection with her loins.

When the song ended, she looked up at Morrison, her eyes bright, her lips moist, arms around his neck. As the first notes of the next song, "Hawaii", spilled from the speakers, she spoke for the first time, purring. "That was the best dance I've had all night. Want to do it again?"

A crimson Morrison backed away, shaking his head, mumbling something about having homework to do as he made his way up the stairs and out the door into the humid August night, leaving a bewildered and bemused Andrea Herman behind as she watched him, hunched over to hide the bulge in his pants, flee the scene. Twice in two months his already volatile teenaged life had been rocked by incidents involving stiff penises and the formerly unfathomable prospect of sex with a partner instead of the usual solo acts he performed on himself. It was too much to take.

He never danced with Andrea Herman again, but he observed her furtively during the next four years as she carved out a well-deserved reputation as the hottest girl in school, the sure thing who would say yes to the most intimate requests, the darling of the school's male population, an object of scorn from the girls. Despite her obvious interest in him at the party, she quickly dismissed him as one of the timid ones, not yet ready for the kind of action she craved, and moved on. As she had learned as soon as her body began to bloom, there was no shortage of adolescent dicks wanting to get into her pants, so Steven Morrison's lack of interest in her did nothing to damage her ego or deter her from her mission. By the time school started in September he was a vaguely familiar face to her with no historical context.

The dual shame he felt as the object of two sexual advances during that fateful year, one from a grown man of God, the other from a precocious nymphette, continued to foster confusion and erode his sense of self-worth during that crucial period of adolescent development, so by the time he graduated from Riverton High he was more than ready to move on to something completely different, a fresh start pursuing his romanticized version of endless summer in California, as far from Riverton as he could get.

9

Although it was a little after seven, beyond the usual evening rush hour, traffic was thick on SR 54 as Morrison approached U.S. 41 in Land O' Lakes. He waited through two cycles of lights at the intersection before turning left and heading toward the poker game at Fuego. Because of the resort's resident nudists and relaxed lifestyle policies, the local legislature had forged a deal with the resort that prohibited any signage on the highway denoting its location, so Morrison reduced his speed as he approached the two-lane road leading to the sprawling complex, not wanting to miss the sign indicating the turn-off in the waning light of early evening.

He was inching along at thirty, cars racing past him on the left, when he spotted the street sign he was looking for and turned right, following the narrow road for a half mile before he reached the entrance to Fuego. He slowed and lowered his window as he arrived at the front gate, and a security guard in an ill-fitting uniform emerged from a small building holding a clipboard. "May I help you?"

"I'm here to visit a friend, one of your members. Wai Tang."

The guard scanned a list on the clipboard for a moment before he looked at Morrison, amused. "Here for the poker game, Mr. Morrison?"

"Yes."

"May I see your ID?"

Morrison handed his Florida driver's license to the guard, who confirmed his identity before handing it back. "Been here before?"

"I have," Morrison replied.

"So you know where to go." The guard stepped back inside the building and activated a switch that raised the gate before emerging once again, handing him a visitor's pass. "Have a nice evening."

Morrison smiled. "I'll try."

He drove slowly to the visitors' parking area opposite the clubhouse building where the game was being held. The night air was still as he exited his car, stars beginning to appear from behind evaporating cloud cover.

He showed his pass to a laconic attendant inside the entrance who glanced at it and looked him over before speaking. "The poker game?"

Morrison nodded. The man indicated an area to their right. "It's in the meeting room next to the pub."

The clubhouse at Fuego was a common area that contained four different bars: a small hotel-like bar in the reception area beyond the entrance, an outdoor bar servicing the main pool area located outside the rear of the building, a disco used primarily for parties and special events, and a replica of an authentic English pub with a name Morrison thought was perfectly suited to the philosophy of the resort: The Hand and Job.

Tang had briefed him on tonight's players, all of whom were residents at Fuego, during a phone call earlier in the week, and he recalled what Tang had said about them. Besides Tang, the attendees included Lauren Caputo, the organizer of the monthly game and a self-professed poker expert who operated her own adult website under her porn name, Monique Monroe; Rick

61

Manning and Elaine Prescott, a husband and wife duo originally from Shaker Heights, Ohio, now both respiratory technicians at Tampa General Hospital; and Duncan Foote, president of the Fuego Residents Association who, along with his wife JoJo, owned and operated a small oil change and automotive repair facility in Port Richey.

Morrison walked past the ornately carved wooden sign for The Hand and Job and into the meeting room where the game was being held. The other five were already seated at the round table in the middle of the room, chatting quietly and sipping drinks. Tang noticed him immediately and was on his feet, a big smile on his face. "Right on time," he beamed. "Let me introduce you to the rest of the players."

When Morrison reached the group, Tang began. "This is Steve Morrison. We worked together for a lot of years in LA. But if you're a fan of adult entertainment, you may know him better as Biff Bratwurst." He paused for a moment, then continued. "Clockwise around the table we have Lauren Caputo, Rick Manning, his wife Elaine Prescott, and Duncan Foote."

"Nice to meet you all," Morrison said as he slid into his chair. "Thanks for inviting me to play."

Lauren Caputo, a buxom brunette in her fifties, looked at him appraisingly, a smile playing on her lips. "Harpoon told us you weren't a cheat," she said, referring to Tang's screen name. "That's good enough for me."

"Hardly," Morrison replied with a smile. "I can barely shuffle a deck of cards, let alone cheat."

Manning nodded approvingly. "Sounds perfect for this game. Glad to have you aboard." His broad face sported thick-rimmed glasses and his hair was thinning on top. Morrison guessed he was in his late fifties. His wife was seated next to him, a petite blond with a dynamic figure who Tang had told him was several years older than her husband. Both were nudists and swingers, as were the rest of the players in the game. On her left was Foote, a short, stocky, dour-faced gray-haired man with a pair of reading glasses attached to a cord around his neck who nodded wordlessly in Morrison's direction.

Tang indicated the vacant seat next to Caputo. "Take a seat so we can get this game underway. Something to drink?"

Morrison nodded. "Beer. Yuengling, if you've got it."

"I think we do." He walked over to a table that had been set up against the wall as a refreshment depot, with bottles of liquor, mixers, wine and soft drinks, along with a cooler of iced bottles of beer. He reached into the cooler, extracted a Yuengling, popped the cap and addressed the table. "Anyone else while I'm up?"

There were no takers. Tang handed the beer to Morrison and sat down between him and Foote. Caputo, who'd been idly shuffling a deck of cards since Morrison had entered the room, offered the deck to Morrison to cut. "Let's play some poker."

Although he wasn't much of a card player, he had studied the structure of Texas Hold 'Em and watched a couple of tournaments on YouTube during the past week so he wouldn't come off as a complete novice at the table. Despite his preparation, it was apparent after the first few hands that he was the least knowledgeable player in the game, especially when it came to calculating the odds surrounding the flop, the turn and the river, so he followed the guideline offered to neophyte gamblers in several of the online sites he'd visited: when in doubt, fold.

They played for two hours before talking a bathroom break. During that time Morrison only played four hands to completion, winning one with a full house, kings over nines, prompting Caputo to remark sarcastically as they both rose from the table, "Don't be afraid to get your feet wet, Rookie. We're counting on your money ending up in our pockets." Before he could respond, she was on her way to the bathroom.

Prescott, who'd overheard the remark, sidled up to Morrison at the refreshment table. "Don't let her bother you. She thinks she's the queen of psychology. She'll do anything to try to unnerve her opponents."

"It's pretty obvious she thinks I'm the mark in this game," Morrison said as he popped a grape from a fruit plate into his mouth. "She's right."

"She's frustrated that she hasn't won much of your money. She hates it when anyone else's chip stack is as big as hers."

Manning joined his wife and the three of them chatted for the rest of the break. Morrison liked the couple; Manning was a frustrated musician, a bass player who attended several open mic sessions in the area when his work schedule allowed, and a fanatical follower of the Cleveland Indians, while his wife was charming, with a dry sense of self-deprecating humor Morrison loved. From his early conversation with Tang, he knew the couple were both left-leaning politically, which put them at odds with Caputo and Foote, who, Tang had advised, were ardent conservatives. "Whatever you do," Tang had advised, "steer clear of politics. Believe it or not, most of the residents of Fuego are big fans of the reality show host now in the White House."

"You're shittin' me," Morrison had responded incredulously at the time. "I thought you said they were all swingers, too."

"They are," Tang said. "Welcome to Pasco County, Florida. It's like Jimmy Buffett says – there's a fine line between Saturday night and Sunday morning."

They played for three more hours after the break. Morrison gained confidence as the evening wore on, winning several hands, including one bluff when it was down to Caputo and him, irritating the poker queen to no end when his false façade of confidence led her to believe he had more than king high, prompting her to fold with a pair of eights. "You've got a lot of balls," she remarked edgily as he raked in his winnings from the hand.

Tang couldn't resist. "You must've seen some of his movies."

10

After another restless night, Rheinhart woke at dawn on Thursday, still hung up on the lack of reporting concerning Chad Middleton's death. He thought watching hockey would distract him, but when Tampa Bay scored three goals midway through the third period to blow open a tight game, his mind drifted back to the enigmatic silence from the media and his curt kiss-off from law enforcement when he attempted to check on progress in the Middleton case, mysteries which kept him awake long after midnight.

He toyed momentarily with the idea of another phone call to Kullmann before recalling that she'd told him that she and Profeta had been removed from the case. What did that mean? According to the crime novels he read, detectives were more reluctant to give up one of their cases than they were to divorce their spouses. Especially a case as juicy as this one appeared to be. The more Rheinhart thought about it, the more he convinced himself that the two detectives were probably as frustrated as he was to be separated from the case.

*****

Gracie Fenton overslept Thursday morning. When she saw what time it was she cursed her boyfriend Hank Milosic, who'd risen at his usual hour of 6:00 am and had failed to reset the alarm before leaving for work in downtown Tampa. She'd told Florence she would arrive thirty minutes early this morning to help with liquor and food deliveries ahead of the weekend. She was going to be late.

It was 9:45 by the time she pulled into the parking lot at Kitty's, her hair still damp after a hasty shower. There was a truck parked in the back lot, its driver and one of the bus boys unloading cartons of chicken wings and breasts.

Florence was waiting for her inside. She glanced pointedly at the clock above the bar. "Late night last night?"

"I'm sorry," Gracie said as she stowed her purse beneath the bar. "Hank forgot to set the alarm for me when he went to work and I overslept." She adjusted her tank top and flashed her boss a smile. "What can I do?"

"They're just about finished with the chicken delivery. Might as well start cutting fruit until the liquor truck arrives." Her tone oozed disapproval as she disappeared into the kitchen.

Gracie bit back a retort and instead forced a smile as she reached for the container of lemons and limes. Gracie knew Florence was under a lot of pressure at home, dealing with several issues surrounding her third husband Walter's adult son Trace from a previous marriage. Trace Smart was forty and had been unable to hold a steady job for years, primarily because of his abrasive personality and an inability to refrain from imposing his uninformed opinions on anyone within range of his booming voice. During those frequent periods when Trace was unemployed, he spent a lot of time at Kitty's acting like he owned the place, running up large bar tabs that his stepmother absorbed, spinning tales of fishing exploits to customers at the bar who wanted only to be able to eat and drink in peace. If Kitty Galore's had been a casino, Trace Smart would've been the establishment's cooler, the person dispatched by management to disrupt the hot streak of one of its patrons. Every time he arrived while she was working, Gracie cringed.

Gracie switched the satellite radio to a classic rock station and sang along to a familiar Tom Petty song as she sliced fruit, wondering if her mystery customer would be in this week. Each Friday for nearly two years, a swarthy, overweight man with graying hair and bushy black eyebrows had taken a seat at the far end of the bar during the lunch hour, ordered a glass of red wine and a plate of pasta, eating in silence before paying his bill in cash and walking out the door. He had a Long Island accent that reminded Gracie of an aging mob boss – she fantasized that he was in the federal witness protection program, referring to him as Guido Vaticanini to Morrison and Rheinhart.

The first time he visited Kitty's the taciturn patron asked for an obscure Barolo produced by a small family vintner outside of Turin she'd never heard of; he was visibly disappointed when she told him they didn't carry that brand. Sensing a level of sophistication in her new customer buttressed by what she suspected was an underlying foundation of wealth, she tracked down the wine and ordered several cases from her liquor distributor once it became clear that he was now a weekly lunch regular. The first time she'd surprised him with his preferred Barolo instead of the house Chianti he'd grudgingly accepted as a substitute, a grin surfaced on his usually impassive face, and the tip he left was double his usual amount. Although Gracie's ingenuity had loosened his purse strings a bit, he remained a silent enigma, continuing to respond to her attempts to engage him in conversation with passive disregard, as if she'd never spoken at all.

Currently, Guido was the only unidentified customer who dined regularly during Gracie's shifts. There had been another, a young man who'd arrived the previous October and had stopped in once a week until April of this year, when he disappeared before reappearing again two weeks ago. When he showed his face shortly after Hurricane Maria had dissipated over the Atlantic, she'd pressed him on his situation, asking where he'd been all summer. It hadn't taken much for the young man Gracie had dubbed Homeless Simpson to tell his story. The young man, whose

68

real name was Jim McIntyre, had graduated from culinary school in Toronto several years earlier but wasn't quite ready yet to settle down. He explained that between May and October he worked as the head chef at a seasonal lodge located on an island in Cache Lake, within Algonquin Provincial Park in Ontario. When the lodge closed in October after Thanksgiving, he drove south to the west coast of Florida, where he lived frugally on his summer earnings, sleeping in his van, avoiding the harsh Canadian winter, until it was time to return in April to prepare for the upcoming tourist season at the lodge.

Florence reappeared from the kitchen, interrupting Gracie's reverie. "The liquor truck's out back. Want to lend a hand?"

"Sure." She wiped her hands and followed Florence to the rear of the kitchen, weaving her way through the tight quarters and the small team prepping for today's meals. She checked each of the beer, wine and liquor orders against the invoices before accepting the delivery and directing the wisecracking truck driver whose nametag identified him as Seamus where they were to be deposited. "No need, lassie," the balding man replied with a grin. "This is my regular route – I know where to leave 'em." He looked appraisingly at Gracie as he pushed a two-wheel cart up a ramp and into the kitchen. "Haven't seen you here before, Miss. Are you new?"

"No, just helping out today. I usually don't start until 11:00."

He made two trips and on his way out tipped his cap toward Gracie. "Pleasure meeting you, Miss. Hope to see you again soon."

She blushed slightly and watched as he climbed into his truck before returning to the bar. Nice man, she thought as she returned to slicing fruit.

When she was done, she washed her hands and turned on the four televisions suspended above the bar, tuning each to the channels her customers wanted to see: ESPN, Fox Sports Sun, the Weather Channel, and the Golf Channel. One of the first pieces of advice Florence had dispensed to Gracie after she arrived from the suburbs of Chicago was that you can never go wrong in Florida showing fishing or golf. Nineteen years later that advice remained as solid as it had been the first time it was offered.

She checked the weekly specials that changed each Thursday, wondering what new items might attract her interest, settling on blackened triple tail with a lime cilantro aioli served with black beans and rice. Hank would probably like that one, too, once she forgave him for forgetting to set the alarm. If he didn't screw up again, she thought, smiling to herself, he might get that for dinner sometime next week.

11

Bored and looking for something to distract him from the Middleton mystery, Rheinhart walked down to Kitty's Friday morning. By 11:00 it was already 75 and the high clouds that filled the sky earlier that morning had begun to break up, leaving broad patches of blue over the Gulf. Bay Street was quiet, deserted, the only sound a leaf blower wielded by a landscaper a block over as he walked to the bar.

He picked up a copy of *Creative Loafing*, a bay area weekly that contained information on cultural events and local political chatter, then peeked inside the bar. No customers yet and Gracie was nowhere to be seen. He nodded to one of the set-up guys stacking clean glasses and headed out the door.

Back at his bungalow, he leafed through the latest edition of the paper, looking for something to do. Using the table of contents as his guide, he passed on a number of musical offerings in St. Pete and Tampa, was intrigued by the review of a new restaurant owned by two Russian emigres from Montreal in Seminole Heights called Vladimir Poutine, but not enough to make an exploratory trip, and ignored the colorful come-ons from a variety of gender flexible escorts advertising personal services on the back two pages.

Frustrated, he was about to go online in search of more options when he remembered that Morrison's friend and scuba instructor DeWayne Bologna had asked Morrison to join him for a lecture on red tide next Tuesday at the Largo Community Center. The principal speaker was Gwen Westphal, former U.S. Olympic kayaker and current champion of Florida water rights, a rising star in the environmental movement with a high profile locally and throughout the state, especially given the recent increase in troubling climate change issues such as hurricane incidence, coastal flooding and algal blooms. Rheinhart knew who Westphal was from the Olympics but was in the dark about her new mission as an ambassador for clean water.

Morrison hadn't been interested but had passed the invitation along to Rheinhart during their lunch the other day. He knew Bologna slightly from attending his Mardi Gras party with Morrison back in March but hadn't given the lecture much thought at the time. Now that he was looking for something to help take his mind off Middleton, it had appeal.

He called Morrison for Bologna's cell number and then dialed the amiable dive instructor who operated his business from a strip mall location on U.S. 19 in Port Richey. He answered in his best Chamber of Commerce voice. "Gulfside Scuba. How can I help you?"

"Hi, DeWayne. This is Zach Rheinhart." No recognition. He continued. "Steve Morrison's friend in Ozona. We met at your Mardi Gras party this year."

"Oh, yeah. How are you?"

"Fine, thanks. Say, I was wondering if you'd like some company Tuesday for Gwen Westphal's talk down in Largo."

His response was enthusiastic. "Sure! Where's your place?"

"You know where Morrison lives in Ozona, on North Street?"

"Yeah."

"My house is on Bay Street, just off Orange. The house number is 245."

"Got it," Bologna said, punching the address into his phone. "The lecture starts at 8:00, so I'll swing by your place at 7:00."

"Sounds good. See you then."

*****

Clement Harkins had endured another restless night, rising twice to use the bathroom and both times having difficulty getting back to sleep. The clatter he generated with his walker in the two-bedroom condo also roused Marcia, who cursed to herself and turned over in her bed, covering her head with a pillow. It seemed that she had barely fallen asleep again when her father, who rose promptly at dawn each morning, commented loudly as he navigated from his room to the kitchen. "Time for someone to start the coffee."

"Be my guest," Marcia mumbled to herself as she shifted position so she could see her bedside clock. Her father had a 9:00 appointment this morning with his neurologist to go over some recent test results. Lamenting another night of interrupted sleep, she rose to a sitting position for several seconds before heading to the bathroom to shower.

When Clement heard the sound of the shower, he howled in protest. "What about my coffee?"

Marcia peeked out from the bathroom door, towel wrapped around her. "I set it up for you last night before we went to bed, just like I always do. All you have to do is hit the ON switch. I'll be out in fifteen minutes." She closed the door.

Clement, using his left hand to support himself on his walker, leaned forward to turn the coffee machine on with his right and stood there impatiently waiting for the dark liquid to fill the pot. After pouring himself a cup he shuffled carefully into the living room and used the remote to turn on the television before sinking into his favorite chair. He switched the channel to Fox News and watched his favorite morning show hosts recap the latest stories as he sipped his coffee and waited for Marcia to get out of the shower so she could make his breakfast. He was feeling like bacon and eggs this morning.

Marcia lingered under the hot streaming water, knowing it would be her final break from her duties as her father's caretaker until after they returned from the doctor and Edith Zeman came up from 506 to watch him while she biked over to Kitty Galore's for lunch. She vowed to pay more attention to the time today – two hours was too long for anyone outside the family to have to deal with the idiosyncrasies of Clement Harkins' unpredictable personality. The incident with Muriel the other day was still fresh in her mind. If either of these women decided to quit, she wasn't sure they could be replaced, which meant she would lose her only respite from her father's smothering presence. That was something too horrifying to contemplate.

She dried her hair and dressed in a pair of cream-colored shorts, a navy polo shirt and a pair of sandals. As soon as she exited her bedroom her father called out from his spot in front of the television. "Bacon and eggs?"

Marcia glanced at the clock on the kitchen wall. "I guess we have time. You want your eggs over easy or scrambled?"

"Scrambled, with onions and cheese."

Marcia made a face. "It's your stomach. Any toast or juice?"

"Orange juice."

Soon the condo was filled with the smell of frying bacon. Fifteen minutes later Marcia called out. "It's on the table."

Clement ate silently, with the intensity of a death row inmate devouring his final meal. While he had slowed down

74

considerably in many areas, his appetite remained as robust as it had been when he first enlisted in the Air Force. He had two portions of scrambled eggs, three pieces of toast and three slices of bacon before pushing back from the table, wiping some crumbs from the corners of his mouth and smiling at his daughter. "A good breakfast is—"

"The foundation for a good day," Marcia finished wearily. It was a line she'd heard thousands of times from her father. She sipped her coffee, eyes on the clock. Dr. Highsmith, Clement's neurologist, had an office in Clearwater, and they'd be battling the tail end of rush hour traffic on 19 when they left.

She placed the dishes in the sink and turned to her father, appraising the appropriateness of the outfit he'd chosen for the day's outing, grudgingly approving it before continuing. "We better get going, Dad."

"What's the difference" he asked, pouting. "I'm not going anywhere else today."

"I am."

12

It seemed inevitable that Steve Morrison would end up in Florida, even without the timely cash influx from his unexpected inheritance. From his youth along the Niagara River in upstate New York to his time in San Diego and Los Angeles, Morrison had always lived near the water, reluctantly moving away from Huntington Beach to Reseda only after his employment situation had soured, forcing him first to rent a tiny apartment inland and then, when even that rent became too high, to move into his road-weary RAV4, parking overnight in different neighborhoods each night, trying to stay one step ahead of the cops. By the time the letter from the attorney handling his uncle's estate arrived at his post office box, he was more than ready for a change of scenery.

He'd heard the stories, all the bizarre weirdness that stubbornly clung to the coattails of the Sunshine State like unwanted cat hair and thought: how could Florida be any weirder than California? Since he had either sold or given away most of his possessions when he moved into his car, packing for the continental trek was not an issue, and after the lawyer handling Benson's estate had sent him a check to help with his expenses, he set off on a leisurely cross-country road trip to his new home. Since it was late November when the check arrived, he opted for a southern route, I-10 mostly, with brief stopovers along the way in Santa Fe, New Orleans and Nashville, three cities he'd always wanted to visit.

From Nashville he cruised down I-75, giving Atlanta and its horrific traffic congestion as wide a berth as possible. After crossing the Florida state line he drove to The Hamptons, a massive retirement community northwest of Orlando, where he spent three days recovering from the rigors of the 3000-mile journey on the recommendation of Harpoon Tang, who had cautioned him the place was a den of inequity, populated mostly by conservative Republicans with a reputation for rampant swinging and, according to Tang, the highest incidence in the nation of Viagra use and, not coincidentally, sexually transmitted diseases. "If you plan to dip your wick while in The Hamptons," he advised, "make sure you're packing plenty of latex."

He'd had an opportunity to do just that when one of the more aggressive widows in the place somehow recognized him from his most visible role, that of Captain Ivan Jakinov in *The Russians Are Coming and Coming and Coming*, an XXX spoof of the 1966 comedy classic about a Russian submarine running aground off Martha's Vineyard. Despite the fact that it had been more than three decades since the release of the porn version, which shifted the locale to Key West and converted the submarine in the original to a fishing trawler out of Havana, the brazen brunette had approached him at a sidewalk café while he was having lunch and announced loudly, "Well, well. If it isn't Ivan Jakinov. What brings you to The Hamptons, big boy? Got any plans for tonight?" Mortified at having been recognized, he dropped two twenties on the table and fled the scene, leaving behind the disappointed dowager and a few curious stares from nearby diners.

He found Ozona much more to his liking, a place where nobody so far had recognized him as a former adult entertainment star and where the leisurely pace suited his post-employment mindset. And if he longed for some connection to his Biff Bratwurst days, Fuego and The Hand and Job pub were only thirty minutes away. Harpoon Tang had predicted the poker game would feel like old home week, and he was right. Morrison felt an immediate affinity with the poker players at Fuego as soon as he entered the room and looked forward to more visits in the future.

Gracie Fenton had been an unexpected and delightful surprise who, along with his inheritance out of the blue, had helped to shift his thoughts back into positive territory again after recent dark times. Once he discovered Kitty Galore's Raw Bar, she cemented their nascent relationship with tales concerning his Uncle Merle, who had been one of Gracie's favorite and more voluble confidantes, relating juicy inside stories about the unorthodox world of rocket scientists and the Cape Canaveral social scene they dominated, like the time the young wife of one of the nation's most well known astronauts had a bit too much to drink and tried to pick up an off-duty cop in a Cocoa Beach bar by performing an impromptu strip tease to the accompaniment of Johnny Paycheck's "Take This Job and Shove It" as it blared from the Wurlitzer in the corner.

Morrison was pleased to learn that Gracie and Merle had been friends; it allowed him to draw a little closer to his uncle through the knowledge he'd imparted to her during their relationship, one in which she described herself as feeling like a stepchild with a really cool new stepdad. "He never judged me, never spoke a word in anger toward me, and he always told me the truth," she said simply. 'What else is there?"

Merle, childless, adopted Gracie as his confidante without reservation, wasting little time in sharing intimacies about his life and his job which heretofore had gone unspoken. Gracie reciprocated, relaying tales of co-workers and customers unfit for public discourse in the fleeting moments when prying ears weren't hovering in the vicinity. Merle had been the first person to whom she pitched her Guido Vaticanini theory once it was formulated; he'd nodded immediately as she was laying out the evidence, seeing the path of her logic, agreeing with her conclusion. He could see Guido as a former mob boss relocated by the feds; from the limited contact Merle had with him, the enigmatic diner appeared to be smart enough to keep his head down and his mouth shut as he played out whatever time he had left in Ozona.

*****

Tang called Morrison on Friday morning, two days after the poker game. "Busy?"

Usually he wouldn't have answered his phone – the only calls he received these days were robo calls from alternative credit saviors. But his phone was face up on the table next to his chair and he could see the call was from Tang. His voice had an edge as he replied. "As a matter of fact, yeah. Watchin' the tube. Wadda ya want?"

"What are you watching?" Tang's English was flawless, without any discernible accent.

"An old cop show from the eighties, *Crime Story*."

"Is it any good?"

"It was, until you interrupted with your call."

"Sorry. Want me to call back later?"

"No. Wadda ya want?"

"Lauren was asking about you, wanted your phone number. I figured I better ask you first."

Morrison sat up. "The poker queen wants my number?"

"Yes. Apparently, you made quite an impression. I think she wants to ask you if you want to be a regular in her game."

"What's her professional name again?"

"Monique Monroe. She does a lot of taboo stuff, mother-son, stepmother-stepson. She has a website. You should check it out."

Morrison thought: why not? "Okay, you can give it to her. Didn't you say she had a day job?"

Tang chuckled. "She used to work in the paint department at Lowe's, but now she's working for FedEx. They must've found out about her website somehow at Lowe's, so she had to move on."

"What else do you know about her?"

"She was born and raised in Maryland, moved to Georgia after high school and became a cop before she ended up in Florida at Fuego."

"A cop?" Morrison was intrigued. "I never would've figured her for a cop."

"I don't know how long she lasted. She doesn't talk about it much."

"Anything else?"

"No, that's it."

"Harpoon?"

"Yes?"

"Tell her not to call before noon."

13

Twenty minutes after Rheinhart's visit to Kitty's on Friday morning, the man Gracie Fenton referred to as Guido Vaticanini pulled into the parking lot in his vintage Cadillac Coup de Ville, taking care to park it in the rear of the lot, away from the other cars. Gracie checked her watch as he clambered onto his usual bar stool at the far end of the bar: right on time. She moved down to greet him, a wide smile on her face. "TGIF," she said pleasantly. "The usual?"

The man nodded wordlessly. Gracie retrieved the bottle of Barolo she'd stored under the bar and poured him a glass, placing it on a coaster in front of him. "Would you like to see the weekly specials?" she asked, even though she knew the answer. Guido always ordered the same dish, pasta with red sauce, regardless of the weekly specials

He shook his head. "Not today. Just the usual," he mumbled in his distinctive accent, what Gracie characterized to Rheinhart and Morrison as Sicily meets Long Island. She reached for the remote and switched the television closest to Guido to the Golf Channel. This week's tournament was from Sun City, South Africa, and he watched the action in silence between sips of his wine.

When Gracie returned to the other end of the bar one of her other regulars, Reb Jadel, leaned in. "How's the hit man doing today?"

"Same as usual, I guess," she said, once again regretting ever mentioning her theory to Jadel, whose verbal restraint was less than ideal when it came to the mysterious customer. "How was your gumbo?"

Jadel held up his empty bowl like a proud adolescent. "It *was* terrific. My compliments to the chef."

"He'll be thrilled."

By noon most of the seats were filled at the bar and Gracie was hustling to keep up with an unusually thirsty lunch crowd. Trace Smart came in, looked around to see if his father and Florence were in the place, didn't see them and walked out in a huff, heading for their office across the street.

"Dodged a bullet there," Jadel observed as he watched Smart cross Orange Street. "That boy can talk all day and not say a damn thing. He ain't quiet, neither." Jadel was a fifth-generation Floridian who worked as a maintenance man for one of the condo associations in Palm Harbor. He was in his fifties, with reddish, thinning hair, several missing teeth and a Confederate flag proudly appliqued to the rear window of his Chevy pickup.

"Got time for another beer, Reb?" Gracie asked, wiping the bar in front of him with a rag.

He looked at the clock on the wall, calculating. He smiled. "Sure do. One more for the road, darlin', start the weekend off right."

"Coming right up."

When Guido's food came out of the kitchen, Gracie intercepted the server and delivered the plate herself. "Another glass of wine?"

The man nodded as he unfolded his silverware from his napkin. "One more."

Like clockwork, Gracie thought as she replaced his empty glass with a full one. Two glasses of wine, a plate of pasta and on his way. Gracie wondered what he did when he wasn't at the bar. In her mind she saw him most comfortable at two incongruously different locations: the race track, among the shady types she felt he would gravitate toward, his ham-like fist clutching betting slips as thoroughbreds raced around the mile-long oval track, and the opera, savoring a performance of Puccini's *La boheme* from a private box at the Straz.

When he was finished with his wine he asked for the check, left a wad of bills on the bar and walked out into the afternoon heat. After Gracie sorted out her tip and placed it in the tip jar, Jadel inquired, "He a good tipper? I hear those Mafia types like to spread it around."

She looked at him appraisingly. "Better than your sorry ass."

Jadel flashed a gap-toothed grin. "That ain't hard."

"That's what she said."

*****

Morrison was reading a book on poker he'd found at the library in Palm Harbor on Saturday afternoon, prepping for his next trip to Fuego, when his cell phone rang. He checked Caller ID: Restricted. He let the call go to voicemail, and in a minute his phone chirped, indicating a message had been left. He dialed into his messages and listened:

"Hello, Mr. Morrison. This is Special Agent Angela Threadgill of the FBI. We'd like to speak with you about a matter currently under investigation. If you could, please call me at our Clearwater office, 727-461-5507, at your earliest convenience to set up a meeting. Thank you."

Why on earth would the FBI be calling him? Maybe it was a wrong number, he thought. There was no reason he knew of for the FBI to call him unless…

His mind flashed to Gracie and her characterization of the taciturn, mystery customer known only as Guido Vaticanini as a member of the federal Witness Protection Program. Could Gracie's theory about him possibly be right? He wanted to call her at the bar to see if she'd been contacted by the FBI also, but remembered it was Saturday – Gracie was off until Monday and he didn't know how to reach her at home.

He'd managed to avoid any direct contact with law enforcement his entire life, with the exception of several parking tickets he'd accumulated in Los Angeles which he'd paid online with a credit card. There had been a couple of random encounters on the set of some of their shoots prompted by neighbor complaints, but the actors never had to deal with them, only the director or, if they were on set, the producer. Being questioned by the FBI would be a journey into uncharted waters.

He decided to wait until Monday to return the call. He wanted to talk to Gracie first, to see what if anything she knew about this. He got up, went to the kitchen and poured himself a glass of water before returning to his book and the chapter on Texas Hold 'Em.

*****

Several miles to the south in Dunedin, Marcia Alvarez was waiting impatiently outside the closed door of her father's bedroom. "What the hell's taking you so long, Dad?"

A minute later the door opened. Clement Harkins stood before her leaning on his walker, clad only in his bathing suit and flip flops, towel draped over his shoulder. "I was looking for my sunscreen."

"We're not going to be at the pool that long," she said in exasperation. Why did everything have to be a project with the old man? "You usually don't stay very long anyway."

"Are there any kids at the pool? I hate it when those little bastards are there, running around, out of control, screaming at the top of their lungs."

Marcia shook her head. "I checked from the balcony a few minutes ago. Besides, it's not a holiday. The only time you have to worry about kids at the pool in November is around Thanksgiving."

Clement looked unconvinced. "Is anybody down there?"

"Just Tim Jordan and his wife from 507, the unit next to Edith's."

"Do I know them?" he asked, trying to match the name to a face and failing.

Marcia tried to remain patient. "Yes. You met them at the condo Christmas party last year. They're retired, from New Hampshire. He used to run a landscaping business. Tall guy, with gray hair and wire-rimmed glasses, always smiling."

"Doesn't sound familiar to me," he said.

Marcia maneuvered the wheelchair into position behind her father and locked the wheels. "You'll see when we get down there. *If* we get down there."

"How about the hot tub? Anybody in it?"

"Not when I looked earlier. But the more time we waste, the more likely it is that someone will be in it on a day like today."

With his daughter spotting him from behind, he released the walker and collapsed onto the seat of the wheel chair. Marcia held it steady until he was settled, then strapped him in with a seat belt before releasing the brakes. She stored the walker in a corner by the dining room table and guided him through the door of the condo and down the walkway onto the elevator. When they reached the main floor she used her pass to unlock the door and pushed him along the pool deck until they were next to the hot tub. Using a nearby chair to help get him onto his feet, Marcia supported her father from behind, hands inserted into his armpits to help with the tricky entrance into the sunken tub.

It took a minute to get him situated and comfortable before she stepped back, reached into her purse and withdrew a cigarette and lighter. She lit up, drawing the smoke deeply into her lungs as she watched him from a few feet away. "How's your ankle feel?"

"It hurts," he replied huffily. "Like always. It hasn't been right since that night when I jumped out of the airplane."

"You jumped out of a plane a lot of times, Dad. You were a paratrooper, remember?"

"Of course I remember," he snapped. "What do you think, I'm an idiot?"

"No, Dad, I don't think you're an idiot," she replied gently. "I just think you get confused sometimes."

"You don't believe me," he said defensively. "You never believed me."

"That you're the real D.B. Cooper? Nobody believes that except you. The real D.B. Cooper died that night when he jumped out of the plane."

"That's what you think, missy. I have proof!"

Marcia exhaled and stubbed her cigarette out in a nearby ashtray. "I've been waiting to see this proof for thirty years now. Where is it?"

Her father turned to look at her, tearing up. His voice was barely audible. "I forgot where I put it."

14

Ten minutes after he picked up the book on poker again, Morrison laid it down. His mind was racing with possibilities, most of them negative, as to why the FBI wanted to talk to him. He simply couldn't concentrate on the odds against betting to an inside straight. He called Rheinhart. "You busy?"

Rheinhart was home, on his computer, researching the woman who was giving the lecture on red tide on Tuesday, Gwen Westphal. "Just poking around the 'Net. What's up?"

"I just had the strangest call," Morrison said. "From the FBI."

Rheinhart was interested. "What did they want?"

"I'm not sure," he admitted. "The call came through as Restricted and I let it go to voicemail. One of their agents in Clearwater left a message, saying they wanted to talk to me about a matter under investigation. Wanted me to call back ASAP."

"I take it you haven't called yet."

"No. I thought about calling Gracie to see if she got a similar call, but I don't have her cell. I thought it might be about Guido, her Mafia hitman in hiding."

Rheinhart laughed. "I doubt that was the reason for the call." Another idea popped into his head. "You haven't been colluding with any Russians, have you? Or Ukrainians? I hear there's a major investigation involving them."

Morrison was in no mood to discern the humor in Rheinhart's query. "Thanks," he spat out sarcastically. "You're a big help."

"There's a simple way to find out," Rheinhart said. "Call them back."

"It's Saturday."

Rheinhart laughed again. "Steve, they're the FBI. They don't take weekends off."

"Maybe I should call an attorney."

"Why?" Rheinhart countered. "You got something to hide?"

Morrison paused for a moment. "I don't think so, but I don't know if I trust those guys."

Rheinhart was incredulous. "The FBI? Why wouldn't you trust them? You don't believe that drivel about them coming out of the White House, do you?"

"I don't know," Morrison replied defensively. "I watch a lot of cop shows. They all say you should always have a lawyer when you talk to the cops."

"Do you know any lawyers in Florida? Besides the guy who handled your uncle's estate, that is."

Morrison thought for a moment. "No, not really. The only other lawyer I know is that woman who advertises on billboards all over the Bay area. Judy Ruliani."

Rheinhart laughed again, a full-throated guffaw. "That's the ticket. Show up at FBI headquarters with that ambulance chaser as your counsel. I'm sure she's defended many accident victims against charges laid by the FBI. I'll bet the feds will be shitting their pants as soon as they see her show up in a Hillary Clinton pantsuit, completely cowed by her big teeth and female pattern baldness."

"Fuck you."

"Forget about a lawyer until you hear what they want to talk to you about," Rheinhart advised in a softer tone. "Remember, you can always walk out at any time. They'd have to charge you with a crime to detain you if you express a desire to leave."

"You sure about that?"

Rheinhart could hear the desperation in Morrison's voice. He tried to reassure him. "Call them back on Monday. You can call Gracie first if it makes you feel any better, but I'm pretty sure she's not involved."

Morrison wasn't sure what he'd expected from Rheinhart when he made the call, but his friend had stilled the anxiety that had escalated since he'd listened to the voicemail message. "Okay. I'll call them on Monday."

"Be sure you call me after you talk to them. You've got me curious, too."

*****

Clement Harkins was born in the tiny hamlet of Northbrook, Ontario and enlisted in the Canadian Forces in 1947 when he was seventeen. Fortuitously, he was assigned to RCAF Station in Trenton, the premier base for flight training in Canada at the time, less than two hours from his birth home. At Trenton he learned to fly both jets and transport aircraft, and when the Korean Airlift was organized in 1950 he eagerly volunteered and was accepted, joining a squad of his contemporaries from Trenton who were shipped to their new home base in Seoul. For Harkins it was a redemption of sorts – he'd wanted nothing more than to have participated in World War II, but he wasn't old enough to enlist until two years after peace was negotiated in 1945. The Korean War was a war he could call his own.

He flew nearly seventy missions in Korea, receiving several commendations for courage in the face of enemy fire, transporting wounded soldiers from the front to medivac units throughout the South Korean peninsula. When his assignment ended, he confounded both his Canadian and American hierarchy by becoming a naturalized American citizen and enlisting in the U.S. Air Force. He was assigned to the Mount Hebo Air Force Station in Hebo, Oregon, where he received training as a paratrooper and also taught basic navigation skills to neophyte pilots in flight training school.

He met his future wife Kay Hendricks while stationed at Mount Hebo. She was a waitress at a diner in nearby Cloverdale where many of the flyboys hung out; according to Clement, it was love at first sight. They were married ten months later in a small civil ceremony on the base, and two years after that Marcia Jean Harkins was born. At 33, Clement was one of the oldest first-time parents on the base, a constant target for ribbing from his fellow pilots, who loved to cite malfunctioning equipment enfeebled by old age as the likely cause for his delayed parenthood. As soon as Marcia was born, his nickname on the base became Grandpa, a nickname that dogged him until he retired.

Marcia grew up as an only child. It turned out that Kay was not the maternal type, her attitude no doubt influenced by Marcia's incredibly difficult childbirth, an ordeal that resulted in a two-week stay at the hospital for Kay after her daughter was born. As a result of the palpable distance that developed between herself and her mother, Marcia grew up adoring her father, who doted on her like she was the only person on earth. She wanted nothing more than to follow in his footsteps while she was growing up; as soon as she turned eighteen, she enlisted in the Army, making it her career. There were a few stumbles along the way, most notably a disastrous two-year marriage to fellow soldier Javier Alvarez, a native of El Paso who used his fists to express his displeasure with his wife's cooking, wardrobe or anything else that pissed him off. It was still a man's army in those days, so rather than file any formal complaints, she applied makeup liberally and wore long-sleeved, high-necked clothing to hide her bruises until she'd finally had enough, requesting a transfer as far from her soon-to-be ex-husband as possible.

The Army granted her request, sending her to Fort Benning, Georgia, where she stayed until she received an honorable discharge at 38. By that time her father's health had begun to deteriorate, so she joined him in Tampa, where he'd been living in an efficiency apartment near MacDill Air Force Base. She helped him find and purchase the condo on the causeway in Dunedin where they had been living for the past fourteen years.

Marcia had traced their history together numerous times since she'd moved in with her father as his caretaker, using the happier days from their past together to justify continuing to stay by his side as both his physical and mental health deteriorated. It was the hardest work she'd ever endured, harder even than the year she spent being a punching bag for a dissatisfied military husband.

As she watched him relaxing in the hot tub by the pool, trying to seek relief for his throbbing ankle, she thought back to the time of the D.B. Cooper hijacking, once again examining long-ago memories, trying to dredge up anything that might lend credence to his claim that he was the elusive Cooper. She'd been in third grade in 1971 and remembered that, for the first and only time, her father had missed Thanksgiving dinner at home that year. When questioned by a bewildered Marcia, her mother told her that her father had been called to work for a secret assignment. "You can never talk about it," her mother had admonished, and Marcia never had.

When her father finally returned home on the Tuesday after Thanksgiving, he was limping badly and there were some unusual scratch marks around his neck which he explained away by claiming he'd had to eject from his F-106 aircraft after its engine had malfunctioned while on his "mission", sending him through a stand of trees that had scratched his neck before finally crashing to earth and damaging his ankle. Once again, both parents advised Marcia never to talk about the "mission." Knowing what she did about military discipline, even as an eight-year-old, she followed her orders and never told anyone about the year her father missed Thanksgiving. By the next week she was interested in trying out for the Christmas pageant at school; any thought of her father's recent absence faded until it was as if it had never happened.

Marcia glanced at her father while she lit another cigarette and wondered: why would her father cling to such a claim for so many years if it wasn't true?

15

As soon as he ended the call with DeWayne Bologna about attending the lecture featuring Gwen Westphal on Tuesday, Rheinhart settled into his comfortable chair and fired up his laptop. He wanted to learn more about Gwen Westphal.

He discovered that she had been born in Boca Raton and graduated from the University of Florida with a degree in marine biology before accepting a fellowship to Stanford, where she went on to earn a Ph.D. in water resources management. It was during her time in Palo Alto that she began to compete competitively in women's kayaking; five years later, she shocked the women's kayaking community by qualifying for the 2000 Summer Olympics in Sydney and then by capturing the bronze medal in her specialty, the 500-meter sprint.

It was the first Olympic medal ever captured by an American woman in kayaking, a sport traditionally dominated by athletes from Europe. But her startling performance was barely given its proper due in the U.S., where canoeing and kayaking were minor sports, well out of the media spectrum when it came to coverage. Beyond her hometown, which held a modest parade for their newly minted Olympic medalist when she returned, and the Stanford University community, her accomplishment was largely unheralded in her home country.

Undeterred by the lack of acclaim, she moved on. After several uneventful years working for the California Department of Water Resources in Sacramento, she returned to Florida, where she accepted a senior position with Clear Sailing Alliance, an advocacy group that had been formed in the aftermath of the Deepwater Horizon disaster, which had spilled millions of gallons of untreated crude oil into the Gulf of Mexico off the shore of Louisiana. The CSA was funded by two venture capitalists from Orlando; one of the two, Todd Schwartz, was an avid backwater kayaker who knew Westphal by reputation and lobbied hard to persuade her to join their fledging organization.

Schwartz's persistence and passion for clean water convinced her. Since her hire she had quickly become the face of the group, travelling around the state, lecturing in local municipalities and school districts as well as testifying before the state legislature in Tallahassee on various water quality issues. At the same time, the alliance meticulously recorded the effect the oil spill had on the population and quality of shrimp in the Gulf and the resulting effects on commercial shrimping, data that Westphal cited with emphasis in her various presentations.

Rheinhart found an interview with Westphal in the *Miami Herald* that featured a picture of her in a tony Coral Gables neighborhood, talking to several residents about the increase in recent tidal surge events which caused significant flooding of local streets. Rheinhart thought she was a knockout, a tall, tan brunette with the tapered physique of an elite-level athlete, shoulder length brown hair and brown eyes above a dazzling smile worthy of a toothpaste commercial. He did the math; she was in her mid-forties, but she looked like she could still compete on the world stage.

He smiled; this was going to be an interesting lecture.

*****

Gracie Fenton had a Sunday routine that varied little. Hank usually cooked them both a big breakfast, bacon, eggs and toast, after which he disappeared into his home office to prepare for the upcoming work week. Gracie cleaned up the dishes, then headed to

94

the pool with her latest book if the weather was decent. This morning the weather was ideal – mostly blue skies, with only a few cirrus clouds forming over the Gulf, an afternoon high predicted to be 80.

She was currently reading a well-worn paperback titled *Escape From Vagina Ridge* given to her by one of her snowbird customers, Carla Kershaw, a retired insurance executive from Pittsburgh who spent her winters in Palm Harbor. She'd pressed it into Gracie's hands one day a week ago as she was leaving the bar, insisting that Gracie read it. "Don't be fooled by the title," she urged. "It sounds like porn, but it's not. It's more like a feminist novel."

Gracie was unfamiliar with the name of the writer. "Who's Parnell Gomez?" she asked, puzzled. "Never heard of her."

"Him," Kershaw corrected. "He's written one other book, but I haven't read it yet. I just finished this one."

Gracie was about a third of the way through so far and enjoying it. Like Kershaw had effused before gifting Gracie the novel, she marveled that a man could write so eloquently about sensitive women's issues. She changed into her bathing suit, grabbed her sunglasses and a large bottle of water and put them in her beach bag with the novel, sunscreen and a towel before heading to the pool.

She liked to coordinate her pool time with Sunday church services to minimize distracting chatter from other sunbathers. This morning she had the place to herself, which made her smile. She set up in the shade beyond the deep end of the pool, one more measure of separation in case one of several residents with small children showed up. Sunday was her day, the last day before she had to return to work, and she did her best to control the environment so she could enjoy the day with minimal

95

interruptions. She worked with people all week long – Sunday was her respite from forcing herself to be nice to others.

She sprayed herself with sunscreen in spite of her position out of the sun, adjusted the lounge chair to a comfortable reading position and opened the book to where she'd left off, with the members of a commune located in the Jay Mountain Wilderness Area of the Adirondacks east of Lake Placid, all of them female, contemplating the fate of the male hunter who'd stumbled onto their compound the day before.

She read for an hour before someone joined her at the pool, a woman she didn't know with two small pre-school children wearing floaties around their tiny biceps, brats in training who immediately began whining about going in the hot tub. Gracie reached into her bag for a pair of earplugs and inserted them, blissfully protecting herself from the ruckus at the other end of the pool as she returned to her book.

*****

At the same time Gracie was lounging by the pool beside Lake Tarpon, Harpoon Tang was on his way to do the same at the large pool at Fuego. As he emerged from beneath the thatched roof of the poolside tiki bar, he shielded his eyes from the sun, looking for Lauren Caputo, wondering if she was awake yet, since Saturday night was another of her regular poker nights.

A large crowd had already gathered by the pool, which surprised Tang. There had been big party at the resort's disco the night before that had not broken up until dawn. He hadn't expected to see much of a crowd by the pool until mid-afternoon, but once again his intuition had been wrong.

He didn't see Caputo among the sun-worshipping crowd, all of them nude, as he walked around the pool area. The variety of body types on display never failed to surprise him: young, old,

96

buff, overweight. Before Tang had moved to Fuego he'd assumed that people who were attracted to nudist resorts were all young, trim and tan. He'd been shocked by the melting pot of naturists and swingers he'd encountered once he moved in – the only things they all seemed to have in common were an utter lack of self-consciousness and tan-lines. Grandmas mingled with college students, investment bankers with heavily inked bikers, their camaraderie driven primarily by the common embrace of public nudity.

He returned to the bar after failing to spot Caputo on his circuit around the pool. He had his cell phone in his hand, about to call her, when he felt a tap on his shoulder. He turned to see Jessica Callaway, one of Caputo's closest friends, with a half-finished muddled drink on the bar in front of her. "Looking for someone?" she asked, smiling.

"I was looking for Lauren," he said, sliding into an empty chair next to her. "Do you know if she's up yet?"

Callaway laughed at the thought. She was a statuesque blond in her late twenties, five nine with a stunning body that was on full display. "I doubt it," she said, smiling. "Last night was poker night at Club Paradise." She glanced at the clock above the cash register. "She might sleep until dinner."

Tang's face expressed disappointment. "I wanted to tell her something. Maybe I'll just send her a text."

Callaway leaned closer. "I hope it isn't anything urgent."

Trying not to stare at her large, unfettered breasts, he shook his head. "Nothing that can't wait."

"In that case, can I buy you a drink?"

Tang had never met a free drink he didn't like. "If you insist." He pointed to her glass. "I'll have what you're having."

She caught the attention of the bartender effortlessly. "Two more mojitos, Raul." She turned back to Tang. "I didn't see you at the party last night."

"Disco's not my thing."

"Me either," she said, finishing her drink before sliding the fresh one onto a coaster. "I was in bed by 11:00."

"Alone?" he asked slyly.

"A lady never tells," she demurred, smiling. "I probably should've been working – I knew I wasn't going to like the party." Like Caputo, whose stage name was Monique Monroe, Callaway operated an adult entertainment website. Unlike Caputo, who cared more about poker than anything else, Callaway was diligent, a hard worker who posted new videos and photo sets each week that were snapped up eagerly by her members. As a result, although she was one of the youngest adult entrepreneurs living at Fuego, she was the most successful of the bunch. Tang was envious of her business acumen and often picked her brain, hoping to come up with some ideas that might help to bolster his retirement funds.

Tang took a sip of his mojito. "That's a switch," he exclaimed. "I can actually taste the rum in this drink. Not like the usual watered-down shit they serve here." He looked at the bartender questioningly, then at Jessica.

She motioned him in closer. When his head was only a few inches from hers, she whispered, "I think Raul loads my drinks because he wants to get into my pants." She glanced downward and continued, smiling. "That is, if I were wearing any."

16

Morrison enjoyed an atypical fall Sunday, sleeping in late, then reading the *Tampa Bay Times* before turning on the football game at 1:00. The Bucs were hosting the Jets; Morrison thought the game would take his mind away from speculating about why the FBI wanted to talk to him, but that wasn't the case.

The game was a snooze fest, featuring nothing but field goals for both teams until the fourth quarter, when first Tampa and then the Jets managed to pierce the end zone. The 15-10 win for the Bucs reminded Morrison of an old cliché – it was like watching paint dry. Instead of distracting him, the monotony of the inept play on his television failed to engage his mind sufficiently to divert his thoughts from the FBI's request that he stop by for a chat.

When the game ended he walked down to Kitty Galore's for a grouper sandwich, which he ate at the bar next to two fans wearing New York Giants' jerseys who were agonizing over their team's pounding at the hand of the 49ers, who'd been winless all season before today. The bar area was packed, with all four televisions over the bar showing the Giants-49ers game, and Morrison gazed in wonder at the passions aroused in the crowd by this most violent of sports. Normally he didn't watch football on Sundays – he wasn't much of a sports fan – but most Sundays he wasn't fretting about what the FBI wanted to talk to him about.

He finished his sandwich, paid his bill and walked home. The sun had just set over the Gulf, and the sky was streaked with vivid slashes of magenta, salmon and indigo as he walked by the marina. A late pleasure boater had just come in and was rinsing his boat off as it rested on its lift. The man waved; Morrison waved back. "Gorgeous sunset," he said.

The man nodded as he sprayed the hull of his Bayliner. "Can't beat the Gulf sunsets. That's why we live here, right?" He looked at Morrison closely in the dim light. "You the guy living in Merle's old house?"

Morrison nodded. "Yes. He was my uncle."

"A good man, your Uncle Merle. We all miss him."

"Did you know him?"

"A little bit," the man said. "He used to tell the best stories about Cape Canaveral. One night he made me laugh so hard I nearly pissed my pants." He smiled, remembering. "You must've been real proud of him. Having a rocket scientist in the family."

"I was," he lied. He felt ashamed. How could you be proud of someone you didn't even know?

The man turned off the hose, disconnecting it from the marina faucet and coiling it in the same motion. "Time for me to get home," he said as he climbed a short stepladder and stowed the hose in a hold on his boat. "The wife doesn't like it when I stay out past sunset." He climbed down and extended his hand. "I'm Paul."

His grip was firm. "Steve. Pleased to meet you."

"Same here. You take care."

Back at his house, Morrison checked the TV listings in the Sunday paper, looking for something to watch but not finding anything that interested him. He thought about calling Rheinhart but was afraid that he might ridicule him again for his concern about the reason the FBI wanted to talk to him.

Instead, he turned on his iPod, settling on some vintage Neil Young. He sank into his favorite chair and closed his eyes, letting the familiar falsetto and guitar riffs wash over him like a cooling breeze on an August day.

*****

When Gracie returned from the pool, Hank was sprawled on the couch in front of the television, watching a movie. He sat up when he heard her come in. "How was the pool?"

She dropped her damp towel on top of the washing machine. "Fine, until two little rugrats showed up with their phone-addicted mother. It went downhill after that." She glanced at the television. "What are you watching?"

"*Field of Dreams*, with Kevin Costner and James Earl Jones." He indicated a spot on the couch next to him. "Care to join me?"

"After I shower."

As she stood under the shower, the hot spray massaging her back, she thought about how glad she was that she didn't have any children. Her mother had pestered her constantly about getting married and having kids as soon as she graduated from high school, choices that were as far from her mind as living on Mars. She'd known since she was a teenager that she wasn't the maternal type. As a young girl she'd preferred playing with her brother's trucks instead of her Barbies, feeling no maternal attachment to Mattel's molded plastic ideal of femininity. Marriage? Maybe. But kids? Not in the game plan.

But her mother wouldn't take no for an answer, riding her hard about when she planned to get married on a regular basis, confident that she'd be able to change her only daughter's mind when it came to having children despite Gracie never having given her the slightest indication that she was looking forward to a white picket fence suburban lifestyle, the kind in which she and her older brother had been raised. When the pressure at home from her mother became too great she packed up and moved out, heading south without a glance in her rearview mirror, as far from Oak Park as she could go.

Florida had been her salvation. She adapted to the warm winters immediately. She met Hank at about the same time she figured that her best shot at earning a decent living, given her high school education, lay behind the bar. She was a natural – Hank called her the Meryl Streep of feigned sincerity. Her ability to project herself as her customers' most sympathetic friend had earned her more than her share of tips at each of the establishments where she'd worked. The money was good, but it wasn't as good as shrink money, which is what she felt she deserved given the amount of counseling she'd doled out over the years to fired employees, jilted lovers and clueless dolts.

Having Hank by her side was a huge asset. He had two grown children from a previous marriage, so there'd been no pressure from him to produce an heir. And he was a patient listener, a sympathetic ear on the days she needed to vent. He had provided crucial balance and support and she loved him for that. All in all, a keeper.

After she'd dried her hair and dressed, she rejoined Hank, who thoughtfully had paused the movie for her until she returned. She plopped herself down on the couch and wordlessly gave him a juicy, earnest kiss.

Taken by surprise, he returned the kiss with some passion of his own. "What was that for?" he asked when they separated.

"You being you," she replied with a smile, reaching over to squeeze his hand affectionately.

Hank picked up the remote and aimed it at the television. "Should we save the rest of the movie for later?" he asked suggestively, sensing she might want to move things to the bedroom.

"Whoa, big boy," she said, raising her arms as if to fend him off. "Kevin Costner first. Then we can talk about dessert."

17

When Morrison awoke, he was still in his chair, the light on the table adjacent to him still on, his iPod shut off. How long had he been asleep? He rose stiffly, stretching dormant muscles carefully as he moved slowly into the kitchen. His fogged mind looked at the clock on the microwave: 3:17.

He did the math. He'd slept for almost seven hours, his usual allotment for the night. No use trying to go to bed now, so he returned to the living room and surfed through the channel guide, looking for a movie to watch.

He settled on *The French Connection*, starting at 3:30 on Turner Classic Movies. The chase scene on the streets of New York was one of his favorites, something likely to hold his attention. Just to be sure, he brewed a pot of coffee, made himself a couple of pieces of toast and sank into his chair, turning out the light next to him, plunging the house into theater-like darkness, the only illumination in the room emanating from the television screen.

When the movie ended it was just beginning to get light outside. By the time he showered, the sun was above the tree line as he selected what to wear. He dressed with more care than usual, the impending call and meeting with the FBI the motivating factor. He chose a collared light blue button-down shirt, short sleeved, khaki slacks and a pair of Top Siders. As he looked at himself in the mirror, he couldn't remember the last time he'd spent this much time contemplating his wardrobe choices. In Florida it was pretty much automatic: T-shirt, shorts and flip flops.

Once again he wondered if he should call Gracie before he called the feds, but he dismissed the idea – he'd have to wait until at least 10:00, the time Gracie started work. He was afraid he'd go crazy by then. Rheinhart was probably right, he reasoned – this interview had nothing to do with Guido Vaticanini.

*****

On Monday Rheinhart woke a few minutes before seven, interrupting an ominous dream. In it, he was back in Jacksonville, in jail, awaiting trial in federal court on bribery charges. His cellmate was a hulking, menacing-looking biker waiting to be arraigned on manslaughter charges to which he had gleefully confessed. The biker was badgering him, daring Rheinhart to start something as he moved closer as an intimidation tactic. Rheinhart feared a physical assault was imminent; he frantically was trying to attract the attention of a guard when he awakened with a jolt, shaken, his brow damp with perspiration.

He sat up, his breathing rapid. He'd just experienced a glimpse that offered him insight into the type of fear Morrison exhibited on the phone the other day concerning the call from the FBI.

*****

At precisely 8:05, hands shaking, Morrison punched in the number Agent Threadgill on his cell. She picked up after the second ring, her voice strong, authoritarian. "Agent Threadgill. How may I help you?"

He took one last deep breath to steady his nerves. "This is Steven Morrison, returning your call from Saturday."

Her voice displayed no emotion; strictly business. "Thanks for getting back to me so soon, Mr. Morrison. I was wondering if you could come into our office to answer some questions concerning an ongoing investigation."

Here goes. "I could come in this morning."

"That would be excellent. Do you know where our office is in Clearwater?"

"Just east of Fort Harrison, on Cleveland?"

"That's it. How soon can you get here?"

Morrison glanced at the time on his phone. "I should be able to be there by nine."

"Perfect. I'll leave word with the receptionist that you're expected; she'll direct you where to go when you arrive. Thanks again, Mr. Morrison."

The line went dead. He stared numbly at the phone in his hand.

*****

His anxiety spiked again as he pulled into the parking lot behind the sleek glass skyscraper at ten minutes to nine. He checked his appearance in the rearview mirror, smoothing his hair one more time before exiting the RAV4 and walking toward the building, wondering how many cameras were recording his approach.

Inside, the reception area was abuzz with activity. Morrison headed toward the Information desk, which was occupied by a burly security guard in uniform. "I have an appointment with Agent Threadgill of the FBI."

The guard, a broad-chested black man in his thirties with a shaved head, packing a large sidearm visible in a holster on his hip, looked Morrison up and down carefully before responding. "Fifth floor." He indicated a bank of elevators behind him and to the left.

Workers were streaming into the multi-story office building, and the ride to the fifth floor was crowded. When the car stopped at five, he was the lone occupant who eased his way past the other passengers. Opposite the elevator doors, six feet away, sat a dark-skinned young woman who smiled brightly as Morrison approached. "May I help you?"

Morrison cleared his throat. "I have an appointment with Agent Threadgill." After a moment he added, "I'm Steven Morrison."

The receptionist, whose nametag identified her as Maria, glanced down at her schedule momentarily before returning her gaze to Morrison. "Welcome to the FBI, Mr. Morrison. If you don't mind, would you please empty your pockets?"

"Of course." He removed his wallet, keys, a comb from his back pocket and his cell phone and placed them on the desk.

Maria swept up his cell phone and placed it in a numbered plastic Ziploc bag. She wrote the number on a piece of paper and handed it back to Morrison. "No cell phones beyond this point," she said apologetically. "You can take the rest of your items back and pick the phone up on your way out." She reached for her phone and punched in a few numbers. "Mr. Morrison is here to see you." After a momentary pause she hung up and looked at Morrison. "Agent Threadgill will be right out." She indicated a row of chairs against the wall to her left. "You can wait here."

While Morrison waited, he furtively checked out the office layout, wondering how many cameras were watching. It looked a typical office setup from the eighties, perpendicular rows of narrow aisles running between a labyrinth of low-walled cubicles in the center of the floor, a number of offices for senior personnel lining the exterior walls. The hum of office activity buzzed in the background; nearby, two men talked to an unseen third person seated in one of the cubicles, their voices too low for Morrison to make out the content of their conversation. Besides Maria, no one seemed to have noticed his arrival.

As he surveyed the floor, he was surprised by the number of employees the FBI had stationed in Clearwater. He figured there would be a large contingent in Tampa, but hadn't figured that Clearwater would require such a significant force. Maybe, he thought, the fact that The Flag, the imposing building that serves as the headquarters of the Church of Scientology, was clearly visible several hundred yards to the south of his current position had something to do with the large personnel deployment.

His musings were interrupted by the approach of a blond woman striding purposefully toward him. He rose as she stopped in front of him and extended her hand. "Glad to meet you, Mr. Morrison. I'm Angela Threadgill. Thanks for coming in."

Her grip was firm, professional. He was conscious not to try to overpower it. "Uh, well, I'm a little confused. I'm not sure what you want from me."

She smiled. "Just a few questions. Follow me."

She led him to a small conference room along the exterior wall, closing the door behind them once they were inside. She indicated a seat on the opposite side of the rectangular conference table. "Why don't you sit over there?" Once he was seated, she took a position across the table from him. She indicated a tape recorder on the table between them. "I hope you have no objections to this conversation being recorded?"

What choice do I have, he thought? "No."

She smiled again. "Good." She glanced at her watch, pushed the Record button, and continued in her professional voice. "It's 9:18 am, November 13, 2017. This is Special Agent Angela Threadgill of the Federal Bureau of Investigation with interview subject Steven Morrison." She looked across the table. "Ready to begin?"

"Ready as I'll ever be, I guess."

18

"Before we start, would you like something to drink? Some coffee or water?"

Morrison's throat was dry. "Maybe some water."

Threadgill rose and extracted a plastic bottle of water from a small refrigerator in the corner, handing it to Morrison, who watched her closely. She was much younger than Morrison thought she would be, in her thirties, a well-toned blond who looked like she spent a lot of time in the gym. Her hair was straight, parted in the middle, just reaching her shoulders, and her eyes were a mesmerizing shade of grey. She didn't look like the menacing type of authority figure he thought he would face – she looked more like a collegiate cheerleader than a federal agent.

"Can you state your name for the record, please?"

"Steven Morrison."

"How old are you, Mr. Morrison?"

"Sixty-five."

"Are you employed?"

"No. I'm retired."

She jotted a something on her notepad, then looked at him, her face neutral. "What did you do before you retired?"

He paused for a second before answering, wondering where this was headed. "I worked in the film industry, in California."

"What did you do in the film industry?"

"I was an actor."

She looked at him intently. "I understand some people in your industry adopt stage names. Did you act under the name Steven Morrison?"

He was beginning to feel uncomfortable. He took a sip of water before responding. "No, I did not."

"Is it true, Mr. Morrison, that you acted under the name Biff Bratwurst?"

The question hit him like a hammer blow and brought an immediate flush to his face. Where was this headed? "Uh, yes, I did." Pause. "How did you know that?" he asked in a low voice.

"We're the FBI, Mr. Morrison. We find out things. It's what we do." She continued. "Did you ever work under a different alias?"

"No."

She glanced at her prepared notes. "Did you ever work on a film in Key West called *The Russians Are Coming and Coming and Coming*? This would've been in 1981 or 1982."

"Yes."

"At that time, was this the only adult film you had worked on outside the state of California?"

"Yes, it was."

"Do you have any idea why this particular movie was filmed in Key West instead of California, like the other films you worked on?"

"That was a long time ago," he said defensively.

"I realize that, Mr. Morrison. Take your time – we're in no rush here."

"Well," he began, "the movie was a spoof of the original comedy, which took place off the shore of Cape Cod. Our version was an update. Instead of a Russian submarine that ran aground, like the original, ours had a Russian fishing trawler out of Havana that became lodged on a reef off Key West."

"Why not film it in California? I'm sure there are places along the coastline there that could pass for Key West."

He nodded. "That's a good question, one I asked the director when they told me during my audition that the film would be shot on location, in Key West."

Threadgill glanced at her notes again. "Would that director have been Les Bent?"

What *didn't* she know about him? "Yes."

"Can you recall what Mr. Bent's reply was to that question?"

"Wow. That was over thirty years ago."

"Do your best."

After a moment he responded. "I think he told me that the principal investor in the film would only guarantee his financial support if the film was actually shot on location in Key West."

"Did you ever meet this investor?"

"No, I didn't. But he must've been loaded, because Bent told me the movie had five times the budget of any movie he'd ever been involved with," he said, recalling. "Transportation to and from Florida and lodging for the actors and production crew in the Keys alone must've cost a fortune."

"Do you have any idea what the nationality of this investor might've been?"

He shook his head. "Nope. It never came up."

"Could it have been someone from outside the United States?"

"Sure. As long as the money was green and kept flowing, nobody cared where it came from."

Agent Threadgill checked her notes again. "Were all of the cast and crew based in California?"

After a moment he responded, shaking his head again. "There was one woman who was hired in Florida as a dialogue coach."

"In your experience, was it normal practice on adult films to hire a dialogue coach?"

Morrison snorted in laughter. "No way. That was the first and last time it ever happened on a movie I was involved with."

"What sort of dialogue did she advise on?"

Morrison shrugged his shoulders. "Beats me. I played the lead Russian in the movie, the captain of the fishing boat, and we never spoke. Bent introduced her to us on the first day of shooting, but after that I don't think I ever saw her again."

"Do you remember her name?"

He shook his head. "No, I don't. It was something Russian."

"Could it have been Natalya? Natalya Bazarov?"

"That could've been it, but I can't be sure." He looked at her sheepishly. "It was a long time ago."

"Do you recall anything at all about her? Physical characteristics, hair color, age, height, weight?"

"The only thing I can remember for sure is that she was pregnant. Really pregnant - she looked like she was ready to pop at any moment. I figured that was why we never saw her on set."

Agent Threadgill removed a photo from her folder and passed it across the table to Morrison. "Is this the woman you remember?"

The photo, showing a woman sitting on a park bench next to a baby stroller, looked like it had been taken at a distance, using a telephoto lens. The woman in it was young, about the right age, with dark hair and soulful dark eyes. "It could be her," he said, handing the photo back to her after a few moments. He screwed up his courage. "What's this all about? Why do you want to know about this woman?"

She ignored his question, responding with one of her own. "Do you know what happened to her after shooting was completed?"

"Nope. Like I said, I never saw her again after she was introduced the first day."

"Were there any other Russian nationals present during the shooting?"

"Not that I knew of."

She glanced at her watch again and spoke directly into the tape recorder. "This initial interview with Steven Morrison is terminated at 11:31 am, November 13." She switched off the machine and smiled. "Thanks again for coming in today, Mr. Morrison. You've been a big help."

Morrison was completely baffled. "If you say so. I've got no idea what's going on here. Why would you be interested in some woman from so long ago?" He knew whatever crime the feds thought she might have committed would no longer be prosecutable because the statute of limitations would've expired by now. Unless, he thought, that crime was murder.

Agent Threadgill stood up, collecting her papers and the tape recorder. "I'm afraid I can't answer that question, Mr. Morrison. It's all part of an ongoing investigation."

An ominous thought occurred to Morrison. "This doesn't have anything to do with the Mueller investigation, does it?"

Agent Threadgill laughed. "Not a thing."

He wiped his brow in mock relief. "That's good. The last thing I'd want is to be drawn into that shitstorm." He glanced at her, embarrassed. "Excuse my French."

She laughed again. "I'm with you on that." She opened the door and motioned for him to follow her. "Maria will give you a validation card to cover the cost of your parking when you pick up your cell phone." She extended her hand again. "Thanks again for coming in, Mr. Morrison. You've been a big help."

"I'm glad you think so."

He followed her back to the reception area. Maria saw them coming and dug out Morrison's cell phone before he could find his claim check and handed it to him, along with a parking validation card.

On his way downstairs in the elevator, he thought: I'm more confused now than I was before I got here. He'd expected enlightenment, a reason behind why the FBI was seeking his assistance, but he was leaving with more questions and few answers.

*****

As soon as the elevator door closed on Morrison, Agent Threadgill returned to her office, shutting the door on the way in. She punched in several numbers on her phone. When a male voice answered, she said. "It's her. Morrison confirmed it."

"Does he know where she is now?"

114

"I don't think so."

"What about Vasilevsky, the money man?"

"He claims he never met him."

"Could he be lying?"

"You tell me. You watched the interview. I don't think he was lying."

The man wasn't convinced. "All the more reason to bring in Rheinhart. I don't believe in coincidences. Run the tape by the analytics group, see what they think."

"I'm on it, sir."

19

"You're not going to believe what happened."

Rheinhart had been on his laptop, playing a game, when Morrison called. "So tell me."

"They wanted to know about a woman I worked with on a film over thirty years ago. Some Russian."

"Russian?" Rheinhart perked up, making the connection. "Does it have anything to do with the Mueller investigation?"

"That's the first thing I asked. She laughed, said no."

"Where are you?"

"In the car, on the way home."

"Stop by my place. I want to hear the details."

*****

They were settled in Rheinhart's compact lanai at the rear of his house, beers in hand, but Morrison still seemed restless, his right leg unable to keep still. Rheinhart noticed his friend's agitation and tried to lighten the mood. "Did they tell you not to leave town?" he asked impishly.

Morrison missed the humor completely, his response devoid of mirth. "No, but just before she turned off the tape recorder she referred to our talk as the 'initial' interview. What the hell does that mean?"

"Hard to figure out the FBI these days. Maybe it means they'll call you back and maybe they won't. My guess is they'll call you back in if they find more evidence."

"Of what?"

Rheinhart shrugged. "That's the million-dollar question." He paused for a second, then continued, thinking out loud. "Something about a Russian that has nothing to do with the Mueller investigation…"

"If you believe the FBI," Morrison interjected.

"Did this woman, Agent Threadgill, give you any indication that she might be lying to you?"

Morrison shook his head. "I don't think so."

"Use your instincts as an actor," Rheinhart advised. "Did she seem sincere, or did it seem like she was feeding you bullshit?"

Morrison took a sip of his beer. "Honestly? I don't know. I was surprised by her youth and how good-looking she was. I kept thinking she was too young to be an FBI agent. I was looking at her body but not noticing her body language, I guess."

"Who was this Russian woman? What did she do on the movie?"

Morrison paused. Although he considered Rheinhart his best friend since he'd moved to Florida, he hadn't revealed the truth to him concerning the kind of films in which he'd acted. He'd shrugged off previous queries from him on the subject, maintaining that the films he worked on were strictly genre films, the kind that never qualified for widespread studio release and thus were largely unknown by the viewing public. Letting Rheinhart in on the reality of his career had seemed too risky until now, but that was before the FBI poked their nose into his business. Maybe it was time to lay his cards on the table. "It's a long story."

Rheinhart leaned forward expectantly. "I've got the time. Let me get us a couple more beers first."

When Rheinhart returned with fresh brews, Morrison laid it all out for his friend. He began by telling him how he'd been a surf bum in San Diego, completely content, when one day while surfing at Black's Beach he met an attractive brunette who introduced herself as Annette Haven. She approached him while he was onshore taking a break and tried to convince him to move to LA to try his hand at acting in adult films. At first he'd been shocked by her suggestion, which had been prompted by her watching him surf the treacherous left that day, admiring his physique molded by thousands of hours of paddling in the ocean.

But as she continued her sales pitch, mentioning that there were plenty of surf spots with better breaks in the LA area than in San Diego, his initial reluctance developed some tiny cracks that she exploited like an insincere politician. She argued that the money he'd earn would be much better than he was getting at the beachside restaurant where he was currently working in Ocean Beach. Plus, she was gorgeous, one of the most beautiful women he'd ever seen. He'd never heard of her before, but if she was typical of the type of women he'd be working with in Los Angeles, he was willing to give the proposal some thought.

Even as he was beginning to warm to the idea, he protested that he knew nothing about acting. She laughed and pointed out bluntly that she'd been watching him closely, and what she'd observed clearly outlined in his skin-tight shorty wetsuit was all the experience he would need to be a big success in adult films.

After considering her offer for about ten days, he decided to make the move. After all, he reasoned, the worst-case scenario was that he wouldn't become an actor but he would still be in Los Angeles, with more breaks to surf than in San Diego and plenty of restaurants in case he needed a job. He gave his notice at Hodad's, packed his meager belongings and lashed his three surfboards to a rack on top of his battered Oldsmobile Vista Cruiser and motored north to Los Angeles. He found an affordable apartment in Huntington Beach, not far from the pier, and when he was settled he called the number Haven had left for him. She remembered him immediately, greeting him warmly and wasting no time in introducing him to several power brokers in the adult film business. Within a month of his arrival, the newly minted Biff Bratwurst had been cast in his first role.

"How did you decide on the name Biff Bratwurst?" Rheinhart asked, transfixed by his friend's bizarre story.

"Two reasons. First, I wanted to change my name so no one in my family knew what I was doing. Second, I thought it was a funny name in a porn sort of way, one that might draw attention to me, get me more roles." He looked at Rheinhart intently. "You can't tell anyone any of this – it stays between the two of us."

Rheinhart started to object but Morrison cut him off. "Nobody, especially Gracie, can know about this. Are we clear?"

Rheinhart recognized the determination in Morrison's voice and nodded. "My lips are sealed. You won't have to worry about me spilling the beans."

"Good," Morrison said, relieved.

"So," Rheinhart continued. "this Russian woman was involved in a porn movie? One that you acted in?"

Morrison nodded. "Yeah."

"What was the name of the movie?"

"*The Russians Are Coming and Coming and Coming.*" Morrison noted the confusion on his friend's face and continued hastily. "It was a porn spoof of a comedy originally released in the sixties that was shot in Key West."

119

Rheinhart's face blanched. "You're shitting me," he said softly.

"No shit, Sherlock."

Rheinhart took a large gulp of his beer, wiping his mouth with the back of his hand before continuing in an excited voice. "I saw that movie, the summer after I graduated from college. A friend was getting married and the best man showed it at the groom's stag party." He looked at Morrison intently. "What part did you play?"

"The captain of the fishing boat, Ivan Jakinov."

"I hadn't seen much porn at all then, but I remember the guys at the party liked it. Some of them thought we should head to Key West right away to service some of those horny women."

"Trust me," Morrison said sagely. "Most of the women in these movies aren't horny. They're just reading the scripts."

"So this Russian woman was in the film? I don't remember her."

"No," Morrison said. "She was hired as a dialogue coach."

"What?"

"That was my reaction when the director told us. In all the years I worked in film, this was the only time there was a dialogue coach. For some reason, the guy bankrolling the film insisted that she be hired. It was his money, so she got the job."

"So, does the FBI think she's a spy?" Rheinhart asked.

"I don't know. Threadgill was pretty tight lipped about why she was asking about her." He paused before continuing. "Funny thing is, I never saw her on the set after that day she was introduced to the crew. She never gave me advice on my Russian accent, and I know none of the other actors who played the Russian fishermen got advice, either, because we used to talk about it."

"And you haven't seen her or heard anything about her since that movie?"

Morrison shook his head. "Not a peep."

"And now the FBI is after her." Rheinhart's British accent was poor, but the reference was clear. "The game is afoot, Watson."

20

After Morrison left for home, Rheinhart jumped back on his laptop and Googled Biff Bratwurst. He scrolled through the results until he found a website whose bare-bones description labeled it a porn movie database. He clicked on it. A Search function appeared in the header, so he typed in Biff Bratwurst again. A list of the films Biff Bratwurst had appeared in materialized on the next page, listed in chronological order.

Rheinhart's jaw dropped as he scrolled through the list. His first listed credit was in 1980, in a film called *Debbie Does Des Moines*. From then until his final credit, *Jurassic Pork* in 2011, Bratwurst appeared in more than 120 films, an average of nearly four a year. Fascinated, Rheinhart dug in, clicking on the films whose names caught his eye, cinematic gems like *The French Erection*, *Close Encounters of the Blond Kind*, *Frisky Business*, *Pulp Friction* and the film that had drawn the interest of the FBI, *The Russians Are Coming and Coming and Coming*.

There wasn't much of a writeup of *The Russians Are Coming*, but what was there matched his distance memory of the film and how Morrison had described it an hour ago. A group of Russian fishermen run aground on a reef off Higgs Beach in Key West, and they slip ashore to find someone to help them. A group of scantily clad female Conch marine mechanics volunteers their services to get the boat running again. A marathon of sweaty, tropical sex ensues.

There was a photo accompanying the writeup, a poster advertising the film. Rheinhart blew up the photo as much as he could while keeping its integrity. Sure enough, the Russian captain with the woolen sea cap leading the stranded men ashore was indeed a youthful Steven Morrison, who, Rheinhart had to admit, looked sexily handsome in his sailor garb, ready to take on all comers.

Porn star was so far down the list of occupations he would've guessed Morrison left behind in California that it wasn't on Rheinhart's radar. From the terse, vague responses his friend had given previously when questioned about his former career, Rheinhart thought that he'd worked in straight-to-video slasher films or some similar genre too narrow for widespread theater distribution.

He smiled to himself. He was looking forward to hearing more of Morrison's story.

*****

Back home, Morrison put in a call to his roofing contractor, leaving yet another message inquiring when they might get around to repairing the hole in his roof. When the call ended he dropped into his favorite chair and closed his eyes. Although the interrogation had not taxed him physically, he felt wrung out, like he'd just completed a marathon.

He was also concerned about revealing the secret of his employment history to Rheinhart, fearing the worst – that the news could, after being scrupulously shielded from anyone in his life for forty years, be exposed and that it would spread through the tightknit Ozona community like an out-of-control wildfire on a gusty day. One thing in his favor was that he knew, from previous conversations, that Rheinhart had already made a gut-wrenching decision to sacrifice his career in order to avoid being personally eviscerated by the publicity of a high-profile trial during the scandal in Jacksonville. It was a tiny grain of hope on a day that, so far, had triggered only fear and confusion.

He was counting on Rheinhart's pledge to keep Morrison's X-rated past to himself. Was that too much to ask?

*****

Marcia Alvarez parked her bike, then stubbed out her cigarette before walking into Kitty Galore's. Gracie was restocking clean glasses in the overhead rack above the bar as she slid onto her usual barstool next to the service bar and called out, "Be with you in a sec."

"No rush," Marcia said as she surveyed the few lunchtime patrons. "Pretty sparse, even for a Monday."

"Funny how that works," Gracie said as she poured a Yuengling for Marcia and placed it on the bar in front of her. "Faye said they had a huge crowd yesterday for the Bucs' game." Faye Tompkins was the daytime bartender on weekends.

"They must've spent a shitload of money on booze to drown their sorrows. I watched the game with my dad. The Bucs looked like a high school team." She shook her head in disbelief. "Against the fucking Jets."

"I wouldn't know," Gracie said diplomatically. "Hank doesn't like football. We watched a movie instead."

"Lucky you." She strained to see the specials listed on the wall above the cash register. "You still have tortilla soup?"

"Let me check." Gracie punched in the order on the interactive cash register screen, then turned back to Marcia. "Still have it. You want a cup or bowl?"

"Better make it a bowl." She drained her beer and placed her empty glass on the bar expectantly. Gracie drew her a second draft, which Marcia grabbed as she rose from her stool. "I'd ask you to save my seat," she said as she withdrew her cigarettes and lighter from her purse. "But I think it's pretty safe. I'll be right back."

As she made her way to the smoking area, Trace Smart stormed past her without a word and entered the bar. Marcia watched him take the stool next to hers as she lit her cigarette. Great, she thought through a haze of blue smoke. She thought Smart was one of the most inconsiderate men she'd ever met, unpleasantly loud and completely full of himself, which was striking when considering her ex-husband had physically abused her. She doubted the sort of behavior she'd witnessed from him at the bar would've been tolerated for very long had his father not been sharing a bed with the owner of Kitty Galore's.

Thinking about unpleasant men shifted her thoughts to her father. She wasn't sure what she was going to do with him. His mood swings were becoming more frequent and volatile as he grew increasingly less mobile. She feared it wouldn't be long until one of his outbursts sent Edith and Muriel on their way, never to return. If she lost them, she'd have to give up her lunches at Kitty's, which were the only therapy currently keeping her sane. Without a daily respite from their domestic battles, she knew it would only be a matter of time before she lost it altogether. She often marveled that she'd made it this far without one or both of them ending up in jail. Or worse.

She finished her cigarette and returned to her seat at the bar. Trace was ranting to Gracie about one of the tenants in the building where he worked. "The guy's a complete asshole," he complained loudly as Marcia sat down next to him. "Painted his bathroom, which is against the rules, then decided he didn't like the color and wants me to fix it." He looked at Marcia defiantly. "Why is his screw-up my problem?"

Gracie, whose face was blank, masking the contempt she felt for him, was glad to cede her role as sounding board on this subject to Marcia, taking advantage of her return to stroll to the other end of the bar to check on a couple midway through their lunch.

"I thought painting *was* your job," Marcia replied brightly, quickly adding, "Along with other things."

"It is," he admitted grudgingly. "But he should've asked me to do it instead of doing it himself."

Marcia thought his logic was ludicrous, but didn't say anything. Just as she was about to change the subject, Smart's phone rang. "What?" he barked into the receiver. He listened for a few moments, then continued, clearly aggravated. "Okay, okay, I'll be there in ten minutes." He turned to Marcia, indicating his half-finished beer. "Tell Gracie to put this on my tab." He got to his feet and walked out, muttering to himself.

Gracie was watching the drama out of the corner of her eye. As soon as Smart was out the door, she returned and said to Marcia, "What was that all about?"

Marcia shrugged. "Beats me. Whatever it was, it got him out of the bar."

"You're lucky. You should see him when he comes in after work."

"No thanks." Marcia finished her beer. Gracie nodded toward her glass. "Another?"

Marcia craned her neck toward the kitchen. "How's my soup?"

"Should be out any minute," Gracie replied.

Marcia thought for a moment. "Maybe just a glass of water. I can't be late again like I was last week. I almost lost my babysitter."

"How's that going? With your dad, I mean."

Marcia looked at Gracie. "Your parents still alive?"

"Yep. Back in Chicago."

She nodded approvingly. "That's the way to do it. Do you see 'em much?"

"Not if I can help it. My mother and I fought all the time when I was living at home. That's pretty much why I moved to Florida."

"I wish I hadn't moved to Tampa after I got out of the Army," Marcia said wistfully. "Biggest mistake of my life."

Gracie arched her eyebrow. "Bigger than your marriage?"

Marcia pondered the choice. When she answered, her face was somber. "I think so. The marriage lasted less than two years. Living with my dad is a life sentence."

"Is he really that bad?"

Marcia's face clouded over. "Have you ever heard of D.B. Cooper?"

Gracie answered as Marcia's soup arrived from the kitchen. "No, I don't think so. Who's that?"

"Some guy who hijacked an airplane back in 1971. He got away with a $200,000 ransom, parachuted out of the plane somewhere over Oregon. They never found him or the money. They wrote songs about the guy, like some folk hero."

"What's he have to do with your father?" Gracie asked, not following.

Marcia took a deep breath. "My father claims he's the real D.B. Cooper. Been sayin' it for years." She took a sip of her soup before continuing. "We're talking long-term delusional bullshit. Really wacko stuff."

"Does he have any proof?"

127

"Not that I've seen."

"Has he ever talked about it with anyone else?"

"You mean like a shrink?" She laughed ruefully. "He'd never do that – he's too paranoid."

"So what do you do?"

"I used to try to talk him out of it, but he accused me of calling him crazy, so now I just nod my head and go along with him."

Gracie tried to sound sympathetic. "Sounds like a good plan."

Marcia grimaced and reached for her cigarettes. "If you've got a better one, I'd love to hear it."

21

The first time Rheinhart met DeWayne Bologna was last March at Bologna's annual Mardi Gras party. He'd been convinced to go by Morrison, who had been taking diving lessons from the former Navy veteran who operated his own dive shop in a strip mall on U.S. 19 in Port Richey. It was an easy sell for Morrison. "Of course you're going to come," Morrison said to Rheinhart when he passed on the invitation. "All you do on Saturday nights is stay home and watch movies. I'm offering some actual human contact with people who are a lot of fun."

Bologna was holding a pitcher of his signature party drink, Bahama Mamas, when the two of them rang the doorbell. He beamed at Morrison and Rheinhart. "Talk about timing," he said, indicating the pitcher. "I just made a fresh batch. Grab a cup, fill it up and meet the group."

About thirty attendees, most of them in costume and wearing beads, filled the modest ranch just off Embassy in Port Richey. Mardi Gras decorations were everywhere, and a steady stream of tropical tunes ranging from Jimmy Buffett to Peter Tosh provided the evening's soundtrack. From time to time small groups of people would disappear into the backyard, where the distinctive odor of marijuana was unmistakeable, and whenever the supply of Bahama Mamas ran out, Bologna appeared as if on cue to mix a fresh batch.

Rheinhart thoroughly enjoyed himself and thanked Morrison in the car on the way home. "That was a lot of fun. I'm glad you talked me into it."

Morrison smiled. "DeWayne's a fun guy. And he throws great parties."

Rheinhart was ready and waiting when Bologna pulled into his driveway Tuesday evening a little before seven. Rheinhart invited him in and offered him a drink, but Bologna declined. "Better get on the road if we want to make it on time," he said. "Besides, I'm driving."

Bologna drove a white Nissan pickup with cap over its bed modified to accommodate the needs of his business and a hand-lettered sign advertising Gulfside Scuba on the driver's side. Accompanying Rheinhart in the front seat were a couple of masks and a damaged regulator, which Bologna scooped up with an apologetic grin and deposited in the bed of the truck through the open window behind him before starting the truck and pulling out of Rheinhart's driveway onto Bay Street.

There was a lively crowd at Kitty Galore's as they drove past, a fleet of Harley's parked in front and music blaring from outdoor speakers. "Is Tuesday Biker's Night?" Bologna asked.

"Not that I know of," Rheinhart replied, turning his head toward the restaurant as they drove past. "Maybe it's somebody's birthday."

"I like Kitty's," Bologna said. "Very laidback crowd. Morrison took me there a couple of times. Good food, too."

"He and I go to lunch there every Wednesday," Rheinhart said. "It felt right from the first moment I walked through the door."

The GPS on Bologna's phone directed them to turn onto Tampa Road, cross Alt 19 and turn right on Omaha Street. From there it was a straight shot through Dunedin and Clearwater to Largo.

They pulled into the expansive parking lot at the Largo Community Center twenty minutes before the lecture was scheduled to begin. Rheinhart was disappointed by the lack of cars. "Don't people care about red tide?" he asked, looking around as he exited the vehicle.

"A lot of people down here take our resources for granted," Bologna stated, shaking his head. "Especially our politicians. We need more people like Gwen Westphal, educating the public."

"Yeah," Rheinhart replied. "If the public shows up."

"If this was the opening of a new Cracker Barrel," Bologna added sardonically, "the parking lot would be jammed."

Inside, they wandered around the expansive foyer with a few other early arrivals, admiring the art on the walls. Rheinhart, who'd never been to Largo before, picked up a brochure outlining the activities offered at the center and was reading about water aerobics' classes for seniors when Bologna gave him a nudge. He looked up; Bologna was pointing at a tall, athletic woman who was talking to a security guard by the entrance. "That's her," he said in a low voice. "The girl of my dreams."

"I thought Donna was the girl of your dreams." Donna Sutherland was Bologna's current girlfriend.

"Donna? No way," Bologna exclaimed. "She's just a rental till the real deal comes along." He stretched to his full height of five eight, sucking in his paunch. "That might be tonight."

"Good luck," Rheinhart said with a smile.

"The heck with luck. Charm is what counts. It's what gets you in the door, especially with a woman like her."

"Really? What kind of woman is she?"

"Smart, accomplished, confident and beautiful. The genuine article."

"Sounds a little out of your league," Rheinhart teased.

"Sonny, you've never seen me play. Pay attention and take notes."

The lights in the atrium flashed off and on, signalling the program was about to begin. Westphal disappeared inside a door leading backstage as Bologna and Rheinhart made their way into the auditorium.

Finding a good seat was easy; the auditorium was about a quarter full. They were handed a small program as they entered by a volunteer and took seats in the middle of the second row, directly in front of the podium. Suspended above the stage behind the podium was a large screen for what Rheinhart figured must be a PowerPoint presentation.

At 8:05 a diminutive man with gray hair and glasses came onto the stage from the wings. Because the microphone had been adjusted for the statuesque Westphal's use, he had to stand on his toes to address the crowd, which produced a few snickers he ignored. "Good evening. We have a special treat for you tonight at the Largo Community Center – one of the shining stars of the clean water movement in Florida, a former Olympic bronze medalist in kayaking, and currently the spokeswoman for the Clear Sailing Alliance, I'm pleased to present Dr. Gwen Westphal."

Generous applause from the sparse crowd greeted the lissome brunette's entrance. She was wearing a sleeveless white blouse and khaki slacks that hugged her curves, seashell earrings and a diver's watch on her left wrist. Rheinhart thought she looked sensational.

She spoke for nearly an hour, and the small but rapt audience hung on every word. She used the screen behind her to great effect, illustrating the pathways of suspected contaminants as they made their way into the Gulf Stream as well the devastating effect red tide had on local marine populations. She debunked the popularly held notion that the sugar and phosphate industries were directly responsible for recent increases in the number and size of red tide outbreaks, which brought a smattering of boos from the pro-environment crowd, but did not rule out that they contributed to their intensity.

When she finished her presentation, she offered to take questions from the audience as the man who'd introduced her hustled to set up a microphone in the middle aisle. Rheinhart waited to see if Bologna was going to ask any questions, but when he failed to make a move Rheinhart, with a wink to his companion, stood up and took his place in a short line of questioners.

When it was Rheinhart's turn to speak, he cleared his throat and grasped the microphone. "Thanks so much for the presentation; it was very informative. I just have one short question: how successful has the Harmful Algal Blooms group at the University of South Florida been in predicting red tide occurrence, and has the Clear Sailing Alliance contributed any data or other resources toward their efforts?"

She looked intently at Rheinhart as she formulated her answer, trying to determine if he was a ringer, a plant from either the sugar or phosphate industries sent to disrupt her talk with a "gotcha" question. Rheinhart gave nothing away, a small smile on his lips as he awaited her reply.

"Great question, Mr. ---?"

"Rheinhart. Zach Rheinhart."

"Mr. Rheinhart. The coalition between HAB, the Harmful Algal Blooms group, and USF has been very fruitful. While we still have not been able to determine the root cause of the *Karenia brevis* algae, those two entities have provided significant breakthroughs in various types of predictive analyses. As for the

Clear Sailing Alliance, we've funded several grants at USF which have helped to keep the efforts moving forward, but have not been involved in providing any data or personnel to the efforts." She paused and smiled. "Does that answer your question?"

"Perfectly. Thank you."

Rheinhart handed the microphone to the next person in line and returned to his seat. Bologna stared at him incredulously as he sat down. "Where the hell did that come from?"

Rheinhart thrived on defying predictions, and he was enjoying this moment immensely. "I did some homework over the weekend." He winked at his companion. "You never know when a little knowledge might come in handy."

There were several more questions, all of which Westphal handled deftly. When the last questioner received an answer, the emcee walked back on to the stage and gratefully accepted the handheld microphone from Westphal, who took a step back from the podium, hands clasped behind her back.

He turned slightly toward her. "Thank you, Dr. Westphal, for that wonderful and enlightening presentation. After tonight, I'm sure we all know a little more about one of the most serious threats to our way of life in Florida." Turning back toward the audience, he continued. "How about a nice round of applause for Dr. Westphal?"

Rheinhart rose to his feet, as did most of the rest of the audience, and gave her a sustained standing ovation. There were several whistles and a lone shout of "More!" from the rear of the room mixed in with the applause.

Bologna and Rheinhart stayed until Westphal and the emcee left the stage, then made their way with the crowd slowly out to the foyer. As they were headed toward the exit, Rheinhart heard a now-familiar female voice call out his name. "Mr. Rheinhart!"

He turned to see Gwen Westphal approaching the two of them. When she was by their side, she extended her hand. "That was a terrific question, Mr. Rheinhart. Are you a scientist, by any chance?"

Rheinhart shook his head; Bologna was speechless next to him. "Just an architect with a passion for the water," he said.

The scientist reached into a pocket and pulled out a pen and a business card. She wrote something on the back of the card and handed it to Rheinhart with a smile. "This is my business card. If you have any more questions, please feel free to give me a call. If you can't reach me at the office, you can call my cell. The number's on the back."

Before he could answer, she spun on her heel and walked away toward the emcee who was with a small group of women by a vending machine at the other end of the hall. Bologna finally found his voice. "I can't believe it," he said in wonder. "She gave you her number."

Rheinhart laid a hand on Bologna's shoulder and flashed a knowing smile. "Sometimes, my friend, knowledge trumps charm."

22

Morrison was already at the bar on Wednesday when Rheinhart arrived for lunch. He and Gracie had their heads close together, speaking conspiratorially, when Gracie noticed Rheinhart's arrival and straightened up. "About time you got here."

Rheinhart was grinning from ear to ear as he sat down next to Morrison. "Sorry I'm late. I lost track of time."

Morrison sipped his beer and turned toward Rheinhart. "How was the lecture last night?"

Gracie looked at Rheinhart in bewilderment. "What lecture?"

Morrison explained as Gracie drew a draft for Rheinhart. "Zach went to a lecture on red tide in Largo last night with my diving instructor."

She placed the beer on the bar in front of Rheinhart. "I didn't know you were interested in science," she said.

"I'm interested in anything that affects my ability to go out on the Gulf in my boat. Red tide has really been prevalent lately. DeWayne was going to the lecture; I just tagged along."

"DeWayne's the diving instructor?" Gracie asked.

Morrison responded. "Yep. Great guy. He's thinking about retiring soon."

"He didn't mention anything about that last night," Rheinhart said.

"He's been thinking about it for a couple of years now," Morrison said. "But the numbers don't work for him yet. He thinks he needs to work another year, maybe two."

"Is he planning to stay in Florida?" Rheinhart asked.

Morrison shook his head. "He wants to move to Saipan. At least that's what he told me the last time we talked about it."

"Saipan?" Gracie was clueless. "Where's that?"

"In the western Pacific, not far from Guam," Morrison replied.

"What's there?" she asked. "What's the attraction?"

Morrison shrugged. "Blue skies and crystal clear, warm water for diving year-round would be my guess."

"Do they speak English there?"

Morrison took another sip of his beer. "They speak English everywhere these days. English is the language of international finance. And tourism." He looked at Rheinhart. "Oysters?"

Rheinhart looked at Gracie. "How are they today?"

"Really big, but not tough. Very tender and tasty."

"We'll take a dozen."

As she punched the order in, Morrison turned back to Rheinhart. "Give it up – why the shit-eating grin?"

Rheinhart tried to play dumb. "I don't know what you're talking about…"

"Bullshit," Morrison replied succinctly. "What happened at that lecture?" His gaze narrowed. "Or was it something else, some other thing?" He paused, then veered eagerly in another direction. "Did you find out something about your corpse? Is that it?"

There were two other couples at the bar, one of them eating, the other just drinking for now, plus Tiny, one of Gracie's regulars who had retired six years ago from the San Diego Chargers. He'd been one of those rare third-down linebackers, adept at both stuffing the run and defending against the pass during a ten-year career. A Fort Myers native, after retiring he'd moved to Sanibel, but soon found he couldn't stomach the traffic, so he sold his place and bought a home on the Gulf in Ozona. He'd remained in top shape during his retirement - not yet forty, Tiny was still close to his playing weight of 245, spread over a six-foot six-inch frame. He was the kind of person she wanted by her side if she was ever cornered in a dark alley.

Tiny caught Gracie's eyes and gave her one of his nods, meaning he was ready for another drink. She raised a finger – I'll be there in a minute – in order to hear Rheinhart's reply. Both Morrison and Gracie looked at him eagerly, anxious for the answer.

"No. Nothing to do with the mystery of the dead body," Rheinhart teased, leaving them dangling.

"So what is it?" Morrison demanded, giving Rheinhart a friendly poke. "Inquiring minds are dying to know."

Rheinhart briefly debated playing them along, but decided they probably weren't going to relent on their questioning until they got what they wanted. "The lecture last night was really good, better than I expected."

"Can you hurry this up?" Gracie asked impatiently, glancing at Tiny and then back at Rheinhart. "I have other customers to serve here besides the two of you."

A light dawned in Morrison's eyes. "It wasn't the lecture you enjoyed so much, was it? It was the lecturer, the Olympic medalist."

Rheinhart withdrew Westphal's business card from his pocket, making sure to place it on a dry portion of the bar. Morrison picked it up. "Dr. Gwen Westphal, Clear Sailing Alliance."

"Flip it over."

Morrison did as he was told, revealing the hand-scrawled phone number on the back. Gracie realized it first. "You got her number!" she exclaimed in delight. "I want to hear the rest when I get back," she said before heading to the other end of the bar to attend to Tiny.

Morrison looked at the card, bewildered. "How in hell did you do that?"

"The old-fashioned way," he said with a smile. "I used my brain."

"Huh?"

Gracie returned, slightly out of breath. "Did I miss anything?"

"Nope. Lover boy's just about to reveal his secret."

"There's no secret. After the lecture there was a short Q&A session. I asked a question, and after the lecture ended, when we were leaving the building, she called out to me. We had a brief chat and she gave me her card." He held it up triumphantly. "With her private cell on the back."

"Must've been some question," Gracie opined.

Rheinhart tried to sound modest. "I spent a little time over the weekend researching her and her work, plus I brushed up on the latest red tide data. It wasn't that hard to pick out something that might catch her attention."

"What was DeWayne doing while all this was going on?" asked Morrison.

139

Rheinhart chuckled. "That's the best part. Before we got to the community center, he was bragging about how Gwen---"

"So it's Gwen now?" Morrison interjected.

Rheinhart continued, ignoring the interruption. "He was bragging about how Dr. Westphal was his kind of woman, hinting that he was going to try to make some move."

"I could see that," Morrison said. "She's all about the environment and clean water. That's right in his ballpark." Pause. "So what did he do when she gave you her number?"

"Tried to pick his jaw up off the floor. He barely said a word to me all the way back to Ozona."

"I have a dive coming up with him this weekend up north on the Rainbow River," Morrison said. "I'll get his version then."

One of the servers emerged from the kitchen with a tray of oysters. Gracie noticed and called out, "Down here, Jess." Gracie looked at the two of them. "Extra cocktail sauce, right?" she asked, reaching into a compartment beneath the bar and placing it on the tray. "Anything else? Fresh beers?"

Rheinhart grinned. "You bet. Lunch today is on me."

Morrison looked at Gracie, then back at Rheinhart, shaking his head in amazement "Well, well. Miracles never cease."

Gracie heard his remark as she returned with two more beers. "This is just the beginning. I have a feeling better things lie ahead."

Morrison looked at Gracie quizzically. "What do you mean?"

"He's springing for lunch because she gave him her phone number. Wait until he actually gets laid."

23

Before Morrison and Rheinhart had finished their oysters, all the seats at the bar were occupied. Gracie was constantly on the move, trying to figure out where all these people came from on a Wednesday – had a bus dropped off a tour group? - as she struggled to keep up with the surge in demand for her attention.

"Looks like Gracie could use some help today," Morrison said as he polished off the last of his oysters, wiping a dab of cocktail sauce from his lower lip before taking a sip of his beer. "I think it's going to take a while for our lunch to arrive."

"We could skip lunch today if you like," Rheinhart offered. "Those oysters were really big."

"Are you shitting me?" Morrison exclaimed in protest. "I don't care how long it takes our food to get here, Valentino. This might be a once-in-a-lifetime opportunity. Who knows how long it will be until the next time you think you've found a girlfriend?"

"Valentino?" Rheinhart fired back. "Couldn't you come up with a more modern reference? Like, from this century?"

Morrison smiled broadly. "Be my guest, Sherlock. You're the one with all the answers. I'm only here for the free lunch."

It took ten minutes for Gracie to work her way through the influx of customers and return to Morrison and Rheinhart at the far end of the bar. By that time they'd both decided on their luncheon choices – Rheinhart opting for a Cobb salad, while Morrison chose one of the specials, baked hogfish smothered in a spicy habanero sauce, served over basmati rice.

Gracie looked at Morrison inquiringly as he placed his order. "Top shelf dining today, I see."

Morrison jerked his thumb toward Rheinhart. "Just taking advantage of Lovestruck Louie's offer. Tell the chef to hurry up before he changes his mind."

Gracie shook her head. "It's going to be a while." She indicated the fully occupied bar. "You've got a lot of competition today. Two more beers?"

"You bet," Morrison replied quickly.

As she collected their oyster tray and turned and walked away, Rheinhart noticed that Tiny was no longer at the other end of the bar, his exit precipitated by the boisterous crowd who'd occupied the bar area with the suddenness of a tsunami. Gracie had told him that Tiny liked room to move and personalized attention; crowds were not his thing.

He turned back toward Morrison, determined to take control of the conversation. "I did some research on you yesterday. Or should I say Biff Bratwurst?"

Morrison tried to appear unconcerned. "Yeah?"

"You've got quite the track record. I did the math – it works out to almost four movies a year."

"Yeah, well, we weren't shooting *Cleopatra*. Most of them were low-budget quickies, shot in a week or less. Except for *The Russians Are Coming*. We were in Key West for five weeks on that one."

"Did you run into Jimmy Buffett while you were there?"

Morrison shook his head. "I had no idea who he was then. I was still listening mostly to Dick Dale and the Beach Boys, West Coast surf music."

"What about the women?"

142

"You mean the actresses?"

"Yeah."

"I was wondering when you'd get around to them," Morrison said, shifting in his seat. His leg had begun to fall asleep. "Wadda you wanna know?"

"What were they like?"

"Desperate, mostly. A lot of them had serious drug problems, heroin, speed and coke. Back then, none of the girls were college graduates, like some of the ones today; it was easy to take advantage of them. Some of them were immigrants, couldn't speak a word of English, but they were good at faking moans and groans. Some were hookers. Their pimps would come to the shoots, dressed to the nines. Everybody ignored them, which really pissed them off. Some were farm girls from Kansas, determined to be the next Judy Garland, sure they were going to have their handprints in the sidewalk in front of Grauman's Chinese Theatre. Someone would tell them that, in order to make it in Hollywood, you needed exposure. The lucky ones ended up on the bus back to Topeka; the unlucky ones were worked hard and tossed aside, left on the curb like yesterday's trash. Some of them ended up dead."

Gracie dropped off their beers without a word and hurried off in the direction of the service bar. She was no longer smiling.

Rheinhart wanted Morrison to continue, but he didn't want to push him too much. He'd already revealed more personal information this week than he had since the two had met; Rheinhart wanted to keep the tap flowing, see what else might spill out. He lobbed his friend another softball. "Did you ever socialize with any of them off the set?"

"The women? No way." He was emphatic. "Didn't hang around with most of the dudes, either. Just showed up, hit my marks and went home at the end of the day. It was work, man, and

143

I don't like to shit where I work. People outside the valley think it's like that movie, *Boogie Nights*, where everyone is one big, happy family. People in the valley know the score."

"Valley?"

Morrison explained. "The San Fernando Valley. That's where most of the films are shot." He paused, then corrected himself. "*Were* shot. Until five years ago, that is."

"What happened then?"

"Measure B passed in Los Angeles County. It required all male actors in the adult film industry to wear condoms whenever penetration was involved. Great for the long-term health of the actors and actresses, but the number of productions fell way off. It turned out that guys didn't want to watch other guys fucking with a rubber on. Some of the production companies moved to Vegas and some new ones sprung up in Florida. My best friend in the business, Wai Tang, was one of the ones who moved to Florida. He kept after me, and when things got bad I was already thinking about pulling up stakes and moving here. That's when I got the letter from my uncle's attorney and found out about the inheritance. Couldn't of been better timing for me – I hadn't worked on a film for four years by then. I couldn't even afford my rent. I was living on the streets, in my car."

"Like Homeless Simpson."

"Who?"

Rheinhart explained. "One of Gracie's customers. She couldn't figure out his story and he wasn't the talkative type, wouldn't give anything personal away. He started coming in last year, a couple of weeks before Halloween. He'd usually stop in once a week, order one beer, drink it and leave. Gracie figured he was homeless, so she made up a name for him, Homeless Simpson. You know, like she did with Guido Vaticanini."

"Was he homeless?"

"Not really. But a couple of weeks ago Gracie finally cracked him open, got him to talk. He was living in his van, but it was by design. He works as a cook at some camp in Canada during the summer, saves as much as he can, then drives to Florida for the winter. He arrived this year about a month ago, and one of his regular stops is Kitty Galore's."

Morrison looked at Rheinhart with a puzzled expression. "How come you know this and I don't?"

"Probably because when she told me the story you weren't here."

Morrison still didn't get it. Rheinhart continued, smiling. "Believe it or not, I sometimes come in here when I'm not with you."

Morrison adopted a pouty look. "You mean I'm not the only man in your life?"

"Hardly."

Rheinhart's snap answer brought a smile to Morrison's face. "Does your new girlfriend know about these other dudes you been hangin' out with?"

Rheinhart protested, his voice rising. "It's not like that." He knew Morrison was playing with him now, but he couldn't let it go. "There are no other dudes." His voice trailed off weakly.

Morrison eased himself off his barstool, smiling. "Keep telling yourself that, Valentino. Right now, I have to squirt." He took two steps in the direction of the men's room, then spun back and hit his friend with the clincher, loud enough so their neighbors at the bar could hear.

"Promise me you won't come out of the closet until I get back."

24

After lunch Morrison walked home with Rheinhart. When they reached Rheinhart's house he invited Morrison in, but Morrison declined, shaking his head. "I think I'll head home and take a nap. Thanks for lunch."

On the way he stopped at the bench next to the Crooked Snook Marina, gazing out at the mangrove islands offshore, wondering: had it been a mistake to reveal his past to Rheinhart? He'd been scrupulously protective of his former life until now. Rheinhart would still be in the dark if Morrison hadn't received that phone call from the FBI and panicked a bit, seeking Rheinhart's advice. He hoped that Rheinhart wouldn't share the information about his career in porn, but who knew anything for certain these days?

He watched from the bench as a pelican glided above the Gulf, looking for dinner. After a minute the inelegant bird tucked its wings into its body and nosedived into the water, emerging moments later with a struggling mullet clenched in its outsized beak. He watched, fascinated, as the pelican floated on the surface, draining its throat pouch of all water and then tossing the mullet a foot into the air with surprising dexterity before swallowing it, still alive, whole. He waited for the bird to become airborne again before rising from the bench and continuing on his way.

At home he washed a stack of dirty dishes that had been sitting in the sink for several days and placed them in the rack to dry before heading to his room to lie down. One too many beers at lunch usually had that effect on him these days.

As he was lying down he noticed his cell phone on the bedside table, where he'd left it that morning. Morrison had grown up in an era where instant gratification via the phone wasn't an issue; he often left it behind when going out. He'd always hated talking on the telephone and had been diligent in not falling prey to the addictive lure of the latest cell phone features insidiously designed to keep users glued to the devices, afraid that they might miss a call or text, no matter how insignificant.

One of the icons indicated that he had a message from DeWayne Bologna. He punched in his access code and listened. It was a brief reminder of their next dive trip, this Saturday on the Rainbow River. He turned the phone off so it wouldn't disturb him while he napped, then laid down and closed his eyes. He was thinking of the prehistoric shark tooth he'd found on a previous dive there when he drifted off to sleep.

*****

Rheinhart watched his friend until he reached the end of Bay Street before turning away and entering his home. He retrieved his phone from a pocket of his shorts and checked the contact he'd added yesterday: Gwen. He toyed with calling her but dismissed the thought almost as soon as it formed. It was the middle of the afternoon on Wednesday, a work day. He might not have anything better to do, he thought, but she surely did. Caution, he decided, was the way to go – overplaying his hand too quickly, as he had several times in the past, could be his worst move. He stared through the phone, wondering how best to approach her when he did call. Dinner? Drinks?

He'd worked through several other approaches that he rejected until the light came on. He smiled broadly. What interested her more than anything else in the world? Water. How could he use that to his advantage?

By asking her to go for a ride on his boat.

147

*****

Morrison's nap was a short one, interrupted by a familiar ringtone. Groggily, it took him two tries to grasp his phone. It wasn't one of his contacts, but it was a local number. Thinking it might be the FBI again, he let it go to voicemail. A minute later a single tone indicated someone had left a message. He punched in his code and listened.

The sultry voice of Lauren Caputo filled his ear. "Steve, this is Lauren Caputo over at Fuego. Harpoon gave me your number, so I thought I'd give you a shout. A bunch of us from the poker game last week are going to Skipper's Smokehouse Saturday to see Free Range Strange, a band from Ocala that Harpoon saw in Orlando a while back. He really liked them. He says you've never been to Skipper's before and he thinks you'll like the place, so I'm hoping you can join us. Rick and Elaine, the couple from the poker game, will be there. Call me back on this number and let me know if we should save a place for you at our table. The show starts at 8:00, and the doors open at 7:00."

He raised himself to a sitting position, staring at his phone. He didn't have to check his social schedule to know that he was free Saturday night. He was free every Saturday night. He did have a dive scheduled with DeWayne during the day on Saturday, but they were leaving before dawn so they could be in the water at first light, and DeWayne had promised him they'd be back by late afternoon. He probably would have time to sneak in another nap if he needed one.

He Googled Free Range Strange and clicked on a link to their website. He selected the "About" icon for the band and discovered they were a five-piece alt country band led by frontman Jerome Cortez, lead singer and mandolin virtuoso who'd also contributed to albums by artists such as The Subdudes and J.J. Cale. He listened to several sample tunes on the website. They were no Dick Dale, but they were interesting, featuring a punkish bluegrass sound with some pointedly political lyrics. Certainly worth a listen.

He exited the website and dialed Caputo's number. She answered on the first ring, as if she'd been holding her phone, awaiting his call. "That was quick."

"It took me awhile to wake up. I was taking a nap when you called."

She chuckled. "I hear that's a favorite practice of senior citizens." She paused a moment before continuing. "So what do you think? You wanna join us at Skipper's on Saturday?"

"I think I will," Morrison replied. "It sounds like fun."

"You know how to get there?"

"I can look it up. How many are going?"

Caputo thought for a moment. "Rick and Elaine, Harpoon, and another friend of mine, Jessica Callaway. She lives here at Fuego, too." She continued. "Harpoon has a couple of guests staying at his house. I don't know if they're coming or not."

"Is there room for one more?"

Her tone was cautious. "Depends on who you have in mind. He or she?"

"He. A friend of mine here in Ozona, Zach Rheinhart."

"Does he know you used to fuck for a living?"

Morrison grimaced at the wording. "Yeah, I told him that I used to work in the industry."

"Is he a swinger?" Caputo asked.

"No. Why do you ask?"

"There's a party at The Hand and Job after the concert that starts at midnight. I was hoping you could join us." Pause. She lowered her voice suggestively. "I thought you might want to spend the night. I have plenty of room at my place."

"Is this the kind of party I think it is?"

She laughed. "If you mean are people going to be naked, the answer is yes."

"I don't know," he said doubtfully. "My friend would probably have a problem with that."

"Then don't bring him," she said succinctly. "Besides, we always have enough men at these parties. What we need is more pussy."

"Can't help you there."

Part 2

25

By the time the crime scene investigators from Pinellas County had finished processing the body and the area where it was discovered on Anclote Key, the sun was hovering just above the surface of the Gulf. Detectives Betty Kullmann and Ted Profeta watched from under the bimini of their own boat as the body, secured in a body bag, was loaded onto the other boat and transported back to the mainland.

As they watched the boat depart, Profeta took a drag on his cigarette and turned toward his partner with a sly smile. "What next, boss?" He gestured around the deserted key, which had been cordoned off all day to pleasure boaters while the crime scene squad investigated. "No doors to knock on here."

Kullmann moved behind the wheel. "Haul in the anchors and we'll head back ourselves. Be nice to dock before dark."

Profeta stubbed out his cigarette and carefully placed the butt in an evidence bag along with the others he'd smoked during this long day, then retrieved each of the anchors and stowed them in an aft compartment. Returning to the bow, he extended a leg over the side of the boat and shoved off from the beach. Once the water was deep enough, Kullmann engaged the power tilt to lower the outboard. She started the engine and eased into deeper water before swinging the boat around and heading back toward Clearwater.

Neither of them spoke during the thirty-minute trip. Profeta, from his position in the bow, was looking for buoys marking crab traps in their path, while Kullmann was running over the meager facts of the case that they knew so far. She'd used her phone to Google Chad Middleton and Junonia Realty while the crime scene squad was at work and had been able to confirm from his picture on the company website that the body discovered by Zachary Rheinhart on Anclote Key that morning had indeed been that of Chad Middleton.

She'd been hoping that the business card found with the body had been a red herring, left by the killer to confuse the detectives and buy some time for the killer to escape. Because if the body was indeed that of Middleton, as it appeared that it was, what on earth had he done to deserve the attention of a professional hitter, a sadistic bastard that cut out the realtor's tongue? It made no sense. More importantly, Kullmann knew that their window of opportunity to gather the kind of critical evidence needed to solve the case was narrow – without a motive, crime scene or an eyewitness, finding a viable suspect in this case would be a formidable task.

*****

After docking the boat and returning to the station house, Kullmann and Profeta were flagged down by Don Cass, the desk sergeant, as they walked through the door. "Captain wants to see you in his office."

"Can I take a leak first, Sarge?" Profeta asked. "We've been on that frickin' island all day."

Cass was unsympathetic. "Grit your teeth and hold it, Profeta. Cap said now. He's late for dinner."

That's a fucking tragedy, thought Profeta as he turned the corner and headed gingerly toward the captain's office, nursing a full bladder. Kullmann followed silently, several steps behind, trying not to grin at her partner's discomfort.

154

Captain Carlos Lopez saw them coming down the hall and waved them into his office. Once they were in, he commanded. "Shut the door behind you."

Kullmann settled into one of the two guest chairs opposite Lopez's desk, while Profeta stood, visibly uncomfortable as he blurted out. "How long is this gonna take, Cap? I really gotta piss."

"Less than five minutes, Profeta," Lopez said, adding. "You can hold it for five minutes, can't you?"

Profeta, defeated, nodded as he sat down gingerly. Lopez continued. "First off, good work out there today. I looked at the notes Kullmann sent me concerning the interview with Rheinhart, and his story checked out – looks like he's just an unemployed architect who discovered the body by chance, like he said."

"It seemed pretty obvious he wasn't the kind of guy who goes around torturing real estate agents," Kullmann offered. "Just in the wrong place at the wrong time."

"Any idea about the cause of death?" Profeta asked. "He looked fine, except for the missing tongue."

Lopez leaned back in his chair, lacing his fingers behind his head. "That's why I called you in here." He looked at Profeta, then shifted his gaze to Kullmann. In a softer tone, he continued. "You two are off the case."

Kullmann, the lead detective, protested, not comprehending. "Are you shitting me?"

Lopez shook his head sympathetically. "I'm afraid not."

Kullmann leaned forward, her tone defiant. "Why? Who's got it now?"

Lopez tried to mollify the visibly upset detective. "There's no good way to frame this, except to say that it doesn't have anything to do with the two of you."

Kullmann wasn't buying it. "Yeah? Well, I don't fucking believe it. Whose idea was it that a woman couldn't run this case and solve it?" Kullmann asked hotly, her face flushed.

Lopez held up his palms, face out, in defense. "Whoa. It wasn't a department decision. By the time the forensic squad returned with the body, the feds were already here, waiting. As soon as the body arrived, they claimed it, took over jurisdiction for the case and drove away."

"Feds?" Profeta asked in wonderment. "How the hell did they know that we found a body? Besides, it hasn't been officially identified yet."

"I don't know how they knew about the body, but they did. They were typical feds – the only words I managed to get out of them was that it was a national security issue, no longer any of our business."

"Realtor, my ass," Profeta muttered under his breath, squirming uncomfortably in his seat.

"What are we supposed to do?" Kullmann asked hollowly, thunderstruck by the turn of events.

"Go home," the captain instructed. "When you come in tomorrow, keep working the cases you already have. And pick up a voucher for meal money before you leave tonight." Lopez held up his hands submissively. "You worked a solid ten in the blazing sun today. The least we can do is feed you for it."

"So that's it?" Profeta asked. "We're supposed to forget about a body we found in Pinellas County today, act like nothing happened."

"Exactly."

Profeta stood up quickly. "Can I piss now?"

Lopez nodded. "Try to make it out the door before you let loose."

Profeta was already on his way, shuffling toward the men's room.

Kullmann watched Profeta hobble off, then turned back to the captain. "How did they know about the case?"

"That's a good question, one I plan to look into." He paused before continuing. "I've been thinking about it since the feds showed up. My best guess is that they had eyes on Middleton for some reason. When I entered the information from the business card that you emailed me into the federal database, it set off some sort of red flag."

"Terrorist?"

Lopez shrugged. "Hard to say. I'll try to do some digging tomorrow, see what I can find out. I have a contact at the FBI office in Clearwater who might be able to shed some light on this."

Kullmann stood up. "Cap?"

"Yes, Kullmann?"

"Keep me in the loop. I want to know why I lost this case." She shook her head sadly. "It's not often you catch a career case in Pinellas County and have it taken away from you on the same day."

Lopez was sympathetic. "Go home, get some sleep and start fresh tomorrow. No sense worrying about something out of your control."

She turned without a word and walked out the door, back to her cubicle, where she sat staring at a dark computer monitor until she was the last dayshift cop in the building.

26

At precisely 11:07 am, Special Agent Carl Breznay's office phone rang. When he picked up, the female voice on the other end of the line was terse. "Found him."

Relief surged through Breznay's body. "Where?"

Special Agent Angela Threadgill continued. "Pinellas County." Pause. "But there's more."

Breznay swallowed deeply before continuing. "Go."

"He's dead."

Long pause as Breznay grappled with the news. "How?" he asked weakly.

"Don't know yet. We picked up the body earlier today. He's with the medical examiner now, trying to figure out the cause of death."

"Are you sure it's him?"

"We ran pictures from the crime scene through our facial recognition software. It's him."

There goes my career, he thought bitterly.

*****

Profeta sat in the dark on the tiny lanai of his manufactured home in Tarpon Springs, cigarette smoldering in the cluttered ashtray, a cold can of Coors Light pressed against his perspiring forehead for temporary relief from the evening humidity. His neighborhood had randomly and miraculously escaped the wrath of

Irma a month earlier, a fact that rankled his partner, whose home had lost major chunks of its fence. When told by Profeta that his place had escaped damage of any kind, Kullmann shook her head, thinking: some people have more luck than they deserve.

The loss of the Middleton case hadn't bothered him at all. In fact, he was glad it was gone, for two reasons. Although the case was fresh, it already looked unsolvable to him, with few clues and no witnesses. A long-term loser, with no upside for his career.

Plus, he enjoyed the fact that having the case yanked from them pissed Kullmann off. She was ultrasensitive to anything resembling a challenge to her ability to command; Profeta savored the indignation and smoldering resentment revocation of the case had produced in his partner. It wasn't like they were joined at the hip – he was Kullmann's partner because he had been assigned to her against his wishes when she'd lost her last partner under cloudy circumstances. He hadn't volunteered for this duty, and he felt none of the outrage seething through her that seemed, in his mind anyway, to distort her sense of reason. They weren't friends; they were business associates.

He took a healthy swig of beer. All he was looking forward to tomorrow was a normal day, one that allowed him to enjoy his after-work beer in daylight.

*****

When Special Agent Carl Breznay of the Fort Lauderdale field office of the FBI realized he'd lost contact with the man he'd been surveilling on Captiva, he immediately contacted the Miami office. But instead of the blistering rebuke he'd expected, the agent in charge of the operation, Cesar Gutierrez, calmly processed the information, asked Breznay a series of follow-up questions, and concluded by trying to assuage Breznay's feelings of guilt, which had seeped into his tone. "Don't worry too much about this, Carl. We'll find him."

"What should I do now?" Breznay asked.

"Stay put, nose around the island a bit, see if anyone knows anything. If he doesn't show up in a couple of days, we'll re-evaluate the operation. Until then, keep your head down and your ears open. Your cover is still solid, right?"

"Airtight." Breznay was posing as Paul Hanson, a private investigator hired by Middleton's ex-wife to track him down in an effort to recoup missing alimony payments. It was a guise that allowed him to surreptitiously shadow the real estate agent and show his photo to anyone on the island for defensible reasons. The Lee County Sheriff's Department had been contacted and was cooperating with the ruse.

"Good," Gutierrez replied. "I'll be in touch."

The line went dead without a goodbye. That's it? Breznay couldn't believe it. He was sure he was going to be reamed for losing track of Middleton, especially on such a contained area as Captiva, with only one road in and one road out. Going into the call he was expecting a demotion; now, after his talk with Gutierrez, he felt like he'd won the lottery. Not the jackpot. A minor prize, something in the thousands.

All he knew about Middleton was that he was in the Bureau's secondary surveillance category, which meant the purpose behind his surveillance was not sufficiently serious enough to require round-the-clock monitoring. Breznay's assignment was to maintain casual contact with Middleton. If he tried to leave the island, Breznay had to alert a backup team in Fort Myers Beach to keep him in sight. As long as he didn't lose Middleton, no one would complain.

It was a plum assignment for a young agent. Captiva represented a different Florida, as far from Disney as it gets, one of the most picturesque barrier islands in the Gulf, home to many publicity-shy celebrities and moguls, an amazing variety of flora and fauna and the fabulous Jensen brothers. With few exceptions, wealth was evident everywhere, from the precision tropical landscaping and towering beachside mansions, many of them colorfully named like boats, to the seaside links golf course and luxury accommodations at South Seas Resort. If you have money and you like to party, you belong in Palm Beach or Miami; if you have money and you like to go to bed by nine, Captiva is the choice.

Fortunately, Breznay was on the Bureau's tab, which remained generous given the feds' recent rounds of belt-tightening in other agencies. Rentals on Captiva, even long-term ones, were among the most expensive in the state, but the FBI had an ace in the hole when it came to a place to stay on the island. They had an agreement with the U.S. Marshals Service to use, when available, the bayside home opposite Buck Key near the southern tip of Captiva owned by U.S. Supreme Court Justice Ramona Hancock.

Hancock, a native of Albuquerque, had owned the Captiva property for a dozen years, purchasing it prior to being appointed as a U.S. District Judge. She visited as often as she could when the court was not in session, but that left the home vacant for most of the year. The marshals, who were responsible for providing security for all members of the federal judiciary, broached the subject of Breznay staying in one of the rooms in the home to Justice Hancock when he arrived on the island a year ago, a month after the election. She accepted without hesitation.

Breznay was in heaven. The lush and spacious home hidden behind a shield of sea grapes, saw palmettos and Australian pines was light years beyond the aesthetic offered by his widower's apartment in Fort Lauderdale. Because Breznay had tracking devices embedded in several key locations, physically observing Middleton involved such light duty that Breznay had to remind himself from time to time that he wasn't on vacation.

Captiva on an expense account offered options both exhilarating and cautionary. Up to the point of Middleton's disappearance, most of his choices had been without consequence. It *had* felt like a vacation – it certainly hadn't felt much like work.

But sometime in the last two days he'd lost the man he'd been assigned to watch, and today that man turned up dead. As a result, the consequences of his failure loomed like a flock of turkey vultures eyeing fresh roadkill.

He was no longer smiling.

27

For some reason she couldn't quite put her finger on, Special Agent Threadgill hadn't thought that Middleton would be found that quickly after he was reported missing. She knew his backstory, why he had been under surveillance and for how long; she figured he was in the wind, long gone, his flight triggered by some circumstance they would likely never discern.

She was among a limited group of agents within the Bureau who knew the true identity of Chad Middleton – that his real name was Yury Bazarov, son of Natalya Bazarov, a Russian national who'd arrived in Florida from Havana in 1982 under murky circumstances. She was eight months pregnant when she was hired as a dialogue coach for the *The Russians Are Coming and Coming and Coming*, an X-rated spoof of the comedy classic *The Russians Are Coming! The Russians Are Coming!* that was about to begin filming in Key West.

Two months before Bazarov's arrival, the FBI had been tipped off to a Russian operation originating in Havana that recruited female party loyalists who had agreed to become pregnant and be relocated in the U.S., where they would give birth. The plan was audacious and far-reaching: to train the offspring of these women to become the deepest of deep cover agents, raised as American citizens and trained by veteran Soviet handlers until they were old enough to enter the work force and begin submitting sensitive data to Moscow.

Chad Middleton was one of those children. His mother Natalya's arrival in the U.S. had been lent legitimacy when she was hired to work on the movie. Her consultant position turned out to be a sham, a no-show job created by the film's mysterious financier Nikolai Vasilevsky to provide legal cover for her emigration to the U.S. It was Vasilevsky who insisted the film be shot in Key West, with one of the most lavish budgets ever associated with a pornographic film. Signing Natalya Bazarov to a contract to coach American actors on how to speak English with a Russian accent legitimized her visa application, paving the way for her authorized entry into the U.S.

The clandestine Soviet program, dubbed Operation Henhouse within the Bureau, had been uncovered by Gordon Downey, a diplomat stationed at the Canadian Embassy in Havana. During the course of his regularly assigned monitoring duties, he'd noticed an unusual number of young women in various stages of pregnancy entering and leaving the Soviet Embassy and reported these observations to his superior. It was immediately clear to Downey that these women were not Cuban; few of them spoke Spanish, and none of them possessed the darker skin tones associated with Cuban natives.

The Canadians passed on their information to the CIA, sparking a detailed investigation. Downey's suspicions were soon confirmed. Natalya Bazarov was identified as one of the pregnant operatives of a Soviet espionage mission to infiltrate the U.S. with impregnated women who would give birth while in the U.S., granting these children American citizenship while they were being trained as Soviet agents.

As soon as Natalya was hired to work on the film at the insistence of Vasilevsky, her visa application to visit the United States was fast-tracked and approved. Three days later she made her way to Florida on a flight from Havana to Miami, by way of Mexico City.

Once she arrived in Miami, a team of FBI agents was assigned to monitor her activities. They followed her down the Overseas Highway to Key West, where she spent a single day on the set of *The Russians Are Coming* before being transported via a gleaming black Cadillac Eldorado to a modest ranch-style home near U.S. 41 in Cape Coral, where she was living a month later when she gave birth to her son. As soon as Natalya and young Yury were discharged from the hospital, Natalya became a virtual shut-in, hailing a cab to go out only when the young family needed groceries. Both mother and son were rarely seen outside the yard of their home until Yury began to attend school when he was five.

The interest of the FBI ticked up when Natalya registered her son for kindergarten as Chad Middleton instead of Yury Bazarov. Agents traced the bogus identity to a two-year-old named Chad Middleton from Bridgeport, West Virginia, who had drowned in a swimming pool accident three years earlier. Providing the boy with a false identity set off alarms among the hierarchy at the Bureau; it indicated to veteran agents that some sort of long-term plan was in the works, one with an as yet unidentified motive and/or target. Once Yury Bazarov became Chad Middleton, his file was tagged with a SO assignation, meaning he was now classified as a Soviet operative, someone who would require lifetime surveillance as long as he remained in the U.S.

So when the name Chad Middleton popped up on the initial entry into the federal crime database filed by the Pinellas County Sheriff's Office, the FBI moved swiftly, swooping in to claim the case and the body before any protest could be lodged by local law enforcement. By the time Special Agent Threadgill, who'd been out of the office that morning, undergoing her annual physical exam, exited the elevator on the fifth floor, the office was abuzz with activity. She gave Maria a puzzled look. "What's going on?"

The words tumbled out of the receptionist's mouth like a runaway train. "They found him!"

"Who?"

"Chad Middleton. The man Special Agent Breznay lost two days ago on Captiva."

Her eyes widened. "Where is he?" She wheeled away and strode purposefully toward her office, instinctively reaching into her purse for her cell to check her messages. She was out of hearing range when Maria replied, "Here, in the building."

Threadgill closed her office door and dialed a familiar number. She barely gave Colton Miller, the agent in charge of the Clearwater office and Angela Threadgill's immediate supervisor, time to say hello before breaking in crisply, "Where is he?"

Miller responded in a measured tone. "Here."

She hesitated a moment, excitement in her voice. "In the building?"

"With the medical examiner."

The adrenaline rush she'd experienced a moment ago when she heard that Middleton had been found just as quickly fled her system. Her voice was laced with disappointment. "What happened?"

"We're not sure yet. There's no obvious trauma to the body, other than his tongue is missing."

"Missing?"

"It appears to have been cut out."

Threadgill struggled to process what she'd just heard. The working theory developed since Middleton went missing two days earlier had been that his cover had somehow been blown and that he had been recalled by his handlers and was either on his way to

Moscow or to some other location in the U.S. for further assignment. Now it appears they were back to square one. "Has anyone notified Special Agent Breznay yet?"

"Not yet," Miller said.

Pause. "I'll do it," she said after a moment. "Can I have a look at the body?"

"Give the M.E. an hour or so first. Call Breznay, then drop by my office before you head to the freezer," Miller replied.

As soon as she hung up with Miller, Threadgill called Breznay. He took the news hard, as she thought he would, her attempts to reassure the distraught young agent sounding hollow even to her. She knew he was worried about how this fuck-up would affect his career – she would be, too, if she'd lost a Russian agent she had been surveilling, someone who turned up dead two days later.

When the call ended, she moved to her laptop and accessed Middleton's file in the Bureau database, looking for something she and everyone else might have overlooked, some clue hidden in plain sight. When in doubt, work the evidence.

It was the only play she had.

28

Now that Chad Middleton had been found dead, Breznay felt there was no need to continue in his guise as private investigator Paul Hanson. Special Agent Threadgill disagreed, suggesting instead that he visit the offices of Junonia Realty as Hanson to see if he could develop any leads from Middleton's client list. "Poke around the office, see what you can find. But be careful. Right now, we're the only people who know Middleton is dead. We'd like to keep it that way as long as we can."

Not quite, thought Breznay. Whoever discovered the body knows he's dead, along with the Pinellas County Sheriff's office. And the killer. "What am I looking for?"

"Anyone who stands out on his client list for any reason. Everyone looking to sell or buy on Captiva has money and wants privacy. Bring me some names."

Junonia Realty was located in a two-story yellow building at the intersection of Captiva Drive and Andy Rosse Lane. The clock on his dashboard read 1:15 when Breznay pulled into the shaded parking lot next to the building. He'd spent countless hours passively observing the building while nursing drinks on the patio at RC Otter's across the lane, but this was the first time he'd been inside.

The reception area was spacious, awash with natural light filtered through a bank of tinted floor-to-ceiling windows. An attractive redhead in her forties spotted Breznay from her spot behind the reception desk as soon as he walked through the door, flashing him a megawatt smile as he approached. Her nametag identified her as Pauline. "May I help you?"

Breznay returned the smile. "I sure hope so. I'm looking for Chad Middleton."

Her smile faded. "Uh, he's not here right now. Is there someone else who can help you?"

He reached into his pocket and withdrew one of the business cards the Bureau had printed for him. "Actually, I know he's not here. I've been hired to try and find him by his mother. She hasn't heard from him in more than a week, and she's starting to get worried."

The receptionist glanced at the card, then at Breznay, measuring him. "He hasn't been to work for three days, Mr. Hanson. Perhaps you'd like to see the manager…"

"No, no, that's not necessary," he replied reassuringly. "His mother is very ill, and he always calls her on a daily basis. Until this week." He smiled again. "I was hoping to get a look at his client list, see if anyone might have any information on where he might be."

Pauline's voice was laced with doubt. "I don't know. We don't usually give out information about our clients."

Breznay retrieved another card from pocket and placed it on the desk in front of her. "My office is coordinating with the Lee County Sheriff on this. You can call him at that number if you like."

She recognized the name on the card but continued to resist for a few more minutes, clearly uncomfortable with the thought of being responsible for releasing the names of any of their clients, most of whom cherish anonymity. She looked around the office for help, finding none. When she returned her gaze to Breznay, he knew he had her. "I can either copy the names in my notebook, or you can make a copy for me if you'd like. In five minutes I'll be out of your hair forever."

"I guess it would be okay," Pauline said. "It's not a very long list."

"Thanks, Pauline. Mrs. Middleton will be very grateful."

She extracted a sheet of paper from a file folder located in one of her desk drawers and walked several feet to a nearby copy machine. When she returned she handed him a list of names and phone numbers. "I hope you find him, for his mother's sake."

"I'll do my best."

*****

The list was short, just six names. Five of the names had notations next to them indicating that they were looking to buy on Captiva. Breznay sat in his car in the parking lot of Junonia Realty, engine running, air conditioning blasting, as he called the prospective buyers. Each of the calls went to voicemail; he left messages for the recipients to call him back, identifying himself as an associate of Middleton's. The messages hinted that Middleton had found a house for them, but that it might not be on the market for long. He hoped the ruse would result in rapid response times.

The other name on the list, Thomas Martin, was indicated as a potential seller. Breznay looked closely at the address; judging by the house number, it was just to the south from Justice Hancock's home, where he was staying. Rather than call, he decided to stop by, since it was on his way home.

He backed out of the parking lot, carefully avoiding tourists on foot and riding bicycles who wandered blithely across Andy Rosse Lane as if it were closed to motor vehicles. He headed south on Captiva Drive, slowing as he passed the Tween Waters Inn to watch two workers struggling to attach a life-sized plastic Santa Claus to a gracefully curved palm tree by the main entrance.

Starting to decorate for Christmas only days after Halloween rankled Breznay; he never put up a single light until December. All the holidays seemed to run into one another now, just like the retailers preferred.

He slowed as the GPS on his phone indicated the Martin house was coming up on the left. Five doors down from the Hancock house he spotted the house number he was looking for on a small sign to the left of the crushed shell driveway and turned in.

The house wasn't visible from the road; it was hidden by the lush tropical foliage, and when it came into view Breznay was surprised. He'd been expecting a mansion, much on the scale of Justice Hancock's home and the others in the neighborhood, but that wasn't what he found. Martin's house was a small ranch just steps from Roosevelt Channel, which separated Buck Key from Captiva, with an adjacent carport and no vehicle in sight.

He checked his appearance in the rearview mirror before exiting the car. He noted an old bicycle in the carport, next to an extension ladder and several cans of paint. He walked up a narrow shell path, rang the doorbell and waited.

In a few moments the door opened. The man on the other side of the door was deeply tanned and shirtless, with longish blond hair, about five eight, wearing only a pair of shorts and sandals. He reeked of marijuana. "Yes?" he asked warily.

"I'm looking for Thomas Martin," Breznay said.

"He's not here."

"Do you know where I can find him?" Breznay asked amiably, looking around. "This *is* his house, isn't it?"

The man nodded. "It's his house, but he isn't here now."

"When do you expect him to return?"

"Tough to say. Why do you ask?"

Breznay could sense the paranoia wafting through the doorway, no doubt aided by the weed he'd been smoking not long ago. He handed one of his bogus business cards to the man. "I'm trying to track down Chad Middleton, and I wanted to see if Mr. Martin could help me out."

The man examined the card, then looked at Breznay. "Who's Chad Middleton?"

"If you'd invite me in, I'll fill you in."

The man shook his head and held up his hand. "We're good right here."

Breznay accepted the refusal stoically. "Are you a relative of Mr. Martin?"

The man shook his head. "Just a friend. I watch the house while Mr. Martin is away."

Stonewalled again. "Chad Middleton is a real estate agent for Junonia Realty."

Recognition dawned in the man's eyes. "Dark hair, a bit chunky, maybe five ten, in his late thirties?"

Breznay nodded. "That's him. Do you know him?"

"Not really. He was around here last summer and fall, wondering if I wanted to sell the place. I told him what I told you, that I don't live here. Tom gets a lot of interest from people who want to buy his place, demolish it and build a bigger house. I figured Middleton was representing some buyer like that."

"When was the last time you saw him?" Breznay asked.

After a moment the man replied. "A year ago, maybe. October, I think."

"You haven't seen him since then?"

"I've seen him around a couple of times – it's a small island. But he never came back to the house again."

It was clear Breznay wasn't going to get any more information here. He extended his hand; the man gripped it tentatively. "If he does come by again, could you tell him I'd like to speak to him. My number's on the card."

"I guess I could do that."

"Thanks for your time."

29

Willie Emerson watched from the doorway as Breznay returned to his car. He looked at the business card in his hand as the car made a tight three-point turn and the man identified on the card as Paul Hanson pulled slowly away. As soon as the car was out of sight he closed the door and reached excitedly for the phone. Thomas Martin picked up on the fourth ring. "To what do I owe this pleasure?"

"You're not going to believe who was just here."

"I'm at work, Willie. I don't have time to guess."

The words came pouring out. "A private dick named Paul Hanson, looking for that real estate guy who was snooping around here last summer."

He had Martin's interest now. "What did he want?"

"He didn't get into specifics, but I didn't get a good vibe."

"Are you stoned?"

"No," Willie lied. "He just stopped in out of the blue, askin' questions, wantin' to come inside the house, but I kept him outside." He paused, then continued. "He felt like a cop to me."

"You should know," Martin said, only half in jest.

"Fuck you," Willie shot back.

"Is there anything else I need to know?"

Willie thought for a moment. "I rode into Jensen's this morning and saw them getting ready to set up the Santa Claus at

Tween Waters. It gets earlier every year. I'm still eating leftover Halloween candy."

"Are you sure you're not stoned?"

*****

Gutierrez had flown to Clearwater the day Middleton was declared missing and set up shop in a vacant office in the building. When Threadgill had called to confirm that Middleton had been found, it was Gutierrez who suggested she give the M.E. an hour before she went to see him, so Threadgill swung by his office to kill some time. He was behind a scrupulously clean desk, leafing through a copy of last month's *Guns & Ammo*, when she poked her head in. "Got a minute?"

Gutierrez looked up and smiled. "For you I've got five." He gestured toward his guest chair. "What's on your mind?"

"Breznay. I'm worried about him."

He straightened in his chair, eyeing her carefully. "How so?"

"For starters, he's going to catch a lot of shit about losing track of a Russian agent who turns up dead two days later. Not exactly a highlight on your CV."

"From whom?"

She couldn't help smiling at his grammatical gem. "Other agents. He's a young guy, just starting out, on the sensitive side. Criticism of the kind he's bound to face in the office could break him. If that happens, we could lose someone I think can become a damn good agent. Already is, in my opinion."

He leaned forward, elbows on the desk, fingers intertwined. "Got any ideas?" he asked, certain that she did.

"Get him the hell out of Dodge. Send him to Cape Coral to talk to the mother. Give him some room to breathe. Maybe we'll catch a break while he's off the island, and when he comes back the shit will have subsided."

"Subsided," Gutierrez mused, scratching his chin. "Don't hear that one every day."

She gave him her most annoying smile. "The least I could do after your 'whom' a moment ago."

Gutierrez, a native Cuban, flashed a smile of his own. "Not bad for someone for whom English is a second language, eh?"

"Don't push it," she warned jokingly.

He quickly returned to the matter at hand. "There *is* a problem with sending Breznay to Cape Coral to interview Natalya Bazarov."

"What's that?"

"We're going to have to bring him into the loop, tell him about Middleton's real identity. All he knows now is that he was supposed to be watching a real estate agent. Once he meets Natalya and finds out she's Russian, he'll put two and two together and wonder why we've been keeping him in the dark about Middleton's Russian roots. She'll be a tough enough interview as it is, but if his mind is clouded by doubts that we're responsible for, by not giving him all the information he needs, it won't help."

Threadgill agreed with Gutierrez's logic – it would boost Breznay's sagging self-confidence for the young agent to know that he was operating with the same level of confidential information as the mission's leaders. "I think you're right. How would you like me to tell him? In person? Or over the phone?"

"I think it would be best for him to hear it from you in person, for a couple of reasons," Gutierrez replied. "But we don't want to bring him to Clearwater, tell him and then send him back again." A barely discernible smile played on his lips. "I think you should take a day or two, drive down there to tell him, get a feel for the island. You've got good instincts – who knows what you might uncover?"

Threadgill liked the idea. It would be good to get out of the office for a change. Her recent promotion to the administrative level of the Bureau meant that she spent almost all her time behind a desk. She missed field assignments. "When would you like me to leave?"

"First thing in the morning. The M.E. should have some solid information for you by then." He rose to his feet and moved from behind the desk, a movement she knew meant their meeting had ended. "Have a little fun while you're down there, but don't stay too long."

She gave him a wide smile as she stood up. "Fun is my middle name."

*****

When Breznay returned to Justice Hancock's house, his housemate, Patrick Henderson, was sitting on the second-story lanai, nursing a beer, gazing at Roosevelt Channel and Buck Key beyond. Henderson was a U.S. Marshall, assigned to Justice Hancock's Florida detail. He was several years older than Breznay, in his late thirties, with short-cropped dark hair, piercing brown eyes and the chiseled body of a lifelong gym rat. Henderson knew that Breznay was staying at the house because he was working on a case, but he didn't know any of the details, which suited him just fine. Henderson was a straight arrow, a man who despised distraction, obsessed with staying in his own lane when it came to protecting Ramona Hancock. As long as Breznay kept to himself and didn't intrude too much in his space, their temporary relationship would survive.

Breznay tapped on the sliding glass door leading to the lanai and slid it open a few inches. "Care if I join you?"

Henderson swung around, a tight smile on his face. "Beer's in the fridge."

Breznay grabbed one and took a seat to Henderson's left. "I could use a couple of these after the day I've had."

Henderson knew Breznay wanted him to bite, to ask what happened today, but that wasn't his style. He nodded slightly but did not reply. Instead, he sipped his beer and returned his stare to the horizon.

Breznay tried another tack. "Do you know anything about your neighbors?"

Henderson turned toward Breznay, his countenance neutral. "You mean here, on Captiva?"

Breznay nodded. "Yeah. I was looking for one of them today, Thomas Martin, lives five doors down, toward Blind Pass."

It was Henderson's job to know everything he could when it came to Ramona Hancock's neighbors. He knew Thomas Martin owned the small house Breznay was referring to, although his primary residence was in western New York. He only visited occasionally, usually on the back end of a business trip.

He knew much more about Willie Emerson, the live-in caretaker of Martin's Captiva house Breznay had met less than an hour ago. He knew about Emerson's checkered past, his battle with drug addiction, his spotty employment record, the devastating accident in the Florida Keys that had nearly killed him several years ago and how Martin, a lifelong friend, had stepped forward to offer his vacation home on Captiva to Emerson while he recovered from the effects of the accident.

"I've seen him a couple of times at the Lazy Flamingo, but haven't talked to him. Last time he was in town was a year ago."

Buoyed by the taciturn agent's response, Breznay continued. "How about the guy that lives there now?"

Henderson's voice was laced with contempt. "The pothead."

Breznay nodded. "Yeah. What's his story?"

Henderson's defenses came up in response to Breznay's interest. Despite the fact that the U.S. Marshall's Service and the FBI were both part of the Justice Department, there existed an unacknowledged ongoing turf battle between the two agencies which often manifested itself in regrettable incidents of mutual distrust and strained relations, incidents which had worsened after the 2106 election. He decided to play the junkie card. "Just another hippie this state could do without."

"You don't think he's dangerous?"

Henderson chuckled, the first time Breznay had heard him laugh since he had arrived. "As long as he doesn't get his hands on a gun and doesn't somehow end up behind the wheel of a car, he's harmless."

30

Angela Threadgill had grown up in Bradenton in a small single-story home on 11th Street West, a five-minute walk from McKechnie Field, the spring training home of the Pittsburgh Pirates. Her lifelong devotion to her beloved Pirates was hereditary, passed on by her grandfather, Thomas Jefferson Threadgill, who'd been born and raised in Aliquippa, Pennsylvania, and moved to Bradenton shortly after his discharge from the Navy.

She'd grown up with no personal memories of her grandfather, just some black-and-white photos from various stages of his life, a life that was cut tragically short the year Angela was born. On a stormy, fog-shrouded morning in May 1980, the freighter *MV Summit Venture* rammed into one of the supports of the southbound span of the Sunshine Skyway Bridge, collapsing a portion of the roadway, sending numerous vehicles, including the elder Threadgill's Chevy Malibu, into the water below. A lifelong early riser, he had been returning to Bradenton from an overnight visit with one of his Navy buddies in Gulfport, listening to the morning news on the car radio, when the road in front of him dropped away and he plunged into the darkness of Tampa Bay.

From the time she was old enough to hear the horrifying story of that foggy, stormy morning, she'd avoided traveling over the bridge, fearful that the same fate which had befallen her grandfather awaited her. First as a passenger, then when she obtained her driver's license, she refused to go over the Sunshine Skyway Bridge, opting instead to take the long way around, either

U.S. 41 or I-75, if she needed to go into Tampa or St. Petersburg for anything.

It wasn't until after she'd graduated from the FBI Academy in Quantico that she decided it was time to face her fears concerning the bridge. She was an FBI agent, one of the most covetous law enforcement assignments in the world. Possessing such deep-rooted fear of an inanimate amalgamation of concrete and steel, she decided, would no longer be acceptable.

As she drove over the Sunshine Skyway Bridge the next morning on her way to her rendezvous on Captiva with Carl Breznay, her thoughts drifted to her grandfather, in particular a photo she had at home of him holding her just weeks after she'd been born. In the photo, which she had displayed on the dresser in her bedroom, her grandfather was wearing his ever-present Pirates cap, grinning from ear to ear, the love of his first grandchild oozing from every pore of his body as he gazed at the tiny baby cradled in his arms. It was her favorite picture of the grandpa she'd barely met.

Once she crossed the bridge, she merged with I-75, resisting the nostalgic urge to drive through her hometown. Traffic was moderate as she accelerated onto the interstate to the sounds of Alison Krauss and Union Station on her satellite radio, analyzing the information she'd received from the medical examiner the day before. Other than the mystery of the missing tongue, the M.E. could find no other anomalies that might indicate a cause of death. There had been no evidence of blunt-force trauma, no gunshot wounds, no bruising of any kind. If he'd still had his tongue, the M.E. declared, he'd have been inclined to consider Middleton's death the result of natural causes, as if he'd fallen asleep and never awakened.

Before she left, he'd told Threadgill that he planned to run more extensive toxicology tests and that he would let her know as soon as the expedited results became available. Given the paucity of clues, he told her he was leaning toward Middleton being the victim of some sort of poison, one that was difficult to trace. "There are so many varieties out there now," the medical examiner cautioned in a sobering tone. "We can only hope we get lucky."

At the same time, Gutierrez had pulled some strings with a friend at the NSA who, when told of a possible Russian connection to the murder, had shared some satellite imagery taken over Anclote Key on the night Middleton's body was dumped there. Anything connected to Russia, especially in the wake of the appointment of Robert Mueller, had the full backing of the intelligence agencies and had fostered a tenuous détente between agencies historically reluctant to share information.

Although the cloud cover that night had been extensive, the images sent to Gutierrez revealed a boat operating without running lights, showing two heat signatures determined to be human, landing on the western shore of the key at 3:49 am. The medical examiner had been able to estimate the time of Middleton's death as sometime between 9:00 pm and midnight, so that meant there had been two perpetrators, with the ability to maneuver a boat without lights on a cloudy, moonless night through the treacherously shallow waters of the Gulf.

Two pros, Threadgill mused as she cruised by Venice, who would be difficult to apprehend.

*****

Breznay had a second beer with Henderson before excusing himself and retreating to his second-story bedroom. He spent the rest of the evening in his room, lying on his bed, munching on leftovers from his dinner two nights earlier at Doc Ford's while watching the Miami Heat and the Milwaukee Bucks square off in what looked to be a half-filled America Airlines Arena. Since LeBron James had bolted from the Heat three years earlier to

182

return to Cleveland, the team had struggled to attract fans to their games. Many fans, Breznay included, had seen their team loyalty wane since their marquee star's departure.

Breznay's phone buzzed just before halftime. It was Threadgill; reluctantly, he picked up. "Hello?"

"Hello, Carl. I hope I'm not interrupting anything."

"Nah. I'm just watching the Heat get their asses whipped by the Bucks. It's not even halftime and they're already down by 27." He tried to inject some enthusiasm into his voice. "What's up?"

"I wanted to give you a heads-up. I'll be coming down to Captiva to see you in the morning, to go over a new assignment we have for you."

Breznay's heart sank. "You're pulling me from the Middleton case?"

Threadgill was quick to reassure him. "No, no, that's not it. You'll still be working on the case, just a different aspect of it."

Breznay wasn't convinced. "What do you want me to do?"

"I'll let you know when I get there," she replied. "I'm going to try to be there a little before noon. I thought we might meet at the Lazy Flamingo for lunch."

"The one by Blind Pass?"

"Yes. That's the only one I've ever been to," Threadgill said, adding, "It's close enough for you to walk, isn't it?"

"Depends on the weather. This time of year, it's usually not too hot."

"Do they still serve the best conch chowder on the island?"

"Yep. The grouper sandwich isn't bad, either."

"Then it's settled," she said firmly. "I'll give you a call as soon as I reach the causeway."

Threadgill ended the call before he could respond. Breznay stared forlornly at the muted television, trying to put a positive spin on this latest news.

Suddenly, he was no longer hungry.

31

Florida is a melting pot of fugitives from all walks of life, many on the run from demons that folks north of the Mason-Dixon line and west of the Mississippi can't fathom. Some of those who flock to the Sunshine State are seeking simple rewards, such as shelter from the elements in a more temperate climate than the one they left behind. Others see the state as the ideal place to hide in plain sight; whatever their own peculiarities might be, they pale in comparison to the seemingly endless supply of petty criminals, corrupt politicians and religious nutjobs featured on the local news each night. There's something about the heat – or is it the humidity? – that seems to ease the transition for both the temporary tourist content to drop a couple of grand at Disney and the refugee fleeing soul-crushing state tax burdens in search of some measure of fiscal sanity.

It was, Angela Threadgill thought, the most fertile landscape in which to pursue the criminal element. She wouldn't live anywhere else; after graduating from Quantico, she had a wide range of potential localities in which to work, but she'd chosen Clearwater, mostly because of her fascination at the time with the Church of Scientology and its cult-like practices. It also didn't hurt that she would be only an hour from her hometown, a simple drive south, especially each spring when optimism bloomed and the Pirates were in town.

As soon as she crossed the bridge spanning the Caloosahatchee River, she left I-75, bored with the monotony of the interstate. She was ahead of schedule, with some spare time, so she decided to take the exit for Dr. Martin Luther King Boulevard.

She followed it toward the Gulf until it merged into McGregor. Less than a mile later she passed the Edison and Ford Winter Estates on her left, which unearthed memories of a field trip she'd taken to the estates when she'd been in middle school. Before then, she hadn't known about the connection between Thomas Edison and Henry Ford, that they had winter homes adjacent to one another in Fort Myers. She remembered leaving the grounds that day buoyed by the sort of interest to further explore the connection between these two American legends that such scholarly excursions are intended to trigger.

Fort Myers, like most areas in Florida, had grown significantly since she had last visited. Strip malls lined both sides of McGregor Boulevard, low-slung portals of retail offering everything from overhead fan repair to custom tattoos, all with limited parking. She stayed on McGregor for several miles until it merged into Summerlin, heading for the causeway and Sanibel Island.

She glanced at the clock on the dashboard: 11:03. Using her Bluetooth app, she dialed Breznay, who picked up on the second ring, and told him she was at the causeway. "I'll meet you at the bar," he said.

"Make sure there's something cold to drink waiting for me."

Breznay had been at the Lazy Flamingo for ten minutes by the time Threadgill walked through the door at quarter to twelve. He was sitting on the far side of the bar, near the men's room, nursing an iced tea. She spotted him immediately and settled in the seat next to him. He gave her an iced tea of her own. "Hope you don't mind unsweetened."

She raised her glass and clinked it against his. "My physician insists on it. She says a steady diet of sugar is worse for your system over the long haul than cocaine."

Breznay gestured toward the booths that lined the exterior walls. "Would you prefer a booth?"

Threadgill nodded. "We'll have a little more privacy. Have you ordered yet?"

"I was waiting for you."

"Know what you want?"

"I do."

He attracted the attention of the bartender, who came over immediately. They each ordered a bowl of conch chowder, and Breznay added a side order of fries before they grabbed their drinks and moved to a booth.

Breznay attempted some small talk. "How was the drive?"

"Easy," she replied. She sipped her drink, then continued. "I made good time, so I got off the interstate and took a swing through Fort Myers. I hadn't been there since I was in middle school. It's really exploded."

Breznay had never been to Fort Myers; the only time he'd come close was when he'd passed through the outskirts on his way to Sanibel and Captiva. With nothing to add, he sat there mutely, feeling like an idiot, until she spoke again. "How's the situation at the house? You and Henderson get along okay?"

Breznay nodded. "He's not much of a conversationalist. He stays pretty much to himself, which is fine by me."

"Have you met Justice Hancock yet?"

He shook his head. "Not yet. She visited once, for Labor Day weekend, but Henderson made me get a hotel room while she was in town. Protocol, he said."

She switched topics. "Gutierrez told me you managed to get a list of names, Middleton's clients, from the realty office yesterday."

He reached into his pocket and passed a copy of the list across the table to her. "Not many clients. Five people looking to buy, one person looking to sell. I called the potential buyers and left messages for them to call me back."

"Any responses?"

"Not yet. After I made those calls I stopped by the seller's house, but he wasn't there. I spoke with the caretaker, a real Florida hippie, but he didn't know much. Then I headed back to the house."

Threadgill scanned the list, but none of the names rang a bell. She slipped the list into her pocket. "I'll run the names through our computer when I get back. Maybe something will pop up."

Breznay's unease grew. He was tired of idle chit chat; he was burning to know what his new assignment was. As if she had read his thoughts, she explained it to him. "We want to shift your focus a bit, broaden the scope of the investigation. We'd like you to talk with Middleton's mother, see if she has any idea what he's been up to."

The fact that Middleton had a mother was news to him. Although he was aware there were tight restrictions on the flow of information concerning Middleton, he felt irked that they'd kept this fact from him. "Where does she live?" he asked, realizing that he'd probably be leaving the cozy existence he'd enjoyed on Captiva.

She looked around the room to see if anyone was listening; no one seemed to pay them any attention. She continued. "Not far, actually. In Cape Coral, a little north of Fort Myers." She pulled a manila folder out of her oversized purse. In it was a fact sheet with everything they knew about Natalya Bazarov. Before she slid it across the table, she spoke again. "You need to know something about Middleton, something you weren't cleared to know until yesterday."

Breznay was mystified. What had they been holding back?

Threadgill continued. "Chad Middleton isn't – *wasn't* – Chad Middleton. His real name was Yury Bazarov."

Breznay was stunned. "Russian?" he managed.

She nodded. "He was born here in Florida to a Soviet national named Natalya Bazarov in 1982. We've had eyes on the mother ever since she arrived in the states, eight months pregnant. When she gave birth to Yury, she stayed in the country. She's been living in Cape Coral ever since." She indicated the file. "It's all in the folder. Take it home tonight and read it. In the morning I want you to go to her house, see what you can find out. We don't have a lot to go on at this point. Anything you can come up with will be a big help."

Breznay was speechless, still trying to wrap his head around the Russia connection. Like everyone else in the Bureau these days, he was particularly sensitive to anything having to do with the Russians. He leaned forward and lowered his voice. "Does this have anything to do with the Mueller investigation?" he whispered.

Threadgill leaned back with an exasperated chuckle, shaking her head. "Why does everyone ask that question?"

32

After they finished their lunch, Breznay offered to give Threadgill a tour of the island. "There's not much to see besides some huge homes and a couple of resorts," he said as she pulled out of the parking lot and headed north across the bridge over Blind Pass. "There's only one stop sign on this road. No high-rise buildings, with a limited business district on the north end of the island before you get to South Seas."

"How did the island do during the hurricane?" she asked, scanning both sides of the road, amazed at the paucity of residual damage evident.

"Henderson said they dodged a bullet. By the time Irma reached Sanibel and Captiva, it had been downgraded to a Category 2 storm. There was a mandatory evacuation order issued for both islands, but they had the causeway connecting Sanibel to the mainland open again the day after the storm. No one had power or water for a week, there were a lot of trees down and there were areas of minor flooding from the storm surge, but according to Dave Jensen, it was nothing compared to what Charley did in 2004."

They passed Tween Waters, the Green Flash, and Twin Palms Marina, all showing various levels of activity. Threadgill slowed as she approached the intersection of Andy Rosse Lane. Breznay reached across Threadgill when they came to a stop, pointing to their left. "That's the office of Junonia Realty, where Middleton was working."

She nodded as she looked at the building. "Where to next?"

"Hang a left," Breznay instructed. "There's a few interesting shops down here. Plus the Mucky Duck."

Threadgill knew of the Mucky Duck by reputation as the only restaurant on the island directly on the Gulf. She drove carefully down the narrow lane, passing several restaurants and shops and a small cluster of high-end rental homes before the road dead ended at the Mucky Duck. Several of the shaded outdoor tables were occupied, and a few steps away on the beach a number of jet skis, kayaks, paddleboards and sailboards sat expectantly, waiting to be rented.

She swung the car around and went out the way she came. At Captiva Road she turned left and followed the road around a tight bend to the left to its end in the small parking area for the island's public beach. She smiled as they passed the colorfully painted drop box for mail outside the Captiva post office. So island like, she thought.

On the way out, Breznay pointed out the entrance to South Seas Resort on their left. "Takes up about three hundred acres. Has a golf course, a couple of restaurants and a few boutiques."

No wonder Breznay had been enthusiastic about the Middleton assignment, she thought as she took in the surroundings. Who wouldn't want to spend time here? It felt like Maui to her - lush tropical vegetation bloomed everywhere, the weather was ideal, the beaches were practically deserted and there were lots of opportunities available for visitors inclined toward an active, outdoor lifestyle.

While Threadgill drove, Breznay pondered his next move. During lunch, she had suggested he find a place to stay closer to Cape Coral while he was interviewing Natalya Bazarov, to avoid the long commute to and from the islands. "It doesn't make much sense for you to fight island traffic, especially if it takes longer than a day."

He had reluctantly agreed. While it wasn't yet high season on the islands, the presence of only one major road connecting the islands to one another and to the mainland presented a constant threat of traffic snarls and lengthy delays for commuters. Still, he hoped he would be able to wrap up his interview with Middleton's mother quickly and get back to the task of finding out who murdered Chad Middleton.

Threadgill slowed to avoid a cyclist she was approaching on her right. As they passed him Breznay glanced at the shirtless man. He gestured excitedly. "That's the guy!"

Threadgill checked her rearview mirror, but couldn't make out his face. "What guy?"

"The guy I talked to yesterday, the one who's staying at the house whose owner was on the list of Middleton's clients, the one looking to sell."

There was no car behind her. She slowed to allow the cyclist to catch up so she could get a better look at his face. But instead of continuing south, he veered left, into Twin Palms Marina. Thinking it wouldn't be a good idea for the man to come into contact with Breznay on consecutive days, she decided to keep driving, which disappointed her passenger – he wanted another crack at the hippie whose demeanor had been so defensive yesterday, an attitude that had raised Breznay's level of interest in the man. He was sure the stoner had been holding something back. But unless he abandoned his cover as Paul Hanson and displayed his FBI credentials, he felt the man was familiar enough in dealing with law enforcement to deny the request of a private investigator seeking further information. He'd need a warrant to gain access to the Martin residence.

"Let him go," Threadgill advised, correctly reading Breznay's frustration. "We can always come back to him if we need to. From what you told me, he's not going very far unless he gets his hands on a vehicle."

"Are you staying on the island tonight?" Breznay asked.

Threadgill shook her head. "I don't think so. Gutierrez told me I could stay a day or two, but I want to get back. I want to figure out how they managed to get Middleton off the island."

Breznay stared glumly out the side window. "You and me both."

*****

While Threadgill was dropping Breznay off at Justice Hancock's home, Miller and Gutierrez were huddled in Miller's office in Clearwater, going over the medical examiner's handwritten notes prepared after his initial examination of Middleton the day before. Cardiac arrest, with two question marks, was underlined twice in the center of the second page, followed by the phrase: **induced or natural???**

"When will the results of the toxicology tests be available?" Gutierrez asked, handing the notes back to Miller.

"End of business today or first thing in the morning," Miller replied. "The lab knows the findings are top priority."

"What do you think?"

Normally, Miller didn't like to pre-judge apparent evidence - he preferred to wait for the lab results to be finalized before offering an opinion. But he felt pressured by Gutierrez, who no doubt was feeling his own pressure from Washington. "Well," he began deliberately, "it could go either way. If his tongue hadn't been removed and he hadn't been dumped on a deserted island in the middle of the night, I'd probably lean toward natural causes. There were no apparent needle marks evident anywhere on the body, no bruising or signs of a struggle that indicate foul play.

From the photos taken by the sheriff's office at the scene, it looks like he fell asleep on the beach and never woke up."

"Looks can be deceiving."

Miller nodded in agreement. "Which is why we need to see the results of his tox screen."

Gutierrez bent in to get a closer look at the satellite imagery supplied by the NSA. "What about these guys?" he asked, indicating the two figures on the boat.

"We're working on identifying them, but there's not much to go on so far. We could really use a break there."

"Do you have anybody on the ground working on that yet?"

"I briefed Threadgill on the photos before she left and told her to poke around a bit while she was down there, see if anybody noticed anyone acting suspiciously," Miller replied. "We'll put Breznay on that once he's done with Natalya Bazarov. Somebody must have seen something."

"Let's hope we get lucky real soon."

Miller was dubious of the effect luck had on investigations, but kept his opinion to himself. "The final report from the M.E. will help. Once we know the official cause of death, that should give us more to go on."

"I hope you're right," Gutierrez said. He stood up to leave, satisfied that Miller was on top of things. "I'll probably head back to Miami tomorrow, but I can be here in a couple of hours if anything develops." He shook Miller's hand. "I'll keep you posted."

"What are you doing for dinner tonight?"

Gutierrez smiled. "I hadn't thought about it. Probably just order room service from the hotel."

Miller stuck two fingers into his mouth, simulating gagging. "That sounds horrible. Why don't you join me for pizza? There's a place on Fort Harrison, a little south of the Scientology building, that has the best pizza in the area," Miller said, adding, "Plus homemade gelato."

"That definitely sounds better than room service. Thanks."

"I'll give you a call at the end of the day. Maybe the lab tests will be back by then."

"I'll be in my office."

33

After dropping Breznay off, Threadgill turned around and drove north, toward the business section of the island. Miller had suggested she ask some questions about any suspicious activity that may have been observed by employees of the three resorts on the island.

She decided to start at South Seas and work back. She drove to the front gate and an attendant rose immediately from his seat in the guard shack and greeted her with a smile. "How may I help you?" he asked in island-tinged English. His name tag identified him as Reginald, from the British Virgin Islands.

Threadgill flashed her identification. "FBI. I was wondering if you could direct me to the reception area?"

Reginald nodded vigorously. "Of course." He opened the half door, stepped outside and pointed to a building just beyond the tennis courts to their right. "It's right in there."

He flipped a switch, which raised the single-bar security gate. "Have a wonderful day," he said pleasantly.

Threadgill smiled and drove through. She parked by the entrance and walked inside. The reception area was spacious, with a pitcher of fresh squeezed orange juice and a stack of plastic cups for arriving guests on a table to her left. The reception desk was in the rear, with three stations. Only one was occupied, by a young brunette typing something into her computer. When she'd finished, she looked up to see Threadgill standing there and motioned her forward. "Checking in?" she asked with a smile.

"Not exactly," Threadgill said, holding her identification out for the young woman to examine. After a moment, the young woman, Fran from Bay Village, Ohio, as indicated by her name tag, responded. "How can I help you, Agent Threadgill?"

"I'm looking for some information about two of your guests, two men."

"Names?" she asked, fingers poised above the keyboard, ready to initiate a search.

"I don't know. To tell the truth, I don't know if they actually stayed here. We think they stayed someplace on the island, so we're asking at Tween Waters and Jensen's, too."

The receptionist's face clouded over. "I'm not sure what we can do for you without names. Do you know what they look like?"

Threadgill shook her head. "I don't. I know I'm asking a lot, but I was wondering if you or any of the other staff might have noticed any guests acting strangely in the last week or two."

"This is Florida," Fran said with a smile. "Define strange."

"Someone with an accent, perhaps, from eastern Europe or Russia. Anyone who looked out of place, like they didn't belong."

Fran thought for a moment. "I don't remember anyone like that, but I can pass the word around. We haven't had many guests since the hurricane, so if they were here, maybe someone saw something."

Threadgill handed her one of Breznay's business cards. "If you could ask around, that would be great. If anyone remembers anything, no matter how small they think it might be, please ask them to call Special Agent Breznay at this number."

Fran placed the card next to her keyboard. "I'll do that."

"Thanks, Fran."

Threadgill waved to Reginald on her way out; he waved back enthusiastically. She stopped at Jensen's and Tween Waters, but the persons she talked to there couldn't remember anyone fitting the vague parameters Threadgill described. She left her business card at both locations.

She hadn't expected much, given the lack of clues or descriptions she was able to pass along, but she still felt disappointed. She was a glass half full person, an optimist when it came to long shots.

Maybe, she thought, Breznay would find something useful in Cape Coral.

*****

Henderson was gone when Threadgill dropped Breznay off at Justice Hancock's home. He went inside and began to pack his belongings for his move to Cape Coral, wondering what lay ahead. Threadgill had left a briefing packet concerning the history of Natalya Bazarov with him, and once his clothes were packed, he grabbed a beer from the fridge and headed for the second story lanai, where he spread out the contents of the file on the table and began to learn about his new assignment.

Natalya Bazarov had been identified as a participant in a covert Soviet operation the Bureau dubbed Operation Henhouse which began shortly after the Mariel boatlift in 1980. As soon as U.S. authorities discovered that Castro had used Mariel as a cover to rid himself of the most venal criminals held in Cuban prisons, as well as a sizeable number of mentally ill patients from their state-run healthcare system, they began to review all travel emanating from Cuba more closely, not just to the U.S. but to other countries as well.

The covert plan to bypass more stringent American immigration monitoring had resulted in Natalya Bazarov's arrival in Miami in 1982, legitimized by the work permit visa she'd obtained legally as the result of her contract position as a dialogue consultant for a film titled *The Russians Are Coming and Coming and Coming*, which was about to commence production in Key West. FBI records indicated she had been paid for her consulting services under a lump sum contract, but any information about actual services rendered under that contract was missing from the file.

Shortly after her arrival on American soil she moved to Cape Coral, where she gave birth to Yury Bazarov. Because she had been identified as a participant in Operation Henhouse, her movements were closely watched, but according to the file there wasn't much to see, as the agents assigned to keep an eye on her reported that she rarely left the house, and then only by cab, to purchase groceries or accompany young Yury on a visit to the doctor.

Breznay sat back and took a sip of his beer. He tried to remember if Chad Middleton had demonstrated any behavior that might have offered a clue to his Russian ancestry while he had been monitoring him on Captiva, but couldn't recall a single thing that stood out. Of course, he had been born and raised in Florida, which meant he looked and sounded like any other Floridian of the era. He told himself he couldn't be blamed for not recognizing something that was never there. Still, he knew he never should've lost him.

He appreciated Threadgill giving him another chance instead of pulling him from the case altogether, which she certainly could've done based on what had happened. In order to redeem himself, he needed to find out why Middleton had been murdered and who had done it. That process would begin first thing in the morning, when he traveled to Cape Coral to interview Natalya Bazarov. Threadgill had come up with a plan for Breznay to continue to use his cover as Paul Hanson. Instead of the story he'd used at Junonia Realty, that he'd been retained by Middleton's mother to find her missing son, he would turn the tables, saying that he'd been hired by Junonia Realty to find a missing employee. Judging the reaction of Natalya to the news that her son was missing would be critical – whether his disappearance appeared to be a surprise to her or if her response to the news was indifferent, as if she already knew that her son was missing.

He heard the door slam downstairs, which meant Henderson was back. Breznay gazed out at the flat water of Roosevelt Channel, wondering when, if ever, he would be back to enjoy this view.

34

Threadgill waited too long to try to leave the island, so she found herself gridlocked on Periwinkle by Sanibel Community Park during the afternoon rush hour as employees of businesses on Captiva and Sanibel jammed the only road connecting to the causeway and their mainland homes. She used the respite in her journey to call her mother and explain why she'd be late for dinner, then dialed Colton Miller to inform him of her meeting with Breznay and her unsuccessful attempts to gather information from the three main resorts on Captiva.

He picked up immediately, his voice cheery. "Good timing, Agent Threadgill."

"Why's that?"

"Agent Gutierrez and I were just about to leave the office on our way to dinner."

"Lucky you," she responded wistfully. "I'm stuck in traffic on Sanibel. I'm going to be late for my dinner. Where are you two going?"

"I thought I'd introduce him to Cristino's. He said good pizza is hard to find in Miami, but I think the mention of their homemade gelato is what clinched the deal. How did it go with Agent Breznay?"

"About like I expected," she said. "He was floored by the news that Middleton was really Yury Bazarov, and a little stung at first that we'd withheld that information from him while he was surveilling him. I left a copy of the case file with him, which made him feel a bit more included; he said he'd be on the road first thing tomorrow to Cape Coral to interview the mother."

"What about you? Sounds like you decided to leave the island rather than stay."

"After I briefed Breznay, I stopped at South Seas, Jensen's and Tween Waters and asked the desk personnel if they'd observed any guests who seemed foreign, anyone out of the ordinary. No luck with any of them, so I decided, rather than eat by myself somewhere on the islands, I'd have a home-cooked meal in Bradenton, stay the night at my parents' house and come back to the office in the morning." Pause. "Any news from the M.E.?"

"Not yet, although he said he was anticipating having some more results for us sometime tonight. I'll call him after dinner."

"If you hear anything new, will you let me know?"

"I'll put your name at the top of my list."

*****

After a restless night, Breznay was up before dawn and had a magnificent view of the sunrise as he crossed the Sanibel Causeway. He had decided he didn't want to arrive at the Bazarov residence before 9:00, so he stopped for breakfast at a family-run café in Fort Myers that he'd seen profiled on the Food Channel.

He ordered shrimp and grits with whole wheat toast and coffee from an impossibly cheerful middle-aged waitress named Stella and read the *Fort Myers News-Press* while he waited for his food, lingering on a wire service report about another Twitter storm from the president, blasting the corrupt leadership and biased agents of the FBI.

His blood pressure spiked as he read the article. He knew there were agents on both sides of the fence when it came to their personal opinion concerning the president – it was a regular water cooler topic around the office. But for the president to declare, in a most public forum, that these agents were unable to disregard their personal opinions while performing their duties as Federal law enforcement officers was incredibly divisive and flat out wrong. He thought the country deserved better than that.

To cool off, he switched to the sports section and was reading about the upcoming Bucs game in Buffalo on Sunday when his breakfast arrived. The shrimp and grits, the restaurant's signature dish, were delicious, the shrimp cooked exactly right, the sauce flavored Southern style, with just the right amount of tang. He devoured the generous portion in minutes, using pieces of toast to sop up the savory sauce. When Stella dropped the check on his table, he paid in cash, leaving a generous tip, and headed out the door.

Morning rush hour traffic on McGregor Boulevard was moderate to heavy. As he worked his way north through several neighborhoods toward Cape Coral, he was surprised by the lack of storm damage evident. Fort Myers had either dodged a bullet like the barrier islands, or municipal cleanup crews had done an extremely efficient job in returning things to normal in a short period of time.

He merged onto U.S. 41 just before the Caloosahatchee River and crossed the bridge bathed in brilliant morning sunshine. Approaching from the south, Cape Coral materialized as a sepia landscape of bleached asphalt and withered, brown lawns. The post-Levittown tract homes along this stretch of U.S. 41 were without shade because the developers of the former sawgrass plain had adopted a clear-cut philosophy early on, removing all trees and brush prior to the start of construction. Thus unchecked, the Florida sun here was relentless; for as far as the eye could see each successive neighborhood resembled the aftermath of a 1950's nuclear test, the local vegetation struggling but failing to bounce back.

Breznay's GPS led him unerringly to Natalya Bazarov's modest ranch home on Charlau Court, just south of where U.S. 41 intersected with Pine Island Road. He pulled into the driveway at 9:09, strapped on his ankle holster and checked his appearance in the rearview mirror before exiting the vehicle. Two doors down, an elderly man with stooped posture gave him a cursory glance as he watered a brown lawn. Breznay resisted the urge to wave and walked to the front door and rang the bell.

He could hear the faint sound of a television on the other side of the door. Good – she was home. In a few moments the door opened a crack, just enough for the woman to see who her visitor was. "Yah?" she replied cautiously in a thick Russian accent.

Breznay used his most nonthreatening tone. "Ms. Natalya Bazarov?"

"Yah."

"My name is Paul Hanson," he said, handing her one of his bogus business cards. "I was wondering if I could speak to you for a few minutes? It's important."

She read the card, then looked him up and down. "Important how?"

"It's about your son."

The door opened a sliver wider. "What about my son?" she replied, anxiety creeping into her voice. "You know my son?"

"It would be better if we could talk about this inside. May I come in?"

She hesitated, weighing Breznay's request. "Are you police?"

"No, ma'am, I'm a private investigator." He showed her his fake identification. "I'd just like to ask you a few questions about Chad."

Her curiosity overcame her reluctance to talk to someone she didn't know. She opened the door wide enough for him to enter. "Come."

Breznay stepped inside. It was easy to see why she was reluctant to invite visitors into her home. The place was a mess. He could see dirty dishes stacked in the sink in the kitchen to his left, and the smell of rotten food in the room indicated to Breznay that the garbage needed to be taken out. The television, tuned to a morning talk show, droned on in the tiny living room. The air inside the house was warm, almost stifling – if the place was air conditioned, it didn't feel like it was turned on. She indicated a small table in the kitchen with two chairs. "In here is okay?"

Breznay nodded, following her. Natalya Bazarov was in her late fifties, about five five, with dark, straight hair parted in the middle, showing gray roots. She wore a plaid robe tightly cinched at the waist, and pink, fluffy slippers. Dark brown eyes highlighted a hardened face that had seen happier days. "Coffee?"

"No, thank you. I just had breakfast."

Her voice was strained. "What about….Chad?"

"I was wondering if you've heard from him recently?"

"Not for few days," she replied. "Last Friday, I think."

"Nothing since then?"

"No."

"Ms. Bazarov, I'm here representing Junonia Realty, the company where Chad works. They hired my firm to look for your son." He watched her intently as he continued. "He hasn't reported to work for several days now. He hasn't called, either. I was wondering if you might have any idea where he may be. They're worried about him."

She stared back at Breznay, concern creeping into her features as the news sunk in. After a few tense moments she spoke, her voice flat. "No. No idea."

"Have you tried to call him?"

She nodded. "Every day. Goes to….how you say?"

"Voicemail?"

"Yes, voicemail. No call back."

"Do you know if he has any friends he may have contacted? No one at work has heard from him since last Friday."

She shook her head, a single tear bleeding from her left eye. "No. Don't know friends."

Her reaction told Breznay everything he needed to know. She was stunned, in shock. Unless she was an award-winning actress, he'd bet the ranch that she knew nothing about what had happened to her son.

He reached across the table, taking the distraught woman's hands between his own. "Would you do me a favor?" She nodded, more tears welling in her eyes. He continued. "If you hear from him, could you please call the number on my business card? It would be a great help."

She looked at the card, then back at Breznay, who handed her a handkerchief to wipe her face. She dabbed at her eyes, then handed it back to him. "Thank you. You will find my son?" she pleaded softly.

"I will do my best, Ms. Bazarov. I promise."

"He is good boy, always sending money," she offered, as if his virtue made the news that Breznay conveyed unthinkable.

Breznay released the woman's hands and stood, nodding toward the front door. "I've taken up enough of your time, Ms. Bazarov. Please give me a call if you hear from Chad."

She remained seated, head bent forward, sobs wracking her stout frame, as Breznay let himself out.

*****

As soon as the door closed behind Breznay, Natalya's sobbing ceased. She rose and walked to the front window, parting the curtain just enough to watch him leave. When his car was out of sight, she walked over to the table next to the chair in front of the television and retrieved a cell phone from its top drawer, punching in a number from memory as she returned to the kitchen table. It rang through to a canned message, requesting the caller leave a message. In a voice seething with fury, she barked, "What have you done with Yury?"

*****

Breznay waited until he was around the corner before pulling over and reaching for his cell phone. He checked the time as he dialed Threadgill's number. She answered promptly. "How did it go?"

"Not great," he replied. "She said she hasn't heard from him since last Friday. She's called him every day since then, leaving messages, but he hasn't called back."

"No surprise there," Threadgill said. "Do you believe her?"

"I think so," he said. "I watched for any tells when I told her the news. She reacted like a mother who's just been told her son was missing, upset and crying. I don't think she has any idea what's going on."

Threadgill considered his words before continuing. "How did the house look?"

"Terrible. It looked and smelled like the house of a cat lady, only I didn't see any cats. If the Russians are subsidizing her, they must be stingy with their rubles."

"Someone's supporting her. According to the intel, she hasn't worked since she arrived in the country."

"She did mention that her son sends her money on a regular basis. But I'll be damned if I know what she spends it on."

"Were you able to plant the bug?"

"Yes. It's on the bottom of her kitchen table."

"Hang around for a couple of days, see if you can find anything else out. In the meantime, send me a report about the meeting." Threadgill instructed. She added hopefully, "Maybe we'll get lucky."

There was an air of resignation in his voice. "About time some good luck came my way."

35

The sound of mockingbirds outside her bedroom window awakened Threadgill before dawn. It felt strange to be sleeping in her childhood bed again – she hadn't done that since she was in college. Her mother had left her room just as it had been when she left for Gainesville twenty years earlier, which prompted nostalgic thoughts as well as a shade of creepiness. It was as if she'd spent the night in some sort of memorial shrine to herself, despite still being alive.

She showered and dressed, made her bed and packed her bag before grabbing a cup of coffee for the road. Her mother protested. "You just got here," she complained. "At least have some breakfast before you go."

"No time, Ma," she said, giving her mother a quick hug. "I'm working a big case, and we have an important meeting this morning." She smiled. "I'll come back again soon. I promise."

"You better," her mother called to her as she carried her bag and her go cup to the car.

The sun was just above the horizon as she approached the Sunshine Skyway Bridge. She dialed Miller's number; he picked up immediately. "Someone got an early start today."

She powered through his attempt at banal pleasantries. "Did you get the M.E.'s report?"

"No, but I did get a text, came in two hours ago. The report is finished, and a copy is on my desk. How soon can you get to the office?"

"Traffic's pretty light. If it stays like this I should be there in less than an hour."

"See me in my office when you get here."

Both Miller and Gutierrez were in Miller's office, huddled over the report, when Threadgill knocked on the door and entered without waiting for Miller's response. "What does it say?" she asked as she approached the pair, out of breath.

Gutierrez was amused. "Sounds like you ran here instead of driving."

"Just from the parking lot. What does it say?"

Miller indicated a vacant guest chair. "Pull up a seat. How about some coffee?"

"Already had some," she said impatiently. "What's the cause of death?"

Gutierrez and Miller exchanged glances. Miller gestured to his superior. "I'll let Cesar tell you. It's his show."

She turned toward Gutierrez expectantly. He smiled. "The official cause of death is cardiac arrest, like we thought."

Disappointment flooded Threadgill's face. "Natural causes?"

Gutierrez shook his head. "Not by a long shot. It took a while to isolate the cause, since there were no needle marks on the body. That's why the report wasn't ready last night – it took the doc until four this morning to finally identify the agent which caused the cardiac arrest."

Threadgill digested Gutierrez's statement before responding. "Poison?"

Gutierrez nodded. "But not just any poison. Doc says the chemical analyses indicate it's a new variant of Novichok."

Threadgill shook her head. "Haven't heard of that one."

"I'm not surprised," Gutierrez continued. "It's Russian, a deadly strain of binary chemical weapons developed in the seventies under the Soviet program FOLIANT. We first became aware of the existence of Novichok in the early nineties, and some breakthrough work in Iran last year finally produced five synthesized samples of Novichok for mass spectral analysis." He had a grim look on his face. "Bottom line is, it's one of the deadliest poisons on the planet, and extremely hard to detect. This particular strain was especially difficult to pinpoint because of the lack of symptoms previously attributed to Novichok. With the other strains, victims manifest obvious physical symptoms such as vomiting and skin irritation. Middleton exhibited nothing like that."

"So it's a new strain, one we hadn't encountered before," Miller added.

Threadgill had a puzzled look. "What's a binary chemical weapon?"

Gutierrez explained. "It consists of two components, like epoxy, which mixes a resin and a hardener together to produce a final adhesive. In the case of Novichok, the fact that the two components don't have to be combined until just prior to application means those components can be transported more easily, with less volatility and danger."

Threadgill stared at Gutierrez, admiration in her eyes. "I didn't know you were so well versed on reactive agents."

Gutierrez deflected the praise. "I wasn't, until I got the text from the M.E. this morning. Thanks to a lot of Googling, I can at least understand the basics."

Threadgill mulled the implications. "So we're talking about Russian agents going to great lengths, exposing themselves to extensive risk, in order to take out one of their own?"

Miller nodded. "It looks that way."

Gutierrez agreed. "We need to find those two guys picked up on Anclote Key by the satellite imagery. They may not know why Middleton was targeted, but I think they can lead us to someone who does."

*****

Two men whose German passports identified them as Klaus Weigl and Karl Meier were having breakfast in the Orlando airport at the same time Miller and Gutierrez were explaining to the lab results to Threadgill in Clearwater. They were waiting for their nonstop flight to Frankfurt on Lufthansa, which was scheduled to leave in two hours. Both men were in their thirties, average height, with short, dark hair and piercing dark eyes. Weigl, two years older than Meier, sported a full goatee, while Meier's fashionable stubble looked like he forgot to shave that morning.

Meier was reading a copy of the *Orlando Sentinel* while Weigl munched on a cheese Danish, his eyes roaming the room in a seemingly casual manner. His gaze settled on Meier. In heavily accented English, he addressed his companion. "What is news today?"

Meier responded without looking up. "Ovechkin score four goals last night. Seven now in two games."

Weigl raised an eyebrow. "Is impressive. Against who?"

"Montreal."

"Kuznetsov?"

Meier scanned the box score. "Four assists." He looked up at Weigl. "They win, 6-1." He added. "Capitals play in Tampa tomorrow."

Weigl regarded his companion with a small smile. "What is it you are saying?"

"Would be nice to see game."

"Some other time. Will be back in Moscow then."

*****

After another restless night, Breznay was up early. He decided to go for a run before it became too hot, so he donned shorts and a pair of Nikes, filled a water bottle, grabbed his iPod and headset and headed downstairs. On his way to the door he passed by the kitchen, where Henderson was seated at the kitchen table with a cup of coffee and the morning newspaper. He gave Breznay a quizzical look.

"Going for a run," Breznay said in explanation. "Be back in an hour."

It was always a good idea to get out before the heat of the day arrived. He did some stretching exercises on the crushed shell driveway before walking to the end of the driveway.

He decided to head north this morning. Because it was early and workers, especially landscaping crews and restaurant supply trucks, were still on their way to their job sites, he crossed over to the southbound lane, where there would be less traffic at this time of day. Captiva Drive was very narrow, with foliage crowding out the shoulder in many areas. He popped in his earbuds and set off at a leisurely pace.

It was five miles roundtrip to Andy Rosse Lane and back. The Killers filled his head as he ran, but they didn't occupy his mind completely. His thoughts drifted to Natalya Bazarov and the

213

uncertainty she must be feeling now that she knew her son was missing. From the condition of her house, she didn't seem to have much in her life about which to be prideful. He'd felt a brief urge to tell her her son would not be coming home, but dismissed it as soon as it arose. Letting his emotions overrule the logic of the moment was an impulse he'd always had to suppress since he was a child. He felt empathy for people, regardless of what side of the law their behavior placed them on.

At Tween Waters he veered onto the beach and continued running along the tide line. There were a number of early morning shell collectors on the prowl, identifiable from a distance by their stooped posture. He breathed the salt air in deeply, thankful to be back on Captiva, at least for a little while.

A variety of adult water toys for rent were already positioned on the beach by the time he reached the Mucky Duck, where he turned around and retraced his steps, heading home, enjoying the rare windless morning. He lengthened his stride, as he always did on the return leg. When he reached Tween Waters he followed a path between the sea oats back to the road and began the push for home, ending with an all-out sprint over the last two hundred yards.

He was a few feet from the front door, bent over, tugging on the hem of his shorts, sucking air, when Henderson, dressed sharply in a charcoal suit, light blue shirt and striped tie, emerged. "I think I heard your phone ring as I was coming down the stairs."

Breznay nodded his thanks, straightened and headed inside, taking the stairs two at a time. His phone, on the bedside table, indicated a message. He punched in his password and listened:

"Mr. Breznay, this is Fran Lopuszynski, from South Seas. I talked to Agent Threadgill yesterday, who told me to call this number with any news. I think I found someone with some information you might be interested in. Call me back."

36

Breznay showered in record time. His hair was still damp when he dialed Fran Lopuszynski, who picked up quickly. "Yes?"

"It's Carl Breznay, Ms. Lopuszynski, returning your call on behalf of Agent Threadgill."

She sounded confused but relieved at the same time. "Oh, thank you, Mr. Breznay, for getting back to me so quickly. I think I have some information for you."

"When can we meet?"

"I'm off tomorrow. Does that work for you?"

Breznay nodded to an empty room, phone to his ear. "Where?"

"I live in Estero, just west of I-75," she said. "I know a place on the mainland, not far from the causeway, a Cuban restaurant that serves the best *Cafe Cubano* around."

"Sounds great. Give me the address and I'll meet you there for lunch. Say, noon?"

"That's good," she replied. "Let me look it up." In a moment she was back. "Do you have a pen?"

"Ready." She read off the address. "Got it," he exclaimed. "I'll see you tomorrow at noon."

*****

After the meeting with Gutierrez and Miller broke up, Threadgill made a copy of the medical examiner's report and took it back to her office. She told Maria to hold her calls and closed her office door, searching the Internet and top-secret Bureau files, educating herself on the history of Novichok.

What she found was ominous. Gutierrez was right – the strains that comprised the Novichok family of poisons were insidious and deadly, some of the most virulent synthetic toxins to surface after the collapse of the Soviet Union. According to Bureau intel, initial development of Novichok began in the early 1970s and continued until 1993. Although the Bureau had long been aware of the research and development program responsible for Novichok, this was the first known instance of its use outside the laboratory, which sent chills down Threadgill's spine. What sort of calamitous situation necessitated the use of such a rare and malign substance, apparently used by Russian agents against one of their own?

It was hard not to wonder if this incident had any connection to the larger FBI investigation into the possibility of Russian interference during the 2016 election. She'd raised the idea during their earlier meeting, but Gutierrez had cautioned her against going down that rabbit hole. "We have to treat this as a separate case, completely divorced from the Mueller investigation. If the evidence leads back there, fine. But until then, the two are not connected."

She'd hoped that Breznay's interview with Natalya Bazarov might yield something, some thread that would move the investigation forward, but that hadn't happened. She wasn't convinced that Natalya was unaware of her son's activities – that was too far a stretch, especially since they knew that Natalya Bazarov had been subsidized by funds from Moscow ever since she'd arrived in Miami thirty-five years ago. She *had* to have some idea of her son's mission; the two had communicated regularly throughout the years, right up until a few days ago when Middleton had disappeared. It went against all of Threadgill's investigative instincts to believe that Middleton's actions had occurred without

216

some knowledge of his assignment making its way to his mother. After Breznay's meeting with Natalya yesterday, she'd prepared an application for a search warrant for Middleton's Fort Myers apartment. It was a long shot, but she was hoping he or his killers might've slipped up, been careless enough to leave something behind.

Her phone buzzed. She picked it up and snapped at the receptionist. "I thought I said no calls."

Maria was apologetic. "I know, but I have Special Agent Breznay on the line. I told him you weren't to be disturbed, but he insisted, says you need to know this right away."

"Put him through." In a moment he was on the line. "Special Agent Threadgill?"

"What do you have for me, Agent Breznay?" she asked with a hint of impatience.

His voice was animated. "I think I have a lead."

"Think?"

"Uh, I actually haven't spoken to the witness yet. I'm meeting her for lunch tomorrow."

"Who's this witness?"

"Fran Lopuszynski, the receptionist you spoke to at South Seas yesterday," Breznay said. "She called me back this morning, after their weekly staff meeting. During the meeting she mentioned your visit and that you wanted to know if any of their guests might've been acting strangely or drawing attention to themselves during the past several weeks. Apparently, someone noticed something."

"Who?"

"Don't know. I'll find out tomorrow."

"So this Lopuszynski isn't your witness?"

"No," admitted Breznay sheepishly. "It's someone else who works at the resort."

"What's their name?"

Breznay could see where this was going. Meekly, he responded, "Uh, I don't know."

"Sounds like you have a few holes to fill in concerning that lead," she said archly. He didn't respond. She continued in a softer tone. "I'm waiting on a search warrant for Middleton's apartment in Fort Myers. You should already have his address - I'll text you as soon as the warrant's approved. Should be any minute now. I want you there, on the scene, when the search team arrives."

The supreme confidence he'd been feeling as he was dialing Threadgill had eroded. Maybe he shouldn't have called until after he'd actually spoken with the witness, when he had an actual lead to pursue. He'd been so eager to atone for losing track of Middleton that he'd jumped the gun. "Sure thing, boss," he said contritely.

"One more thing."

"Yes, boss?"

"Good work."

*****

When the call went out over the intercom that passengers were cleared to board Flight 465 to Frankfurt, Klaus Weigl nudged his traveling companion, Karl Meier, who was staring at his phone, watching some dated footage of comedian Yakov Smirnoff on YouTube. Meier removed his headset and looked at Weigl questioningly. "What?"

"Is time to board plane."

They gathered their carryon bags and made their way casually toward the boarding corridor marked Business Class. Weigl, constantly vigilant, looked around for signs of any suspicious activities, while Meier put his headset back on and continued watching Smirnoff on YouTube. Satisfied that they weren't being watched, Weigl nudged Meier. Annoyed, Meier removed his headset once more. "What?"

Weigl pointed to Meier's phone. "Who is that?"

"Russian comedian, Yakov Smirnoff. Is from Odesa, Ukraine. Very funny."

"Smirnoff? Like vodka? Never heard of him."

Meier smiled. "Is not surprised. Too much like work you are."

A female voice came on the intercom. "At this time, we'd like to invite all Business Class customers to board Lufthansa Flight 465 to Frankfurt." The line tightened and began inching toward the tunnel leading to the plane. Weigl and Meier, boarding passes clutched in their hands, made it past the final attendant without incident, shuffling with the crowd to their seats.

They stowed their bags and settled into adjacent seats in the third row. Meier continued to watch his phone, laughing occasionally, while Weigl, his eyes restless, scanned the plane. He knew that international flights usually contained one or more air marshals. He tried not to draw notice to himself as he covertly observed the passengers as they boarded the plane, trying to identify anyone who might be an undercover agent.

It took thirty minutes for all the passengers to stow their luggage and find their seats. Once they were seated and a head count matching the flight manifest was completed, a male attendant stood just behind the entrance to the cockpit, holding up the flight instruction manual in one hand. He spoke into a handheld microphone, going over the flight details and safety information in both English and German.

When he was finished, he slipped into an area hidden from the passengers' view as the plane began to back away from the terminal. Twenty minutes later the plane was in position next to their designated runway, and when it was clear, the pilot steered onto the asphalt and gunned the engines. Meier continued to be absorbed in his video, while next to him Weigl's heart was pounding in his chest as their speed increased. As soon as he felt the plane lose contact with the ground and nose skyward, he felt a huge surge of relief.

They'd gotten away with it. They were going home.

37

Breznay arrived at Middleton's apartment building ten minutes before the search warrant arrived. It had taken him nearly an hour to make the drive to the north side of Fort Myers, in the middle of the day. He figured it would be more tedious during rush hour. Of course, realtors worked odd hours, often not adhering to a strict 9 to 5, since most of their work involved showing properties in the evening or on weekends, when most potential buyers were available.

The building was nondescript, a two-story structure with areas of chipped and peeling paint near the corners and a small garden flanking either side of the main entrance that looked like it hadn't been weeded in months. It was the only multi-unit building on the block – the rest were all single homes, most of which were in need of some level of repair. To Breznay it looked like the perfect place to hide in plain sight.

While he waited for the search team, he called Threadgill to tell her he was on the scene. Maria took the call, telling him that this time she *really* couldn't be disturbed. He could sense the irritation in her voice, probably because she blamed him for insisting she put his last call to her through. Tough titty, he thought after he hung up. He hadn't twisted her arm.

When the team arrived, in two cars, he exited his ride and donned a blue windbreaker with the large yellow **FBI** emblazoned on the back, grabbed a couple of pairs of latex gloves and plastic booties for his shoes, checked to make sure his weapon was on his hip and strode toward the group.

"You Breznay?"

He nodded. "That's me."

He thought he heard a snicker from one of the team, but he couldn't determine its source. He knew the story was out about how he'd lost the man whose apartment they were about to search and he expected some heckling. As long as no one accused him of colluding with the Russian, he figured he could take the heat.

Special Agent Smithwyck, who'd initially addressed him, spoke to the entire group. "Gloves and booties on. We're looking for any electronic devices that might contain data, plus any receipts, bank records, legal documents or personal correspondence. Take your time – it's not a race. Any questions?"

Silence. "Okay, let's go. Be thorough."

The building super, a squat, swarthy bald man who resembled a sumo wrestler, was waiting for them inside the foyer. "Middleton's place, right?" he said, dangling a large key ring.

Smithwyck replied. "That's correct."

"Apartment 2C, upstairs" the super said, indicating an elevator and next to it, a stairwell. "You can ride or walk."

The elevator was too small to accommodate the entire group, so Breznay and one other agent, a young black man who towered over Breznay, opted for the stairs. He gave Breznay a sideways glance, but didn't say anything as they ascended to the second floor. It didn't matter; Breznay knew exactly what he was thinking.

The super opened the door. Smithwyck was all business. "We'll take it from here," he said brusquely, addressing the super. "We'll let you know when we've finished."

The apartment was a mess. Breznay thought: like mother, like son. But it soon became apparent that much of the disarray in the one-bedroom unit resulted from a hasty search, likely performed under duress by the murderers or someone associated with them. There was no sign of forced entry, so whoever had tossed the place had either been invited in or had a key of their own.

They went through the apartment methodically, from top to bottom. Breznay concentrated on the bedroom, searching between the mattress and box spring, unscrewing and peering inside the heating vents, checking drawers for false bottoms, looking for anything that might shed some light on when and why he'd been snatched. There was a cell phone charger plugged into a socket behind a small bedside table, but no sign of a phone. A lone picture hung on the wall behind the bed, an abstract that made no sense to Breznay, but he dutifully tagged it and placed it with the other evidence.

They spent four hours combing the place, but didn't find much else of interest besides a small address book with five names, first names only, next to corresponding phone numbers. Pretty old school, thought Breznay, as he bagged and tagged the book. Most people these days kept their contacts stored on their cell phones. Paper was so analog, so last century.

They found no cell phones, tablets or laptops, although there was a wireless modem, now unplugged, in a small closet in the bedroom, which indicated the presence of a computer. There was a stack of bills, both paid and unpaid, sitting in a haphazard pile on a table next to a Barcalounger in front of the television that the team collected, along with the contents of his medicine cabinet and a hairbrush, with strands of hair entangled between the bristles that likely belonged to Middleton.

By the time all the evidence was collected it was early evening, the sun on its daily descent into the Gulf. Breznay called Threadgill, impatient. He wanted to switch his attention back to

Fran Lopuszynski and the tantalizing lead her voicemail message offered. She answered immediately. "What do you have for me, Agent Breznay?"

"The evidence is all bagged, tagged and ready to transport. We just finished."

"Any electronic devices?"

"No. Just a modem in the bedroom. We're bringing it in for analysis."

Although Threadgill hadn't expected much of value to be found at Middleton's apartment, that didn't quell the disappointment she felt after hearing Breznay's assessment of the search. They needed something to help maintain their momentum. Right now, it felt like they were losing what little wind had filled their sails. "Okay. I want you to follow up on that lead with the clerk at South Seas. Once you've met with her, I want a full debrief, then I want you back on the mother. We're convinced here that she has to know more than she's let on so far."

"Yes, ma'am."

*****

Breznay arrived at the restaurant the next morning an hour before their scheduled meeting time and called Threadgill. "I have an idea."

Threadgill's voice remained neutral. "About what?"

"I think that Paul Hanson has run his course," he said, referring to his cover identity. "I think I could get better results as an FBI agent than I would as a PI."

Threadgill mulled the suggestion for a moment before responding. "I want to reserve judgment on that until we find out what kind of lead your receptionist has for us. I don't want Natalya

224

Bazarov to know that the FBI is interested in her and her son. Not yet."

"Has the bug picked anything up?"

"Just one short call. She called someone as soon as you left her house, asking what they did to her son. She definitely knows more than she's letting on."

Breznay was elated. "Who did she call?" he asked eagerly.

"We don't know. Because the call went to voicemail, we had enough time to trace the number to a burner located at or near the Orlando airport. No clue who was on the other end."

Disappointment. "Oh."

Threadgill continued. "It's not all bad news. Based on that call, we think she has a pretty good idea who was involved with her son's disappearance. All we have to do now is find them." She offered the crestfallen Breznay a bit of encouragement. "Thanks to your bug, we now have a chance that she might lead us directly to them. She didn't sound like a woman prone to giving up, especially when it comes to her son. She'll keep calling until she reaches them."

"I hope you're right. I wish I could've gotten into her phone instead of planting the bug in the kitchen."

"Ears in the kitchen are better than no ears at all." She could sense the fragility in his voice and moved quickly to shore up his confidence. "If your lead today pans out, it'll move to the head of the pack. You're the only person who's provided any credible information since Middleton disappeared."

Breznay watched a slim, young brunette exit an older Ford and walk inside the restaurant as he weighed the sincerity of his superior's words against the reality of the situation as he saw it. "What does Fran Lopuszynski look like?"

"Brunette, brown eyes, slim, in her mid-twenties."

"I think she just pulled into the parking lot."

"Go get her, Tiger."

38

Fran Lopuszynski was sitting alone at a corner table when Breznay came through the door. It was a small restaurant, family owned and operated, with only eight tables and a lunch counter in front of the small kitchen. A single waitress hovered near the end of the counter, pretending not to watch the dynamic as he approached her table. "Fran Lopuszynski?"

She had a concerned look on her face. "Yes. Agent Breznay?"

He smiled, showing her his ID. "Please call me Carl," he said. He indicated the seat opposite hers. "Mind if I sit down?"

She blushed. "Of course not."

When he was seated he moved quickly to reassure her about the reason for their meeting. "I want to thank you for responding so quickly to Agent Threadgill's request. Also, there's no reason for you to appear so worried."

She dropped her eyes, avoiding his gaze. "Is it that obvious?"

"It's a natural reaction. Very few people ever receive a visit from an FBI agent. There's no playbook on how you should react, but I want to personally assure you that your assistance is truly appreciated. Citizens like you make my job easier." He smiled broadly. "Thank you."

Her cheeks remained flushed. "I'm not sure how much I can help…." Her voice trailed off.

"Let me be the judge of that," he replied as he extracted a small tape recorder and placed it on the table between them. "I hope you don't mind if I record our conversation?"

She hadn't expected that. She hesitated as he continued. "It's standard operating procedure, in case what you have to say qualifies as admissible evidence somewhere down the road."

"I guess it's okay."

"Good," he said as he activated the recorder. "This is Special Agent Carl Breznay, interviewing subject Fran Lopuszynski. Ms. Lopuszynski, can you tell me why we're here today?"

She nodded. "The other day, Agent Threadgill of the FBI questioned me at work, asking if I had noticed any of our guests acting strange during the last couple of weeks. The next morning, during our staff meeting, I mentioned Agent Threadgill's interest in our guests, and one of the supervising housekeepers told me that she had seen something she thought was strange several days earlier."

"What day was that?"

She thought for a moment. "A week ago today. Last Friday."

"What did she observe?"

"We had two German guests who stayed with us for two weeks in one of our Land's End villas. Our weeks run from Friday to Friday, so our housekeepers have a slim window, two to three hours, where they clean the rooms and prepare them for the next arriving guests."

Breznay broke in. "How did you know they were German?"

228

"When they registered, they had to provide proof of their identity in order to register their credit cards. All subsequent charges incurred at the resort are thus placed on the credit cards that we have on file. We make a photo copy of both the ID and the credit card for each guest before returning them. They both presented German passports when they checked in."

"Do you remember their names?" he asked.

She reached into her purse and withdrew two sheets of paper, which she pushed across the table to Breznay. "I made copies of our copies. You can keep those."

Breznay stared at the sheets of paper before him, studying the faces of the two men intently. The quality of the prints was poor – he could see they were both dark-haired, but not much beyond that. Their dates of birth indicated they were each in their thirties. "Let the record indicate that these documents identify the two men as Klaus Weigl and Karl Meier, ages 36 and 34." He looked at Fran. "Continue."

"Well, our housekeeper crew went to their room last Friday at 10:00 am and rang their doorbell, but there was no answer. They tried a second time, as per our protocols, and when they didn't receive a reply the second time, they used a master card to enter their room. The room was messy, but it appeared the two men had gone. There was no luggage or other personal items left in the room."

"Go on."

"When one of the women emptied one of the trash cans, she found three empty bottles of vodka, with some foreign language on the labels, strange looking letters."

"How were they strange?" Breznay asked eagerly.

"She told me they didn't look like letters from our alphabet. She said they looked funny, like they were Greek or something."

"Did they save the bottles?"

Fran shook her head. "No. They collected them and placed them in the recycling bin." Breznay's heart sank as she continued. "But she did take a picture of one of the bottles to show to her husband." She reached into her purse and withdrew her phone. She scrolled through her picture gallery, then handed the phone to Breznay. "Here it is."

He stared at the picture intently, heart racing. The letters weren't Greek; they were Cyrillic. Russian. Trying to contain his excitement, he asked, "Are there surveillance cameras on the resort?"

She nodded. "Everywhere."

"Would it be possible that there might be some footage of these two?"

"There's a camera behind the reception desk that records all guests checking in and out. They should be on there."

If the tapes hadn't already been erased. "How long do they keep that footage?"

"I don't know," she replied. "You'd have to ask someone in security."

"Who should I contact?"

"Conrad Ellis. He's our chief of security. Just call the main number for the resort and they'll connect you."

"What's the name of the woman who took this photo?"

"Eva Molina. But she won't talk to you."

"Why not?"

She bent toward Breznay, turning her head away from the tape recorder and lowering her voice to a whisper. "She's an illegal from El Salvador. She won't talk to any person connected with law enforcement. She's afraid she's going to be deported."

Breznay couldn't blame her, given the current contentious debate over illegal immigration. "Can you send me the photo of the vodka bottle in an email?"

"I can do that right now," she said. "What's your address?"

Breznay gave her his Bureau email address. He watched as she typed it in, attached the photo and sent it on its way. "That should be a big help," he said. "Do you have anything else for me?"

Fran shook her head. "Just the vodka bottle, for now."

Breznay pushed one of his business cards across the table. "If you come up with anything else, please give me a call." He turned off the tape recorder and slid it into the pocket of his suit coat before standing. "Thanks very much, Ms. Lopuszynski. You've been a tremendous help."

She had a confused look on her face. "But we haven't eaten yet."

Breznay withdrew two twenties from his wallet and dropped them on the table. "I have to send this photo on to Agent Threadgill and see if I can catch Conrad Ellis, so I won't be able to stay. Lunch is on the FBI." She started to rise, but Breznay motioned her back into her seat. "No need to get up. Thanks again for your patriotism."

She watched as he walked briskly out the door. The waitress came over to her table, concern on her face. "Everything okay? He left in an awful hurry."

"He had some business to attend to," Fran said. "Do you have any lunch specials today?" she asked.

"Soup of the day and half a Cuban sandwich for $7.95."

"What kind of soup?"

"Black bean."

"Sounds perfect."

*****

As soon as he reached his car, he dialed Threadgill. She picked up immediately. "What do you have for me?" she asked expectantly.

"Two names. Klaus Weigl and Karl Meier. Their passports identify them as German, but it's likely they're Russians, based on the photo I'm about to send you. As soon as I hang up with you I'm going to call the chief of security at South Seas, see if they have any video footage of the two."

"Good work, Breznay. Keep me posted."

39

While Breznay tried to chase down any surveillance video that might exist of the two German nationals at South Seas, Threadgill and Miller were huddled in Clearwater, going over the limited options available to them to advance the investigation into Middleton's death. When Gutierrez returned to Miami, he sent a copy of the Operation Henhouse file, which lay splayed out in front of them on the conference room table as they looked for some new threads to pursue.

Threadgill was poring over Natalya Bazarov's file, searching for her visa application. She raised her head for a moment and noticed Miller staring out the window like a student on the last day of school. "Penny for your thoughts?" she said slyly.

Miller turned toward her, a smile on his face. "You're way too young to have that cliché in your vocabulary. Besides, inflation has pushed that penny to at least a quarter by now." He turned serious. "I think we need to bring Rheinhart in. Other than a half-assed interview he gave to the Pinellas County detectives, nobody's talked to him. He's the guy who discovered the body. I'm thinking he probably saw that Middleton's tongue had been removed. Maybe he saw something else, something that he doesn't realize is a clue. Right now, he's the only lead we have."

Threadgill demurred. "If he did notice the missing tongue, he has to be wondering why there's been no media reports about a dead body with missing body parts. He's a smart guy, an architect.

Smart enough to figure out that a media blackout means that he stumbled onto something big."

"*If* he stumbled onto the body," Miller corrected. "We don't know that for sure. He could be a part of this."

"It doesn't look like it to me," Threadgill responded with conviction. "We ran a background check on him. We're pretty sure he's exactly what he appears to be, a disgraced architect who moved across the state to lick his wounds while he tries to resurrect his career. No links to Russians of any kind so far."

"What about associates?"

"Only one to speak of in his new location. He goes to lunch every Wednesday with Steve Morrison, another relatively recent arrival on the west coast of Florida."

"What's his story?"

"Morrison's?"

"Yeah."

She reached for another file folder and withdrew a document, reading from it. "He moved to Ozona from Los Angeles two years ago after inheriting some property from his late uncle. Since the move he hasn't worked or done much of anything, except take scuba diving lessons, which leads me to believe he received some money along with the house, since he hasn't applied for Social Security yet."

"What did he do in LA?" Miller asked.

She leafed through the file, then looked up, a grin on her face. "He was an actor."

Miller, who regarded himself as a film buff, with expansive knowledge of all genres, didn't recognize the name. "Never heard of him. What was he in?"

Threadgill's eyes twinkled. "There's a reason for that. He acted under a different name. Biff Bratwurst."

Miller was perplexed. "Never heard of him, either. Why on earth would anybody pick a pseudonym like……" His voice trailed off as he realized why. He looked at Threadgill intently. "Porn?"

Threadgill's smile widened. She was having fun with this. "Is that a guess or a bit of knowledge you recalled from viewing his work?"

"Simple logic," he replied calmly, ignoring her dig. "No one in their right mind would choose a surname like Bratwurst to act in mainstream films." He analyzed this new revelation before continuing. "So Rheinhart's only friend has a depraved past. That doesn't mean Rheinhart's not involved."

Threadgill was concerned that revealing their hand to Rheinhart by bringing him in for an interview at this time would result in little probative value and would likely prove more harmful than good. "Why don't we do this instead? Why not do a flyover on both of these guys, Rheinhart and Morrison, to see where it leads? It shouldn't take long to find out if we're on the right track. Meanwhile, Breznay will try to find some video and keep an eye on the mother. Right now, that's all we have."

Miller considered Threadgill's suggestion. He could see her point, but he wasn't convinced yet that leaving Rheinhart as a dangling witness would be productive as they moved forward. He did agree that keeping eyes on the mother and monitoring whatever they could pick up from the recording device attached to the underside of her kitchen table should be their primary focus, at least until they received video of the two mysterious Germans with a penchant for Russian vodka. "How soon do you think Breznay will be able to come up with some video of the Germans?" he asked.

"Should be sometime today. He said there's cameras everywhere on the resort. Records indicate they stayed for two weeks – there should be all sorts of footage as long as they didn't erase it already."

"Call me as soon as you have something we can look at. In the meantime, we'll do deep background checks on Rheinhart and Morrison." He looked at Threadgill, a faint glint of hope in his eyes. "Maybe we'll get lucky."

*****

As soon as Breznay finished his call with Threadgill, he dialed Conrad Ellis. The call went to voicemail, so he left a detailed message, explaining that he was looking for some video and then headed back to the island. He'd just pulled into the driveway of Justice Hancock's home when his cell buzzed. "Special Agent Breznay. How can I help you?"

"It's Conrad Ellis, Agent Breznay, returning your call. I have some video you might be interested in seeing."

Breznay's pulse quickened. "When can we see it?"

"How soon can you get here?"

Breznay gave a triumphant fist pump. "I'm on the island. Tell me how to get to your office."

"I'm in the real estate office, near the rear of the resort. You'll go around an S curve. On the right you'll see tennis courts. I'm just beyond the tennis courts, in the building on the right."

"See you in ten minutes."

Ellis was waiting for him when he arrived. The security chief was in his sixties, with gray hair cut close to the scalp, piercing blue eyes, and a significant paunch. After Breznay presented his ID, Ellis indicated a chair he'd pulled next to his own, disdaining pleasantries, all business. "Let's watch some video, Agent Breznay."

Ellis had downloaded three files: a short clip of when the two Germans at the reception desk when they had arrived, similar video when they checked out, and a two-minute clip of the two of them ordering drinks at the tiki bar next to the main pool. They watched the clips several times as Breznay's excitement grew. The two men were revealed in much sharper focus than they had been in the copies of their passport photos Fran Lopuszynski had provided for him. He turned to the security chief. "Can you send those files to me in an email?"

Ellis expression never changed. "I can do better than that. I captured a couple of screen shots of these two that are better than mug shots. Give me your address and I'll send them all to you."

"Let me see the stills."

Ellis had consolidated two individual shots of the men into a side-by-side. Breznay bent forward to get a closer look. Both men were in their thirties, with short, dark hair and coal-black eyes. The one who'd identified himself as Klaus Weigl had a neatly trimmed goatee, while Karl Meier had a slightly receding hairline and stubble indicating he hadn't shaved for several days. Breznay was especially attracted by their eyes; they looked dead, as if there was nothing of substance behind them. The eyes of assassins.

Breznay's phone pinged, indicating the email from Ellis had arrived. He forwarded the files to Miller and Threadgill before turning his attention back to Ellis as he stood up. "You've been a great help, Chief Ellis," he said, extending his hand.

Ellis's grip was firm. "My pleasure, Agent Breznay." He hesitated, then spoke again. "I used to be on the job in

Philadelphia. Twenty-three years." He smiled. "It's nice to be able to work with the feds without any bullshit for a change."

Breznay nodded. He knew of previous turf squabbles between local LEOs and the feds that had interfered with or seriously delayed investigations of importance that he'd worked on since he'd joined the Bureau. "I agree, Chief. I prefer cooperation over obfuscation every day of the week."

"I know this is an ongoing investigation, but if you could keep me in the loop…" he said suggestively.

Breznay smiled. "I'll do whatever I can," he promised.

40

As soon as Threadgill received the files sent to her by Breznay, she ran them through the Bureau's facial recognition software. When the results of the analyses were complete, confirming their hunch, she called Miller immediately, her voice pulsing with excitement. "We've identified those Germans on Captiva as two agents associated with the GU."

The GU, also known as the Main Intelligence Directorate, was one of the agencies that had risen from the ashes of the Soviet KGB after its dissolution in 1992. Miller's response was restrained, considering the import of Threadgill's news. "I'll be right down."

He strode into Threadgill's office without knocking, closing the door behind him. She was at her desk, hunched forward, scrolling through her laptop. She looked up, indicating her guest chair with a nod. "Bring it around so you can get a look at this." When he was seated, she continued. "Once the software identified these two, I ran their names through a CIA database we were granted access to after it became obvious the Russians had interfered in the 2016 election."

"Hooray for agency cooperation," Miller deadpanned.

Threadgill continued. "The two men identified as Klaus Weigl and Karl Meier by their German passports are actually Anatoliy Mishkin and Alexander Chepiga, two mid-level Russian operatives of the GU."

Miller digested the revelation before replying. "Does Washington know this yet?"

Threadgill shook her head. "I was waiting to show you the results before contacting them. I figure you or Agent Gutierrez should be the ones to pass along news like this."

Miller regarded his colleague with admiration. There weren't many agents who would defer taking credit for a discovery as significant as this one, especially since the initiation of the Mueller investigation five months earlier. Anything attached to Russia was red hot these days; her reticence at taking credit for such consequential information was noteworthy. "What's the certainty level of the identification?"

"Ninety eight percent. A virtual lock."

"So we have Russian-on-Russian crime." He voiced the question both of them were pondering. "What did Middleton do to incur the wrath of the Main Intelligence Directorate, to push them to kill a deep cover agent, one of their most precious assets, someone born here, raised on U.S. soil?" He looked at Threadgill intently before shifting back to the two Russian agents. "Do we have anything from Homeland Security yet on the whereabouts of these two?"

"Yes," she replied. "According to the TSA, they flew from Orlando to Frankfurt last Sunday. There's been no activity on their passports since then, which means they likely used their Russian passports to return to Moscow from Frankfurt. I can't imagine they'd linger in Germany for any reason. Their superiors would want a debrief as soon as possible."

Disappointment flooded Miller's features. He knew the futility of tracking down suspects within the Russian borders. "If they're back in Russia, they're lost to us."

Threadgill agreed with her boss, but tried to spin it in a positive way. "Unless there are some loose ends still out there."

Miller wasn't buying it. "The Russians don't usually leave loose ends. I'm thinking Middleton might've been the loose end. That's why we need to stay on the mother, find out who she's trying to call."

"The call she made after Breznay visited her was traced to a burner phone abandoned at the Orlando airport," Threadgill recalled. "Could that be a coincidence?"

Miller shook his head, his face grim. "Not in a million years."

*****

Natalya Bazarov paced between her living room and kitchen, furious. Following Breznay's visit, she'd continued to call the number of the Russian agent who'd contacted her after checking in to South Seas, but the calls all went directly to voicemail. She was livid, because she knew her inability to get through to the Russian painted a grim picture. She was certain that the story he'd fed her was a lie: that he was here to meet with her son and detail a new assignment for him, one that would have him incommunicado for some time. The realization that she might never see her son again had settled in like a swiftly moving virus, leaving her sapped of enthusiasm and bitter to her core.

In retrospect, she should've seen something like this coming when Nikolai Vasilevsky, the man responsible for her legal arrival in the U.S., informed her that his superiors in the Kremlin had decided to rename Yury Chad Middleton a year before he was scheduled to begin kindergarten. There had been no consultation, no opportunity for her to voice a protest at the time – by the time they shared the news with Natalya, the name change was already underway. When the KGB came to a decision, there was no appeals process.

She was ashamed that she'd never stood up in defense of her son's birth name. She'd feared that the slightest indication that she was being uncooperative would signal an end to the monthly checks she received from Vasilevsky's production company, Conch Republic Films. Those checks were her only source of income – she had no other marketable skills. Without them, she'd have to try to land a cashier's job at Winn Dixie or McDonald's, which wouldn't come close to providing the minimum amount needed to support even her austere lifestyle. She was trapped, with no way out.

*****

Threadgill was in her office, contemplating what to do about lunch, when Ellen Feeney, a young Bureau lab analyst assigned to the evaluation of the evidence collected at Middleton's apartment, knocked excitedly on her door.

Feeney looked flushed and out of breath, as if she'd run all the way from the lab. Threadgill motioned her in, pointing to her visitor's chair. "Do you have something for me, Agent Feeney?"

Her voice was buoyant, filled with excitement. "I think so," she said, pushing two photos across the desk. "These are photos I took of a painting that was hanging on the wall in Middleton's bedroom, one of the front, one of the back."

Threadgill looked at the front view of the abstract painting, shaking her head in confusion as she handed it back to Feeney. "Art is not my thing. Tell me what I'm looking at here."

Feeney nodded. "This a print of a Russian painting called *The Knifegrinder Principle of Glittering*, sometimes referred to as just *The Knifegrinder*. The original was painted in 1912 by Kazimir Malevich; it hangs on the wall at the Yale University Art Gallery in New Haven. Without going into too much detail, it's considered a major Russian work linking cubism and futurism."

"I'll have to take your word for that," Threadgill commented drily. "Looks like a Rorschach test to me."

Feeney continued as though Threadgill hadn't interrupted. "We subjected both the front and the back of the painting to spectral analysis, to see if there might be any subliminal messaging. We didn't find anything on the front of the painting, but we discovered something significant on the back." She indicated the photo of the back of the painting. "In the lower right corner, on the back, we found a series of ten numbers, which we determined to be a telephone number, a landline. It doesn't come through on this photo I snapped from my cell phone, but I wrote it down for you." She passed the number across the desk to Threadgill, who examined it with interest. "Area code 305. That's the Keys." She looked at Feeney. "Any idea who it belongs to?"

Feeney nodded excitedly. "We traced it to a Russian national named Nikolai Vasilevsky. He owns a condo in Marathon. Or at least he did until Irma came through. According to the Monroe County sheriff I talked to, it suffered a lot of damage from the hurricane."

Threadgill's excitement level was nearing Feeney's. "I know that name. He's the guy who sponsored Natalya Bazarov's original visa application. His company has been sending her support checks for more than thirty years." She paused a moment before continuing. "Did you try it?"

"I couldn't get a ringtone. I called the phone company; they told me the landlines in Marathon are still down. They say it might be months before service is restored to everyone in the area."

"Excellent work, Agent Feeney." Threadgill could feel the adrenaline pulsing through her system. Another lead linked to another Russian. She was exuberant - they were finally getting somewhere. "When can you get me a detailed report on what you discovered?"

"Sometime this afternoon."

Threadgill stood up and gestured toward her office door. "What are you waiting for?"

41

As soon as his phone call with Threadgill ended, Miller called Cesar Gutierrez in Miami and relayed the latest developments in the case. Gutierrez, listening without comment, waited until Miller finished before speaking. "Russians everywhere," he observed. "And it all seemed to start in the Keys back in '82. Vasilevsky, Bazarov and that movie...what was the name of it again?"

Miller took a few moments to look through his case file before replying. "*The Russians Are Coming and Coming and Coming.*"

"Do we know anything else about the movie? Any cast or crew?"

"A little," Miller replied, reaching for another section of the file. "One of our younger analysts, Gavin Tremayne, was able to find a website that listed Vasilevsky as the executive producer and Natalya Bazarov as the dialogue consultant on the film. The director was a guy named Les Bent, who coincidentally also lives in the Keys now, in Islamorada. He also found the cast list, but I don't know how helpful that will be. Most of the names on the list look as phony as a three-dollar bill. Biff Bratwurst, Audrey Heartburn, Kandy Kane, names like that."

Gutierrez weighed their options. As long as Mishkin and Chepiga were in Russia, they remained untouchable. As much as he'd like to interrogate them, it was out of the question unless they left the country, which wasn't likely. That left Vasilevsky and

Natalya Bazarov, who so far appeared to be a Soviet pawn, merely one of a number of unwitting fertile conduits crucial to Operation Henhouse. Her continuing relationship with Vasilevsky throughout the years had been strictly financial in nature – with her son now dead, she no longer served any purpose to the Kremlin. Gutierrez figured her days were numbered.

The phone rang, interrupting his reverie. His executive assistant was on the line. "I have Special Agent Miller on the line."

"Put him through."

Gutierrez could hear the exuberance in Miller's voice. "We found something of interest in Chad Middleton's apartment, on the back of a picture that was in his bedroom, a phone number linked to Nikolai Vasilevsky."

"Linked how?"

"To a landline in Vasilevsky's name in Marathon. He owns a condo on the ocean side. We called, but we couldn't get through at all. The Monroe County sheriff's deputy said that area really got slammed by Irma. He said all the landlines are down and probably will be for weeks."

Another link to the Keys. Gutierrez evaluated the new intelligence for a moment before replying. "We need to send someone down to the Keys, to see what we can find on Vasilevsky. We also need to find out more about that movie – that seems to be ground zero for all the players. And I'd like to have some eyes on Bazarov. Now that her son is dead, she becomes expendable. If the Russians send someone after her, maybe we'll get lucky."

"I agree," Miller said. "I think we should send Breznay down to Marathon. He's no longer a viable prospect for monitoring Bazarov because of his previous contact with her. She thinks he's a PI - if she spots him again, it could drive her underground. I have one of our agents set to monitor Bazarov going forward, a Hispanic female posing as a local house cleaner. If Bazarov notices her more than once, she won't be suspicious."

"Are you sure about Breznay?" Gutierrez asked.

"Absolutely," Miller replied without hesitation. "He's been busting a nut trying to make up for losing track of Middleton. Plus, he found the painting in Middleton's apartment. He's already up to speed – he can be there tomorrow."

Miller's confidence convinced Gutierrez, who added, "What about access and a place for Breznay to stay?"

"I'll contact Monroe County, see what they suggest. The know the local conditions better than anyone."

"One more thing," Gutierrez said. "We need to find out more about that movie. Have Tremayne keep digging. See if he can track down anyone else who worked on it."

*****

Breznay was at Justice Hancock's home reviewing his notes on the surveillance video of the two Russians for his latest report to Threadgill when his phone rang. He smiled when he saw who was calling. "I'm working on the report right now. I'll have it for you by the end of the day."

"That's not why I'm calling," Threadgill said. "We have a new assignment for you."

Breznay's heart sank. He was hoping he would be able to extend his stay on Captiva a bit longer. "Where?"

"Marathon, in the Keys. Or as close as you can get to there. We're working with Monroe County to find you a place to stay. I'm putting together a file for you – I'll attach it to an email and send it to you when it's ready." She paused for a moment before continuing. "I'm sending someone down with a four-wheel drive vehicle – there's still a ton of debris everywhere down there. They should be there by tonight."

"What's the assignment?"

"Vasilevsky. We found his phone number hidden on the back of the painting you collected at Middleton's apartment. We need to find him ASAP; he has a condo in Marathon, which means he probably evacuated ahead of the storm. Bring comfortable shoes – you may be doing a lot of walking."

Breznay swallowed his disappointment. "You want me to leave in the morning?"

"Yes. As soon as we find a place for you to stay, I'll send the address to you via email."

The line went dead before Breznay could respond.

*****

Irma made landfall as a Category 4 hurricane at Cudjoe Key on September 10. Although the cleanup efforts had been underway now for more than a month, the devastating effects of the storm continued to dominate the landscape: mobile homes destroyed, shredded by the storm, their aluminum components scattered everywhere, trees downed, boats lifted from their moorings and deposited on land as if they were weightless. Initial efforts had concentrated on clearing debris from the Overseas Highway so that humanitarian aid, in the form of food and water, could be delivered to those who had chosen not to evacuate, as well as determining the structural integrity of the numerous bridges in the Keys. When the roads and bridges were deemed passable, utility trucks, some from as far away as New York, began to arrive in order to begin the lengthy process of restoring power to the region.

An exhausted Monroe County deputy examined Breznay's credentials at a police roadblock in Florida City and waved him through. Breznay had seen some of the images on television that dominated the Weather Channel in the aftermath of the storm, but he'd been unprepared for the visceral impact of the damage as he slowly made his way south. It took him more than four hours to travel seventy miles from Florida City to Marathon, and the remnants of broken dreams were visible all along the route.

It was dusk by the time he reached the Marriott Hotel in Marathon, where Monroe County officials had managed to secure him a room that he would be sharing with a Florida Power and Light employee from Sebring. No one was in the room when he arrived, so he deposited his gear on the unoccupied bed in the room and headed out on foot to the Overseas Pub and Grill, the first restaurant in town to reopen after the hurricane roared through.

He found a seat at the surprisingly crowded bar and waited patiently while the beleaguered lone bartender did his best to keep up with the demand. He'd been forewarned that the restaurant offered only a limited menu, but after what Breznay had observed on the drive south, he was amazed that they were able to serve any food at all.

After a few minutes the stocky, bearded, heavily inked bartender greeted him with an apologetic tone. "Sorry to keep you waiting. What can I get you?"

"A burger, medium, and a beer. Anything that's cold," Breznay said.

The bartender turned on his heel and delivered Breznay's order to the makeshift kitchen. Most of the other customers appeared to be utility workers, identifiable by their haggard, unshaven faces and work vests with luminescent vertical orange striping. The conversation was subdued; it looked to Breznay as if the collective level of exhaustion among the workers left them with barely enough energy to down their food, let alone socialize.

249

The bartender, who introduced himself as Aaron, returned with Breznay's beer. He took a long draught before speaking. "Looks like you folks are doing an amazing job."

"Thanks," Aaron replied wearily. "It's been a helluva month. I can't remember the last time I had four hours sleep without interruption. You with one of the utility companies?"

Breznay shook his head. As Gutierrez had suggested, he kept his response vague. "I'm with the federal government."

Aaron's face hardened. "FEMA?"

"No, I'm afraid not."

Silence. Then, "That figures. Those bastards are never there when you need 'em. You'd think they'd have figured it out after the way they fucked up with Katrina. Look what's going on now in Puerto Rico. Fucking paper towels." He shook his head as he turned away. "Unbelievable."

"Not a good sign," Breznay conceded.

Aaron looked askance at Breznay. "That's being charitable."

42

When the mandatory evacuation order was issued for all Keys' residents several days before Irma reached the mainland, Nikolai Vasilevsky was in Tampa, preparing to attend his first American football game. Coverage of the storm spanned all media platforms, and he began to grow anxious about his condo in Marathon as the storm neared. It was located on the Atlantic side, close to the projected path of the hurricane according to the consensus of various computer modeling results that had monopolized local weather reports for the last ten days.

When the football game was cancelled, he briefly considered returning to the Keys. He had some documents hidden in the bedroom of his second-floor unit that could be disastrous for him should they see the light of day. He didn't want to take that chance, hope they'd remain secure, but when the governor closed Highway 1 to all traffic, exempting first responders, that decision was taken out of his hands.

Irritated and nervous, he called his oldest friend in the Keys. Maybe he had decided to stay in defiance of the mandatory evacuation notice. His friend answered cautiously on the third ring. "Hello, Nikolai."

"Mr. Les Bent!" Vasilevsky boomed in a distinct Russian accent. "How are you, my friend?"

"Fine, except for the fucking hurricane. And you?"

"I am fine also. Have you remained in the Keys?"

"No," Bent replied. "I left last week before the storm hit." He hesitated for a moment before continuing. "Don't tell me you're still there."

"I am not," Vasilevsky replied. "I have traveled to Tampa to see the Buccaneers, but they have cancelled the game. I am in a hotel now, waiting to hear about when I can return." Pause. "Where are you?"

"Actually, not far from you," Bent replied. "I'm staying with a friend in Land O' Lakes."

"Where is Land O' Lakes?"

"About thirty minutes north of Tampa. When it became obvious that I had to leave, I called my friend, who graciously invited me to stay with him. He's the only person I know on either side of the state who doesn't live near the coast."

"So you are inland?"

"A little bit, yes."

"Have you heard anything about the status of your home?" Vasilevsky asked.

Bent, whose home was located on the Gulf side in Islamorada, responded. "I called the Monroe County Sheriff's Department. All they could tell me was that they were checking addresses of homes in the order requests came in from full-time residents before they checked on any seasonal homes. I'm not sure that the power is back on yet."

"So you will stay in Land O' Lakes for how long?"

"As long as I have to. My friend has been very gracious about offering me shelter until I can return to my house."

"Do I know this friend?" Vasilevsky asked, probing.

"You might know him by reputation," Bent replied. "We used to work together in LA. His name is Wai Tang, but most people know him as Harpoon Tang. Biggest Asian dick in porn."

Vasilevsky, whose lone connection to the porn industry was his one-time backing of *The Russians Are Coming and Coming and Coming* thirty-five years ago, hesitated before replying. "I am not familiar with this name."

"He's retired now. I think he moved to Florida about five years ago."

Now that Vasilevsky knew that Bent wasn't currently in the Keys, his interest in the conversation had waned. "Lucky for you to have such a friend. Much better than me, living in hotel."

"If you'd like, I can ask him if you could visit," Bent offered graciously. "I think you might like the scenery here."

"Where in Land O' Lakes does Mr. Tang live?"

"Fuego Resort and Spa."

*****

After finishing his burger and downing a second beer, Breznay walked back to his hotel. Instead of going up to his room, he wandered out by the pool in the back to call Threadgill. She answered immediately. "How is it down there? Is it as bad as it looks on the news?"

"Worse," he responded grimly. "The side roads are impassable, mounds of debris as far as you can see. No landline phone service, spotty electric. On the bright side, I get to share a room with some guy from Florida Power and Light. Most of the hotel parking lot is filled with their trucks."

She was unsympathetic. "From what I hear, you're lucky to get a room at all. Most places still aren't open."

253

He wasted no time making his case for early withdrawal. "Vasilevsky can't still be here, boss. He's not the type to try to ride out a hurricane – I'd bet my life on it. He's an aging Russian. Even the Russian mob guys are scared shitless of hurricanes. He evacuated like everybody else."

"You're probably right," she answered. "But as long as you're down there, check out his residence, make sure he's not there. Ask some questions. Maybe they know him at that bar where you had dinner. If they do, maybe they have some idea where he would go."

Breznay was skeptical. "I think it's a stretch that we'll find anything of value, but you're right – I'm already here. I wouldn't mind eating at the Overseas again. The bar has a ring of ice around it that keeps your beer really cold. Never seen anything like it."

"I'm glad you're keeping your observation skills sharp, Agent Breznay," she observed drily. "They're the most important tools in your kit."

"You've trained me well, Agent Threadgill. I owe it all to you."

After the call ended, Breznay returned to his room. The television was on when he came in, and a man was sprawled out on one of the beds, clad only in gym shorts, hair wet, smelling of a recent shower, watching Fox News. He turned toward Breznay. "You the fed?"

Breznay nodded. "That's me. Carl Breznay. You must be the juice man."

The man nodded. "Pete McGrath. I guess we're bunking together." He returned his attention to the television.

Breznay figured he was in his late thirties or early forties, military haircut, a physique sculpted by hours in the gym that was beginning to soften around the middle. "Where you from, Pete?"

"Alachua." As an afterthought. "Near High Springs." His tone flat, discouraging further questioning. Breznay changed the subject. "Mind if I take a shower?"

"Go for it."

As he stood under the soothing spray, he formulated a plan for tomorrow. At first light he'd have a look at Vasilevsky's condo. The sheriff's department was on board; Threadgill had called ahead, alerting them to Breznay's presence but remaining vague as to the details of his agenda.

He doubted he'd find anything – Vasilevsky had ample warning that Irma was on the way. Plenty of time for him to gather anything sensitive and head for the hills. The Overseas Pub opened at 7:00 for breakfast, so he'd be able to get an early start. He might as well get a closeup of the damage and work up a thirst before it gets too hot.

He dried off, toweled his head and donned a pair of his own shorts. He felt like a new man; he bet there weren't a lot of places between Florida City and Key West that had hot running water. He dropped onto his bed. McGrath was still watching television, so Breznay watched, too. Fox wasn't his network of choice – he was a YouTube guy – but a different point of view every once in awhile wasn't a bad thing.

McGrath watched until ten, then shut off the television. He looked at Breznay. "Early day tomorrow."

Breznay waved him off. "No problem. I'd like to get an early start, too."

McGrath shut off his bedside light and rolled over, showing his backside to Breznay. After a few minutes, when McGrath's breathing became regular, Breznay took a photo of Vasilevsky out of the file and studied his features closely, marveling at the bushy eyebrows that reminded him of Brezhnev. The picture was the latest they had, ten years old, but recent enough that he'd still be recognized by the staff if he'd been a patron of the Overseas. Where does a Russian spy go when he's flushed from his American home? Florida was a big state, with lots of nooks and crannies.

The possibilities were endless.

43

As soon as Miller ended his phone call with Gutierrez, he dialed Gavin Tremayne's number. The young analyst picked up immediately. "Tremayne."

"Special Agent Tremayne, this is Special Agent Colton Miller. We spoke the other day."

"Yes, sir, I remember. About a movie."

"Exactly," Miller said. "Do you think you can find some more information about that movie?"

Tremayne thought: no problem. "What do you need?"

"Names. The real names of the cast and crew members, if you can find them. It's obvious some of the names listed in the credits are bogus."

"Shouldn't be a problem, sir," Tremayne replied cockily. "These actors all file their taxes under their real names, which means paychecks would also have been made out to those real names. If I remember correctly, the film was shot in Key West. There aren't a lot of banks there; I can start with the ones that were in business back then and are still in business now. If that doesn't pan out, I have a connection at the IRS."

Miller didn't need to know all the details. "I don't care how you do it, Tremayne. Just get me those names."

"I'm on it, sir."

He started on eBay, searching for a videocassette of the film. Not many porn films from the early days of video had been converted to DVDs, but there was a chance that a VHS or Betamax copy might be out there.

Thirty minutes of searching by title, character names and actors proved fruitless, so he switched to the tube sites. They were all the rage these days: sites that urged owners of previously purchased material to upload anything from brief clips to entire movies to their sites. He started with the most popular of the tube sites, Pornhub, where after twenty minutes of targeted searches he managed to find a short clip from the beginning of the movie that included a full list of the credits.

He mentally patted himself on the back as he downloaded the clip and ran the grainy copy through the Bureau's visual acuity enhancement software, which produced a tighter, cleaner copy he was able to enlarge. From the credits he was able to determine the movie had been produced by Conch Republic Films. He jotted the name down in his notebook before doing the same with the complete listing of cast and crew. He smiled to himself. He'd struck gold in under an hour.

*****

Something was bothering Miller, something he couldn't quite put his finger on. He was sure it had to do with the movie Tremayne was investigating. He leaned back in his chair and closed his eyes, trying to visualize what he felt was a link, some connection he was missing. Something to do with the cast…

His eyes opened as he sat upright. How could he have been so stupid? He reached for the phone, heart pounding in his chest as he dialed Threadgill's number. She picked up on the first ring. "Special Agent Miller. It's been ages."

Miller ignored the sarcasm in his colleague's voice. "I knew I was right about Rheinhart!' he exclaimed. "We need to bring him in right away."

Threadgill balked. "I thought we decided the other day that we would keep an eye on him, but not spook him by bringing him in."

The excitement in his voice was palpable. "That was the other day. Things have changed."

"How so?"

"The porno we talked about a couple of days ago, the movie about the Russians in Key West."

"What about it?"

"Guess who acted in it?"

Threadgill was growing impatient. "Who?"

"Biff Bratwurst," he crowed triumphantly, waiting for her reaction.

"That sounds familiar..."

"It should. That's the screen name of Steve Morrison. The same Steve Morrison who is the only known associate of Zachary Rheinhart since he moved to the Gulf coast from Jacksonville."

The light went on. "The guy who found Middleton's body."

"Exactly. The best friend – the *only* friend - of the guy who discovered the body also starred in the film that kicked the whole process into gear thirty-five years ago. What are the odds that those two things are coincidental?"

He had a point. "Not good," she admitted.

"So you've changed your mind about bringing Rheinhart in for questioning?"

"I guess I have."

They spent the next few minutes considering the options. They agreed that there were only three viable choices: calling

Rheinhart and Morrison in individually, one before the other, or bringing the two of them in together. Miller dismissed the latter immediately and Threadgill concurred, which left them with individual sessions. After some give and take, they agreed to bring Morrison in first, then Rheinhart. If they brought Rheinhart in first, it would give the two a chance to compare notes before they had a chance to talk to Morrison. Calling Morrison in first, on a generic request for assistance in an ongoing investigation, would arouse no suspicions in Rheinhart, whom they felt was likely unaware of Morrison's possible link to the case.

"So we call Morrison in on Monday, and Rheinhart after that," Miller said. It was a statement rather than a question.

Threadgill nodded. "We see what Morrison has to say and what Tremayne can find, then proceed from there."

*****

By noon the next day Tremayne had the material Miller requested. Of the six cast members listed in the credits – Biff Bratwurst, Audrey Heartburn, Kandy Kane, Honey Potts, Dick Cox and Lance Hardman – only two were still alive. Biff Bratwurst, real name Steven Morrison, currently resided in Ozona, Florida, while Audrey Heartburn, birth name Margaret Ann Woodard, was in an assisted living facility in Stockton, California. Kandy Kane and Honey Potts had both succumbed to AIDS during the late 1980s, when the disease spread unchecked through the adult entertainment industry. Dick Cox, birth name Arnold Peabody, died as a result of injuries sustained in an automobile accident in Flagstaff, Arizona in 1997, while Lance Hardman, aka Dexter Cosgrove, was gunned down a year later by an irate husband who discovered Hardman, fortified by a dose of blue steel, banging his wife with enthusiasm after following the couple to a seedy motel in Long Beach.

The most interesting nugget of information uncovered as far as Tremayne was concerned involved the director of the film. He was sure that Les Bent was an alias, but was surprised to find that Leslie Charles Bent, currently living in Islamorada, Florida, was the director's birth name. The only other member of the crew listed in the film's credits was the writer, Carlton Doorman, whom Tremayne discovered to be Francis Carnegie, who'd left the industry shortly after *The Russians Are Coming and Coming and Coming* was completed for an editor's position at a small publishing house in Oxnard that specialized in scientific textbooks.

He input the data into an Excel spreadsheet, then called Miller, who answered on the first ring. "What do you have for me?"

"Not a lot," Tremayne conceded. "Only two of the cast members are still alive, one in Florida, the other in California. The director is living in Florida as well."

"Les Bent?"

"Yeah. Believe it or not, that's his real name." Pause. "How would you like me to send this to you?"

"Attach it to an email."

"I'm sending it to you now." Two clicks later, it was on its way.

"What else are you working on at the moment, Agent Tremayne?"

"Not much," he said. "Doing research for an extortion case involving the Scientologists, but there's no urgency connected with it that I know of."

"How'd you like to do one more thing for me?" Miller asked.

"What do you need?"

261

"Anything you can dig up on Zachary James Rheinhart, age fifty-five, current address 245 Bay Street, Ozona, Florida. Especially any connection he might've had with Steven Morrison before both of them moved to the same hamlet on the Gulf Coast."

Part 3

44

Rheinhart was up with the sun Thursday morning, roused by the piercing chatter between a pair of parrots that had a nest in a palm in his neighbor's yard, beyond the rear boundary of his lot. He didn't mind the avian wakeup call – he'd planned to get an early start today anyway. If he was going to ask Gwen Westphal out on his boat, he wanted it to perform flawlessly on their initial date. It had been sitting on the boat lift at the marina since he'd discovered the body on Anclote Key, and this morning he wanted to take it out in the sound to make sure there would be no surprises if she were to accept his invitation.

He loaded an extra five-gallon gas container in his car and drove down to the 7-11 at the corner of Tampa Road and Alt 19 to fill it, then drove to the marina, parking in the small lot reserved for members. As he exited his car, he noted the low cloud cover and smiled; as long as it didn't rain, he preferred a slightly overcast day on the water to a sunny one. Better visibility when the sun wasn't reflecting off the surface of the Gulf, especially during crab season.

He lowered the boat to the surface before topping off his tank and starting the engine. It turned over immediately; as the engine warmed up, he went through a five-minute instrumentation check. Satisfied that everything was in working order, he backed the boat away from the dock in a gentle circle until the bow was pointing toward the Gulf, then shifted into forward and idled through the channel past the mangrove islands until he reached the end of the no-wake zone.

It had been less than two days since Rheinhart had attended Gwen Westphal's lecture and returned to Ozona with her phone number, and he marveled at the change in his attitude the chance encounter had produced. He'd been obsessing about the dead body he'd discovered for weeks; it had dominated his thoughts, leaving him frustrated and depressed. This morning, as he exited the channel and buried the throttle, bringing his skiff onto plane, his mind was bursting with optimism, a smile plastered on his tanned face. Nothing like the prospect of some female companionship to extricate his spirits from the depths where they'd been hovering for several years, since the disaster in Jacksonville. It seemed like ages since he'd looked to the future with any sense of anticipation.

He sped north past Three Rookers, his eyes on the water ahead, looking for crab traps and monitoring the depth finder in the shallow sound as he approached Fred Howard Park. The only sign of life this early at the peninsular park was one of the county employees on a compact four-wheeler with a rake attached to its rear, cruising the tide line, smoothing the sand on the beach before the arrival of today's visitors.

*****

In Miami, Cesar Gutierrez was in his office, going over the evidence compiled so far in the Middleton case, trying to piece together the biggest outstanding mystery stalling the investigation: the motive behind two Russian assassins murdering one of their most valuable assets, a deep cover covert agent who had been living and operating in the United States his entire life.

He'd gone over the monthly reports Breznay had compiled as a result of his monitoring of Middleton in detail, and one of the more interesting trends that emerged was the lack of variation in Middleton's daily routine. He drove to the office each morning on Captiva, put in a full day's work, then returned to his apartment in Fort Myers, which he left only rarely for trips to purchase food or to visit his mother in Cape Coral. He'd been working at Junonia Realty for seven years with middling success in a highly competitive field; without subsidy payments from Moscow, his commissions would have scarcely covered the monthly rent on his studio apartment. Why had he stayed so long in a job for which he seemed barely competent? His handlers must have wanted him on Captiva, in the real estate business, for some reason. The list of Middleton's current clients Breznay had acquired from Junonia Realty was sparse, but Gutierrez's instincts led him to believe it offered the most logical thread for further inquiry.

Also, why had his murderers removed his tongue? They'd killed him with a new strain of poison that was virtually undetectable. If they'd left his mouth intact, it might've taken months for the true cause of Middleton's death to be determined. Was there a personal aspect to the killing, or was the removal of the victim's tongue merely a red herring designed to send law enforcement in the wrong direction?

He wasn't confident that Breznay would find anything of value in Marathon, which was unfortunate. With the two suspects in Russia, out of their reach, they needed to find Vasilevsky, or some evidence from a different source that would point toward a motive. Without that, they were just pissing into the wind.

*****

Because Miller had minced no words about the importance of his new assignment, Tremayne worked twenty hours straight, fortified by Mountain Dew and Oreos, and had the results of his investigation into Rheinhart's background ready for Miller when he came into the office the next morning. Once he'd found Rheinhart's Social Security number by utilizing a backdoor into the IRS mainframe, a task that took him less than five minutes, it was simply a matter of how far back to go. A quick call to Miller confirmed he was primarily interested in the period of time since

Rheinhart moved to Jacksonville, so the young analyst concentrated on that.

Like many of his colleagues at the Bureau, Tremayne had grown uncomfortable with the current administration's assault on the intelligence community, so an assignment that on its surface had nothing to do with Russia or Russians was a welcome relief, one into which he plunged with enthusiasm. This sort of short-term, intensive research that Miller had requested was the perfect device to keep him away from being sucked into the sort of volatile chatter by the water cooler that had the potential to derail one's career.

Zachary James Rheinhart had been born in Ridgewood, New Jersey, in 1962, the only child of Thomas and Elaine Rheinhart. After a standout academic record at Ridgewood High School, he'd received a scholarship from the Rhode Island School of Design, where he graduated *magna cum laude* in 1984 and accepted a position with a major architectural firm in New York City, primarily to remain in proximity to his mother, who had been diagnosed with Stage 4 breast cancer during the fall semester of his senior year of college.

After his mother died in May of 1985, Zach continued to work in Manhattan, moving up the corporate ladder with alacrity, reaching the position of vice president before he turned thirty. But he was uncomfortable living and working in the most populous city in the country, and he began to discreetly explore other employment options. When Gunn Design, headquartered in Grand Island, New York, ten miles north of Buffalo, offered him the position of Director of Design of the firm's new Corporate/Commercial Group, he accepted the challenge eagerly. He was forty-two.

Five years later he was offered a similar position in another new division of the firm, the Federal Contracts Group, but with it came a stipulation – relocation to Jacksonville, Florida, to oversee the design and construction of the new federal courthouse building in Duval County. He sold his home in New York, purchased a condo overlooking the St. John River in downtown Jacksonville, where his carefully crafted career slowly began to unravel as the courthouse project encountered a string of schedule delays and resultant cost overruns that eventually halted the project, bringing Gunn Design to the brink of litigation, costing Rheinhart his job and precipitating his move to Ozona, on the Gulf Coast.

The only connection Tremayne could find between Rheinhart and Morrison prior to both of them moving to Ozona was hardly a connection at all. Steven Morrison had been born in Niagara Falls, New York and raised in the area until 1970, when he left home and moved to San Diego. That was more than twenty years before Rheinhart moved from Manhattan to Grand Island, a few miles south of Niagara Falls. Tremayne dismissed any significance to the apparent geographical link, chalking it up in a footnote to the report as mere coincidence.

But when Miller sat down and read a copy of Tremayne's research report, he wasn't about to dismiss that earlier connection between the two men as cavalierly as the young analyst had. Experience had taught him that coincidence, particularly in his line of work, almost always failed to hold up under intense scrutiny.

Especially when investigating persons of interest.

45

The Overseas Pub and Grill had been the first business in the middle of the Keys to reopen after Irma roared through, and the dedication of a small band of employees who'd stayed behind to ride out the storm rather than evacuate had transposed the haven for long-time Conchs and refugees from faster paced and colder climes in the north into Recovery Central in the aftermath of the hurricane. Before the storm, they opened at 11:00 am for lunch, but somehow the restaurant had managed to temporarily add breakfast to their menu despite manpower shortages and the difficulty of arranging food deliveries from the mainland.

When Breznay arrived shortly after seven the next morning, he was amazed at the number of trucks in the parking lot as he walked through the door. Inside, the place was a cacophony of sound as police, firefighters, EMTs, utility workers and a few hardcore locals filled every seat in the place. Shaking his head in amazement, he continued on to the outdoor bar in the back, usually reserved for the smoking crowd, where he was able to find a seat at one of the tables adjacent to the small stage area reserved for musical performances.

He scanned the restaurant, looking for his roommate who had already left the Marriott by the time Breznay woke up, but didn't see him. The close-mouthed McGrath had offered no clue the night before as to where he would be working today – judging by the raucous scene around him, he might not have known where he was going until he received his orders earlier that morning at the restaurant.

He shifted his attention back to the menu, taped to his table, which offered toast, English muffins, bagels, coffee, tea and orange juice only. There were no waiters or waitresses – all employees were working in the kitchen – so when Breznay decided on coffee and a bagel, he trudged up to the door to the kitchen and placed his order with a harried young man who looked like he hadn't slept in days. The man jotted his order down on a pad of paper and asked Breznay his name before telling him, "Check back in fifteen minutes."

He returned to his table and tried his cell phone – no service available, just as he'd figured. Agent Threadgill had supplied him with a secure satellite phone before he'd departed, but had cautioned him to use it only if absolutely necessary. "We're pretty low on the necessity totem pole down there," she'd advised.

While he waited he went over his plan for the day, which hinged mightily on whether or not structural damage to the complex would prevent him from accessing Vasilevsky's second-floor unit. He scanned the crowd, looking for someone who might be associated with FEMA, but it was a hopeless task. Only the police and a few of the utility workers wore outfits defining their affiliations; most of the crowd was dressed like him, in slacks, cotton shorts, work boots and hats to protect against the tropical sun.

When his food was ready he gulped down his coffee and took his bagel with him. He'd parked in the rear of the building, near the original route of the Overseas Highway before it was destroyed during the great hurricane of 1937. He waited patiently, munching on his bagel, as a steady stream of vehicles heading south passed by before a gap appeared and he was able to turn left onto the highway, heading north.

271

Vasilevsky's condominium was several miles to the north, on the Atlantic side, and as he drove he once again marveled at the extent of the destruction the storm had wrought, wondering how much worse the damage could be further south, where the storm had made landfall. Mounds of twisted metal flanked both sides of the highway, remnants of homes and lives now consigned to the scrap heap, many of them unlikely to be rebuilt.

He drove slowly, carefully as he approached the access road to the complex. Most of the road signs were down, so he was using some overhead satellite imagery he'd downloaded before he left Captiva. When he saw the road he thought was the right one, he turned onto it and immediately pulled as far off the pavement as he could to check the imagery, which agreed with his decision.

Fifty yards ahead, the access road was blocked by downed trees and power lines, so he parked his truck, grabbed a backpack he'd loaded with some basic tools, including heavy-duty bolt cutters and his service weapon, and continued on foot. The air was warm and humid as he proceeded slowly, scanning the ground for snakes and other wildlife that might've been displaced by the storm, careful to avoid the live power lines that were strewn along the south side of the road.

It took him nearly an hour to reach the condominium complex, but he knew that his mission was futile long before he reached his destination. From the condition of the access road, it was obvious no efforts had occurred thus far to clear the damage on the way in, which meant the complex was untouched as well, in the same condition it was after the storm had moved north, toward Naples and the mainland.

He was sweating profusely by the time he reached the three-story complex. As per code, the first level of the structure was open, used for vehicle parking, storage of beach paraphernalia and as a conduit for storm surge during a hurricane event. The building's structure looked largely intact, with about half the windows blown out, as Breznay searched for a staircase to reach the upper floors. The Monroe County official he'd spoken to two days earlier warned him about trying to access any building that hadn't yet been structurally assessed, which, he admitted, were most of the buildings in the Keys. "You're on your own down here," he'd advised gravely. "If you fuck up and you're by yourself, there's no Plan B. Nobody will be coming to your rescue."

He walked carefully among the debris around the exterior of the building until he spied a door in the middle of the complex that led to a staircase. He tried the door; it was locked. Unfazed, he shrugged the backpack off his shoulders, donned a pair of latex gloves and extracted a pry bar, which he managed to insert between the door and the frame enough to lever the door open after fifteen minutes of concentrated effort.

A pungent mixture of mildew and decaying food overwhelmed him as he ascended the staircase. He slipped on a surgical facemask as he exited onto the second floor and began looking for Vasilevsky's door, his flashlight illuminating the darkened hallway. About half of the doorways had been left open by residents before they departed, heeding the advice of state officials who'd informed the residents that open doors could help to minimize damage caused by high winds.

Vasilevsky was not one of those compliant residents; his door was closed and locked, so Breznay pulled out the pry bar and worked on the door until he'd managed to pop the lock. Inside, the place was a shambles: broken glass was everywhere on the floor, as Vasilevsky had either not attempted to board his windows in any way or had run out of time to do so as the storm approached. He proceeded to the master bedroom, stepping carefully over the shards of glass in his path. If the Russian had left anything of value in the condo, Breznay figured it would be in his bedroom, possibly in a wall safe.

His hopes were dashed as he entered the room and scanned the walls of the room and the small, walk-in closet – there was no safe. The carpeting under his feet was soaked and made a squishing sound as he swallowed his disappointment and began a methodical search of the room. He checked the mostly emptied drawers for false bottoms, but found none. He checked between the mattress and box spring, but came up empty. There was a shelf above the headboard of the king-sized bed that contained a few books, mostly paperbacks, and he riffled through the pages of each one by one searching for a scrap of paper, anything, that might yield a clue, but was disappointed again.

His gaze fell on a chest of drawers against the wall, opposite the end of the bed. He'd inspected each of the drawers, finding nothing of interest. But he noticed a small space between the bottom of the piece and the floor of the bedroom, a space certainly large enough to conceal the kind of information he was seeking. He wrestled with the chest, moving it away from the wall and twisting it sideways before toppling it over on its backside.

Pay dirt. Underneath the chest of drawers, taped to the underside of the unit, was a manila envelope that had suffered some damage from the water that had infiltrated the bedroom through the windows blown out by the storm. He went into his backpack, extracted the largest evidence bag he had, gingerly removed the envelope and placed it in the evidence bag, which he promptly taped shut and labeled before placing it inside the backpack.

He was elated. He'd found something he hadn't expected to find – a reason to get out of the Keys immediately and return to Captiva. Or maybe Threadgill would want the envelope delivered directly to Clearwater, which certainly wouldn't hurt his standing among his fellow agents, most of whom had dismissed him as incompetent or worse after he'd lost track of Chad Middleton.

As much as he wanted to know what was inside the envelope, he fought off the urge to open it. The last thing he needed to do was something stupid like interrupting the chain of custody protocol that applied to the collection of newly discovered evidence.

Although he felt he already had the holy grail he'd been seeking, he continued to process the entire unit for another hour, finding nothing, but covering his ass as far as the thoroughness of his search was concerned.

When he was finished, he exited the room, making sure he'd left nothing behind, and made his way down the stairs to ground level. As he walked through the door into the parking lot, he pulled of his facemask, revealing a grin so wide it could illuminate a darkened room,

Things were definitely looking up.

46

An insistent bladder, the bane of uninterrupted sleep worldwide, forced Steve Morrison from his bed shortly after dawn Thursday morning. Figuring it was futile to try to get back to sleep, he slipped on a pair of shorts and brewed a pot of coffee as he turned on the television to check the day's weather. When he first moved to Florida, he'd been baffled by the local populace's obsession with the weather. Having spent more than forty years in California and its similarly mild climate, he'd been much more concerned with the traffic, only giving the weather a thought when it threatened his ability to get from Point A to Point B.

But he soon found that monitoring the weather, sometimes on an hourly basis, was as critical to Floridians as the intake of food and water, especially among retirees, the segment of the population for whom travel during periods of inclement weather was largely voluntary. Talking about the weather was the universal common ground, a sure-fire conversation starter when faced with an unfamiliar social situation. Everyone in Florida had an opinion about the weather.

So he switched on The Weather Channel and walked outside to get the morning paper, which was deposited daily at the end of his driveway by a former auto worker from Flint whose pension had been downsized after his retirement. As he straightened with the paper in his hand, he glanced down toward the marina and saw Rheinhart lowering his boat from its lift onto the water. He smiled. His friend hadn't logged a single hour in his boat since he'd discovered the body. It was about time he climbed back into the saddle again. He wondered why his friend hadn't mentioned an outing on the water during their lunch yesterday. Maybe it was an impromptu decision, simply a result of getting up on the right side of the bed this morning.

Morrison stifled an urge to wave and instead went back inside his house. He spent ninety minutes reading the paper from front to back, sipping his coffee, The Weather Channel droning on in the background as the sun cleared the treeline, gradually filling his front room with morning light.

When he'd finished with the editorial page, he set the paper down and contemplated the weekend ahead. He was afraid he'd overbooked for Saturday, trying to squeeze an early-morning dive in on the Rainbow River with DeWayne Bologna before meeting the crew from Fuego at Skipper's Smokehouse for some live music the same evening. This morning he was leaning more toward a trip to Skipper's – there would always be another opportunity to dive, with the cooler weather approaching, but Skipper's was a place he'd wanted to experience for months. The local public radio station he listened to from Tampa sponsored a lot of concerts there, and the folks at Kitty Galore's, especially Gracie, all had high praise for the ramshackle outdoor music venue and restaurant. "Great people, great music, great food," Gracie had enthused yesterday when Morrison mentioned that he was planning to visit on Saturday. "There's nothing like listening to great music under the live oaks and the stars."

He decided to wait until 11:00 to call Bologna, who was a night owl. He filled in the time by comprising a grocery list for the upcoming week and calling his roofing contractor again. When no one answered, he left yet another message indicating his patience with their response time to his damaged roof was ebbing, then hopped into the shower.

When he was dressed, he dialed the dive shop. "Gulfside Scuba."

The voice was familiar, but not Bologna's. After a moment's pause he responded. "Pops?"

Vinnie "Pops" Ranalli was a retired postal worker from New Hampshire who was Bologna's right-hand man, both in the dive shop and on the water. He answered in a voice tinged with impatience. "You got him. What can I do for you?"

"It's Steve Morrison, Pops. I was looking for DeWayne."

"Hi ho, Steverino," Pops replied. "DeWayne's having the oil changed in his truck this morning. Should be in about noon. Anything I can help you with?"

"Uh, yeah, there is. Could you take my name off the list for Saturday's dive on the Rainbow River? Something's come up and I can't make it.

"What's her name?"

Morrison blushed at the other end of the phone. How did he know? "Uh, it's not like that…"

The dive shop assistant wasn't buying it. "Whatever you say, Steverino. As far as I'm concerned, there's only two reasons to cancel a dive trip – a funeral or pussy. You don't sound too broken up, so I'm goin' with the latter."

Morrison tried to change the subject. "Tell DeWayne not to worry about the deposit. He can keep it, bein' the last minute and all."

"No need to worry about that. It's probably paying for his oil change as we speak."

They chatted for a few more minutes, mostly about the water quality lately, before Pops asked, "You plannin' to join us on our trip to the Keys next month? We'll be divin' the reef in Key Largo, lookin' for bugs."

Morrison smiled at the diver's slang for lobster. "Sign me up. We stayin' in the same place as last year?"

"Yep. DeWayne gets a good deal from those folks. He's been stayin' there for years." Pops hesitated before continuing in a mock serious tone. "You gotta let us know in advance if you're bringin' a date. Might mean the difference between sleeping in a bed or on the couch."

"I've never brought a date before, Pops. What makes you think I'd bring one this year?"

"I don't know," he said airily. "There's just something about a man who cancels a dive trip at the last minute…"

*****

Gracie glanced at the clock on her dashboard as she waited impatiently for the light at Tarpon Avenue and U.S. 19, already late for work. She'd been unable to start her car this morning and had to wait for AAA, since Hank had left for work hours ago. The attendant showed up in thirty minutes, tested her battery and declared it dead. She fumed and fidgeted, calling the bar with the news she would be late while he retrieved a new battery from his truck and installed it, shaking his head and muttering, "Nothing kills a battery like the Florida sun."

By the time he finished and she was on the road, it was 10:05. She was scheduled to start work at 10:00, so she'd notified Manolo, one of the bus boys, that she'd be about half an hour late. "Is Florence in yet?" she asked anxiously.

He responded in his accented, clipped English. "I have not seen her."

As she drove, her thoughts turned to Marcia Alvarez. The chain-smoking lunch regular had not shown up at the restaurant for three days, and she was worried that something might have happened involving her father – either he'd finally pissed off the

279

two women who watched him for an hour while Marcia snuck away to Kitty's each day, causing them to quit, or his health, always fragile, had worsened. Whatever had occurred was dire enough to prevent the beleaguered daughter from the only respite she enjoyed each day from the overbearing, caustic Clement Harkins. For Marcia to miss lunch for three consecutive days, it had to be something serious.

She pulled into the parking lot behind the restaurant at 10:31. Pretty good time, she thought to herself, as she walked rapidly over the crushed shell surface, through the back door to the kitchen. She was greeted sarcastically by Polly, the day shift manager, who was in the kitchen, sampling the soup of the day as Gracie scurried by. "Glad you could make it," she crowed between tastings. "Power go out?"

"Dead battery," Gracie replied flatly as she headed for the entrance to the bar area. Manolo was behind the bar, slicing lemons and limes in her absence, a sheepish grin on his face when she appeared. He put down his knife and stepped aside. "You made good time."

"Only hit one light," she said as she stowed her purse beneath the bar before walking over to him and giving him a big hug. "Thanks for covering for me."

"You owe me one."

"Still no Florence?" she queried, looking around.

Manolo shook his head. "I asked Polly if she was coming in. She said Florence and Walter were headed to a cabin in Georgia for a long weekend."

Gracie made a face. "The last time they took a trip like that, we ended up with a stuffed moose head on the wall."

Manolo, who'd refined his English skills by devouring Hollywood classics, grinned from ear to ear. "Maybe they'll come back with a toothless banjo player this time."

Gracie gave him a playful nudge. "I'd prefer Burt Reynolds."

47

The answer came to Gutierrez at 4:45 Friday morning. He'd awoken as he always did to pee – he drank too much coffee; once again, he promised himself he would cut back – and had trouble getting back to sleep. Restless, he went over the evidence again in his mind as he lay in bed, trying to connect the dots between Middleton and the as-yet unknown motive for his murder. The other question yet to be answered was this: did Middleton have an assignment at the time of his murder, or was he merely waiting for one? In either case, there likely was a link to the elusive motive.

It was that link that materialized as he gazed at the ceiling of his bedroom. Suddenly, sleep was no longer an option. He grabbed his phone from his bedside table and called Miller, whose slurred response told Gutierrez Miller had been asleep. "What is it, sir?"

"How soon can you get to the office?"

Miller glanced at his phone in the darkness, still laden with sleep. "What time is it now?"

"A little after five."

"I could be there by six."

"Good," Gutierrez said. "Call Threadgill and have her there, too."

"What's so important?" Miller asked sleepily.

"I think I figured out what Middleton was up to when he was killed."

*****

Threadgill had grumbled a bit when Miller's call woke her up, but she managed to make it into the office at 6:10. "This better be good," she stated flatly as she collapsed into Miller's guest chair. "You interrupted the best night's sleep I've had in a month."

"He woke me up, too," he replied defensively. "Sometimes I think he doesn't sleep at all, just works."

The light from Miller's corner office was the only illumination in the darkened office as he dialed Gutierrez's number and placed the phone on speaker mode. Gutierrez picked up on the first ring. "Is Agent Threadgill with you?"

"Right here, sir."

"Good. What's the latest at your end?"

The two agents in Clearwater exchanged glances. Threadgill nodded toward Miller: you tell him. "Agent Breznay found a manila envelope in Vasilevsky's condo in Marathon, taped to the bottom of a chest of drawers in his bedroom. It's being processed right now. We should have the results later this morning."

"He didn't look inside the envelope?"

This time Threadgill answered. "No sir. Just bagged and tagged it and drove straight here with it yesterday."

"Let me know what the lab says ASAP." He paused for a moment before continuing. "I couldn't sleep last night and was going over the clues we had so far when it hit me. Why would the Russians want Middleton to stay in that realtor's job when he wasn't very good at it? The history you dug up on his sales performance and commissions at Junonia Realty were mediocre, at best. So why did he stay?"

Miller and Threadgill looked at one another, puzzled. Gutierrez continued, his voice rising as he answered his own question. "He stayed because of the mantra of all realtors; location, location, location. He stayed at Junonia Realty because his mission involved someone on the island, someone the Russians wanted to get to."

Miller broke in eagerly. "That's a good theory, sir. Captiva is loaded with celebrities, business tycoons, all sorts of retired millionaires and billionaires from the U.S. and overseas. It's a target-rich environment for some sort of Russian operation."

"Exactly. But you forgot the least visible, most likely target of them all. Supreme Court Justice Ramona Hancock."

Dead silence. Finally, Miller spoke, his voice filled with wonder. "Why do you think it's her?"

"Because of Middleton's client list. It took me a while, but I finally figured it out. There were only six names on the list Breznay got from the receptionist at the realty office. Five of those names involved people who were looking to buy on the island, your usual run-of-the-mill folks with more money than they know what to do with, looking to buy their own piece of paradise." He paused for effect. "But there was only one name on that list that was being solicited by Middleton himself, only one client whose property *he* was interested in. So interested that he went back to the property multiple times, trying to get the owner to sell, without any luck. According to Breznay's report, Middleton never even connected with the property's owner, just the hippie who's staying there, the caretaker or whatever he is."

Threadgill was scrambling though her notes, eventually finding the item she was looking for. "Thomas Martin's property."

"Yes," Gutierrez said decisively. "Thomas Martin's property. He owns one of the last small cottages on the island. Most of the other original properties like his had been knocked down and replaced with statement homes, really big places. So I think Middleton's play was this – he was posing as the agent for an unknown, secretive buyer who wanted to do exactly that, buy Martin's property and knock down his shack to replace it with a McMansion. But he couldn't get past the caretaker to even make an offer to the owner. The Russians wanted that property very badly, and when he couldn't deliver, they decided to take Middleton out, to try to reach Martin with someone else who could convince him to sell. The plan may even have been to simply remove Middleton and replace him with another agent, swap new for old. But something might have gone wrong, and those two Russian agents ended up killing him instead of simply relocating him. If that's the case, then the reason for removing his tongue becomes plausible – it was a red herring designed to throw law enforcement off the real scent."

Miller and Threadgill considered Gutierrez's theory. Although it had some holes, it made as much sense as anything offered thus far. It was Threadgill who finally spoke. "But why did the Russians want that particular property so badly?"

"Because of its location," Gutierrez replied. "It was the ideal spot in the ideal neighborhood for what they had planned."

"Which was?" Miller asked.

"The assassination of a sitting Supreme Court Justice, perhaps the most liberal justice currently seated. The Honorable Ramona Hancock. Her vacation home is five doors down from Martin's cottage, easily accessible via Roosevelt Channel. If they could take possession of Martin's house, they'd be only several hundred feet by water from their target."

Miller considered Gutierrez's idea for a moment before responding. "It fits, I suppose, but there's still a lot of conjecture involved, a lot of threads unconnected by tangible evidence. As far as we know now, there's nothing to indicate the Russians' interest in such a brazen plot."

"You're right," Gutierrez allowed. "But at this point, it's better than anything else we've dug up. If we can find something linking Middleton to Hancock, I'd bet the *casita* that we're on the right track." Pause. "The Russians are on a roll. They fucked with the election, manipulating it enough so their guy became president, against all odds, with no repercussions so far, at least until Bob Mueller files his report. Right now, they're flush with confidence - they think they can get away with anything, so why not take a shot at one of the liberal court justices? If their candidate could push another conservative through the nomination process onto the court, it would be several generations before that kind of judicial influence could be turned back in the other direction. If the president gets re-elected, it might take as long as fifty years to undo the damage."

The two mulled Gutierrez's bold theory for a few moments before Miller responded. "What's our next move?"

"We need to find a connection between Middleton and Hancock. Something that tells us we're on the right trail." Gutierrez continued. "Call me as soon as the package Breznay pulled out of Vasilevsky's condo is processed. I want to know what was important enough to conceal under his dresser, but not important enough to take with him when he left the Keys."

"It may be something as simple as his little black book," Threadgill said. "We know he has a taste for high-priced pussy. Or maybe he just forgot it when it was time to evacuate."

"Could be," conceded Gutierrez. "Or it could be something that points us in the direction that confirms my theory." He chuckled lightly. "I've always been a glass-half-full guy. I'm hoping optimism carries the day here. We could use a break."

Miller remained cautious. "I hope you're right." He thought Gutierrez's theory was a real longshot, but he didn't want to dissuade his boss from his optimistic stance. "I'll let you know as soon as the new evidence is processed."

"I'll be waiting."

48

"What do you think?"

The conference call with Gutierrez had ended, and Miller and Threadgill were in Miller's office, door closed, sipping coffee as the rest of the office began to slowly come to life. Threadgill shrugged her shoulders. "At this point, I'm willing to try anything. We don't have much to go on."

Miller, who had concerns with some of Gutierrez's assumptions, was careful not to second guess his superior in front of Threadgill. "I agree. That's why I want to bring Rheinhart in, shake the tree, see what falls out."

"I guess it can't hurt," Threadgill conceded. "How do you want to play it?"

"I want you to interview him alone, since you're the one who interviewed Morrison. I'll be watching through the glass."

"When?"

"Today, if we can."

*****

Rheinhart slept in Friday morning. He'd stayed up late watching a movie, one of his favorites, Hitchcock's *Strangers on a Train*, and hadn't made it to bed until nearly 2:00 am, hours past his normal bedtime. He was just finishing drying himself after his shower when his phone rang. It was 8:52. "Zach Rheinhart."

"Mr. Rheinhart, this is Agent Angela Threadgill of the Clearwater office of the FBI. Is this a bad time?"

Stunned, it took him a moment to respond. "No, no, not at all."

"I was wondering if you could come in today and answer a few questions about one of our ongoing investigations. Strictly voluntary, of course."

"Does this have something to do with the body I discovered on Anclote Key a few weeks ago?"

"I can't reveal that sort of information over the phone, Mr. Rheinhart," she replied in a neutral tone. "I can tell you that it shouldn't take more than an hour or so, and there's no need for you to bring counsel with you. It's just an informal chat."

Rheinhart wondered if there was any such thing as an informal chat where the FBI was concerned. "I have some time today. I could probably be there by 11:00."

"That would be wonderful, Mr. Rheinhart. You know where we're located?"

Morrison had described the office in detail after his interview. "On Cleveland, just off Fort Harrison?"

"That's it. I look forward to seeing you at 11:00."

Rheinhart was elated – despite Agent Threadgill's refusal to answer if this was about the dead body, there was no other reason for the FBI to be interested in anything he had to say. Finally, someone wanted to hear his version of that morning. But the FBI? Why were the feds interested in the death of a real estate agent, even one whose tongue had been excised?

His mind was churning with possibilities as he shaved and dressed. Checking himself in the mirror to make sure he hadn't drawn blood with his new blade, he donned a white polo shirt, tan khakis and boat shoes without socks, his formal wear. He contemplated calling Morrison before he left, but decided against it

– he'd have a lot more to talk about once he found out what the FBI was interested in learning from him.

Traffic was unexpectedly heavy as Rheinhart turned onto Alt 19 from Tampa Road. It seemed the high season, with continually congested roads, lasted all year now, the result of highly successful promotional campaigns initiated by several local Chambers of Commerce, causing the locals, a group in which Rheinhart now included himself, to grumble about the traffic constantly. Real First World problems, the White Privilege edition, Gracie Fenton had stated, heavy on the sarcasm, when he'd complained about the constant traffic at the bar.

He followed a minivan with Wisconsin plates all the way through Dunedin into Clearwater, where he turned left onto Cleveland. It was a pleasant morning, a little overcast, temperature in the high 70s, and Scientologists dominated the pedestrian traffic in Clearwater in their distinctive outfits: white dress shirts or blouses, dark slacks or skirts. Rheinhart wondered if the location of FBI headquarters less than a block from The Flag, the anchor building of the Church of Scientology, was a coincidence.

Morrison had told him there was a covered parking area behind the building, so he pulled in and used the walkway to enter from the rear. He scanned the building's directory in the foyer, and filed into the elevator, hitting the button for the 5th floor.

He exited from the elevator. Several feet ahead sat the receptionist Maria, who gave him a warm smile as he approached. "I'm here to see Agent Threadgill."

"Mr. Rheinhart?" He nodded. "I'll take you to her office."

After she'd relieved him of his cell phone, he followed her through a maze of cubicles to one of the outer offices, where a youngish blond woman sat at her desk, intent on the computer screen in front of her. She looked up when Maria tapped timidly on the glass, waving him in as she rose to her feet. "Come in, Mr. Rheinhart," she said, offering him a firm handshake. "Can I get you something to drink? Coffee? Tea? Water?" She indicated a guest chair opposite her desk.

"Water would be nice," he said as he settled into the chair. Threadgill was attractive, in her mid thirties, younger than he had expected. Maria turned quickly and was back in a moment with some bottled water. She closed the door on her way back to the reception area.

"I hope you don't mind if I record our session, Mr. Rheinhart," she said, indicating a recorder on the table between them. "It's standard operating procedure."

"Fine with me." He leaned forward, elbows on his knees, eager to find out why he was here.

Threadgill turned on the recorder, recited their names and the date and time and then looked expectantly at Rheinhart. "Ready?"

"As I'll ever be."

"Good. To the best of your recollection, can you tell me your whereabouts on the morning of October 13 of this year?"

Bingo. "I was up early, out in my boat, hoping to take some pictures of a small boat I had seen on Anclote Key the day before. It looked like it had been washed ashore during Irma."

Threadgill looked at him intently. "If you were on the key the day before, why didn't you photograph the boat then?"

"My phone had run out of its charge, dead as a doornail. I decided to come back first thing the next morning, before another storm could shift it or even sweep it away. It was on the high tide line, but if another storm blew in, I was afraid it might be gone."

"Did you see anything else while you were there that first day?"

Rheinhart nodded. "The boat's engine – at least I figured it was the boat's engine. It was lying in the sand near the boat, the cowl missing, filled with sand."

Threadgill jotted a note, then looked up. "Are you a professional photographer, Mr. Rheinhart?"

He shook his head. "Hardly. It's a new hobby of mine, something to keep me busy."

Threadgill knew about his employment situation, how he had left Jacksonville in disgrace, so she didn't follow up. Instead, she asked, "So there was nothing else that first day that you saw that was unusual?"

"No. Just the boat and motor."

"What about the next day, when you went back?"

Rheinhart took a deep breath. He hoped Threadgill hadn't noticed. "I got to the sandbar just after first light, a little after six. I wanted to shoot the boat and motor in the morning light. I beached my skiff on the eastern shoreline, where I normally do, and began to walk across the sand toward the boat, which was on the Gulf side. That's when I saw him."

"Him?"

"A man, sitting in one of those low rider beach chairs. There isn't much elevation on the south end of the key, but he was sitting on the highest point of land." He smiled. "Maybe two feet above sea level."

"What did you do next?"

"I waved, but he didn't move or respond in any way, so I moved closer. I thought he might've fallen asleep in the sun and I didn't want him to get burned, so I moved in to jostle him, try to wake him up. That's when I discovered he wasn't sleeping – he was dead."

"How did you determine that?"

"His skin was cold to the touch, so I bent down to get a closer look, to see if he was breathing. He wasn't."

"What did you do next?"

"I called the Pinellas County Sheriff's office. They sent a couple of boats out, one to process the crime scene, one with a couple of detectives who asked me the same sort of questions you're asking me today."

"How long did the questioning last?"

"Most of the day. It was late afternoon when they finally said I could go home."

"What happened next?"

"Nothing. The detectives who interviewed me, Kullmann and Profeta, never followed up with any additional questions. I thought that was strange, especially because of ___." Rheinhart stopped, unsure of how to proceed. He still hadn't told anyone in law enforcement about the other pictures he took.

"Because of what?" Threadgill was looking at him intently, pen poised above a pad of paper.

They'd reached the point Rheinhart had worried about for a month now – how to handle the additional pictures he'd taken on his Nikon, pictures he'd concealed from the Pinellas County detectives. Pictures of a man without a tongue. He'd told himself he would avoid the subject if he could, but if he was asked directly about it, he would tell the truth. He told her the truth. "Because I noticed that someone had cut out the man's tongue when I bent down to see if he was breathing."

No reaction. "What else did you notice?"

Rheinhart took a nervous sip of water. It was like she was reading his mind. "There was a business card in the man's right hand."

"Did you read it?"

Rheinhart nodded. "I accidentally knocked it out of his hand when I pulled back after feeling how cold he was. I panicked a bit, I guess. I picked the card up off the sand and read it before I put it back in his hand. I told the detectives about that."

"Can you remember what the card said?"

"Chad Middleton, Junonia Realty. It had a phone number and email address on it, but I don't remember those."

"Did you take any pictures of the body?"

Rheinhart exhaled. Here goes. "I did," he admitted. "I took two closeups of the man's mouth, without the tongue, and I photographed his business card."

Threadgill extracted a sheet of paper from the file in front of her, read it, then glanced up. "According to the report written by the detectives, there was no mention of any photographs." She looked at him intently. "Why is that?"

"Because I didn't tell them I had my Nikon with me," he confessed sheepishly. "I hid it in one of the live wells in my skiff, under some cloth. They never searched it."

"What was your plan in withholding those photos from the police?" Non accusatory, merely curious.

"I've asked myself that question a million times, but I still don't have a good answer. Maybe I thought I could sell them to the *Tampa Bay Times* when the story broke, but it never did. I searched everywhere on the Internet, looking for a story about the discovery of a dead real estate agent who'd had his tongue cut out, but there was nothing." He took another sip of water before continuing. "I couldn't understand how that could happen in the Internet age, where everything goes viral in real time."

"Do you still have those photos?"

Rheinhart nodded. "They're still on my camera."

"Have you shown them to anyone or told anyone about them?"

"I haven't showed them to anyone, but I did talk about them with a friend who didn't believe my story."

"Did you tell anyone else about the existence of those photos?"

"No."

"What's the name of the friend to whom you showed the pictures?"

"Steve Morrison. He's a friend of mine in Ozona."

Threadgill jotted down another note as Rheinhart continued. "You interviewed him on Monday of this week."

She looked up, surprised. "He told you about that?"

He nodded. "He did. It's not every day you get interviewed by the FBI. He couldn't figure out why you were interested in some movie he made years ago in Key West."

"Are you aware of Mr. Morrison's alias?"

"His screen name? Sure. He told me about it after your interview with him last Monday."

"But not before that? How long have you known Mr. Morrison?"

"Ever since I moved to Ozona, about two years ago. As far as telling me about his acting career, you could probably tell from interviewing him that getting him to give up details about his personal life is like getting blood from a rock. The guy isn't exactly the chatty type."

A faint smile appeared on Threadgill's face. "That's an interesting observation. So you think he didn't share the information about the body or the pictures with anyone else?"

"The pictures, no. We told the story to Gracie Fenton, but made her promise not to tell anyone else."

Threadgill wrote down the name. "Who's Gracie Fenton?"

"She's the weekday bartender at Kitty Galore's Raw Bar in Ozona. Morrison and I have lunch there every week."

Threadgill was dubious. "Bartender? What makes you think she'll keep your secret?"

"She's not some ditz – she's a pro, been tending bar her whole life, probably for nearly thirty years. She knows how to keep a secret – especially where future tips are involved."

Threadgill straightened up, placing her pen on the pad of paper in front of her. She smiled at Rheinhart as she spoke again. "This concludes the interview with Zachary Rheinhart," she said, turning the recorder off as she rose to her feet. "Thank you for your cooperation, Mr. Rheinhart," she said, extending her hand. "You've been a big help."

Rheinhart rose. "That's it? You don't want to see the photos I took?"

"That's not necessary – we have the crime scene photos from the Pinellas County Sheriff's office. You can pick up your cell phone and parking validation slip from Maria on your way out."

Rheinhart hesitated. "Am I free to leave town?"

Threadgill smiled. "As long as it's voluntary."

49

Morrison decided to have lunch at Kitty's on Friday. It was a spur-of-the-moment decision, one he made at 11:30. He called Rheinhart to see if he wanted to join him, but the call went directly to voicemail and Morrison didn't leave a message. Instead, he walked by Rheinhart's bungalow and noticed his car was gone. Probably running errands, he thought as he continued walking. Maybe buying his new love interest some designer chocolates.

The bar was crowded when he arrived, but he managed to find a single seat under the moose head at the far end. Gracie spotted him and came over with a beer. "Flying solo today?"

Morrison nodded as he took a sip. It was cold and refreshing. "I walked by Rheinhart's house on the way over here, but his car was gone."

"A date with his new lady friend?" she asked impishly.

Morrison shook his head. "I don't think so. I think he's planning to take her out on his boat for a first date, seeing as how she's the clean water queen. He took his boat out yesterday for the first time since he discovered that, um, thing."

Gracie nodded knowingly. "At least he's back in the saddle again."

"About time."

"Oysters today? They're from Apalachicola this week, nice size."

"Let me think on that a bit."

"Take your time." She was off in the other direction in a flash, responding to a tentative wave from a needy customer at the opposite end of the bar.

Morrison surveyed the bar area as he sipped his beer. He'd spent enough time at Kitty's since he'd moved to Ozona, downing oysters and beer, that he could read the crowd like a long-time regular. Most of the butts on barstools belonged to regulars – they were easy to spot because they never needed a menu to order and knew that the specials were on a neon display on the wall behind the cash register. The remaining customers at the bar during lunch were mostly first-timers, usually in groups of two or four, full of questions for Gracie about the menu and where the nearest beach was.

He glanced at his watch: 12:27. Part of the reason he'd decided to come today was to get a good look at Guido Vaticanini, who was one of Gracie's Friday regulars. He wasn't here yet; neither was the Alvarez woman, whom Gracie had identified as a Monday through Friday regular, someone you could set your watch to. She also hadn't been in the place two days ago when he and Rheinhart met for their weekly Wednesday lunch. He made a note to ask Gracie if she knew why.

He decided to pass on oysters today despite Gracie's recommendation, opting for the Cobb salad instead when Gracie returned to replenish his beer. "Health food today, eh?" she said as she punched in his order on the touchscreen cash register. She returned to Morrison, bending low, dropping her voice. "Don't stare, but Guido just walked in behind you, dark hair and beard, a body like Yogi Bear."

Morrison waited a few moments before turning his head casually to get his first glimpse of Gracie's mysterious customer. He fought back a smile – her description of Guido's appearance was spot on: dark hair and beard, sloping shoulders, and a sizable gut likely crafted over the years by a carb-rich diet and a dearth of exercise. He looked flustered, standing behind his usual stool which was occupied today by a stout woman from Hoboken with blond hair, grey on either side of her middle part, wearing a red Rutgers T-shirt and white golf visor. She was with her younger sister, and their food had just arrived, which accounted for Guido's hesitation about where to sit.

Gracie came to his rescue with a glass of his favorite red wine. "It's on the house," she said, pointing to a two-top against the wall. "I should have a spot at the bar for you in five minutes." Guido accepted the drink without comment and slid into one of the chairs she'd indicated, a scowl on his face. He wasn't used to compromising when it came to his seat at the bar.

Morrison caught Gracie's eye and motioned her close. "No Marcia Alvarez today?"

Gracie shook her head, concern flooding her features. "Last day she was in was Monday. She never misses a day. I hope she's okay."

"Doesn't she have an elderly parent she takes care of?" Morrison asked. "The guy who thinks he's D.B. Cooper?"

She nodded. "Yeah. Could be something happened to him. I don't think he's too mobile these days." She looked at him intently. "You're still planning to come over on Thursday, right?"

"Thursday?" Morrison didn't follow.

Gracie gave him a disapproving look. "For Thanksgiving. Remember?"

Morrison nodded sheepishly. Since they had no family in the area, Gracie and Hank hosted what she called Orphans' Thanksgiving each year, inviting friends who were also alone in Florida to share their feast. Both he and Rheinhart had attended for the first time last year and had been impressed by Gracie's culinary skills, especially the Baconator turkey, which she wrapped completely with strips of uncooked bacon before inserting it into the oven. Morrison had never tasted such a moist turkey in his life. "What am I supposed to bring?"

"A key lime pie. Rheinhart's bringing the rolls."

"What time?"

"Dinner's at 5:00, but you can come earlier if you'd like to watch the football games."

*****

While Gracie and Morrison were discussing her situation, Marcia Alvarez was at the VA hospital in Tampa, where she'd been since her father, Clement Harkins, had suffered a stroke Monday evening. They were in the condo then, watching *Wheel of Fortune*, when the old man made a gurgling sound, eyes rolling back in his head, and slumped to his side, unconscious. Marcia recognized the symptoms immediately and called 9-1-1. The paramedics arrived in six minutes, and after a brief discussion, opted to transport him to the VA facility in Tampa near the USF campus instead of the nearest local hospital because of his veteran status.

She'd been there for four days, waiting for her father to regain consciousness, growing increasingly irritable because the hospital allowed no smoking anywhere on the property. She had to walk across the street to a strip mall, where she stood under an awning in front of a consignment shop, out of the relentless sun, smoking two cigarettes at a time, one after another, before returning to her bedside vigil.

The lack of information coming from the medical staff added to her frustration. When she asked the attending physician, Dr. Harbinder Gill, when her father might emerge from his coma,

300

the diminutive doctor shrugged his shoulders. "Could be tomorrow. Could be next year." Pause. "Maybe never."

"Fuck you very much," she snarled, walking away in a huff, on her way to mainline another pair of cigarettes.

What bothered her the most was the last scenario the doctor had offered. If that was the case, if her father died without regaining consciousness, their last conversation, her final memory of her father while he was alive, was a vicious argument the two had while Marcia was doing the dinner dishes Monday night. A demand from Harkins for mango ice cream for dessert had escalated into a shouting match that could be heard on three floors of the Causeway Tower condominium complex. Marcia finally walked away, fuming, to smoke a cigarette on the tiny balcony overlooking St. Joseph Sound.

When she finished, she came back inside, turned on the television and slumped down on the couch without a word. Her father, settled in his favorite chair, switched the channel to *Wheel of Fortune*. Five minutes later, Marcia was dialing 9-1-1.

The old man was a pain in the ass – there was no doubting that – but the thought that she might never speak to him again tore her up inside. She knew she was considered by most who knew her as a world-class hardcase, prickly to the point of unsociability, but deep inside she loved the old coot. He'd done the best job he could raising her after her mother died when she was a teenager – she knew that now despite the fact she'd enlisted in the army as soon as she was old enough, primarily to get out of the house, away from Clement Harkins. Compared to the husband who had used her as his personal punching bag, her old man was Gandhi.

She'd called Muriel and Edith and told them about what had happened that first night from the hospital. They'd both expressed genuine concern, asking if there was anything they could do to help, despite the abuse they'd endured from him on an ongoing basis. They were sweethearts, she thought. No matter how this turned out, she promised herself she was going to do her best to make amends with the pair, maybe send them on a cruise to the island of their choice.

She'd been holding off on the hardest task of all: calling her father's lawyer. He knew he had one because he'd written her name down in his shaky block printing when she'd asked last year if he had a will, but not before he shot her a withering look upon hearing the request. "Can't even wait till I'm in the ground, eh? Don't worry – you get it all."

She wasn't sure what 'all' meant, and her father's surly response discouraged any further inquiry. She regretted the inference he'd drawn from her innocent, responsible question, so much so that she dropped the subject, never bringing it up again. Now, staring at him in his hospital bed, a maze of tubes connected to a variety of machines monitoring his vital signs, she feared that call would occur much sooner than either of them had anticipated at the time.

She wiped a tear from her eye, then looked around quickly to see if anyone had noticed. Outside their room, the hospital throbbed with activity, nurses striding by purposefully, on their way to the latest crisis, oblivious to the drama behind the closed door.

50

After another phone call from Vasilevsky where everything the Russian said implied he'd love an invitation from Harpoon Tang for temporary housing until he could determine the extent of damage to his condo in Marathon, Les Bent acquiesced, fronting the request to Tang, who was hooked immediately. "Did you say Russian?"

"From Moscow."

The excitement in Tang's voice was evident. "Do you think he might be a target of Mueller?"

*****

When Bent called back, informing Vasilevsky that he was welcome to stay at Harpoon Tang's home as long as he'd like, the Russian thanked him profusely until Bent cut him off. "For fuck's sake, Nikolai. It's just a room."

Maybe to you, he thought after he hung up, but not to me. No one would think to look for him at a nudist resort in Land O' Lakes, which would give him enough time to figure out his next move. The package he'd left behind at the condo was a problem – he needed to get it back. He was already formulating a plan, hoping to find some young guy at Fuego who would drive to Marathon and pick it up for him, no questions asked. Money was no object. "Please tell Mr. Tang I am very grateful."

"You can tell him yourself when you get here."

In less than an hour Vasilevsky was on the road to Fuego, heeding Tang's warning that, because of the controversial nature of the resort, directions to the complex on U.S. 41 were nonexistent. Pasco County was one of the more conservative counties in Florida, as red as any in the Panhandle; county officials didn't want anyone knowing they had the highest per capita number of nudists of any county in North America, so they cut a deal with the four largest resorts in the area that restricted all advertising or mention of the resorts in proximity to any major thoroughfare in the county.

With no sign indicating the turnoff to the resort other than the street sign that fed into the complex, Vasilevsky slowed as he approached the turn. He drove down a narrow two-lane road until he reached the gate, where he chatted briefly with Bernard, the security guard, who'd been alerted to the Russian's arrival by Tang. Bernard handed Vasilevsky detailed directions to Tang's home when he pulled up to the gate, indicating which direction to go with a smile and polite nod. "Enjoy your stay at Fuego."

Vasilevsky returned the smile. "I will try very hard."

He drove slowly past the main clubhouse and reception area, head on a swivel, as he took in the sights. A nude couple in a golf cart waved as they passed him, going in the opposite direction, and several power walkers, equally naked, strode past purposefully as he followed the directions he'd plugged into his phone, looking for Tang's address. He drove past a two-story building of condos next to the main pool area, past a pair of volleyball courts, until he spied the sign for Tang's street.

His house was the third one in on the left, a sprawling, two-story contemporary with a red tile roof that featured a three-car garage. Vasilevsky pulled into the driveway, impressed – he had no idea porn paid this well. As the producer of *The Russians Are Coming and Coming and Coming*, he'd barely broken even, despite the relatively high gross revenue the film had produced. Of course, making money had not been the objective of that film.

He was removing his suitcase from the backseat of his Escalade when Les Bent emerged from the front door, followed closely by an Asian man that had to be his host. Bent hurried over, a grin creasing his deeply tanned face. "Let me help you with that, Nikolai."

Vasilevsky shrugged off the help. "Is okay. I can manage." He was relieved that both men were fully dressed – apparently, nudity was optional at Fuego instead of mandatory – as he approached the front steps. Bent, who was dressed in a short-sleeved white polo shirt, grey shorts and sandals, indicated their host. "Nikolai Vasilevsky, Wai Tang. Better known as Harpoon."

Tang stepped forward, offering his hand in greeting. Vasilevsky put his suitcase down. "Is very nice to meet you, Mr. Harpoon. Your kindness is very appreciated."

Tang's grip was strong. "It's my pleasure, Mr. Vasilevsky. Les has told me a lot about you. And please – call me Harpoon." He swung his had toward the front door. "My home is your home. If you need anything, just ask." He looked at the Russian with concern. "Les told me you have a place in Marathon. Do you know how much damage it incurred?"

Vasilevsky shook his head. "Not yet." He smiled ruefully. "I am old man. I was hoping to find young man here to go down and see." After a moment he added, "I will pay well."

Tang smiled. "That shouldn't be too difficult. Florida is filled with young men who have more brawn than brains."

Confusion spread across the Russian's features. "I do not know brawn."

Bent flexed his bicep to demonstrate. "Muscles. More muscles than brains."

"If you say so."

For the next week, Vasilevsky took advantage of Tang's hospitality while he worked on a plan to move forward. He was concerned about Natalya Bazarov. She was no fool; sooner or later she would figure out that her son was not missing, but dead. He was afraid she would do something rash, something that would lead the authorities to link him to Middleton's disappearance. With the two assassins, Mishkin and Chepiga, back in Russia, he and Bazarov were the last loose ends, and he was well aware of what the Russian intelligence service thought of loose ends. He'd expected to be recalled to the Kremlin after Middleton's murder, but the call hadn't come. The silence from his superiors was chilling.

He spent most of his time at Fuego by the main pool, under one of the shaded lounge chairs, reading. He'd become a fan of American fiction, mysteries especially. They helped him improve his English; more importantly, they offered a welcome distraction from his current dilemma. Tang and Bent gave him plenty of space. They were both enthusiastic gamblers, a vice he'd never acquired, and they liked to stay up late, playing poker in games organized by one of the other residents of the resort Tang had introduced him to, Lauren Caputo. They often slept until noon, sometimes later. At times it felt as if he was staying in the spacious home alone.

The scenery was another pleasant distraction. He wasn't comfortable being naked in public but he still had a pulse, and he couldn't help enjoying the abundance of naked female flesh in and around the pool. He'd been surprised by the range of ages and body types that frequented the resort; like most non-nudists, he thought that they would all be young, beautiful and nubile. The amount of sagging flesh and grey hair around the pool area that he'd observed was totally unexpected, as was their total lack of shame.

On Wednesday Tang had introduced him to Calvin Meade, one of the maintenance men at the resort. Meade was in his mid-twenties, with several visible tattoos, not too bright, but very willing to drive down to Marathon to retrieve some personal items, especially when Tang told him that Vasilevsky was willing to pay. He stared at Vasilevsky with eager but vacant eyes. "How much we talkin' about here?"

"I was thinking one thousand dollars, U.S.," Vasilevsky replied. "Plus expenses, with receipts, of course."

Meade smiled, sensing an opening. If a grand was his opening offer, the old guy was bound to go higher. "Make it two grand and a rental car, an SUV, and we have a deal."

Vasilevsky was in no position to barter. "Is deal. I will pay half now, half when you return." They shook hands. "When can you leave?"

"Right after work on Friday. I get out at five."

Vasilevsky had been hoping he could leave today, but Friday was acceptable. He went to his room and returned with ten crisp hundred-dollar bills, which Meade snatched eagerly. "SUV will be here Friday," the Russian said.

"Pleasure doing business with you, Igor," Meade said as he stuffed the bills into his pocket.

Vasilevsky's reply had an edge. "Is not Igor. Is Nikolai."

"Whatever."

As soon as Meade departed, Vasilevsky looked up rental car companies and scheduled a Honda Pilot to be delivered to Tang's address on Friday afternoon. Next, he sat down and wrote out a detailed list of where he wanted Meade to look and what to look for. He added a few items to the list that didn't exist because he'd resented the brash young man's attitude, but quickly deleted them when he realized that looking for nonexistent items would delay his return. He wanted that envelope and its contents in his hands as soon as possible.

51

Natalya Bazarov was pacing between her kitchen and living room, smoldering, incensed by her inability to reach Vasilevsky. There had been no word from her son for three weeks now. She felt he was probably dead – if he was alive, he would've found some way to reach out to her by now, to let her know he was okay. He knew how much comfort she drew from their regular talks, how much it meant to her just to hear the sound of his voice. He wouldn't have gone dark, abruptly cut off all communication without some sort of explanation unless something dire had happened.

She blamed her elderly Russian benefactor. She'd always feared him, especially the power he continued to hold over her because of her inability to speak English well enough to feel comfortable in a foreign land and the control he wielded over her as her sole source of financial support. It was history repeating itself: he would tighten his influence over her as he had more than thirty years ago when he sponsored her exodus from Havana to Key West, seducing her with crumbs until she became totally dependent on his support. She had no leverage to improve her lot, no pathway forward to get by on her own without his assistance. She was at his service, at her peril.

She picked up her phone and dialed the only number she knew by heart. As it had for the last three weeks, the call went directly to voicemail. She fought off the despair she felt once again by failing to reach him. The message she left for him in a strong, unwavering voice hadn't changed.

"Nikolai. Where is Yury?" She returned the phone to its base and picked up the business card that private investigator had left behind. Maybe she'd give Paul Hanson a call, see if he had any new information concerning her son.

She was running out of options.

*****

From his shaded lounge chair by the pool at Fuego, Vasilevsky saw that Natalya was calling and let the call go to voicemail. Time for a new burner. Or maybe Moscow would send another cleaning crew to take care of the last loose end. He felt Natalya's desperation for news about her son would only increase, tempting her to resort to reckless avenues in order to find the truth. Avenues the Kremlin would prefer to remain unexplored.

Thinking about loose ends made Vasilevsky uneasy. Suppose Moscow didn't consider Natalya the last loose end of this debacle? What if Moscow sent a cleaning crew after him?

*****

On the way home from his interview with the FBI in Clearwater, Rheinhart glanced at the clock on the dashboard: 2:04. Impulsively, he pulled into the crushed shell parking lot at Kitty Galore's. He needed a drink. Maybe two.

The lot was mostly filled as he found a spot in the rear. He walked through the back door of the restaurant, squinting to adjust his eyes to the darker interior of the bar. Gracie spotted him as soon as he rounded the corner, waving and gesturing toward the other end of the bar. He followed her gesture and saw Morrison seated there, involved in what looked like a two-way conversation with Guido Vaticanini, seated to his right. There was a vacant seat to the left of Morrison. Rheinhart made a beeline for it.

Morrison looked up from his conversation with the swarthy man of mystery and saw Rheinhart as he approached, a broad smile on his face. "Couldn't live without me, eh?" he called out.

Rheinhart turned to give Gracie the hand signal that he wanted a beer, but she was ahead of him, already on her way with a fresh draft. "Well, well, well. You're the second surprise of the day," she said as she placed his beer on a coaster, nodding toward Morrison.

"A pleasant surprise, I hope," Rheinhart said after he sipped his beer.

"Let's just say things continue to look up," she replied impishly. "Would you like to look at a menu?"

Rheinhart shook his head. "Not necessary. I'll have the grouper sandwich, blackened, with fries."

"Coming right up." Gracie retreated to enter his order.

Morrison looked at his friend with interest. "What brings you to Kitty's on a Friday?"

Rheinhart looked past Morrison, toward Guido. "I could ask you the same question."

"Hunger and thirst for me," Morrison said, a smile playing around his lips. "How about you?"

"The second," Rheinhart said as he took a longer sip of his beer. "I had an unusual morning."

"Really?" Morrison wanted more.

Rheinhart looked at Guido, who was on his feet, withdrawing a few bills from his wallet which he placed on the bar under his empty wine glass. Gracie noticed from the middle of the bar. "Need any change?" she called out.

The enigmatic Vaticanini shook his head, turned and left the bar without a word. When he was gone, Rheinhart turned to Morrison and stated flatly, "I hope it wasn't my breath."

"He's not exactly a chatterbox, like Gracie said," Morrison offered. "But I did find out his real name. We actually had a conversation before you showed up and spooked him."

Gracie was straining to hear their conversation as she mixed a vodka and tonic for a customer seated in the middle of the bar. When she was finished she hurried back, looking at Morrison with amazement. "You found out his real name? How did you do that?"

"It was simple. I introduced myself. He responded." He let his answer hang, which prompted an impatient response from Gracie. "Okay, wiseass. What's his name?"

"Arnold Berman, from Southold, Long Island." It was Morrison's turn to smile, a smile he directed toward Gracie. "And he has nothing to do with the Witness Protection Program."

Although he was bursting to tell them about his session with the FBI, Rheinhart couldn't resist, sucked in by the melodrama. "What's his story?"

"A lot less interesting than Gracie's fantasy. Two years ago he retired and moved to Florida with his wife, Charlene. A year ago they were in the right-hand lane on 19, headed toward the Cracker Barrel for an early dinner, when some guy sped out of a restaurant parking lot without looking and T-boned their Lexus, a direct hit on the passenger's side where Charlene was sitting. She was killed instantly. He's been a recluse ever since, only coming out once a week, on Friday, to have lunch at Kitty's because it was her favorite restaurant."

Gracie was puzzled. "I don't remember seeing him in here before, with his wife. He's only come in alone." She paused. "How could this be her favorite restaurant?"

"She didn't come in with her husband. She came in with a group of women, neighbors in the complex who played bridge together. Arnold never knew where they went for lunch on those outings until one of the other women mentioned it to him at the wake. Now he comes in every Friday, has a glass of wine and her favorite meal, and then goes home."

A light came on for Gracie. "Now that you mention it, I think I remember that group. They used to sit at the big table, by the door to the parking lot out back, so I didn't have much contact with them. They stopped coming in about a year ago."

"Right after she died," Morrison said.

"It's been a good month for Gracie," Rheinhart said. "First, she finds out the truth about Homeless Simpson, now she knows about Guido Vaticanini. Two mysteries solved." He paused. "Speaking of which, you'll never guess where I was this morning." He looked expectantly at them both.

"The suspense is killing me," Morrison said acidly.

"At the FBI office in Clearwater. I had an interview session with Special Agent Angela Threadgill." He looked at Morrison. "Name sound familiar?"

Morrison, suddenly all ears, shifted to face Rheinhart. Gracie leaned in expectantly. "You're shitting me," Morrison blurted.

Rheinhart was savoring this exchange. "No shit, Sherlock. She wanted to know about the body I found on Anclote Key. The reason the detectives from Pinellas County never got back to me was because the FBI took over the case. Kullmann and Profeta

313

couldn't answer my questions because they didn't know the answers."

Morrison looked at his friend quizzically. "Why on earth would the FBI be interested in the murder of a real estate agent? Even one with his tongue cut out."

"That, Sherlock, is what I've been trying to figure out ever since she started asking me questions." He paused for effect, looking directly at Morrison now. "She asked me about you, too. Wanted to know how we met, how long we've been friends. She knew all about your acting career, too."

"Maybe this all has something to do with the Russians," Morrison mused, forgetting that Gracie was not as informed concerning his personal history as Rheinhart was. "That's all she wanted to talk about."

Gracie picked up on the slip immediately. "Acting career?" She shifted her gaze between the two men, settling on Rheinhart after watching Morrison's face sour. "Tell me more."

Rheinhart, grinning, nodded toward Morrison. "Ask Biff here. He'll fill you in."

52

The material Breznay had collected at Vasilevsky's condo in Marathon was processed by the lab overnight and delivered to Miller's office Friday afternoon. As soon as he heard that the results were in, he called Threadgill. "We have the evidence from Vasilevsky's condo."

"I'll be right there."

As he waited for Threadgill to arrive, he dialed Gutierrez and told him the news. "Put me on speaker," Gutierrez demanded. "I want to know what our boy found."

Threadgill knocked once and barged in. Miller had the evidence spread across his desk so she could take it in. There were four sheets of paper: a group photograph of the current U.S. Supreme Court members, a head shot of Justice Ramona Hancock, a printout of a Zillow listing for Tom Martin's property on Captiva Road, and an aerial photo taken from the rear of Justice Hancock's Captiva home, likely taken by a drone hovering slightly above the mangroves along the banks of Roosevelt Channel.

Threadgill drew in her breath sharply. It was all there, compelling evidence to back up the theory Gutierrez had laid out a few days earlier. She and Miller exchanged glances, both of them thinking the same thing – admiration for the deductive instincts of their senior colleague in Miami who, based on these documents, seemed to have nailed it.

Gutierrez's impatience at the silence coming from Clearwater got the best of him. "What is it? What did he find?"

"There'll be no living with you after this, Cesar," Miller said with open admiration. "We have four pictures here, all of them related to Justice Hancock. An aerial shot of her home, a head shot of her in her judicial robe, a group photo of all the Supreme Court members, and a printout of a real estate listing for a nearby house, the one Middleton was actively seeking to be listed. It all seems to fit with the theory you posed the other day – the motive for taking out Middleton had something to do with Justice Hancock."

Gutierrez took the praise in stride, his voice unemotional, all business. "Send me some pictures. ASAP."

"Cell phone pics okay?" Threadgill asked

"Of course. Send them to my Bureau email."

Threadgill collapsed into Miller's guest chair as Gutierrez clicked off abruptly. Miller remained standing, both palms on the desk as he leaned over the photo array, studying them, trying to shake the nagging thought that the photos weren't what they appeared to be. He finally broke the silence, addressing Threadgill. "What do you think?"

She looked at the photos, then up at her boss. "They look like they confirm Cesar's assumption, that Hancock was in Middleton's crosshairs…" Her voice trailed off.

Miller noted the doubt in her voice. "But?"

After a moment she continued. "It looks too neat. What are the chances that, in the first place, Vasilevsky would leave such an incriminating series of photos behind? It would've been easy to grab the envelope before evacuating from the Keys. Leaving behind four photos that, side by side, provide critical links between Vasilevsky, Middleton and Hancock doesn't seem to me like something a veteran KGB agent would ever do, no matter how much stress he was under."

316

Miller nodded in agreement. "That was my first impression, too. There were too many goodies in that envelope. One photo I could live with. Maybe two. But four, all directly connected? That seems too good to be true to me."

Encouraged by Miller's cynicism, which dovetailed into her doubts, Threadgill took the supposition a little farther. "Two of the photos, the group shot of the Supreme Court and the close-up of Justice Hancock, look like photos from the public domain, probably downloaded from Google Images or a similar service. But the other two, the aerial photo of the house and the copy of the document printed from the real estate web page, are items that have human fingerprints on them. Someone created them specifically, with some purpose in mind."

Miller reached into his pocket for his cell phone and snapped photos of the four items, which he attached to an email for Gutierrez in Miami. "Do we have anything new on Vasilevsky's whereabouts?" he asked.

"Nothing since he left the hotel in Tampa two weeks ago. No activity on his passport, so it's likely he's still in the country somewhere."

"We need to find him before he's called back to Moscow or disappears for good."

Threadgill cocked her eyebrow at Miller. "You think they would take him out? An asset that has been in the country for thirty-five years?"

Miller nodded grimly. "They didn't hesitate to do it with Middleton. If Vasilevsky is still in the country, he's probably gone underground. Finding him won't be easy."

"I agree. Any idea where to start?"

"Only one," Miller replied. "The porn director, Bent. If anyone knows where Vasilevsky might be, it would be him." A smile appeared on his lips. "Put Tremayne on it. I like what he did for us before."

"What about Breznay? He's the one who found the envelope."

Miller shook his head. "Different skill set. Tremayne knows the web inside and out. If Bent's still in Florida, Tremayne's the man to find him."

*****

At ten after five, Calvin Meade departed from his single-wide in Wesley Chapel, driving the burgundy Honda Pilot Vasilevsky had rented for his journey. The maintenance man had packed the night before and had begged off work an hour early, telling his supervisor he was headed out of town for a wedding.

He had to admit the Pilot wasn't bad for a Jap car. It drove like a car instead of a truck and held the road well, better than he had expected, as he dashed in and out of traffic on I-75. He cursed the slower drivers as he darted from lane to lane, Kacey Musgraves blasting from the satellite radio. He was determined to make good time despite the early weekend traffic that had already started to build; his only stop was in Homestead, where he grabbed a couple of burgers from the drive-thru lane at Burger King and topped off his tank before descending on the Keys.

He arrived in Marathon just past midnight. It wasn't until then that he realized he didn't have a place to stay. Fucking Igor hadn't said a thing about hotel reservations. He tried two places, the only two places that looked open, a rundown motel just off the highway and the new Marriott, but they were both full. The clerk at the Marriott had actually laughed when Meade had requested a room, telling him, "Check back in about six months."

From the Marriott he drove back to a bar he'd noticed just up the road that still had its lights on. Might as well have a brewski or two before looking for a spot to park and sleep, he figured.

When he pulled into the Overseas Pub and Grill, the bartender was cleaning the bar, preparing to close. Meade pestered him for a few minutes before the bearded bartender agreed to pour him a draft. "Only one," he told Meade in a no-nonsense voice. "I've got to be back at six to open for breakfast."

"Don't worry," said Meade as he settled into a stool at the deserted bar. "I drink fast." He downed half the beer in a single gulp. I shoulda bought a six-pack, he thought as he wiped some foam from his lower lip. "I noticed you have a parking lot out back. I just got into town and there's no place to stay anywhere. Do you think I could park my truck back there for the night?"

The bartender's face darkened. "I don't know…."

Meade peeled one of Vasilevsky's hundred-dollar bills from a roll in his pocket and dangled it in the bartender's face. "I'll make it worth your while."

Even though the bartender knew he was the last employee in the place, he looked guiltily around the bar as if he were afraid he was being watched before snatching the bill from Meade's soiled hands. "I can't promise you won't get rousted by the sheriff."

Meade smiled, revealing bridgework eroded by crystal meth. "Me and the law get along just fine. Shouldn't be no problem." He finished his beer in a second gulp, pushing the empty glass across the bar. "I figure that Benjamin oughta cover my beer, too," he said as he stood up.

"Park in the back, by the dumpster. Nobody should see you there."

"Much obliged, Mr. Bartender."

319

*****

Trucks started pulling into the parking lot shortly before seven, creating a racket that jarred him awake from a fitful sleep. He groaned as he rolled over, his neck stiff, his right ankle asleep, trying to get his bearings. He'd slept in the back after the lowering the two back seats, using his backpack as a pillow. As he crawled out the back door to stretch his legs, he saw the remnants of Irma, aluminum, wood and plaster stacked in a haphazard pile that towered over the dumpster just a few feet away. He'd watched the coverage on the local news – Christ, it was the only thing they showed for a week before and a week after the hurricane struck – but being there, not far from where the storm had come ashore, was a whole different ballgame.

As it continued to get light, Meade started his truck and pulled out onto the Overseas Highway. Debris was everywhere, as far as he could see as he drove slowly north. For the first time he worried about what he was getting into; when he'd asked Igor about the condition of his condo, the man just shrugged his shoulders. "Is a mystery."

If the Russian hadn't made him agree to take a photo of himself that included the condo complex to prove that he'd been there, he would've left then and there, headed back, claiming not to have found what he'd been instructed to look for. It was a hurricane, for Christ sake. No fuckin' envelope could survive that.

The Honda's GPS delivered him to the road where Breznay had turned down two days earlier. He drove in as far as he could, parked and locked the vehicle, continuing on foot with his backpack, which contained a selection of tools Igor had suggested for the job.

Fuck it, he thought as he stepped over tree limbs and twisted lawn furniture as he approached the building. When he was

320

close enough to see the extent of the damage the building had endured, his mind was made up.

He tried the door to the staircase. It was unlocked, so he climbed to the second floor and walked along the hallway until he saw the number of Vasilevsky's condo on the door. He switched on the flash attachment for his camera phone and took two selfies, one at the door which included the condo number, and one inside the bedroom, showing the chest of drawers tipped over on the floor in the background. Nothing was taped to the bottom, in contrast to what the Russian had said.

Satisfied that he'd fulfilled his end of the deal, Meade made his way down the staircase and back to his truck. He checked his watch and smiled; if he was lucky, he'd be back in Wesley Chapel in plenty of time to watch Florida State against Wake Forest on ESPN.

He backed carefully down the road until he found a place to turn around, then drove out to the highway. He'd get some coffee at a convenience store, maybe a Danish or two, then head home. He'd have to lay low, stay out of sight at least until Sunday before calling Igor with the bad news. That wouldn't be hard – Trevor, one of the bartenders at the tiki bar by the pool at Fuego, told him the Russian spent all his time next to the pool, reading a book and staring at titties. Meade couldn't blame the old man; he probably didn't see many naked babes where he came from.

He turned up the volume on the radio and smiled as he set the cruise control for forty, Kenny Chesney's baritone and guitar filling the SUV. He lit a cigarette and rolled down the window, resting his arm as he drove, smoke trailing behind. He was thinking about scoring some more meth – what he always did when he had a few extra bucks in his pocket. Darryl, his dealer, would be surprised – not by the request, since Meade was a regular customer, but by the hundred-dollar bill he'd nonchalantly toss his way as payment. Usually he paid with a fistful of grubby bills and change, money he'd scrounged or stolen from unsuspecting resort residents who were foolish enough to invite him inside for a drink of water or lemonade on those steamy afternoons when he worked on their property.

He took a drag on his cigarette and smiled. Maybe Igor had some other jobs he could do for him. He'd make sure he'd ask for more next time – he was afraid he'd left money on the table during their previous negotiation. The Russian smelled like money, a real meal ticket if he played his cards right, someone he could string along for months as long as he didn't get greedy and overplay his hand.

A regular Russian sugar daddy.

53

Clement Harkins passed away Saturday morning, never having emerged from his coma after being stricken on Monday. Marcia was asleep, curled up in the guest chair in her father's room when two nurses, alerted by flatlining monitors attached to her father's sallow flesh, barged into the room in a vain attempt to revive him. The flurry of activity jarred her back to consciousness. Half awake, she sat up and watched silently as the two checked her father's vital signs, finding none. After several minutes the taller of the two looked at her watch. "I'm calling it at 5:27 am," she said.

The other nurse went over to Marcia, bent down and whispered in her ear. "We'll give you a few minutes alone with him, if you'd like."

"He's gone?" she asked in confusion.

"Yes. I'm sorry for your loss," she said gently. "We'll be outside in the hall. Take your time."

Marcia struggled to her feet and went to her father's side. He looked as he had all week, eyes closed, motionless. Her initial reaction to the death of her father was relief instead of grief, followed swiftly by pangs of guilt. He was her father, despite his flaws and eccentricities. She should be feeling more, a deeper sense of loss, but it wasn't there. Instead, she felt like a parolee with a new set of clothes and a ticket to the destination of her choice, a chance for a fresh start.

She spent a minute studying his face for a final time before bending down and kissing him on the forehead. "Safe travels, you old bastard," she whispered affectionately, her voice catching as she straightened to look for the nurse.

*****

After informing the nurse of her father's request to be cremated and promising to make the arrangements as soon as she spoke with his attorney, Marcia went back to the condo in Dunedin and stripped off her clothes as soon as she was inside the door. She stood under the shower for a long time, letting the hot water wash over her, cleansing her of everything associated with the hospital, especially the antiseptic smell used to mask the odors she now associated with decay and death.

When she was dressed she called her father's attorney and left a message that Clement Harkins had died and that she wanted to proceed with the next phase – whatever that was – as soon as possible, hopefully early next week. Since it was Saturday, the call was forwarded to the attorney's answering service.

After she hung up, she went to the liquor cabinet, removed a bottle of single malt that she had been saving for the holiday season and poured herself a generous glass. She went out onto the tiny balcony, closing the sliding glass door behind her, and sat down. She placed her glass on the table beside her and lit a cigarette, inhaling deeply, lost in a jumble of thoughts both light and dark as several boats maneuvered on St. Joseph Sound in the morning sunlight.

*****

Rheinhart decided to call Gwen Westphal Saturday morning. It had been four days since he'd attended her lecture, just the right amount of time in his mind to let her know he was interested but not too eager in following up her invitation to call. He'd rehearsed what he planned to say in front of his bathroom

324

mirror the night before, like a socially inept high school sophomore about to ask the best-looking girl in the class to go to the prom.

The call went directly to voicemail, as if her phone was shut off. He drew a deep breath and spoke clearly as soon as her greeting message ended. "Hi Gwen, this is Zach Rheinhart. I attended your lecture on red tide in Largo on Tuesday. We spoke briefly after it ended, and you gave me your number. I was hoping you might like to go out on my boat sometime. Give me a call when you get a chance." He hung up, his heart pumping, his hands clammy as he put down the phone. Not too bad, he thought as he went into the kitchen and poured himself a cup of coffee.

*****

Morrison was awakened from a sound sleep Saturday morning at 6:00 by an incoming call to his cell phone, which rested on his bedside table. He struggled to grab the phone, wondering angrily who the hell was calling him at this hour. He groaned when he saw the Caller ID: DeWayne Bologna.

Morrison's voice was agitated. "DeWayne. Didn't Pops tell you that I cancelled for today?"

Bologna's voice was way too cheery for the morning hour. "He did, but I wanted to check to see if you changed your mind. I'm about five minutes from the rendezvous spot and thought I'd touch base, just in case."

"It's six fucking o'clock in the morning. I was sound asleep when you called."

"Rough night? Too much demon rum again?" Bologna's voice was light, teasing.

Morrison was in no mood for his friend's attempt at humor. He struggled to keep his emotions in check as he responded. "Not at all. I had some trouble sleeping, is all. I was looking forward to a coupla more hours of shuteye."

325

"Oops. Sorry about that."

"Goodbye, DeWayne. Bring me back a shark's tooth."

He hung up and tried to get back to sleep, but after tossing and turning for thirty minutes, he gave up, still perturbed as he rose from his bed and made a pot of coffee. As the pot was brewing, he turned on The Weather Channel to check on the weather for tonight's outing to Skipper's. Lauren had said it was mostly an outdoor venue, and he was relieved several minutes later when the local weather scrolled along the bottom of the screen, calling for a 0% chance of rain this evening.

As he sipped his coffee he thought about the implications of Rheinhart's interview with the FBI yesterday. His friend had seemed almost relieved that the FBI had called him in – at least Rheinhart now knew why there had been no follow-up from the Pinellas County detectives. Their interest in his relationship with Rheinhart was intriguing – other than their weekly get togethers for lunch at Kitty's and an affinity for life near the water, they had very little in common. Rheinhart was cerebral, always questioning the events in his life as if he could discover some sort of connection, some purpose behind what Morrison was convinced were simply random occurrences, while Morrison was a plodder, a stoic who accepted whatever came his way and tried to make the best of it. He'd had his dark periods, particularly when he had been living in his car in LA, but the inheritance from his Uncle Merle had given him a new lease on life.

He was looking forward to the outing tonight. He'd spent some time earlier in the week on YouTube, watching some video of previous live performances of Free Range Strange and also some concert footage taken at Skipper's, a rousing three-song medley from Southern Culture on the Skids, getting himself in the mood for a rare night out.

He wondered how invested Lauren Caputo was in luring him back to Fuego after the show. The post-concert party she'd mentioned sounded interesting, but he wasn't sure exactly where he fit into the lineup. Was his inclusion merely an afterthought, his invitation a nod to his longstanding friendship with her neighbor, Harpoon Tang? Or was there a deeper, hidden motive, something a little more personal behind her not-so-subtle invitation? He smiled; he was looking forward to finding out.

After he downed his second cup of coffee, he had a bowl of cereal with some freshly sliced mango he'd purchased the day before at the local produce market. When he was finished eating, he placed the dishes in the kitchen sink and walked into his bedroom to select his clothes for the evening. Harpoon had said Skipper's was ultra casual, which fit nicely with his limited wardrobe, primarily T-shirts, shorts and sandals. He decided to step it up a bit with the after party in mind, choosing a colorful guayabera shirt he'd purchased ten years ago while on vacation in Zihuatanejo and a pair of off-white baggies.

He made his bed and laid the shirt and shorts he'd selected for tonight on the quilted afghan he used as a bedspread. Next, he called Tang, who answered cheerily. "Steve! What's up?"

"Just checking on the time we're supposed to meet tonight."

Tang thought for a moment before replying. "The show starts at 8:00 and the doors open at 7:00. We're going a little earlier to have dinner there – I think we agreed we'd try to get there by 6:00. You're welcome to join us for dinner if you like."

"I might do that," Morrison said. "How many did you say would be there?"

"For dinner? Just me and my two houseguests. Unless Lauren and Jessica decide to join us."

"Houseguests?"

"I have two refugees from the hurricane staying with me. They both have places in the Keys that they had to leave behind because of the mandatory evacuation order." Pause. "I think you might know one of them, a guy I knew in the industry, Les Bent. I seem to remember you telling me the two of you had worked together."

Small world. "Yeah, I know Bent, but I haven't seen him in years. How is he?"

Tang chuckled. "Still intense. You'd think living in the Keys would've had some effect on him, but he's still the same, wired guy I remember from the valley."

"Who's the other guy?" Morrison asked.

"Bent's friend from the Keys, an older guy, a Russian named Nikolai. Can't remember his last name."

54

As soon as she returned to her office after her meeting with Miller, Threadgill was on the phone to Gavin Tremayne, who listened eagerly as she filled him in on Vasilevsky's background and the urgency with which they needed to locate him. She promised to send him digital files of the material found in Vasilevsky's condo before she added the clincher. "Special Agent Gutierrez has your back on this. Any advanced security clearance you may need, anything at all, just call him in Miami." She paused. "We need to find him before the Russians do. Once they reach him, he'll be lost to us forever."

"Don't worry, ma'am," he said confidently. "If he's in the country, I'll find him."

"I'll need daily updates."

"You'll get them."

"Good luck, Agent Tremayne." The line went dead.

He'd immediately grasped the implication she'd laid out plainly for him: that the Russians wanted to reach him as badly as the Bureau did, and if they did, Nikolai Vasilevsky would never be heard from again. He smiled with anticipation; this was going to be fun.

*****

On Saturday mornings Fuego felt like a ghost town, its streets and lanes deserted, the only sounds those of sandhill cranes and northern songbirds that congregate near the numerous ponds on the sprawling resort property. This lack of early-morning activity was primarily a result of Friday parties and other events that extended far into the night, some of them winding down as the sun was coming up. The residents of Fuego were night owls, especially on the weekend, so human presence on these mornings was chiefly limited to lawn maintenance and landscape personnel.

Vasilevsky was an early riser who enjoyed the solitude of the morning, usually up with the sun. This Saturday was no exception – he was out the door by 6:30 for his morning constitutional, a brisk walk from Tang's home down to the main clubhouse and back that usually cleared his head of the dark thoughts that had been plaguing him since the arrival of the two Russian assassins Mishkin and Chepiga.

Not this morning. He was anxious about Calvin Meade's mission to Marathon to retrieve the documents he'd foolishly left behind. He didn't know much about the young maintenance man Tang had vouched for and that disturbed him. It wasn't the way he liked to do business; usually he knew more about his associates than their immediate families. Meade was the extreme opposite, an unknown quantity that he'd been forced to align with out of desperation. His worst fear was that Meade would take the down payment and not follow up by traveling to Marathon and checking his condo for the documents – that's why he'd insisted on a photograph of Meade at the condo before paying him the additional thousand.

He was hoping Meade would return with the documents, but his instincts told him that was unlikely. What to do in case he returned empty-handed dominated his thoughts as he strolled around the resort this morning. He'd have to make a value judgement then – were the documents swept away by the hurricane, or were they retrieved by a first responder or someone from the law enforcement community? If he decided it was the latter, his next move would involve an emergency exit strategy that put distance between himself and both the Americans and the

Russians. If caught in the U.S. he would be tried and incarcerated; if the Russians found him after he'd blundered so badly, his days would be numbered.

He was looking forward to tonight's outing as a welcome respite from the grim reality of his situation. He'd come from a musical family in Kiev – both his father and older sister had played the balalaika in a local musical group that often performed at weddings in the Kiev area. The event at Skipper's tonight as described by his host might be the last entertainment he'd be able to enjoy for some time, since he expected Meade to return tomorrow. He planned to make the best of it.

*****

After Agent Breznay delivered the manila envelope he'd retrieved from Vasilevsky's condo, he'd expected a follow-up assignment related to his find. But aside from a brief thank you from Agent Threadgill when he'd handed the sealed package over to the Bureau's lab technicians, nothing had happened. Frustrated, he'd finally approached Threadgill in her office and asked her what she wanted him to do next.

She looked up from a stack of reports she'd been reviewing, formulating her answer. After a few moments she said, "I think you should go back to Captiva to pick up your things and return to Miami. Special Agent Gutierrez will want an in-person briefing to corroborate that you followed Bureau procedure in finding and securing the evidence."

"Does that mean I'm off the case?" he asked, unable to keep the bitterness out of his voice.

Threadgill shrugged. "That would be up to Special Agent Gutierrez. He's still running the show." She stood and extended her hand. "You did good work for us, Agent Breznay. I look forward to working with you again." They shook hands and she sat down, returning to her reports.

So that was it, he thought as he shuffled slowly out of her office, closing the door behind him. Game over. At least for him.

*****

As soon as Morrison ended his conversation with Tang, his thoughts shifted to his interview with the FBI earlier in the week. The woman agent who'd interviewed him had zeroed in on the movie he'd shot in Key West with Les Bent, who, according to Tang, might be part of the group at Skipper's tonight along with an older Russian named Nikolai. He considered calling her back, letting her know that Bent was in town, at Fuego, along with an unknown Russian, but dismissed the notion. What if Tang was mistaken and his two houseguests decided not to join the festivities tonight? He'd look like a fool if there was an FBI presence at the concert and those two were no-shows. Better to wait; if they did show up, he'd ask Bent if the Russian staying at Harpoon's place was the mysterious financier of *The Russians Are Coming and Coming and Coming.* Bent had no idea Morrison had talked to the FBI; he was determined to keep it that way.

He fixed himself a peanut butter sandwich for lunch and then took a nap, trying to regain some of the sleep Bologna had stolen from him this morning. He turned off his cell phone and was asleep for a little more than an hour before an insistent knocking at his front door roused him. Groggily, he opened the door to find an unknown man standing there, clipboard in hand. Behind the man, in the truncated crushed shell driveway, was a white pickup truck with the lettering **GULF ROOFING** stenciled on the side. His roofing contractor.

The dark-haired man was slim, average height and looked to be in his thirties. He deduced from Morrison's disheveled appearance and confused state that he'd been sleeping and was

332

immediately apologetic. "Did I wake you? I'm so sorry. We tried calling, but your phone was turned off. I finished up another job in the area and wanted to stop by to tell you we can start on your roof on Monday." Pause. "If that's okay with you," he added hastily.

About fucking time, he thought. "Monday would be great," Morrison said affably. "What time should I expect you?"

"We like to start early, around seven, before it gets too hot. Is that okay?"

Morrison nodded. "I'll make sure I'm awake."

"Sorry about waking you up, Mr. Morrison. I'll see you on Monday."

Morrison watched as the man retreated to his truck and drove away, then headed for the bathroom. So much for catching up on my sleep, he thought, as he stared into the mirror, trying to decide if he needed to shave. He reached for his razor. There was a party back at Fuego after the concert; it wouldn't hurt to smooth out a couple of his rough edges, just in case.

After he finished shaving he showered, staying under the hot spray for longer than usual as his mind returned to Bent and the Russian. He considered calling Rheinhart to see what he thought, but quickly ruled it out for the same reason he'd backed off on calling the FBI. Better to be sure first – there'd be plenty of time after tonight to get his input. Plus, if Tang was right and the two did show up, he'd likely be able to gather more information for both the FBI and Rheinhart. No need to jump the gun until he had the goods.

When he was dressed he checked his appearance in the mirror. Not bad, he thought. He wondered what Lauren Caputo would be wearing tonight. Probably, he thought with a lascivious grin, something that would be very stylish and easy to remove. Clothes for her were something she wore only when she had to, according to Tang, who assured him she was much more comfortable being naked and preferred her men the same way.

Morrison smiled. He had considerable experience being naked himself, although he might be a little rusty. He was unconcerned, though – he was confident he'd rise to the occasion when the time was right.

He hoped that would be tonight.

55

As soon as Gutierrez received Miller's report on the processed evidence recovered from Vasilevsky's condo in Marathon, he passed it on to his superiors in Washington. He'd hesitated briefly before deciding to share the information, primarily because of the upheaval throughout the Bureau following the firing of the Director of the FBI by the President in May, but in the end decided that the Russian components of the case were serious enough to warrant inclusion into the expanding case file regarding Russian interference in the American political process.

For Gutierrez, the evidence indicated a strong possibility that Chad Middleton, aka Yury Bazarov, had been involved in some sort of plot against U.S. Supreme Court Justice Ramona Hancock, possibly an assassination attempt. But for some reason as yet unknown, the mission had been scrubbed by the Russians and an extremely valuable, long-time deep cover Russian operative had been poisoned by a pair of Russian assassins as part of a bizarre kidnap/murder plot before he could complete his mission.

Gutierrez could see a motive behind why the Russians would want to brazenly murder a sitting Supreme Court Justice. Justice Hancock was the flagship liberal on the court; if she was no longer there, the current administration would undoubtedly appoint a new justice with conservative leanings, changing the balance of the Court for generations to come. Such a change would be eagerly welcomed by Putin, whom the Bureau and other intelligence agencies knew considered the current president to be weak and malleable.

But something had gone wrong. Instead of killing Hancock, they decided they had to kill their own agent instead. Finding out why such a radical decision had been made would be the focus of the investigation moving forward.

*****

Tremayne began his search for Vasilevsky by examining his financial records. Because he was a known Russian agent operating in the United States, there was a considerable file on his banking history already in existence at the Bureau. He had two checking accounts listed, one for his personal use and a business account servicing Conch Republic Films, which had made monthly payments to Natalya Bazarov since she'd arrived in America from Havana. These payments had been deposited into Bazarov's account on the 10th of each month for more than thirty years.

But there had been no deposit for November, the current month, and no other activity on that account. His personal checking account, which included a debit card, showed no activity in the last two days before Hurricane Irma made landfall. He also had a credit card from a major U.S. bank that had not been used for nearly two months.

Tremayne frowned. No activity on either bank account or his credit card was a strong indication that Vasilevsky had tapped into what the Bureau referred to as "get lost" money, a cache of cash and documents all agents kept in reserve in case they needed to relocate with little advance notice. If so, he could already be on the run, with a considerable head start.

Or he was already dead.

*****

Lauren Caputo finally stirred in her bed a little before 3:00 Saturday afternoon. She had played in a monthly poker game the night before at a private swinger's club called Night Moves in north Tampa and hadn't returned to Fuego until 7:00 am that morning. She'd set the alarm for 2:15 but had hit the snooze button on her alarm several times before finally deciding it was time to get up.

Still in bed, she raised herself onto her elbow to light a cigarette and called Jessica Callaway, who answered almost immediately. "I didn't think you'd be up this early. Didn't you have a game last night?"

Caputo exhaled a plume of smoke. "Yeah. I didn't get home until after the sun was up."

"Ouch. How'd you do?"

"I won a little, about fifty, I think. I didn't count it."

Jessica smiled. Lauren always said she won, which Jessica knew had to be false. If she was as accomplished a poker player as she claimed, why did she have a day job with FedEx, especially since she also operated a MILF website out of her home in Fuego? She was always scrambling for money; more than once she'd asked Jessica for a temporary loan "just until payday." That was the type of request that came from a problem gambler, not a successful one. "First drink's on you tonight, then."

"So you are coming to Skipper's with us tonight? The last time we talked you were up in the air about it."

"I filmed two clips this morning while you were sleeping on your sack of winnings," Jessica, who operated her own adult website, replied brightly. "I'm looking forward to seeing this band."

"Harpoon says they're pretty good. Says the lead singer is a friend of John Travolta up in Ocala." Lauren's tongue felt like sandpaper. She took a sip of water from a bedside glass before continuing. "Harpoon and his houseguests are planning to go early, get dinner before the show. Are you interested in joining them?"

"Who else is going from Fuego?"

"Rick Manning and his wife, Elaine, but they're coming directly from work, so we're going to meet them there. And I invited Steve Morrison, a guy I met at a poker game at the resort a couple of weeks ago."

"You've been holding out on me," Jessica replied reproachfully. "Who's this Morrison character? You haven't mentioned him before."

"He's a friend of Harpoon's. They used to work together in California. His screen name was Biff Bratwurst. He's been living in Florida for a couple of years now, in Ozona."

"Never heard of him. Will I be impressed?"

Lauren yawned. "Probably not. He's older, but Harpoon says he's a lot of fun once he loosens up." Pause. "I invited him to the party tonight after the concert at The Hand and Job."

Jessica bore in. "Will he be staying over?"

"I think so. He did say he'd be meeting us early for dinner."

"Sounds like fun," Jessica said. "Count me in. Do you want to drive, or would you like me to?"

"I'll drive. Why don't you stop by at 5:30? That should get us there in plenty of time."

"I'll see you then."

After the call ended Lauren took a shower. The hot water was therapeutic, helping to rouse her a little more, but she made a note as she stood under the spray not to schedule so many events during her long weekend off from her duties at FedEx in the future. By the time tonight's party at The Hand and Job ended, long after midnight, she knew she'd be exhausted.

She dried off and, with a towel wrapped around her damp hair, picked out her wardrobe for tonight. It was going to be pleasant, in the 70s, with no chance of rain, so she selected a purple short-sleeved knit top with a plunging neckline that always drew attention to her breasts and a pair of skinny jeans that accentuated her hips and ass. Harpoon told her Morrison was a boob man, and her surgically enhanced pair were her best features, a solid 38C. She was confident they would command his attention, especially since they'd be unfettered in the top she'd chosen to wear this evening.

She grabbed her cigarettes and lighter and went out on her lanai, naked except for the towel wrapped around her head. Her backyard was small, about thirty feet from the rear of her home to the edge of her property. A small paved pathway used by walkers and joggers separated her yard from a pond that attracted a variety of tropical water fowl in the mornings. At least that's what her neighbors told her – Lauren was a chronically late sleeper, rarely awake before noon, so she hadn't observed their early morning feedings amid the reeds along the marshy shoreline of the small pond.

She lit a cigarette and inhaled deeply. From the direction of the clubhouse she could hear faint shouts coming from the pool dedicated to water volleyball. There was a spirited core of aquatic volleyballers at Fuego who played every Saturday afternoon; they'd tried to recruit her on several occasions, to no avail. Her exercise regimen was a simple one: sex. She felt any voluntary activity that produced sweat and didn't culminate in an orgasm or two was a waste of time. The closest she came to actual involvement in any sport was her passion for college football and her beloved Georgia Bulldogs, the team she'd adopted when she'd been a cop in suburban Atlanta. She watched as many of their games as she could.

She ground out her cigarette and glanced at her watch. Time to get ready.

56

Vasilevsky waited until noon on Saturday before calling Meade. But there was no answer, so he left a brief message. "Is Nikolai. Please call."

He wandered into the kitchen and found a can of tomato soup in the cupboard. He heated it up in a pan he found in a drawer beneath the oven and ate it in Tang's kitchen with some crackers he'd found in one of the cupboards as he pondered once again the wisdom of employing Calvin Meade to perform such a vital task. He hadn't heard a word from him since Wednesday, when he'd agreed to make the journey to the Keys, and he was starting to get nervous.

When he was finished eating he rinsed out his bowl and placed it in the dishwasher before heading upstairs to shower. He brought his phone with him into the bathroom and laid it on the sink, within reach if Meade should call while he was showering.

*****

Meade was between Islamorada and Key Largo, on his way home, when his phone chirped. He smiled; it was fuckin' Igor. Let him stew a bit longer. He had to see a man about some meth.

*****

Rheinhart was also keeping his phone close, hoping for a call back from Gwen as he cleaned his small bungalow in case they decided to return to his place after their boating date. There had been no need for him to clean the place thoroughly for months – his only guest was Morrison, who was the last person likely to comment on the slovenliness of another man's living space, the man whose previous home before moving to Ozona had been his car.

He vacuumed the living room and the bedroom, emptied the garbage beneath the sink and placed it in the blue container under the carport before scrubbing the bathroom and, inspired by the chance for romance, changing the sheets on his bed. He worked cheerfully, the Stranglers providing the soundtrack on his iPod as he methodically removed several weeks worth of dust and dirt. He proceeded as it the house was for sale and he was hosting an open house, even using an old toothbrush to scrub away the mildew that had accumulated on the grout between the tiles of the shower walls.

Two hours later he surveyed the results with a fatigued smile. Now all she had to do was call him back.

*****

Traffic was heavy as Morrison made his way down State Route 54, all three eastbound lanes congested with Floridians on their way, he figured, to chain restaurants for the Saturday night dinner special. He'd left himself some wiggle room in case traffic was bad, so he wasn't worried about being late. He was listening to Bela Fleck and the Flecktones on satellite radio, one of the jazz channels, head nodding to the beat as he periodically checked the vehicles adjacent to him to see if any of the drivers were on their cell phones. He had an inordinate fear of distracted drivers, a fear he'd developed on the freeway death traps of southern California as the use of cell phones had proliferated. He hadn't thought it possible when he first arrived, but it didn't take long to convince him that Florida drivers were even worse than those in California.

There was some congestion at the juncture with U.S. 41. He waited for two light changes before being able to make the right-hand turn toward Skipper's. Checking his mirrors, he merged into the far-left lane and accelerated through a yellow caution light as Weather Report followed Bela Fleck. He passed the turnoff for Club Paradise on the right, the second largest nudist facility in the county behind Fuego.

Traffic was lighter on 41 as he headed south. The clock on his dashboard read 6:03 as he turned left onto Skipper Road and then made a quick left again into their parking lot. Tang had been right – the place didn't look like much from the outside, a series of loosely connected ramshackle structures that looked like they'd been assembled by an enthusiastic but underskilled high school shop class. A sign between the front door of the restaurant and the road confirmed that Free Range Strange was tonight's headline act.

He drove slowly through the pothole-infested parking lot before finding a space behind the restaurant. His group was already there, studying menus, when he walked through the door. Tang saw him first, a broad grin on his face as he waved Morrison over, indicating an empty seat next to him. "Welcome to Skipper's," he said, adding in an aside to the group assembled around the table, "It's his virgin visit."

"You weren't kidding when you said the place had a few rough edges," Morrison observed drily as he slid in next to Tang. "From the road it looks more like a junkyard than a music venue."

"Wait till you see the stage and seating area," Lauren said from her position to Morrison's immediate left. "Did Harpoon tell you to bring disinfectant?"

"Don't listen to her," Tang advised. "Anything less than the palace at Versailles is a dump to her."

There were six of them at the table. On Tang's right was Les Bent, thirty years older but still recognizable to Morrison. Next to him was an older man in his sixties who Morrison deduced was Tang's other houseguest, looking uncomfortable next to a

343

sensational-looking blond who Morrison judged to be in her late twenties. The blond was seated next to Lauren Caputo, who flashed him a seductive smile when she caught his eye.

Tang continued. "This is my friend Steve Morrison," he said in introduction. "This is Les Bent, whom I think you know."

Bent flashed a million-dollar smile. "Steve? I always thought his name was Biff." He extended his hand across the table. "Been a long time."

"Harpoon tells me you're living in the Keys now, Les," Morrison said as he shook Bent's hand.

"Yep. Got a nice little place in Islamorada." He paused, his face clouding over. "At least I used to. Haven't been back since the hurricane."

"Still drinks like a fish," Tang complained facetiously. "My liquor bill is out of this world since he moved in." He indicated the older man next to Bent. "This is Nikolai, another evacuee who's staying with me." Tang smiled. "Fortunately, he doesn't drink nearly as much as Bent does."

The man nodded toward Morrison. He spoke in heavily accented English. "Very nice to meet you, Mr. Morrison."

"Next to Nikolai is Jessica Callaway, another resident of Fuego. And you know Lauren."

"Not well enough," Lauren said suggestively. "But the night is young."

Morrison nodded toward Jessica. "Nice to meet you, Jessica. I've heard a lot of nice things about you from Harpoon."

She gave Tang an inquiring look. "Is that so?" She shifted her gaze back toward Morrison. "Maybe you can fill me in later."

"It would be my pleasure," Morrison said. Lauren kicked him under the table and gave him a dark look.

"We went ahead and ordered some oysters," Tang said, handing Morrison a menu. "You're welcome to share them or get something else for yourself. Still a beer man?"

"Yuengling, if they've got it."

"They do."

Morrison pretended to study the menu; he'd checked the menu online earlier in the day and already knew what he wanted to order. From time to time, he glanced surreptitiously at the elder Russian across the table from him, wondering what his connection was to Harpoon. He could tell Bent was ahead of the others in the alcohol department - he'd always been an early starter. He was having difficulty not staring at Jessica, whose blond hair fell just below her shoulders, her azure eyes mesmerizing. It wasn't hard to see why her website was so popular.

Bent corralled a waitress as she was walking by, holding up his glass. "Another mojito, my dear, and a Yuengling for my friend here," he said, indicating Morrison.

The waitress, a dishwater blond with a sturdy build and the expression of someone who's seen it all, twice over, looked around the table. "Anyone else?" she asked.

Nikolai raised his hand timidly. "Glass of water, please. With lemon."

She looked around the table. There were no other takers, so she walked back toward the kitchen, shaking her head.

When she was out of sight, Bent turned back to Morrison. "What are you doing these days, Biff?"

"It's Steve," he said, irritated. "I'm retired."

"So you decided to move to God's waiting room with all the other shuffleboard players?" Bent needled, glancing sideways to see if Jessica appreciated his humor.

Same old Bent. Always has to be the youngest guy in the room. He caught the glance Bent sent toward the young blond and thought: good luck with that. "I figured it was time for a change. Florida was as good a place as any." He smiled at his antagonist. "Seems to suit you just fine, Les."

"There's Florida, and then there's the Keys. Two different worlds." He smiled. "You remember what it was like in Key West, back in the day. It's nothing like that any more, but it sure as hell beats living in California. Must have a coupla million beaners there now, and not a single fucking one of them knows how to drive."

Nikolai was confused. "What are these beaners?"

"Mexicans," Tang explained wearily.

"Whatever you say."

57

Morrison ordered the fried catfish dinner. Both of the women ordered salads, while Bent tried to convince Nikolai to order the gator ribs. Nikolai was having none of it. "Alligator? Who eats alligator?"

"It's one of the most popular items on the menu," Bent lied. "Tastes just like chicken."

Nikolai knew Bent as well as anyone at the table and recognized his bullshit. He looked at his antagonist. "Then why not order chicken?" He turned to the waitress. "Chicken sandwich, please."

Tang ordered the grouper Reuben and Bent settled on chicken wings and another mojito. The small rectangular dining area was mostly full, an older clientele, definitely not the Red Lobster crowd, folks who'd been around the block once or twice sprinkled among two young families and their well-behaved adolescent children, the oldest of which appeared to be no more than eight. Two waitresses handled the room, pros who knew when to hover and when to disappear. There was a hint of anticipation in the room; diners going to the show seemed more animated than those there solely for dinner.

Posters touting previous performers were plastered to the walls of the dining area. Morrison recognized several of the groups and performers, people who had gone on to play on some of the nation's most esteemed stages. The place certainly had a musical pedigree.

Morrison also observed the group dynamics while they ate. The five with roots in the adult entertainment industry interacted like long lost friends, picking up conversations after years had passed as if no time had passed at all. But Nikolai seemed ill at ease as raunchy tales flew back and forth across the table, eliciting gales of laughter and additional tales more debauched than their antecedents, never smiling, just continuing to munch on his chicken sandwich, his gaze averted. Morrison had the impression the Russian regretted his decision to accompany the group and that he would be more comfortable in any setting other than the one in which he currently found himself.

Bent, now on his fourth mojito since Morrison had arrived, finally connected the dots between Morrison and Nikolai. "You haven't said boo to Biff since he got here, Nikolai. Don't you recognize him?"

Morrison's voice had a malevolent edge. "It's Steve."

"Steve, Shmeve." Bent waved his hands as if dismissing Morrison's correction. "Nobody knew you as Steve when we were filming back then."

Lauren had picked up on the tension. "Filming what?"

"A true cinematic classic," Bent said with unabashed pride. "The highlight of my career as a director. *The Russians Are Coming and Coming and Coming*."

As soon as the words passed Bent's lips, Nikolai looked up from his sandwich at Bent, alarmed. Bent continued. "Biff, er, Steve here was the star of that epic. Captain Ivan Jakinov. You must remember him, Nikolai."

The Russian shook his head, avoiding eye contact. Morrison thought he looked like a cornered rat, unable to find an avenue of escape. He looked at Nikolai more closely, calculating.

348

It had to be him. Tang's houseguest had to be the mysterious money man behind that film, the man the female FBI agent had casually questioned him about on Monday. She'd probed him about Russians, about the woman who'd been hired as a dialogue consultant. And she'd asked him what he thought at the time was a throwaway question about the film's financial backer: were there any other foreign nationals on the set?

Morrison decided to press the Russian. "So you were the money man on that film, eh? I never knew that before." No response from the Russian. Morrison continued. "I'd like to buy you a drink, Nikolai. That was the best shoot of my life, my favorite role. I hope you made a lot of money from that film." He looked around for the waitress, hoping to get her attention.

Nikolai was appalled that he was the object of this conversation. He shook his head hastily. "Is no need to buy drink, but thank you."

Lauren appraised the three men – one drunk and teetering on obnoxious, one grateful, one terrified. "Must've been some movie," she offered as a prompt.

"It was one of a kind," Bent said proudly. "Back then we did a lot of spoofs of real movies, box office hits. We'd change the title a little, make it more suggestive, but not so different that fans of the original wouldn't recognize it."

"When was it shot?" Jessica asked, jumping in.

Bent leered at the young blond. "Before you were born, sweetheart. Back in the early eighties." He reached back, remembering. "Before Key West got so fashionable and expensive."

"It was shot in Key West?" Lauren asked, leaning in.

"Yep," Bent answered. "First and last time I shot in the Keys." He gestured toward Nikolai. "Thanks to this man. He insisted we shoot in Florida, to make it more realistic. I liked it so much that I ended up moving there. So did Nikolai."

Morrison chimed in. "Not right away, though? You went back to the valley for a while, didn't you?"

"I did, but it kept getting more crowded, more expensive, way more traffic. I got fed up and came back to the Keys. Been happy as a clam ever since."

"Until the hurricane," Tang said with a smile.

Bent nodded. "Until the hurricane. I'm still waiting for a status report on my house. It's been two months now and I haven't heard a thing. Nikolai, either." Bent smiled. "That's why he sent one of the maintenance guys from Fuego down to Marathon yesterday, to check on his place." He grimaced. "I should've given him my address, asked him to stop in Islamorada on his way home." He turned toward Nikolai. "You heard back from him?"

Nikolai shook his head. In a small voice he replied, "Not yet."

Morrison was taking it all in, digesting the revelations, recalling that the FBI agent who'd interviewed him on Monday, Threadgill, insisted her questions had nothing to do with Mueller's investigation. Reflexively, he patted his wallet, nestled in the pocket of his shorts. The FBI agent's card was in there. He made a note to ask Tang about the maintenance man's trip when the two of them were alone, see what he knew about that.

The waitress appeared from around the corner. Bent noticed her first, lifting his empty glass and pointing at it, indicating his need for a refill. Morrison turned toward Tang, who was still nursing his first Arnold Palmer. "I hope he's not driving."

"No chance," Tang said with a resigned smile as the waitress ambled over, a neutral look on her broad features. "I used to work with the guy, too. I remember having to peel him off a number of barstools in Pasadena."

The waitress surveyed the group. "Can I get anyone else anything?"

Tang looked at his watch; the doors would be opening in five minutes and he was anxious to get a good seat. "Just the check, I think. We're here for the show."

The waitress's neutral face brightened. "I love Free Range Strange. Especially Jerome." She looked around the table. "Separate checks?"

"Jerome is Travolta's friend," Tang added in explanation as he reached for his wallet. "Just one check tonight."

"I'll be right back."

When she returned a few minutes later, no one protested when Tang reached for the check. He glanced at it to make sure the charges were correct, then handed it back to her with his credit card.

Jessica spoke first. "That's very kind of you, Wai." She was one of only a few who called Tang by his given name.

"Don't mention it," he replied with a smile. "You can get the next one if you like."

"Deal."

When the bill was settled, the ladies visited the rest room and the men waited for them by the entrance to the stage area, where a small line waiting to be admitted had just begun to move. Lauren and Jessica returned, makeup refreshed. Morrison moved quickly toward the diminutive man with dark hair and a moustache who was taking tickets. "This one's on me," he insisted to the rest of the group, reaching for his wallet as he addressed the man. "How much?"

The ticket taker counted heads. "Six of you? That'll be ninety bucks."

He extracted a hundred and handed it to the man, who held it up to an ultraviolet light used mainly to illuminate hand stamps. "Don't see many of these," the man said, apparently satisfied that it was authentic as he withdrew a ten from his cash drawer and handed it back to Morrison. "Enjoy the show."

58

Rheinhart was dozing in his chair when his phone rang. It took him a moment to orient himself before he located the phone on the table beside him. His pulse spiked; it was Gwen. He tried to keep the excitement out of his voice. "Hello?"

"Zach? This is Gwen Westphal, returning your call from this morning."

He took a deep cleansing breath. "Thanks for getting back to me so quickly. Uh, I was calling to see if you might want to get together sometime."

"I'd love that," she said warmly. "What do you have in mind?"

"I thought we might go out on my boat. Somewhere in the Gulf."

"You have a boat?"

"Yes," he said. "It's not very big, a little Hewes skiff, but as long as the chop's not too bad, it's a decent boat, especially on the flats."

"Sounds cozy." Pause. "I'm free on Wednesday – it's my day off. Does that work for you?"

"That's perfect." Could she read his eagerness? "I'll check the weather, make sure it's not supposed to rain."

"It sounds like fun, Zach," she said. "Where do you keep your boat?"

"At the Crooked Snook Marina in Ozona."

"I know that place," she said. "I live in Tarpon Springs. I can meet you at the marina if you'd like."

This was going better than he'd expected. "I'll check the weather and the tides and get back to you. Are mornings okay for you?"

"Best time of the day to be on the water."

"Great. Then I'll call you back after I check the conditions for Wednesday."

"I'm looking forward to it."

*****

Tang took charge once they were in the performance area, known as the Skipperdome. It was an open-air space nestled beneath a couple of ancient live oaks that provided a natural ceiling above the stage area. There was a section of covered seating in the middle, separated from the compact stage by a dance floor and from the elevated rear section by the mixing board. Rows of picnic tables with benches on either side of the center section were uncovered and favored by folks uncowed by adverse weather predictions.

The people in line ahead of them had opted for the center section, but Tang walked briskly past them to the rear section, where there were a number of tables and comfortable chairs, a service bar and the merchandise area where bands hawked CDs, T-shirts and other related items. Even though they were as far back as they could go without spilling over into the parking lot, they were still only thirty feet from the stage, with excellent sightlines because of the section's elevation. The entire rear area was under a slanted roof that protected those seated beneath from the elements.

Tang indicated a pair of round tables. "How's this?"

"Looks good to me," Lauren said, grabbing a chair with a substantial cushion, surveying the crowd as they trickled in. She lit a cigarette and turned to Tang. "What kind of music do these guys play again?"

"Bluegrass, with an edge that's sort of punk. Very high energy," Tang replied.

Jessica lit a cigarette of her own. "Is there an opening act?"

"I don't think so," Tang said.

Bent drained his glass. "Whose turn is it to buy?"

"Harpoon paid for dinner and Steve bought the tickets," Lauren observed archly. "Looks like you're up, Les."

While they were getting settled, Morrison was watching the taciturn Russian closely. He appeared to be relieved that they were no longer talking about *The Russians Are Coming*, the Keys or anything related to that time long ago. Like Morrison, it was his first visit to Skipper's, and his head was on a swivel, drinking it all in. A mural on the wall to the left of the stage, beyond the picnic tables, piqued his interest. He turned to Tang. "Who is that man on wall?"

"Jerry Garcia. He used to be in a band called the Grateful Dead. That mural was a spontaneous thing, painted by one of the customers. As time went on other people added little bits here and there. Looks just like him." Tang continued. "The Grateful Dead are pretty big here. Every Thursday night is Grateful Dead night at Skipper's. Uncle John's Band plays, and the admission is free."

While Nikolai was engaged in conversation with Tang, Morrison slipped his phone out of his pocket and took several photos of the unsuspecting Russian. If he was who Morrison thought he was, Special Agent Threadgill would surely be interested in some photographic evidence. He raised the phone to his ear, pretending to make a call as he snapped several photos of the Russian's face and profile.

Lauren noticed what he was doing and raised her eyebrows. Morrison lifted his index finger silently to his lips, warning her to be quiet. She gave him a long, inquiring look before turning back toward Jessica. It was the kind of look that implied a conversation to be had down the road; Morrison nodded silently in agreement.

Rick Manning and his wife Elaine arrived just as the band appeared on stage. Introductions were made as they found chairs and joined the group at the table. Most of the seats in the Skipperdome were filled and there was a buzz of anticipation in the air. Morrison caught a whiff of weed as the owner of Skipper's, beer in hand, made his way to the microphone to introduce the band. He waited patiently until the bustling crowd quieted a bit. "Let's give these guys a big Skipper's welcome. From Ocala, please put your hands together for Free Range Strange."

Generous applause as the frontman of the band, Jerome Cortez, stepped up to the mic. He was tall, thin, with a permanent grin seemingly fixed on his face. "It's great to be back at the Skipperdome, one of our all-time favorite places to play. We're going to start with something off the new album, *Hollow Promises*, which is available from Sherry at the merch table at the back." Pause. "We hope you like it."

It was an interesting lineup. Two guitars, two mandolins and a banjo burst into a blistering instrumental whose tempo reminded Morrison of "The Orange Blossom Special." Fingers were flying as a group of band devotees, true believers who followed the band from gig to gig, flocked to the dance floor from their seats in front of the stage, heads bobbing in approval like incontinent chickens.

They slowed it down a bit after that, with two tunes that could almost be considered ballads. Cortez's voice was strong and

clear, and the band's harmonies reminded Morrison of the Beach Boys in their prime. Harpoon was right – these guys were good. They played for ninety minutes before taking a fifteen-minute break, then came back for another hour before finally calling it quits. Jessica tried to get Lauren to dance with her during the encore but she refused. Bent was quick to lurch forward. "I'll dansh with you," he slurred, grabbing her hand and dragging her toward the crowded dance floor before she had a chance to refuse.

Applause and whistles filled the Skipperdome as the band finished their encore and took their bows before ducking quickly backstage. They had a date in Boca Raton tomorrow night, and they wanted to get on the road as soon as possible, while the adrenaline was still surging.

Tang turned to Morrison, practically shouting to be heard above the crowd noise. "What did I tell you?"

Morrison nodded. Even Nikolai had gotten into it, tapping his foot and bobbing his head to several of the tunes. Morrison was able to snap several more photos of the enigmatic Russian, who was absorbed by the music and didn't notice. The ever-alert Lauren did notice; he'd explain to her when they were alone at the party later on.

He managed to pull Tang aside as they waited for the crowd to file out. "Is Nikolai going to the after party?"

Tang laughed. "Hardly. He's been at Fuego for two weeks and I don't think he's taken his clothes off to shower. One of our parties would give him a heart attack."

After dissuading Bent from ordering one last mojito for the road, Tang and Morrison supported him as they made their way to Tang's car. They poured him into the back seat, where he collapsed, barely conscious, Nikolai watching it all warily before getting into the front passenger seat. Tang slid behind the wheel

and rolled down the window. "See you at the bar. I left word at the gate that you're my guest. Don't let them give you any shit."

Morrison stepped back as Tang pulled out. He was about to make his way to his own car when he felt a tug on his shirt from behind. He turned to find Lauren and Jessica standing there. "So what were those pictures all about?" Lauren asked pointedly.

"It's complicated," he said, buying time. "I'll explain at the party."

She took a drag on her cigarette. "I suggest you make it quick. I've got some ideas about how to spend the rest of the night that don't include conversation."

59

Meade skidded into his driveway fifteen minutes before kickoff, grabbed the six-pack and jumbo bag of popcorn he'd picked up from Wawa and was in his seat, glass pipe within reach, in time for the coin toss. He'd called Darryl right after he'd passed Sarasota and told him he was looking to buy. Darryl was holding and told Meade to stop by, the earlier the better because he was going out tonight. Meade reassured him. "I should be there in about forty-five."

Now it was time for a little football. Right after a few hits of his latest purchase.

*****

The Saturday night parties at Fuego were themed affairs, highly anticipated by members and residents. Lauren had warned Morrison that tonight's party at The Hand and Job carried a pirate theme. "It's Buccaneer Night," she'd advised. "Dress accordingly."

Morrison wasn't the costume type, so he'd ignored her advice and hadn't put together a different outfit. Besides, the object of these parties was to get as many people naked as quickly as possible; going to elaborate steps to create a specific wardrobe that would then be removed within an hour of arrival seemed counterproductive. He knew he'd probably be in the minority, but he didn't care. He was a guest who would be gone by first light.

He was held up slightly at the gate by the security guard, who'd received instructions from Tang to admit Morrison but still insisted he sign in. By the time he'd parked his car and made his way to the front door of the English pub, Lauren and Jessica were

waiting for him in full costume, dressed nearly identically in short skirts, knee-high black boots and low-cut white peasant blouses that showed off their impressive cleavages. They each had a sash tied around their heads, Jessica's black, Lauren's red.

Lauren spotted him first, rushing to his side, linking her arm with his. Jessica followed, doing the same on the opposite side. "Might as well make an entrance while people are still sober enough to notice," Lauren said saucily. Noticing the confusion on Morrison's face, she explained. "We're both wenches. Jess is the ale wench, and I'm the mead wench. We're here to provide for your pleasure."

A wide grin creased Morrison's face. "Sounds perfect to me."

Both women were statuesque, Jessica five nine, Lauren an inch shorter. They were also well known at the resort, veterans of many of these parties, so their entrance with an unknown face caused a bit of a stir among those not yet paired off. Eyes followed them as they made their way by the dimly lit bar to an unoccupied couch in the far corner of the room, where Lauren and Morrison sat down while Jessica continued on, toward the cloak room. She returned a moment later with three large beach towels. "For when our clothes come off," she explained with a wink to Morrison.

Morrison sat back, soaking it all in, music throbbing through expertly concealed speakers throughout the pub. Apparently, Lauren and Jessica had made up their minds that they were going to share Morrison tonight without consulting him. He had no problem with that, but was slightly surprised that Lauren was willing to share him with her much younger friend. He'd had the impression from their earlier conversations that Lauren was planning to keep him all to herself.

Since it had been so long since he'd found himself in a situation like this, he'd resorted to the crutch that had extended his

career in adult entertainment, a small blue pill that he'd swallowed before leaving the parking lot at Skipper's. Just in case, he told himself as he swallowed the pill with a sip of water. The last thing he wanted was to be unable to rise to the occasion when it presented itself – the pill was his insurance policy.

He already felt a stirring in his loins, sandwiched between the two wenches as they both lit cigarettes and searched for an ashtray. The smoke was thick in the room as Morrison turned to Lauren, raising his voice to be heard above the music. "I thought smoking was illegal in bars in Florida."

She exhaled in the opposite direction, then turned back. "This is a private club that was in operation before the ban took effect. Since it's on private property, smoking was grandfathered in, so the pub isn't required to adhere to the new law." She went on. "There is one bar on the property that is non-smoking, but hardly anyone goes there. Most members here and swingers I've known like to smoke and drink…a lot."

Just like the porn business, Morrison thought. He'd been one of the few people, cast or crew, who hadn't been a smoker. He reasoned that people willing to have unprotected sex with strangers were wired differently. They cared little about lifestyle choices that might affect their health – they were hedonists, here for a good time instead of a long time.

Lauren leaned in, her left hand caressing his inner thigh. "So what were those pictures all about at Skipper's?"

Morrison had rehearsed what he was going to say to Lauren on the drive back to Fuego. "You heard Bent comment that Nikolai and I worked together before, right?"

"Actually, I didn't. But go on."

"We did, although I had never seen him before tonight. He was the money man on a film I shot in Key West, but he never showed up on the set. He called the shots from somewhere else. I've been curious who would spend that much money on a porn shoot ever since. I didn't know he was coming with us tonight, and I certainly wouldn't have known who he was if Bent hadn't been drunk." He looked around the room. "He's not here, is he?"

"Bent? Hardly," she replied. "He could barely walk. Harpoon told me he and the old man had to carry him inside."

"Harpoon's here?"

"I saw him when I first got here," she said, sliding her hand up his thigh to caress the growing bulge in Morrison's shorts. She looked at Morrison's crotch, then into his eyes. "Your friend here tells me we've spent enough time talking." She released her grip on him just long enough to pull her blouse over her head, releasing her breasts, nipples already erect, before her hand returned to give his cock a friendly squeeze.

Following Lauren's lead, Jessica also removed her blouse and rose to her feet to wiggle out of her skirt, standing before the two of them clad only in her black boots. Morrison noticed she was completely shaved as Lauren squeezed him again before searching for his zipper, drawing it down slowly, then reaching inside to grip his shaft again. He wasn't wearing any underwear, and her hand felt warm and soft against his rigid flesh.

The rest of the night was a cascade of pleasure unlike any he'd experienced before, Lauren and Jessica alternating in addressing his obvious need while delaying their own. And when he needed to rest and recuperate the two of them concentrated on each other, their coupling providing a visual incentive during his recovery process. He didn't know how long they spent at the pub before they returned to Lauren's condo, still naked, clutching their clothes, to continue their explorations, which continued until the first light of the morning appeared above the line of palms surrounding the pond behind her place. They'd moved from the bedroom to the lanai and back to the bedroom again where the three of them, exhausted from their couplings, fell asleep sprawled across the bed, a tangle of naked limbs, the aroma of sex pungent in the cool morning air.

*****

Tremayne checked his watch. It had been nearly thirty-six hours since he'd been assigned to find Vasilevsky and he'd run into a brick wall. He was tired, in desperate need of a few hours of sleep but afraid to abandon the search. So far he had nothing positive to report to Threadgill, and he didn't want to slack off until he had something, anything, that would resemble a clue to the Russian's current location.

He'd tried hacking into Vasilevsky's phone, but he was no longer using the number the Bureau had on file for him. Exactly what I would've done if I was trying to lay low, thought Tremayne – ditch the phone and use a burner.

He'd circulated the latest photo they had of Vasilevsky to all the airports, train stations and bus terminals between Miami and Charlotte, but had come up empty. There continued to be no action on his credit cards or withdrawals from the bank account that had funded Natalya Bazarov, further deepening his gloom. He'd run into dead ends like this several times in the past, and in each of those incidences his quarry had turned up dead. Not a good sign.

He stood and stretched. Maybe a shower would clear his head. He sniffed his armpit and recoiled, trying to remember the last time he'd bathed. Was it only two days ago? He made a note to check out some new deodorant options the next time he left his apartment and grabbed a fresh Mountain Dew from the refrigerator before shuffling into the bathroom, leaving the door open behind him as he shed his clothes and stepped under the cold spray designed to jolt him back to life.

There had to be a way to locate Vasilevsky. All he had to do was figure out how to do it. Fast.

60

It was nearly 2:30 by the time Morrison woke up on Sunday afternoon. Jessica was gone. Lauren snored gently beside him as he tried to shake the cobwebs from his brain and get his bearings. Carefully, he rose from the bed, trying not to disturb Lauren, whose rhythmic breathing indicated deep sleep, and went looking for his clothes. He found his shoes just inside the front door, and his shirt and shorts in a heap on the floor in front of the refrigerator. Had they eaten?

He washed his face in the bathroom and patted his cowlick down with some water. He'd had little to drink, two beers at Skipper's and one back at Fuego, so he knew he was okay to drive. When he was dressed he retrieved his phone from the pocket of his shorts and checked the photos he'd taken the night before. Not bad; he was no professional, but the pics he'd taken the night before were good enough for someone who knows what Vasilevsky looks like to identify him.

He extracted Threadgill's business card from his wallet. He dismissed a fleeting thought that this was Sunday and decided to call her to tell her what he had discovered. Like he'd told Rheinhart, the FBI doesn't take the weekend off.

She answered on the fifth ring, slightly out of breath. "Special Agent Threadgill. How can I help you?"

"Agent Threadgill, this is Steven Morrison. I hope I'm not disturbing you."

"Not at all," she demurred. "I was out by the pool, reading. What's on your mind?"

"I have some information you might be interested in. It concerns our interview last week."

"Go on."

"I think I found the Russian you're looking for."

She was interested, but wary. "Why do you think that?"

"Because there was an older Russian with Les Bent last night. The three of us went to see some music at Skipper's Smokehouse."

"What was this Russian's name?"

"Nikolai. He never told me his last name."

"What did he look like? Can you describe him to me?"

"I can do better than that," he replied. "I took some pictures of him. I figured you'd like to see them."

"You figured right, Mr. Morrison. Can you send me those photos via text message to my phone?"

"Sure. You want them all?"

"Send me whatever you have."

"Okay, but I'm going to have to hang up to send you the pictures," he explained sheepishly. "I'm not very tech oriented."

Urgency crept into her voice. "Before you hang up, Mr. Morrison, will you be available if I want to talk to you again after I see the photos?"

"Sure. I'm about to drive home from Land O' Lakes, but I don't have a hands-free setup in my car. I should be home in less than an hour."

"Perfect," she exclaimed. "Send me those pictures, and I'll be in touch." Pause. "Thanks again, Mr. Morrison."

There were seven photos in all. Morrison sent them one at a time, making sure each one had been transmitted before sending the next. When they were all sent, he got into his car and selected a jazz station on his satellite radio to accompany him back to Ozona, listening to Pete Malinverni's "August in New York" as he swung onto U.S. 41.

*****

As soon as she hung up with Morrison, Threadgill strode quickly to her home office and called up the latest photos the Bureau had of Nikolai Vasilevsky. The photos from Morrison came through on her phone a moment later, each announcing its arrival with a resonant tone. She blew up the only unobscured frontal shot of the group as much as she could and held her phone next to her laptop.

It was him. A bit older, a few more lines around his eyes, a little more gray in his hair, but she had no doubt it was him. She resisted the urge to call Miller or Gutierrez; instead, she dialed Tremayne. "Any progress?"

The young agent's voice was subdued. "Nothing since we talked last."

"I'm going to send you a photo. I think we found him. Someone spotted him at a concert last night in Tampa."

Tremayne responded excitedly. "Are you sure?"

"I have some photos taken on a cell phone at the concert. I can't be a hundred percent sure without further analysis, but if it's not him, it's his twin brother."

Tremayne shuffled through the array of papers strewn around his home office before responding. "According to the file, he doesn't have a twin brother, Agent Threadgill. Only an older sister."

"I was being facetious, Agent Tremayne."

"Huh?"

"Just making a joke." She continued in a motherly tone. "How long since you last slept, Gavin?"

He was taken aback. It was the first time she had ever addressed him by his given name. "Uh, Thursday night, I think."

"I suggest you get some rest. We're going to need you alert and at your best to close this out."

"Yes, ma'am."

Time had never moved slower for Threadgill as she monitored the time on her phone, calculating how long it would take Morrison to reach Ozona. She made herself a tuna sandwich and gulped it down with some lemonade, then did a load of laundry and checked her email. When she decided he'd had enough time to make it home, she dialed Morrison's number. He picked up on the second ring. "Perfect timing. Just got home five minutes ago." He took a deep breath. "Is he the one you're looking for"

"I think so. I have a few more questions for you, if that's okay?"

Her tone was out of character. If that's okay? "Shoot."

"Thank you, Mr. Morrison. Was Les Bent with the Russian gentleman?"

"Yes. They're both staying with a mutual friend in Land O' Lakes. They live in the Keys and can't go back yet."

She held her breath before continuing. "Do you have the address of this mutual friend handy?"

"I think it's in my address book," he replied. "Would you like me to check"

"Please."

He returned in a minute. "Do you have a pen and paper?"

She tried not to sound impatient. "Go ahead."

"They're staying at the home of Wai Tang. He lives at the Fuego Resort in Land O' Lakes, 375 Aruba Lane."

She scribbled furiously. "Do you know how long they'll be there?"

"Bent and Nikolai? Probably until they're allowed to go back to their homes, I'd guess."

"You don't know of any plans for Nikolai to leave?"

He decided to have a little fun with her. "No, ma'am. I'm pretty sure he likes the scenery where he's at. I could check with Harpoon."

"Who's that?"

"My friend, the one who owns the house where they're staying. That's his nickname."

She was all business. "I would advise against any further contact with Mr. Tang until we speak again. We are interested in speaking with this Nikolai, and I wouldn't want you or anyone else to spook him or make him nervous enough to leave before we get a chance to do that. Is that clear?"

It was clear she was not in a humorous mood. "Yes, ma'am," he replied meekly.

"One more thing. Do not under any circumstances discuss this conversation or the substance of it with anyone else. To do so would interfere with an ongoing investigation of the highest priority. Is that clear?"

"Crystal."

"Good. You've done a real service for your country, Mr. Morrison. We'll be in touch."

61

The plan to apprehend Nikolai Vasilevsky came together within an hour of Morrison's phone call to Threadgill. She contacted Miller, who dialed Gutierrez into their conversation. The three of them concurred that they needed to move swiftly before the cagey Russian could move on from Fuego.

Gutierrez made a phone call and within an hour obtained a warrant to detain Vasilevsky on the grounds that his visa had expired, rendering him deportable. There wasn't enough evidence to charge him with Middleton's murder, not yet, but they hoped that Vasilevsky understood how his detention would be viewed by his superiors in the Kremlin and perhaps give up the information they were looking for in exchange for immunity from prosecution and/or deportation. Gutierrez was banking on Vasilevsky realizing his chances for survival were considerably brighter in the U.S. than they were in Russia.

By 6:00 pm on Sunday, the FBI apprehension team, warrant in hand, was assembled and on its way to Fuego. Six black Escalades rolled up to the gate; two agents emerged from the lead vehicle, holding their FBI identification up so the guard could see. The confused guard, a portly man in his sixties, made a move for the phone, but one of the agents moved swiftly to cut him off. "We're here to serve an arrest warrant on a person who is currently a guest of one of your residents," the agent said, moving the guard back from the phone. "Until we have this person in our custody, there will be no communication between you and anyone on your staff, or with any of the residents."

The guard was overwhelmed by the show of power, his head on a swivel as he took in the size of the FBI presence. He addressed the agent who'd snatched the phone from his hand. "You must want this guy pretty bad."

The agent remained impassive as the five vehicles rolled past the guardhouse, through the gate. One vehicle remained behind in case Vasilevsky somehow made it past the apprehension team and tried to make a run for it. Special Agent Miller, who was calling the shots, was in the lead vehicle. As per their hastily conceived plan, the five vehicles headed toward Tang's home. One of them stopped at the clubhouse in case Vasilevsky was at the main pool, while the others proceeded to the residence.

They parked a block away, around a slight bend in Bimini Lane so the vehicles couldn't be seen from Tang's house. Two agents made their way to the rear of the home in case the Russian tried to slip out the back; the rest remained out by the road, vests on, weapons raised. When Miller was satisfied everyone was in place, he addressed the squad. "Nice and easy. We are not to initiate any gunfire. Fire only if you've been fired upon first. Is that clear?" Nods all around.

Warrant and identification in hand, Miller walked up to the door and rang the bell. After a few moments Tang opened the door. He saw a number of semiautomatic weapons aimed toward him. He looked at Miller, gape mouthed. "What is this?"

"Wai Tang?" Miller asked brusquely, holding up his ID. "We're from the FBI. We have an arrest warrant for Nikolai Vasilevsky. Is he on the premises?"

Tang nodded, eyes wide. "We're just having dinner. He's in the dining room."

"Is anyone else with him?" Miller asked. He turned slightly and gave a thumbs-up sign that propelled four of the agents to his side

Tang nodded again. "Les Bent is here."

"Step aside please, Mr. Tang."

The agents moved swiftly inside the house, weapons raised, down a short hall and into the dining room. Vasilevsky saw the agents first; his first instinct was flight, but he was quickly flanked by two of the agents whose presence made flight impractical

Bent, who was still nursing a lingering hangover from the night before, raised his head and saw the team, his fuzzy brain not quite comprehending the scene before him, right hand clutching a Bloody Mary.

Miller stepped over to Vasilevsky, who remained seated. "Nikolai Vasilevsky?"

The Russian nodded mutely. Miller continued. "I'm Special Agent Colton Miller of the FBI." He held up the warrant. "I have a warrant here for your arrest. Would you please get to your feet and put our hands out in front of you?"

Vasilevsky did as he was told. He looked at Miller as the agent slipped handcuffs around his wrists. "What is charge?" he asked coolly.

Miller ignored the question as the agents surrounded the Russian. "We have a vehicle waiting for you outside." He indicated the door. "Nice and slowly please."

One of the Escalades had been moved into Tang's truncated driveway. A rear door was open. The agents herded him into the car, where two of them flanked him in the back seat.

Tang and Bent, still gripping his drink, followed the agents as they escorted Vasilevsky to the vehicle. They watched, dumbfounded, as the vehicle backed out of the driveway. Across the street, several neighbors who'd noticed the influx of official-looking SUVs on their quiet little lane during the Sunday dinner hour stood on their front lawns, watching the drama unfold. Two of them, a man and woman in their seventies, were naked.

After the agents were gone, Bent turned toward Tang. "What the fuck was that?"

Tang shook his head, bewildered. "Your guess is as good as mine."

Bent's eyes brightened. "I'll bet it has something to do with the Mueller investigation."

*****

Calvin Meade was fuming, impatient. He'd called Vasilevsky an hour earlier, telling him he was back in town with the information from the Marathon condo, anxious to get his hands on the rest of his money.

But when he'd arrived at Fuego, a man in a blue jacket with the letters **FBI** stenciled in yellow on the back had held up his hand, directing him to park on the side of the road, refusing to allow him to enter. "Official business."

"What kind of business?" the exasperated maintenance man inquired. He received no reply from the stolid agent. Meade continued, his frustration spilling out. "How long is this going to take?"

A faint smile cracked the lips of the agent, who'd made Meade as a meth head seconds after he'd emerged from the Honda Pilot. "As long as it takes."

Meade walked back to his car. Once inside, he pulled out his phone and dialed Vasilevsky's number. The Russian's phone, which had been gathered and placed in an evidence bag before they left Tang's home, rang on the seat next to Miller, who glanced down and smiled as they prepared to leave Fuego, on their way back to Clearwater. Leave a message, he thought to himself.

When the call went to voicemail, Meade left a terse message. "Mr. Vasilevsky, this is Calvin Meade. I'm at the gate, but they won't let me in. I'll be there as soon as they do."

Two minutes later, five black Escalades rolled slowly past the gate, toward U.S. 41. Meade watched with apprehension as the agent who'd detained him at the gate got into an identical vehicle as the other five and followed them toward the access road into the resort. He knew cops when he saw them, and these were important cops. More feds, probably.

As soon as the SUVs were out of sight, the security guard motioned to Meade, signalling it was okay for him to enter. He knew Meade as an employee of the resort and waved him through without questioning.

Meade drove straight to Tang's house, parking in his driveway, verification photos clutched in his left hand as he strode briskly toward the front door. He rang the bell twice, impatiently. When Tang answered, he blurted out, "Igor here? Tell him I've got the stuff he was looking for and I want to get paid."

Tang looked at the young man and smiled. Meade noticed and bristled. "What's so fuckin' funny?"

"You're a little late," Tang replied. "He just left."

Meade was apoplectic at the news. "Wadda ya mean, he just left? I called him an hour ago, told him I'd be right over."

"He had a more pressing appointment," Tang said in way of explanation, adding, "With the FBI."

The presence of the FBI and their interest in Vasilevsky didn't bother Meade nearly as much as the sudden realization that the thousand dollars he was owed was now seriously at risk. "Is that what those guys in the Escalades were? FBI?"

Tang nodded. "Yes."

"And they arrested Igor?"

"Right again." He smiled, adding, "Come to think of it, I'll bet they'd be interested in talking to you, too. Maybe you should give them a call."

62

Tang finished his dinner, then called Morrison while Bent was loading the dishwasher. "You'll never guess what just happened here."

Morrison played dumb. "At Fuego?"

"Yes."

Morrison tried to make his voice sound innocent. He let the question dangle for a few moments before responding. "The FBI arrested Nikolai?"

Tang was gobsmacked. "How did you know?" he asked in bewilderment.

Morrison told him the whole story: how he'd been interviewed by the FBI last Monday and how the agent asking the questions was particularly interested in the work he did on *The Russians Are Coming and Coming and Coming.* When he'd seen Vasilevsky with Bent and the rest of the crew the night before at Skipper's, he'd put two and two together and snapped a couple of photos of the Russian on his cell phone camera and sent them to the FBI, who confirmed that Vasilevsky was the guy they were looking for.

Tang listened to the story, incredulous. When Morrison finished, Tang spoke up, irritation in his voice. "Why didn't you give me a heads-up that they were coming? They burst in while we were having dinner," he said, adding a little embellishment.

"They warned me not to breathe a word of what I knew to anyone, especially you. They identified you by name. I guess they figured an Asian like yourself might be sympathetic to a Russian criminal, might help him escape."

"That's bullshit!" Tang exclaimed hotly. "I'm not__"

Morrison interrupted. "Geez, Harpoon, I was kidding. Lighten up." He changed the subject. "Was Bent there, too?"

"The three of us were all at the table, eating, when they showed up."

"How's he feeling?"

"Hungover. He didn't wake up until nearly three this afternoon, still smelling like rum."

"Some things never change."

*****

Vasilevsky was silent on the trip to Clearwater, trying to keep calm, figure out his next move. His captors didn't help – there was no conversation at all among the four agents accompanying him, including the one who'd appeared at the door and identified himself as Miller; the man in charge. He was riding in the front, in the passenger seat, seemingly oblivious to the prisoner in the back seat flanked by two equally impassive agents.

He knew the American justice system allowed him to speak with an attorney and would even provide him with one if he couldn't afford to pay. He could afford to pay, and he knew who to call, a man the Russians had on retainer in Tampa. All covert agents in Florida were aware of this attorney and had instructions to contact him as soon as possible if they were ever taken into custody. He had the man's card in his wallet, but he'd never considered the possibility that he would actually need his services one day.

When they arrived at Bureau headquarters in Clearwater, they conveyed him from the parking garage in the rear into the building via a secure hallway especially designed to keep high-profile suspects away from the media glare, avoiding the front door where members of the press would assemble once the news leaked out that a Russian spy had been arrested.

The agents escorted him to a secure interrogation room with a rectangular table and two chairs, one on either side of the table. After they'd searched him and removed the contents from his pockets, Vasilevsky was led to the chair on the far side of the table facing a reflective glass surface which he knew to be a two-way mirror, where Agent Miller removed the handcuffs and stepped back, observing him silently for several moments, eyes locked with the Russian prisoner as he read him his rights.

When Miller reached the part about his right to have an attorney, Vasilevsky finally broke his silence. "Would like attorney." He nodded toward the wallet at the end of the table. "Is card in wallet."

Miller donned a pair of latex gloves and extracted a business card, holding it up for Vasilevsky to see. "Is this the guy?"

Vasilevsky nodded. As if he had telepathic powers, an agent entered the room from his observation point in the hallway with a cell phone which he handed to Vasilevsky. Miller handed the card to the Russian, who dialed the number. It rang seven times before switching over to an automated response. "Morton Abramowitz is no longer associated with the firm Bellino and Cairns. If you would like to speak to another attorney in our firm, please press 1. Have a nice day."

Vasilevsky was shaken, but managed to control his reaction. He knew Miller was observing him closely. He pressed 1, not yet willing to give up. In a moment a female voice came on the line. "How may I direct your call?" she asked pleasantly.

"Am looking for Mr. Abramowitz, please."

She sounded apologetic. "Mr. Abramowitz is no longer with the firm. Is there something I or another attorney can do for you?"

"Do you have new number for him?"

"I'm afraid I can't give out that information." Brusque now, businesslike.

His heart rate soared. What to do now? If he hung up, his one call would be finished and he'd be assigned a court-appointed attorney, someone no doubt unsympathetic to his specialized needs and background. He stalled, trying to decide what to do next. This alternative hadn't been covered during his training.

The woman on the other end of the line was growing impatient. "Are you still there, sir? Is there anything else I can do for you today?"

Miller was watching keenly as Vasilevsky struggled with the bad news, encouraged by the way things were going. The more isolated the Russian felt, the more likely it was that they might extract something useful from him. Not being able to find or contact his go-to attorney was a better outcome than he could've expected.

Finally the Russian spoke, his voice resigned. "Is nothing else. Thank you." He handed the phone back to Miller. "Would still like attorney," he said to Miller.

"I'll have one of my men put in a call to the public defender's office," Miller said. "Would you like something to drink? Some water, perhaps?"

Vasilevsky nodded wordlessly. In a few moments, the same agent who'd supplied the phone returned with some bottled water and placed it on the table near the suspect. Vasilevsky took a healthy swig, then returned the bottle to the table and looked imploringly at Miller: it's your show. Let's get started.

Miller placed a tape recorder between the two of them, turned it on and looked at the Russian agent. "Are you Nikolai Vasilevsky?"

Silence. Miller tried again. "Are you aware of your current visa status?"

More silence. Miller leaned over the table. "Is this the way you want to play it?"

Vasilevsky crossed his arms over his chest and leaned back in his chair. "Attorney."

"We're working on that. But I have to tell you, Nikolai – once your attorney arrives, he'll advise you to keep your mouth shut. Most of our public defenders are right out of law school, not talented enough to land a job with a reputable firm. Whoever shows up will never have represented a covert Russian agent. He or she won't have any idea how to deal with your unique situation. Right now, you're probably your own best attorney – nobody but you realizes the kind of deep shit you're in here. But if you talk now, you can help wrap this up a whole lot faster, and you can be on your way."

Vasilevsky stared at Miller, thinking: how dumb do you think I am? Expecting me to roll over and give it up? He wasn't sure yet what he'd been hauled in for – Miller had stated earlier that they merely wanted to question him as part of an ongoing investigation, but had given no clue what the investigation concerned. He was better off keeping his mouth shut, hoping that his attorney would have some advice he'd be willing to follow.

Realizing Vasilevsky wasn't going to talk, Miller tried another tack. "How well do you know Les Bent, the man you were having dinner with earlier tonight?"

The Russian's face remained impassive, but his brain was on fire, synapses crackling. Could this be something about Bent and not him? After considering it briefly, he dismissed that notion. They wouldn't have showed up with a swarm of agents in Kevlar vests with semiautomatic weapons locked and loaded if all they wanted to do was ask him a few questions about Les Bent. This had to be about Middleton's murder – there was no other reason he could think of that would justify such a show of force.

When the Russian failed to respond, a small smile appeared at the corners of Miller's mouth. "Have it your way. We'll wait for your attorney." He stood up and grabbed his handcuffs, motioning Vasilevsky to place his hands in front of him. Vasilevsky gave him a questioning look. Miller shook his head. "You didn't think I'd leave you in here alone, uncuffed, did you?"

He snapped the cuffs on and left the room, leaving Vasilevsky to stew in his own thoughts.

63

Threadgill was waiting in the hall when Miller emerged from the room. He handed the evidence gathered from Vasilevsky's pockets, his wallet, a comb and a set of keys for a rental car, to one of the agents and told him to file it. He turned back to Threadgill, who said. "What next?"

Miller shrugged. "We wait for his attorney. He's too smart to talk to us before then."

Threadgill was thinking. "Maybe not. Maybe there *is* a way to get him to open up before the public defender arrives."

Miller looked at the blond agent intently. "What's on your mind, Agent Threadgill?"

"If we wait for a lawyer to arrive, he'll be lost to us. But if we confront him with the photos that Breznay found in his condo now, before the lawyer arrives, it might rattle him enough to get him to say something."

Miller smiled approvingly. "Very good, Agent Threadgill. I think you're on the money." He didn't tell her that Gutierrez had suggested the same tactic when he and Miller had spoken earlier, on the way to apprehend Vasilevsky. "But first we'll let him sit awhile, let him think things over." He looked at his watch. "I haven't eaten a thing since lunch. I'm starved. Can we get a couple of pizzas delivered?"

One of his subordinates nodded vigorously. Miller continued. "Two large, one with onions, peppers and mushrooms, the other with meat. Lots of meat." He looked at Threadgill. "That okay with you?"

"Sounds good to me."

While they waited for the pizzas to arrive, they went over the strategy for presenting the photos. They both agreed that the key photo in the array was the overhead shot of Justice's Hancock's Captiva home, taken by a drone. Miller wanted to embellish the truth around that one, suggest that they'd found the owner of the drone, who had spilled his guts. Threadgill, who'd been pondering investigative strategy since she heard they'd nailed down Vasilevsky's location, threw Natalya Bazarov's name into the mix. "We need to make him think we have her and she's talking. We want him to think she told us all about Operation Henhouse, that we know all about his involvement and what it means."

Miller was nodding. "I like it. Hell, we've got nothing to lose at this point."

Forty minutes later the pizza arrived, and they ate with gusto. Miller wiped his mouth with a napkin when he finally came up for a breath and smiled. "I hope he can smell the garlic on my breath when I go back in."

"Shouldn't be a problem, boss," Threadgill said, playfully holding her nose and leaning away from her colleague. "My mother could probably smell it in Bradenton."

By the time Miller returned to the interrogation room, Vasilevsky had been alone for ninety minutes. As he was uncuffing the Russian, he noticed the bottle of water on the table beside him was empty and requested another one, which was promptly delivered. As he rubbed his wrists to get the blood flowing again, Vasilevsky's eyes were fixed on the slim manila folder Miller had placed on the desk between them, next to the recorder.

Miller started in immediately. "We both know how this works, Nikolai. Once news gets back to the Kremlin that we have you in custody, one of two things will happen. We'll negotiate over your fate, work out some sort of exchange, one or more of our agents for you, depending on how valuable they feel you still are to them. That might take months. Or years." He paused. "Or they'll decide you're no longer a valuable asset. In that case, they'll either decide to leave you with us, in one of our finer prisons, where you'll spend the rest of our life, or they might send Mishkin and Chepiga back here to do what they did to Chad Middleton, eliminate the final loose end."

Vasilevsky's eyes widened at the mention of the two Russian assassins. How did they know about them so quickly? He struggled to remain composed, aloof, as the seriousness of his situation dawned on him.

Miller noted the Russian's reaction to his mention of Mishkin and Chepiga and bore in. "If I were you, Nikolai, I would opt for the first choice. If we can work out some sort of deal, then you can return to the homeland to live out the rest of your life in Russian splendor. But for some sort of deal to be arranged, you'll have to give us something. Something worthwhile, something big. If you don't, we have no incentive to negotiate, and you'll die here, in prison, probably not from natural causes."

Miller let his words sink in for a few moments before continuing. "What'll it be, Nikolai? Door A or Door B? Living out the rest of your life in the land where you were born and where you remain, at least so far, a national hero? Or wasting away in one of our less luxurious detention facilities?"

Vasilevsky, who'd arrived in Clearwater confident Abramowitz would have him released by morning, was shaken by this turn of events. Not being able to reach the attorney, the man he'd been told would be his ticket to freedom should anything ever go wrong for him in Florida, had been troubling. But on top of that, they knew about Mishkin and Chepiga. He glanced at the manila folder again. What else did they know?

Miller continued, reaching for the folder, carefully extracting the four photos and spreading them on the table for Vasilevsky to see. "I'm sure you'll recognize these photos, Nikolai. We found them in your condo in Marathon."

Vasilevsky looked at the photos in disbelief. It couldn't be – Meade had told him earlier today that he'd found what Vasilevsky was looking for, would bring what he found to Tang's house. How could the FBI have copies of the photos if Meade claimed he found them? He thought back, trying to recall Meade's exact words. The maintenance man had said he had the proof that would trigger the final payment. Vasilevsky had assumed that had meant Meade had found the package of photos the Russian had left behind. Apparently, the man had been lying to him, leading him on to make sure he received the thousand he was owed.

Miller interrupted his reverie. "It was a rookie mistake, Nikolai, leaving those photos behind. What on earth were you thinking? All you had to do was take them with you and you would've been home free, probably back in Moscow by now. What happened? Too frightened by the hurricane to think straight? Or is it just old age, your memory rotted by the passing of time?" Miller walked around the table and stood next to Vasilevsky, bending down until his face was inches from the Russian's, continuing in a taunting tone. "You blew it, Nikolai. You cooked your own goose, made your own bed, decided your own fate, however you want to describe it. We have you by the short hairs and we're not about to let you go until you start to talk."

As Vasilevsky struggled with his emotions, Miller returned to the other side of the table before he spoke again. "Here's what we think, Nikolai. Chad Middleton, aka Yury Bazarov, was on a mission to assassinate Ramona Hancock. He'd been groomed since birth for this role, ever since you brought his mother over from Cuba to work on that ridiculous movie in Key West. We know you've been supporting Natalya Bazarov since her arrival in the U.S. – she admitted that to us, plus we have the bank records to prove it."

"But then something happened. For some reason, the Kremlin decided to call off the hit, to back off. But they didn't stop at that. They decided to send two assassins here from Russia to murder Middleton, a deep cover agent you'd been nurturing for years, one of your most coveted assets." He picked up the document that contained the real estate information on Thomas Martin's house on Captiva. "We think it was Middleton's job was to secure this house, close enough to Justice Hancock's house to allow easy access to the back of her house for an assassination attempt. But he couldn't close the deal, couldn't even get a meeting with the owner of the house. Instead, that hippie living in the house brushed him off, sent him on his way." Miller chuckled. "All that time and money invested in Middleton, and he turned out to be really bad at his job, just the opposite of what you needed."

"What we want to know, Nikolai, is two things. Are we right about the plot to assassinate Justice Hancock? If so, why did the Kremlin pull the plug on the job? We don't really care why they decided to kill Middleton – it wouldn't be the first time someone's been murdered by some of your associates for the sin of being incompetent. If you can help us understand why the mission was scrubbed, maybe we can work something out with Moscow. It's as simple as that."

Vasilevsky had remained silent during Miller's speech, taking a sip of water, his expression steely, unwavering. But inside he was in turmoil. The Americans knew much more than he'd given them credit for, much more than Moscow had suspected. The only thing they'd gotten wrong was allowing Mishkin and Chepiga to slip out of the country and make their way back to Moscow. Everything the arrogant FBI agent had said was true, especially concerning his fate with his colleagues back in the Kremlin. Once they found out that he was in custody, he would be lost to them, worth nothing, certainly not worth the effort it would take to bargain for his release. He was an old man, one who'd proven to be, like the FBI agent had said, incompetent. If by some miracle he didn't end up in a U.S. prison and regained his freedom, they would send Mishkin or Chepiga or someone like them to make sure he never had a chance to be incompetent again. No lawyer would be able to help him now; he had to help himself.

Vasilevsky looked up at Miller, a sad smile on his face. "What do you want to know?"

64

Marcia Alvarez spent a restless night Sunday, unable to sleep, troubled by her impending meeting with her father's attorney Monday morning for the reading of his will. Marcia knew she was his only living relative and would inherit whatever was in her father's estate. She felt certain that he hadn't adjusted his will since Marcia had struck a deal with Muriel and Edith to give herself a bit of a break each day, and Marcia wanted to make sure she gave each of them a little something to demonstrate her appreciation for the abuse they'd endured.

She'd been struggling with her emotions since her father had slipped away Saturday morning. The old man had been a royal pain in the ass, loud and raunchy, an old-school pessimist who regularly filled the air with invectives against anyone who crossed his path, especially his only child. She had long wished that he would stop his rantings, but now that he was gone, the silence in the compact condo they'd shared for thirteen years was unsettling, so much so that she'd had trouble sleeping the last two nights.

Her father's attorney, Judy Ruliani, had returned Marcia's call as soon as she picked it up from her answering service Saturday morning, full of sympathy and understanding. She adjusted her Monday schedule to fit Marcia in at 10:00.

She gave up trying to get back to sleep shortly before 6:00, rising to brew a pot of coffee, lighting a cigarette, pondering the day ahead. Ruliani's office was in downtown Tampa, in one of the large buildings fronting Ashley Street. It would take her at least forty minutes to make the drive from Dunedin, so she wanted to leave by 9:00 at the latest. She wasn't hungry, so after two cups of coffee and another cigarette she took a long shower, soothed by the hot spray, reluctant to leave the unexpected comfort it provided her this morning.

There was no rain in the forecast, so she decided to wear a simple summer dress, pale yellow and sleeveless, along with a pair of fashionable beige flats. It was the sort of outfit she never would have worn when she was married to Javier, who regularly left bruises on her arms and neck when she did something to upset him. As soon as her divorce was final, she'd gone out and splurged on two sleeveless dresses with scoop necklines, grateful that she no longer had to hide the evidence of the abuse she'd suffered beneath long sleeves and high necklines.

When she was dressed, she checked herself in the mirror, pleased with what she saw. Not bad for an old broad, she thought, as she shifted to a side view. Her breasts were still firm; now that she no longer was a fulltime caregiver, maybe some intelligent, caring man would notice them. She smiled wistfully; she couldn't recall the last time a man had touched them.

Traffic was thick, the tail end of the morning rush hour, and she pulled into one of the surface lots near the museum at ten minutes before nine. It was a beautiful morning, in the mid 70s, brilliant sunshine and just a hint of breeze coming across the Hillsborough River, so the five-minute walk was exhilarating, bringing a smile to her face. An old cliché flashed through her mind: today was the first day of the rest of her life.

Ruliani's office was on the seventh floor. She rode up alone in the elevator, emerging to find a sign declaring Ruliani and Associates directly across from the bank of elevators. She opened the door and was greeted warmly by the receptionist, who'd been prepped by Ruliani concerning the schedule change. "Good morning, Ms. Alvarez. Ms. Ruliani will be with you in a moment." Her face grew serious. "So sorry for your loss."

Marcia was taken aback. "Thank you," she managed as she took a seat in the waiting area.

She'd been surprised when her father told her that he'd decided Judy Ruliani would be the one to draw up his will five years earlier. She knew the brash woman from her steady barrage of commercials on local television and the numerous billboards scattered around the Tampa Bay area that featured her smiling face. Marcia thought she had the biggest teeth she'd ever seen, wondering more than once if they were her own. She wouldn't have been Marcia's first choice as personal attorney – she thought the woman to be an insufferable loudmouth - but then again, she and her father had rarely agreed on anything.

Ruliani emerged from a door bearing her name and strode toward Marcia, offering a sympathetic hand. "Pleased to see you again, Marcia. I wish the circumstances were different, though. How are you holding up?"

"Fine, I guess. I'm having a little trouble sleeping, but other than that I'm okay."

Ruliani indicated her guest chair. "Please have a seat."

There was a slim file on the desk in front of Ruliani, slimmer than Marcia thought it should be. The attorney flipped it open and began. "As you're both the executor and sole person mentioned in the will, this shouldn't take too long." She handed Marcia a copy of the will. "As you can see from the document, your father had a limited number of assets and no outstanding debts. The condo at Causeway Tower, which now is yours, was paid for in full, so going forward you'll only incur the annual maintenance fee. In addition, your father had a savings account which contains $137,692, and a certificate of deposit with Sun

Trust worth $88,799 that matures in four weeks and three days." She withdrew a small key from the file in front of her and passed it across the table to Marcia. "Your father also rented a safety deposit box at a Sun Trust branch in Dunedin on Curlew Road. Box number 4432. As executor of his estate, you're authorized to access the contents of that box at any time after today."

Marcia was stunned. She had no idea her father had that kind of cash put away. She turned the key over to see the numbers 4432 etched neatly on the other side. The existence of a safety deposit box was also news to her. She wondered what could be inside. Papers, documents probably. She looked at Ruliani, her face slack. "I had no idea he had a safety deposit box. I knew about the other account and the CD, but not that."

Ruliani smiled, her immense bridgework gleaming. "He sent me the key to the safety deposit box in the mail about three years ago, I think, along with instructions on how to alter his will. He wanted it to be a surprise for you."

Marcia smiled ruefully, still holding the key. "He was right about that."

"Do you have any additional questions?" Ruliani asked.

Marcia shook her head. "I don't think so."

Ruliani stood offering her hand across the desk again. "If you do, don't hesitate to call me." She smiled. "Now you know where to find me."

Marcia rose and shook Ruliani's hand, thinking: was that a sales pitch for me to have my will done, too? Just like a shark, constantly feeding, constantly on the move. And those teeth. She flashed a smile of her own. "Thanks so much for squeezing me in today."

"My pleasure." She walked around the desk and escorted her to the door, holding it open for her. "I hope to see you again soon."

Marcia drove home on autopilot, hardly conscious of controlling the car, her mind crowded with emotions that the reading of the will had stirred up. She'd done the math in her head – there was over two hundred grand in cash coming her way. How in hell had her father managed to save that much? He'd always been a cheap bastard, tighter than the skin on a wiener where she and the expenses connected to the condo were concerned, but she hadn't imagined he'd managed to put that much in the bank. There would certainly be enough for a couple of nice checks for Muriel and Edith. She imagined how surprised they'd be by the gift, the thought leaving a warm feeling inside as she merged onto 275, headed for home.

She'd managed to get by since her retirement from the Army on her federal pension combined with what her father received monthly from the Air Force, and had been worried about making ends meet now that her father's monthly checks would cease. But this morning's meeting had erased her fears, filling her with optimism moving forward.

She took the exit for the Veterans' Expressway and then Hillsborough Avenue, playing with the radio, landing on a classic rock station. Pink Floyd's "Comfortably Numb" filled the interior of her car as she drove, singing along when she knew the words, humming when she didn't. She pulled into a convenience store, bought a pack of Marlboro Lights and a twelve-pack of Yuengling and continued west, at the last minute driving past the juncture of 580, her usual route home, staying on Tampa Road instead, heading for Kitty Galore's. She'd checked her watch at the convenience store; based on the traffic, the restaurant would just be opening when she arrived. She felt like celebrating.

She crossed U.S. 19, the Rolling Stones' "Sympathy for the Devil" replacing Pink Floyd. At Orange Street she turned right, barely avoiding a middle-aged woman in a golf cart coming from the opposite direction who'd wandered across the center line, eyes on her phone instead of the road.

She was the first car in the parking lot, patting herself on the back. Perfect timing, she thought as she emerged from her car, lighting a cigarette. She smoked outside, seated on the bench outside the restaurant. Across the street, The Barbecued Pig was opening as well, a young woman wiping off the surface of several tables in front of the entrance.

Marcia stubbed out her cigarette and walked into the bar. Gracie was alone inside, slicing fruit, her head down. "Who's a woman have to blow to get some service in this bar?" Marcia asked loudly, sliding into her familiar seat next to the service bar area.

Gracie looked up, her mouth dropping open in surprise, concern in her voice. "Marcia! Where have you been? Is everything all right?"

"It's a long story. Bring me a Yuengling and I'll tell you all about it."

65

On Tuesday night Rheinhart called Morrison and cancelled their regular Wednesday lunch. When Morrison asked why, Rheinhart replied enigmatically. "Other plans."

"Other plans?" Morrison exclaimed incredulously. "On a Wednesday?"

"Yep."

Despite Morrison's badgering, Rheinhart wouldn't tell him the reason for the cancellation. "Are you still planning to go to Gracie's for Thanksgiving dinner?" Morrison asked.

"Yes," Rheinhart replied. "I'll tell you about my other plans on the way to her house."

*****

Morrison picked Rheinhart up at his house at 2:00. He was dressed in his usual Florida casual outfit, navy polo shirt, khaki cargo shorts and Top Siders. As he slid into the front seat, Morrison turned toward his friend, wasting no time. "So, what was so important that you had to cancel our lunch yesterday?" he said as he backed out of Rheinhart's driveway.

Rheinhart was loving this. "Can't a man have a social life?"

It took Morrison a moment before he got it. He turned to his friend, not quite believing it. "You had a date with the clean water babe, Gwen."

"I did."

"What did you do?"

"Took her out on my boat."

"And…..?"

"You'll have to figure that part out for yourself," Rheinhart declared teasingly.

Despite numerous efforts from Morrison as they drove to Gracie's condo on Lake Tarpon, Rheinhart refused to divulge any more information, which only frustrated Morrison more. He pulled into the driveway, and as the two exited the car, Morrison gave it one last shot. "Are you going to see her again?"

Rheinhart gave him his best smile as they walked up a slate path to the front door. "You'll be the first to know."

The football game was on the television in the background as Gracie opened the door, clad in an apron. "Right on time, boys. Can I get you something to drink?"

"Beer, if you have it," Morrison said. "I think you know my brand."

She turned to Rheinhart. "Yuengling for you?"

"Perfect."

The smell of the turkey wafted out from the kitchen as Gracie led the two into the family room. "Smells delicious," Rheinhart said.

"Wait till you taste it." She indicated a man sitting in a Barcalounger directly in front of the sixty-inch Samsung television. "You know my partner, Hank."

Hank turned his head and waved to the two, indicating an empty couch beside him. "I saved you guys some prime seats."

Rheinhart looked around. "Is it just the four of us?"

Gracie shook her head. "No. I invited Marcia Alvarez, too." She lowered her voice. "Her father died on Saturday. She didn't have anywhere else to go."

"The old guy who thought he was D.B. Cooper?" asked Morrison, looking around. "Is she here yet?"

Hank hooked a thumb toward the sliding glass door which led to a small lanai. "She's out there, having a smoke."

"What happened to her father?" Rheinhart asked with concern.

"He had a stroke a week ago Monday," Gracie explained. "He never came out of it. He died at the VA hospital in Tampa on Saturday." She looked at Morrison. "Go easy on her," she warned.

Morrison held up his hands in mock defense. "Why am I always the bad guy?"

Rheinhart offered. "If the shoe fits…"

Morrison turned to his friend. "Fuck you."

Gracie returned with their beers, a Yuengling for Morrison, a Big Storm Wavemaker for Rheinhart. She gave Morrison a disapproving look before returning to the kitchen to check on the turkey.

Morrison took a healthy swallow as he sunk down into the couch. "Who's winning?"

"The Packers are up by fourteen. The Lions haven't crossed the fifty-yard line yet on offense," Hank replied.

"No surprise there," Morrison said flatly.

The glass door slid open and Marcia Alvarez returned to the room. She looked at the two newcomers on the couch. "I'm Marcia. Which one of you is Morrison and which one is Rheinhart?"

Morrison raised his hand. "Morrison here."

She looked at Rheinhart. "You must be Rheinhart, then." She smiled. "Find any more bodies lately?"

"No," Rheinhart answered, chagrined. "I'm sorry to hear about your father."

Marcia waved off his concern. "He lived a long life. And he was in no pain in the end. I hope I can say the same when my time comes." She looked at Hank as she settled into a chair next to the couch. "Detroit score yet?"

"Nope. There's a minute left in the third quarter."

They watched as Green Bay controlled the baa for most of the fourth quarter, eating up the clock with an impressive ground game. With two minutes left, Gracie called to Hank from the kitchen. "Time to mash the potatoes."

As he left the room, Marcia turned to Rheinhart. "Whatever happened to that body? I never saw a word about it in the papers or online."

Rheinhart and Morrison exchanged glances. "I still haven't heard anything," he lied. "It's a big mystery."

"Must be, to be kept a secret for so long," Marcia said. "How long ago did you find it?"

"In October. Five weeks ago."

"Christ, you couldn't keep a secret like that in the Army for an hour," Marcia said as she sipped her beer.

Morrison looked at her more closely. "You were in the Army?"

Her head bobbed. "Twenty fucking years. Excuse my French."

"Did you get to travel much?" Rheinhart asked.

Marcia looked at him with disdain, like he was a member of the media. "Well, yeah, I guess so, if you consider Kuwait and Nicaragua travel destinations."

Gracie saved Rheinhart from further embarrassment by poking her head out from the kitchen. "Dinner's on in five minutes, as soon as Hank removes the bacon and slices the bird." She pointed down a narrow hallway. "Bathroom's down there if you'd like to clean up."

Marcia headed toward the lanai, unlit cigarette dangling from her lower lip. Morrison looked at Rheinhart. "After you, lover boy. Make sure you wash all the fluids off those hands."

Rheinhart stifled a retort, instead heading down the hall. Morrison rose from the couch and peered into the kitchen. Gracie was making gravy, and Hank was plucking slices of bacon from around the turkey and placing them in a bowl. Morrison was intrigued. "You eat the bacon?"

Hank smiled. "You don't think I'd throw it away, do you?"

By the time Marcia finished her cigarette and washed her hands, everything was on the table in the dining room. Turkey, cranberry sauce with sliced walnuts, cornbread stuffing, mashed potatoes, roasted turnips, green beans and gravy.

When Marcia returned, Gracie removed her apron and directed her three guests to take a seat. "I'm at one end, Hank's at the other. Sit wherever you like." She held up two bottles of wine, one white, one red. "Wine, anyone?"

Nods all around as they took their seats. Gracie handed the wine to Hank, along with a corkscrew, then took her seat at the opposite end of the table.

Morrison was still intrigued by the Baconator turkey. "I don't think I've ever seen anyone make a turkey like that before," he marveled.

"Wait until you taste it," Hank said. "You've never tasted a moister turkey in your life." He looked around the table. "We're glad you could join us for our Orphans' Thanksgiving. We're not very religious – would anyone like to say grace?"

"Grace," Morrison blurted.

"Perfect," Gracie said, smiling. "Let's eat."

EPILOGUE

Two days before Christmas, Marcia Alvarez drove to the Sun Trust branch on Curlew and cashed in the CD her father had bequeathed to her. She'd been watching the stock market for the last month, educating herself on its nuances and pitfalls. She'd never had enough money on her own before to consider investing it, but she had some pretty concrete ideas on what to do with the cashier's check that one of the bank managers prepared for her while she waited patiently.

The manager, a well-dressed woman in her late forties with autumn hair and a mole on her left cheek, smiled as she reached across the desk to hand Marcia the check. "You know, we'd be happy to deposit that check for you if you'd like."

"Thanks," Marcia said, "But I'm planning on investing this in the market."

"That's pretty risky," the bank manager warned.

"Maybe," Marcia said. "But you're only young once, right? You gotta take your shot when it comes along. This is my last inheritance – I'm not getting another chance."

"Whatever you say, Ms. Alvarez. Is there anything else I can do for you today?"

She reached into her pocket for the key to her late father's safety deposit box. She passed it over to the manager. "I'd like to look in this safety deposit box."

"Wait right here," the manager said, rising to her feet. "I'll get the duplicate."

Marcia looked around the bank as she waited for the manager to return. There was only one other customer in the bank, an elderly man with a cane discussing something in earnest with one of the cashiers, their heads close together. Marcia couldn't hear what they were saying, but she saw the young cashier smile and shake her head. The old coot probably asked her for a date, she thought.

A moment later the manager returned. "Follow me."

She trailed behind the manager as she led them to a locked gate in the rear of the bank. She inserted a key into the lock, opened the door and motioned Marcia inside to the restricted area. She scanned the wall to her right, looking for the proper number. When she found it, she motioned Marcia over and handed her the second key. "You'll need to insert both keys in order to access your box." She smiled. "Would you like some help?"

"No thanks," Marcia replied. "I can take it from here."

"Very well," the manager said. "I'll be right outside in case you need any assistance." She turned and went out the door, closing it behind her.

Marcia was alone in the vault area. She took a deep breath to steady herself. Her father had rented one of the largest boxes the bank had to offer, big enough to stuff a small golf bag into it. What on earth was in it?

She inserted both keys, turned them a half turn. She heard a click. She removed the box and laid it on a broad table nearby to examine the contents, hesitating to lift the lid for a moment before she gathered her nerve.

She opened the lid and gasped. Before her were bundles of musty twenty-dollar bills, with bank wrappers binding them together, stacked one of top of the other, three deep filling the entire box. She picked up one of the bundles and examined it, riffling it like a deck of cards. The bills were all old, dated either 1963 or 1969, most of them from the Federal Reserve Bank in San Francisco. She counted the stacks and did some rough math in her head. Must be at least a hundred fifty grand here, she thought.

She took a step back. She had been holding her breath; she released it now. She felt a little light-headed, like it was all a dream.

She stepped forward again to look into the box, to see if there was anything else there. The only other item in the box was a business envelope, with Marcia's name printed on the front in her father's unmistakeable scrawl. Holding her breath again, she tore the envelope open with one of her nails, careful not to disturb its contents. She extracted the folded piece of paper, opening it and laying it on the table next to the safety deposit box. It was a short sentence, in her father's handwriting:

Do you believe me now?

Made in the USA
Columbia, SC
21 September 2019